I WILL LIVE FOREVER IN YOUR SMILE

I WILL LIVE FOREVER IN YOUR SMILE

ROSE GATE

THE I WILL LIVE FOREVER IN YOUR
SMILE TEAM

Thanks to our JIT Readers:

Jan Hunnicutt
Lex Robertson
Billie Leigh Kellar

Editor
SkyHunter Editing Team

CHAPTER ONE

Limerence: The state of being infatuated or obsessed with another person typically experienced involuntarily and characterized by a strong desire for reciprocation of one's feelings but not primarily for a sexual relationship.

<u>Garbiñe</u>

"No, no, no, no, no!"

I had fallen asleep? Really? I never fell asleep!

I opened the closet door, possessed. I don't even know what I selected. My neurons wouldn't work. "Something comfortable" was the only thing I managed, and I grabbed the first soft garment that fell into my hands after I pulled hard on the shelf. All the others tumbled onto my head. I would pick up the mess later.

I pulled a comb through my hair. My new haircut was brightened by highlights, which I had expressly requested not be California blonde. I went into the kitchen and drank a cup of coffee, even at the risk of affecting my migraine or irritating my colon. Today I needed it!

I was like a kid on the first day of school. Such were my nerves the night before that I couldn't fall asleep until five in the morning. I had dark circles under my eyes that made Kung Fu Panda look like a L'Oréal model next to me, and on top of that, I had slept through the alarm clock.

The course started at nine o'clock, and it was five past nine. I even wondered whether it was worth going, but if I didn't, I would have to cancel.

Paula and Colmenares had been beating on me about it for a week. Besides, the course was very interesting, and I was looking forward to it.

I slipped on my shoes and ran the brush through my sparse mane. The stylist had insisted that blonde would brighten my natural brown, but I hadn't expected him to be Edward Scissorhands' little brother.

I grabbed the cup, and in my haste, scalded my tongue. Shit!

I threw the rest down the drain. When I drank coffee, I had it black. I did a couple of jumps to finish getting into my shoes and ran. I did a sprint that I couldn't have bested even in my time as an athlete. Maybe my athletics championships were too far away, but she who has it keeps it.

At a quarter past nine, I pulled on the glass door of the meeting room. I pulled so hard that I was afraid it would come off. For how thin I was, I had a lot of strength, although maybe the old hinges took some of the blame.

When the door opened, there was absolute silence, and a score of eyes fell on me.

Come on, give me a break! It was the first course I had ever attended that started on the hour.

I had hoped that they would have entertained themselves chatting, and as usual, the course would start half an hour late, but no. There they all sat at a table designed so that no one would miss anything, listening like attentive schoolchildren until I arrived.

I hate being the center of attention! Did I tell you? Well, now you know. If there's one thing I can't stand, it's having all eyes on me, especially for doing something wrong like being late. I'm disciplined to the point of being boring, and I like being that way. It's one of the few things I still have from my father, and I don't intend to change it.

The male faces were all turned toward me, some wearing superior smiles that increased my discomfort.

I hated being late. I hated breaking the rules, and I hated being the center of attention!

Well, there I was, the only woman who had signed up, although I didn't understand why. In Tenerife, there was more than one female civil guard, and the course was open to local and national police. It was logical that there would be a couple of us, although that was the least of it. I had never felt uncomfortable working with men, or I wouldn't have chosen the police as my profession.

I tried to compose myself and offered my apologies, which were accepted with a condescending smile from my superior, who was sitting in the righthand corner. I focused my attention on him to calm the tightness that had settled in my chest.

Fucking anxiety! I was sick to death of it. You don't know what it is until you suffer it, and I was unlucky enough to have it as a part of my life for this past year. If I tell you how shitty my last two years have been, I might not start the course today.

I was ready to occupy the only empty chair at the gigantic table, but before I could reach the seat next to my partner Colmenares, the commissioner stopped me.

"Navarro, since you are late, don't sit down yet." I looked at him, puzzled. I hoped he wasn't thinking of giving me some kind of punishment, facing the wall like at school. That would be all I needed. The commissioner continued, "We were trying to recreate a scene of domestic violence with police intervention, and we were missing a woman to play the victim. As you can see, women are conspicuous by their absence today. I came close to going to the lost and found for a wig and offering the role to Núñez."

Núñez, a bald man with a thick mustache, looked at him with horror, then gave me a pleading look. I'm sure he was imagining himself wearing a wig left behind by one of our many tourists. They were oddly colored and caked with strange fluids, kept until the fifteen days passed. Then the cleaners threw them in the landfill.

"Don't worry, sir, I'll be happy to do it."

I wasn't going to object after being late. I left my things on the table and went to the center with the instructors.

I hadn't even glanced at them. I thought about the talk I had with Paula yesterday when she tried to boost my morale.

I *was* depressed. I had had a very complicated few months between my health problems and my recent separation. Those made me fall into a pit blacker than a cricket's belly until my best friend and Colmenares, my partner, started to work together to get me out of the lethargy into which I had fallen.

"Don't torture yourself anymore, Garbi. Truly, he did you a favor. Sooner or later, it would have happened. It was foretold. Only a matter of time," my friend had said, playing down the importance of my separation.

Paula had been my only support in the whole affair. My sisters were going their own way. For them, changing boyfriends was as difficult as choosing a handbag in their gigantic dressing rooms. They had turned my room in my parents' apartment into their own mini-mall, where they played dolls with my mother. When they got bored, wham! Off to the next man. Few models were left for them to try.

I wasn't like that.

I had never been with anyone other than Dario, my ex. I still choked when I thought about him. I had always been such a perfectionist, such a believer in lifelong love, that I did not cope well with my failed marriage.

"Here we go again. I think your Wi-Fi antenna has failed. You should check the connection or call Technical Support. With a bit of luck, the phone company will be good and fix it for you." I looked at Paula without understanding. "You've disconnected again!"

"I'm sorry. I seem to be having a hard time today. What did you say?"

"I was wondering if you are finally going to sign up for that course they give at the barracks. It would be a great way to clear your head. You've always been motivated by those things. I think it's just what you need to give you a lift. Besides, who knows? Maybe the instructor is hot, and you could pick him up."

"As if that were so easy!" Paula was the attractive one, and I was the bland one. You could walk past me several times and never see me. For my job, it was great, but for men, it wasn't the best. The only thing that stood out was my eyes.

"Flirting? Have you *seen* me? Men like women who have something to hold on to, not a stick they have to pick up so wind doesn't blow it away." I had become very thin, and my clothes hung on me. It had been years since I was thirty-six, and now I was skinny and baggy.

"You are exaggerating. Many would kill for your model silhouette. The only thing wrong is that you don't know how to take advantage of it."

"I never knew how to do that. I got involved with Dario because he came to me by chance. If he hadn't, I would never have dared take a single step. Besides, I'm not in the mood for guys right now."

"Well, it's about time you were. Look, I accept that you don't sleep with a different guy every week as your sisters do, but a little joy for your body wouldn't hurt. I think one nail drives another nail, and the hardware store is full of them."

I snorted since men were at the bottom of my priority list.

"Don't snort. You know I hate it. You need to start proving to yourself that the new Garbiñe exists. That she's not a myth. You promised you were going to change and think more about yourself, and I see you behaving just as always."

I ducked my head at the rebuke. "I'm not like you," I muttered under my breath.

"I don't even pretend that. Let's see, next, you're not going to tell me you're not sexual."

I shook my head in embarrassment.

"Don't give me a hard time. What happened is that you had one at home who spent all day playing outside, and it's been proven that when you stop using it," she pointed at my crotch, "it turns into an amoeba. But if you water it a little bit," she wiggled her hips happily, "you get the bug again. Don't tell me you don't want someone to give you a good fuck. The kind that makes your eyes turn upside-down."

I let out a weak laugh. "I don't know if I've *ever* had one of those."

"Well, that's all the more reason. Call the barracks right now and tell them you're going to that course tomorrow. See if you can get a master's degree."

"I'm not going on a flirting course, let alone getting the instructor into my bed."

"Okay, so you'll go to clear your head, learn whatever they teach you, and above all, prove to yourself that you're on the road to a new life," she said in a warning tone. "Isn't that what you told me you wanted when you finally had the guts to ask your ex for a divorce?"

I nodded.

"Well, this is it. The day has come. Call right now on the phone, and let me hear you tell them you'll be there."

I knew Paula wouldn't leave me alone until I did. When she

got this way, she was much more stubborn than I was. Deep down, I was glad to have such a persistent friend.

"All right, all right." I gave in, and she grabbed the cell phone from on top of the coffee table and held it out to me.

I called Colmenares, and he told me he had already reserved the place since he was convinced I would go in the end. He had been my support at work. He was much more than a colleague with whom I shared the patrol car. Maybe not at Paula's level of confessing my nonexistent sex life, but I would put my life in his hands.

"Done." I hung up, earning a smile from my friend.

"All right, it's time for a tune-up. Your skin and hair have seen better days, and the 'Duchess of Alba' look is no longer in fashion."

"But I don't have curly hair," I protested.

"I meant the dry thing. And look at your ends. They're wide open, not like your legs. Go on, get your things. We're going to the hairdresser. They've opened a new salon in the mall that they say works wonders."

"A new salon?" I thought about it. I didn't know that someone had opened one in the mall.

"Yes, one of the franchises of that girl who won *GH Singles*."

"The one with the multi-colored hair?" I asked in horror. I couldn't rock *My Little Pony* hair.

"Yes, but don't worry. They do everything. I haven't gone to the extreme of wanting to see you with weird hair," she joked. "I'm content with seeing you look a little better. Let's take advantage now that you have time and Ruben is with his father." I smiled at the thought of my son. He was my driving force.

They say that when a woman separates, the hairdresser gets ready. There is no separation if it is not accompanied by a change of look. It's like signing a declaration of intent to say you're coming back on the market.

"Great. Now I'm going to be chard."

"Not chard. You know I'm not much of a vegetable person unless it's a good cucumber. In your case, I had thought more about turning you into an object of desire, like an iPhone."

"You're not going to stop insisting, are you?"

"You know I won't."

I stood up, resigned. Maybe a good haircut wasn't a bad idea. Paula could be right. I should just let her drag me along and enjoy an afternoon with my friend.

Now you know me a little better. I might do well at work, but on a personal level, I'm a failure. That's why I'm terrified of anything that takes me too far out of my comfort zone.

I had to take small steps, or that unpleasant feeling of drowning would shake me like a hurricane.

It was best for me to focus on what my superior had just asked me to do and help the instructors carry out the demonstration.

I shot a glance at them.

CHAPTER TWO

Ikigai: Your vocation or reason for living.

Garbiñe

My goodness, it was the *Mossos*!

My partner had not warned me that the people teaching the course were the autonomous police force responsible for law enforcement in Catalonia. We had a bit of animosity toward them. The salary gap between the different police forces made them targets of envy. They were the pretty girl, the plugged-in *par excellence*. While a *Mosso d'Esquadra* just out of the academy received about thirty-four thousand euros gross per year, a new national police officer or civil guard received ten thousand euros less. In short, for the same work, the Mossos received thirty percent more. Was it not something to be angry about?

I tried not to let it show, but the injustice got on my nerves. Another of my many virtues. I knew that deep down, they were not to blame. It was a question of politics, but it pissed me off. Same profession, same conditions, same risks, right?

Well, no. That splinter we all had stuck in us was getting crusty, causing a nervous twitch to settle in my eye.

When I managed to lift my chin to meet the two faces, it was another shock. Paula had suggested I should pick up the instructor. What a guy!

My eye twitched, and the instructor squinted at me in surprise.

I'm sure he thought I was flirting. I swear I wasn't, or not consciously. Sometimes my eye twitched when I got nervous, and with a specimen like that, I had to be.

If I could have, I would have forced myself to leave the barracks, walk around the block ten times, and finish with a hundred pushups to calm the uneasiness I felt at seeing the uniformed Catalan. I'd thought Dario was handsome! That brown-eyed brunet made me want to drink his eyes. Well, his whole body!

He was over six feet tall, with an athletic build and a tough but mischievous expression that broke down all my defenses. Jesus! That was a real test.

The other was more normal. I breathed a sigh of relief since otherwise, it would have been impossible for me to produce words, not coherent ones.

They introduced themselves by shaking hands with me—first the normal one, Carles Tarradellas, and then the hunk.

God, did I think that? Paula, get out of my head! I threatened my friend. I never talked like that, and I never had impure thoughts. It must be my friend who, using witchcraft, had possessed my brain.

"Sergeant Áxel Montoya," the hunk introduced himself, melting my neurons.

"Like the deodorant?" I found myself asking stupidly. It had the same effect on me as it did on the women in the ads.

He let out a laugh. "Almost, but with an 'L' at the end." He winked at me without the others seeing him.

He sounded like the star of a soap opera with that voice. My eye, encouraged by his, twitched again, plunging me into an embarrassment that caused him great amusement.

By all the saints, these things didn't happen to me. As far as I knew, they only happened to the protagonists of the Turkish soap operas I was fond of watching when my husband wasn't home. Okay, I confess I'm not very proud of it, but they allowed me to disconnect. If I put on documentaries, I ended up asleep, dreaming that I was being devoured by an alligator. With the Turks, I dreamed about different things.

Áxel's tongue stuck out between his lips, and I wanted to jump him. Gender violence? Ha! If they left me alone with him in my current state of mental derangement, the least they were going to charge me with was rape with malice aforethought. Not much aforethought, though.

Yeah, baby! I mentally heard my friend Paula exclaim. *Besides, his last name is Montoya. If I were you, I'd peel him like an onion. He's going to make you cry, but with pleasure, not like Dario the asshole.*

"Shut up!" I exclaimed, which perplexed Áxel, who blinked a couple of times.

"I beg your pardon?"

I blushed. "I was putting myself in the role. In gender violence, there is always an argument. I'm sorry if I jumped the gun. I should have warned you."

He gave me another of his devastating smiles. At this rate, I would have to go to the locker room to take a cold shower.

"It's okay. I like women of action, but I want to know your name before we proceed."

"Yes, sorry. I haven't introduced myself." I cleared my throat uncomfortably. "Sergeant Garbiñe Navarro, at your service, sir."

"I might have the name of a deodorant, but you have the name of a tennis player," he replied. "It seems we are fated."

"Predestined?" I babbled. What did our names have in common?

Uh-huh. What would become of a good tennis player if she stank? Her reputation would be gone in two days. No one wants to get close to someone who stinks. The joke made me smile. It was a good thing he had said it softly, and the rest of the people in the room were minding their own business while we chatted—if that could be considered chatting.

"Are you ready, Garbiñe?"

My name took on another dimension in his mouth. How could it affect me so much?

There I was, my nerves shot with embarrassment and the sodium bicarbonate that must have been injected while I was sleeping since I felt the blood in my veins bubble.

"We begin," Sergeant Montoya announced in a loud voice, then gave the appropriate explanations.

I looked around the room wistfully. I had missed this environment very much, I realized. I would never again let myself become depressed.

After so many months immersed in the ordeal, I could see myself enjoying the new concepts presented by the Mossos with the competence of those who know what they are talking about. Finally, although it had cost me, I could see myself smiling again. My work was my vocation and my life, and no one could take that away from me.

Sergeant Montoya took on the role of aggressor. Every time he touched me, sparks erupted wherever his hand landed. My breath hitched, and his partner demonstrated how to reduce the subject.

My head had come out of psychotic mode, putting Dario and my collection of illnesses aside. I was immersed in a jumble of keys, restraints, electric shocks, and laughter among colleagues from different police forces that made me feel alive again.

I had signed up for an open Taser course. You know, that gun that, instead of shooting a bullet at you, gives you electric shocks. Many said they were dangerous because of the adverse effects, but others countered that and turned it into a defense tool. That's what today's training was about.

After breaking the ice and getting comfortable in my environment, I told Áxel that the sensation I was getting from that little device, which I was using to break up the people, was not that bad. Rather, I perceived it as a jolt of the kind you get in a physiotherapy session to relieve muscle pain. Nothing that shocking.

His gaze sparkled, like a good glass of Coca-Cola, which was forbidden me.

"You think so?"

I nodded cockily.

"Come here. I'm going to shock you somewhere that is more sensitive." Oh, my God, had they turned on the heat? "I hit you in the quadriceps before, and since it's a big muscle, the perception is different. May I shoot you here?"

He ran his index finger along the inside of my arm just above the triceps. What the gun didn't do for me, his finger did for me. It gave me such a shock that I had to look twice to make sure he didn't have anything in his hand. His magic touch made my whole body vibrate.

"Yes," I answered with a dry mouth, barely remembering the question.

When he triggered the gun, aiming it at the place he had touched, my whole arm went numb. That caused a giggle I couldn't contain.

"Do you like it?" he asked, attentive to my answer.

"I haven't been shot enough to be sure."

He arched his eyebrows in amusement, as did the others present, who seemed more intent on us than on the course.

"You don't know, do you?" I said, biting my lip. Since when did I bite my lip?

"All right, tough girl. Let's see how sensitive you are."

He placed me in the center, and to the astonishment and amusement of the others, fired his Taser at me. It wasn't he who was causing the laughter. It was my joking comments about how, if that was all he could do with that thing, I doubted it would be of much use to us.

Either the Catalonian poachers were lazy, or he couldn't understand why, after several shocks, I was still as fresh as a daisy. I was sure that if he could have, he would have given me such a jolt to silence my protests that I would have been sucked dry. However, it was time for the second part of the course, and he had no choice but to hold his tongue.

Áxel was in charge of presenting the Taser, giving us theoretical data, and showing us videos to prepare us for what we would witness next.

It was time to use the theory he had taught us. My dear Mosso asked for a volunteer for the next exercise. He said that so far, he had been playing with us, but now we were going to see for real what happened with an accurate shot.

I believed that theory was not enough and practice was a fundamental part of a course. However, I must have been the only one who felt that way since my male counterparts were looking around, trying to blend in with the furniture so as not to be chosen. No one wanted to go out in the open and find out how powerful the device really was.

The instructor's dark eyes swept the room but stopped when I raised my voice to say, "I will do it."

His smile widened. I wasn't sure if it was for the pleasure of revenge or because he liked my boldness. "All right. Come with me, Sergeant."

Colmenares elbowed me before I got up. "Are you crazy? It's not to shoot. It's to have him shoot *you*."

"I know that, but if I don't understand what it feels like, I won't learn. I'd rather go out than behave like a chicken in front of the Catalan. You all look like you've had your balls cut off."

After the reprimand, I stood up with my pulse pounding and a glorious warmth spreading over every place the brunet placed his gaze, not that there was much to see. I would have given a lot to have a physique like Damaris' or Elisa's right now or to have chosen my outfit with more care. The unflattering drab gray sweatshirt dulled my skin tone.

As soon as I reached the center of the table doughnut, the president of AUGC (*Asociación Unificada de Guardias Civiles*) asked me if I was sure, and as my partner had done, he emphasized that I was going to be shot, not shoot.

I stared him straight in the eye as my father had taught me. "I understand, sir. I know what the exercise is about, and I volunteer to be shot. How else would I know what happens when someone is hit?" The commissioner, the president, and everyone else looked at me with admiration. I think even my favorite instructor did.

I was once again the center of attention, with a mixture of pride, bravery, and the feeling that, instead of eating the doughnut, it was going to eat me.

Áxel approached my back, his scent bursting like a rock festival in my nostrils. Don't get me wrong. It was not because he smelled like a sweaty rocker, quite the contrary, but because of the intense aroma in which I was enveloped. I felt like closing my eyes and breathing in.

What would I have said to him if he had caught me? What would I have done to find out if he smelled like deodorant?

He asked for two volunteers to support me, remarking that he only needed them to hold me so I wouldn't hit the ground with my teeth. I wanted to burst out laughing and tell him that I had shown him that his little gun was not enough to knock me down, but his serious look did not invite me to do so.

I swallowed hard when I was flanked by two large guys who looked at me as if I were going straight for the edge of the cliff. My pulse was racing, and the self-assurance I'd shown faded. What if I was wrong, and that thing would knock me down?

The best thing to do was not to think. As my father used to

say, "*A lo hecho, hecho.*" "What's done is done." I looked at the ceiling, thinking that he would be proud of me.

Áxel's command to hold tightly to my companions so as not to collapse took me by surprise, and the air left my lungs. Not now. I couldn't have an anxiety attack in the middle of the exercise. I wouldn't allow it. I needed to believe in myself. I was in control, and I could face the fear.

I concentrated on his voice, which echoed in my head. I heard Áxel explain to the others what he was going to do, and when he finished, he stepped so close that his chin brushed my earlobe.

"Let's see. Remind me what your name is."

Had he forgotten my name? Had I made so slight an impression? Through gritted teeth, I answered, "Garbiñe."

"Oh, yes. The tennis player."

Laughter reached my ears. I needed to erase his humor, even though I was at a distinct disadvantage. "Shoot and cut the crap. I don't think my name is important for you to shoot me."

More giggles came from behind our backs.

"What about your last name? I don't like to use my 'gun' with strangers."

Sure, he didn't like to use it with strangers. Who was he kidding? He had such a cheeky face that I couldn't stand him. He moved away, and I tensed. What if it was a distraction maneuver?

That theory gained strength in my head. I was almost sure. It wasn't that he didn't remember my name. He was trying to throw me off, like that TV quiz show where they throw questions at you, and when you least expect it, gates open under your feet so you fall, scaring you to death. I was mentally congratulating myself when "Navarro" died on my lips.

My whole body became tight and stiff. It felt like something was going to break, and my mind functioned strangely. I felt no pain, though my lips kept pleading "Stop, stop!" and "It hurts, it hurts!"

Montoya did not take pity. He was there to do his job, which he enjoyed. You could see it in his smile and expression.

He waited for the Taser sequence to end. Five fucking seconds. That was all it took for me to swallow my words and end up with my morale on the floor as well as my body. Never had such a short time felt so long.

On top of that, the wonderful pistol had the option of giving a second shock since, although the sequence was over, the hooks were still clinging to my skin like ticks. They had not been released, and I was still hooked, at the mercy of the tough instructor. He gave me another shock so those present could see the possibilities of his toy. I wanted to tell him that if he was so eager, I would give *him* a few shots from behind, but I don't think he would have understood what I meant.

I fell silent and stopped begging him not to give me anymore, still proud.

He must have felt sorry for me since he stopped frying me like a KFC chicken and explained how to unhook the barbs from my skin.

I made the most of the moments of respite, trying to catch my breath and relax. My feeling of being out of control resurfaced. I still couldn't shake the anxiety, even though the attack I had just suffered had left me half-dead.

Once free, I made use of the low temperature of the floor to compose myself and crawl until I managed to stand up with as much dignity as I could muster. Morale battered, I tried to make my way to my chair without whimpering.

I did not raise my head again until the morning session ended with a lunch break.

I glanced sideways at Áxel, who was surrounded by agents. He didn't even notice me getting up and leaving the room with Colmenares. He was too busy being congratulated by everyone.

On the way to the elevator, my partner asked if I was going to eat with him and the guys or if I was planning to go home.

When I started to answer him, I was interrupted by the president of the AUGC, who invited me to have lunch with them. "Excuse me, Sergeant Navarro. We were very proud of your performance today and would be honored to have you with us for lunch. If you don't mind, I would like you to tell us how you felt when you were shot. We are very interested in your opinion since you were the only one who dared to do so."

I glanced sideways at Colmenares, who nodded. It was a good opportunity to interact with the guild's bigwigs.

"It would be an honor, sir."

The man smiled. "Well, if you would wait for us right here, we will be right out." Arturo Valdepeñas—that was the president's name—made a slight gesture and returned to the interior of the room.

"Take advantage, Navarro," my partner murmured. "It could be a great opportunity for you. One must have contacts even in hell. You never know. I'll see you later."

He gave me a light tap on the shoulder and disappeared down the elevator with the rest of the men.

I stared at the door. Before long, he would appear, coming out of the same space as me, and I wouldn't know how to behave. I didn't want to make a fool of myself.

Throw yourself at his neck, wolf! Paula said in my head.

No way. That guy fried my thighs. I'm not ready to throw myself on him, I reproached her. Maybe I was losing it.

I ran my hand over the place the shot had hit at the top of my legs, under my ass. I could still feel the tingling. I was massaging the spot when a shadow loomed over me.

I knew it was him. He'd caught me licking my wounds, and that filled me with courage. I lifted my chin, and his unwelcome smile made me stand up straight.

"Too much for you, tennis player?" he asked.

"No, though you should admit you were ignoble."

He looked at me strangely. "Why?"

"Because you shot me in a sensitive spot." The corners of his lips turned up, and the traitor in my chest almost burst out.

"There are more sensitive points," he purred. "Maybe someday I'll show you."

I held my breath. Was he flirting with me? I wasn't an expert on the subject, but I had the feeling that his statement was meant as a joke. I didn't dare ask since I wasn't ready for the answer.

Luckily, the others were quick to fill the awkward silence in which I was caught in his gaze. I just hoped it wasn't my turn to sit next to him, or I'd end up drooling all over my shirt.

Damn my luck. A Mosso!

CHAPTER THREE

Serendipity: An unexpected and fortunate finding that occurs when you are looking for something else.

<u>Áxel</u>

Who would have guessed when I agreed to come to Tenerife to give the course that I would meet someone so interesting?

I glanced sideways at the sergeant/tennis officer. She was not sitting directly in front of me but two seats to the right. That allowed me to look at her without being overly noticeable. I couldn't help but smile again when her frown tightened as she tried to concentrate on what the officer sitting next to her was telling her.

When she entered the room, she did not cause me undue pressure, but during the morning, her boldness and tenacity and the shy brazenness framed by translucent green eyes made me want to know more.

The girl had guts and a lot more balls than the rest of her fellow professionals had shown, and it was turning me on. When I went to shoot her with the Taser in the back, my eyes involuntarily strayed to her ass, which seemed perfectly round. My finger missed, and the hooks ended up anchored in her thighs. When I hit her, I couldn't believe it, but I had to continue, even though that had to hurt like hell.

She was not a dazzling beauty who would make that much of an impression on me. However, there was something about her that made me unable to take my eyes off her for more than a few seconds. She was not the typical woman who walked by you, and you turned around to compliment her. She didn't have one feature that stood out except the color of her eyes.

She was slim, had brown hair with blonde highlights, a very ordinary face, and emanated a strange energy that made me want to get to know her. Maybe it was that I had been alone for too long or that the warm air of the island was affecting me, but I could not stop thinking about what that woman was hiding under the giant sweatshirt.

Sergeant Navarro was the real thing, and that made her all the more intriguing. Even though I wasn't in my prime to go treasure-hunting, with her, I felt like becoming a pirate.

I looked at her ring finger. She wasn't wearing a wedding ring, but she had the mark. Was she married and had taken off her ring to come to the course?

Or maybe she had just separated? *That's what you would want,* said the sharp voice of my conscience.

The president of the AUGC had just asked me a question I had not heard. I was blankly staring at Garbiñe, lost in her figure. "Can you repeat the question? I was lost in thought and didn't pay attention to you. Excuse me, sir."

"I was telling you what a surprise Sergeant Navarro was, wasn't she?"

Garbiñe's cheeks were flushed, and she looked uncomfortable. The president had blurted the question aloud, and she had heard him.

"A very big surprise for such a small body," I said loud enough for that pink hue to increase in intensity. She looked adorable with her cheeks on fire. I drank some water, savoring her offended mood. I didn't expect her to turn her face around to face me.

"Just because I'm thin doesn't mean I'm deaf or don't have stamina," she said, facing me. "I have very sharp ears and could challenge many in hand-to-hand combat."

Mmm, one-on-one with her was just what I was thinking about. I liked to tease her, to watch her turn on that inner warrior she seemed to possess. I was going to spur her on and see what happened. "I noticed it when you begged me not to give you the second shock and unhook you at once."

Her grin contracted. The pink tone gained intensity. "I'm small, not dumb. I had already tasted what your gun had to offer and didn't want any more."

I could only smile and raise my glass to her challenge. If it had been another gun that had hit between her thighs, I would have wanted a repeat by the tennis sergeant, who had turned all the officers into her ball boys.

The meal was pleasant and relaxed. We discussed various aspects of the course in broad strokes. We were joined by a journalist who was very interested in knowing the possible adverse effects of the gun. There was a lot of disagreement among politicians about the consequences of its use.

I was barely able to interact with her. Most of the time, I was answering questions that would be part of an article that would be published in the newspaper, which made me even more eager to get to know her. I didn't have much time. I was going back to the peninsula the next day, so I would have to do something about it.

After an accelerated dessert, we returned to the conference room to resolve any doubts that might have arisen among the participants. We evaluated the sensations of each one and got lost in an endless number of anecdotes, some told by me and others by officers who had used the weapon in the line of duty.

It was one hundred and twenty minutes of approach more than theory, and the eyes of my favorite sergeant did not stop sparkling like precious stones.

Garbiñe

I looked at the clock. It was five in the afternoon, and I had to meet Paula in ten minutes. The course was over, but I couldn't stop staring at him. What was wrong with me? It wasn't like he was the first handsome man I had ever seen. There was something about him beyond his obvious beauty. Something that drew my attention strongly and made me want to know more. Much more.

"He's an amazing guy, isn't he?" Colmenares asked. "He seems to know a lot. Did you like it?"

I almost jumped out of my chair. Fuck, he could tell! "What?" I asked, pretending to be clueless.

"The course, what else?"

A wave of relief coursed through me. "You might as well be asking me about the food since I haven't eaten with you." I went off on a tangent. He shook his head in denial. "Yes, I liked it very much. Thanks for insisting and saving my place. I owe you one."

We had both packed up and were on our feet. The other officers were saying goodbye to the instructors in a huddle.

"I can't stop thinking about it. He is an example to follow," said Colmenares.

His comment threw me off my game. "Who?" I asked without understanding.

"Sergeant Montoya. I thought the subject would have come up at lunch. I didn't have time to explain his life to you. If you had arrived sooner..."

"I fell asleep! How many times has that happened to me in my life?" I answered. "And if you're going to tell me some gossip, forget it! You know that's what *Sálvame* is for, and I don't care about those things."

"It's not gossip. He told us about it when he made the presentation."

"Surprise me." I snorted, thinking that nothing he said could shock me.

"Montoya has terminal cancer. In his last visit to the doctors, he was told that he has three months to live, and there he is, as if nothing is wrong, giving courses all over Spain."

I think if I didn't faint or fall on my ass, it was a pure miracle. I felt my jaw unhinge. I wanted to burst into tears and bang my head against the wall. It had to be a joke. It was impossible!

"What do you mean, three months?" I exclaimed in disbelief. "If you're pulling my leg about something so serious, I don't think it's fucking funny, Colmenares."

"Do you think I'm such a jerk as to joke about something like that? If it wasn't a joke, he made my day. There is no way that man has ninety days to live. The sergeant is all about self-improvement. Have you ever seen anyone more full of life than him? He is like the Energizer bunny!"

Now what? Fuck, fuck, fuck, fuck! I had become infatuated with someone who would disappear in no time, and not because he was going back to his native Catalonia. That man was leaving everything, and the worst thing was that if I had felt attracted to him before I heard the news, now he had awakened something in me that I didn't know how to categorize.

It was not pity. On the contrary, it was a shot of adrenaline that filled me with euphoria. No, don't look at me funny. I know you don't understand. It's not about an obsession with sick people. I'm not a weirdo who's into strange things. It's not about that.

I understand you may have thought that since you don't know anything about my life or what I'm going through. No wonder you judge me. We hardly know each other! But give me time. It's hard for me to confide my problems to others, and you and I have just met.

That he is terminally ill and behaves as if he has his whole life ahead of him has been a revelation. Okay, I know I sound like a freak, but seriously, give yourself a chance to get to know me so you can understand me better.

I need to get close to him. To feel him and have his vital energy recharge mine. No, it is not selfishness. I guarantee you I am the most detached person in this world. It is a necessity. I need him. You have no idea how much because I'm not even aware of it myself yet.

My partner and I stood waiting for our turn to approach and say goodbye, even though I didn't feel like it.

We continued commenting on sensations and exchanging opinions until there were six of us left in the room. The commissioner insisted that we take a group photo and that I should stand between the two instructors as the star pupil.

I felt like one of those crazy fans standing next to their favorite star at the end of a concert.

A simple brush of sleeves with Áxel made me bristle all over. That had been a full-fledged shock. It had left me trembling, unable to move or speak a word. If I was like that after a simple touch, I didn't even want to imagine what a hug would do to me.

"Let's go for a coffee. Are you coming?"

The question bounced in my ears, I tilted my head up and there he was, with his dark gaze on mine. I would have loved to accept. Unfortunately, I had a commitment I could not avoid. I felt like dropping everything and saying yes, but it was impossible to skip that date, no matter how much I wanted to.

"I'm sorry. I can't," I mumbled.

Áxel nodded at my refusal.

Paula was waiting for me at the clinic for her first mammogram. It was not my plan to leave her alone in a circumstance like that. She needed me, she trusted me, and I could not leave her stranded. I also didn't want to miss the opportunity to get to know him better. I don't know where I got enough strength or courage to say, "If you are staying here tonight, I have no plans for dinner." Had I been too bold?

The left corner of his lip turned up. "That sounds even better. If we go out to dinner, I'll call you."

I swallowed hard. I wanted to convince myself that I had nothing more important to do. No one was waiting for me at home, and it was better to be accompanied by people who would give me conversation than to enjoy an evening alone with my problems.

Well, that, and I liked that Catalan more than the spicy *mojo picón* my mother prepared.

I said goodbye to everyone and thanked them, then left to go to the clinic, where my friend was waiting for me. Luckily, she had not yet been brought in. She was in the waiting room, reading a magazine.

"Sorry," I excused myself, oozing with guilt. It was the second time I was late today.

"Don't worry. These places are always late. I'm not in a big rush to get my tits smashed."

"Are you afraid?"

She waved her hand. "I know it won't be anything bad. It's just a precaution. I hope the doctor is good."

"Is it a guy?"

"It seems so. Unless, instead of Manuel, it's Manuela, and they made a mistake on the plaque."

I looked at the plaque my friend was talking about. "Aren't you ashamed to have your tits groped by someone you don't know?"

"He's a doctor!" she protested.

"And a man."

"Don't fuck with me! So what? If I had to choose, I'd rather have my tits touched by a man than by a woman. Besides, they're very nice," she said, weighing them.

I didn't say anything else, but I would be wary.

"I would like you to get all that sanctimonious stuff out of your head. By the way, how was the course? Was the instructor any good?"

I thought about Áxel, and heat overcame me.

Paula's eyes widened. "Wait a minute, wait a minute. What was that?"

"What?"

"You've turned red, and you never turn red."

That was a half-truth. She hadn't known the teenage Garbiñe who would light up like a Christmas tree when my ex came over to tell me something.

"It must be the temperature in here," I dissimulated unsuccessfully.

"Nope. You're going to tell me why your face looks like a strawberry, and I want the truth," she said in a warning tone.

"Paula Carrington Maruenda?" a man called from the doorway, saving me from a confession. My friend raised her hand and smiled at the doctor, who was not bad.

"Don't think you're going to get away with it," she whispered in my ear. "As soon as the doctor stops squashing my tits, I'll come for you, and you'll confess every last letter of the alphabet. Go, compile it all. I don't want you to be unprepared."

With a friend like her, it was impossible not to smile. I waited for her to come out so we could go to a bar and I could submit to her interrogation, which was much worse than the ones we used to do to the accused at the Guardia Civil's headquarters.

After we were seated at a bar table and I told her what was

going on, Paula kept blinking. "So, the hunky instructor is terminally ill with three months left? If so, we've made a full house."

I was taking a sip of water, and I almost spat it in her face.

"Don't get me wrong, but with three months left, you're his best option. If you don't get him, it's because you don't want to. The guy has thrown you the lure. You have to be the one to move."

"You donkey!" I guffawed, feeling bad about her nonsense.

"How many times have the stars aligned for you to feel this way about a guy?"

"Once," I confessed.

"Well, God is doing you a favor and a big one by sending you a guy who is very hot and who will soon be leaving us. You have to learn to relativize things. His state of health gives us a lot of advantages. Don't get me wrong, I'm sorry for him and all that, but what I'm thinking about is you and the great favor you're going to do him. You can look at it that way too, if it makes you feel better."

"What do you mean?"

"You're a textbook freak when it comes to guys. Knowing you, you'd be afraid to start anything involving the word 'future' with anyone. With this Áxel guy, you have it easy. It might sound crude, but in three months, 'Ciao, bacalao.' You don't have to wonder if your son will like him, what explanations you will have to give to your family for going out with a guy other than Dario, or going through the dreaded 'what if I fail again?'

"You avoid all that. Secondly, to make your benefactor soul feel better, you have to think that you are doing a good deed. You're going to help that poor man leave this world happy."

"Paula!" I complained helplessly.

"Didn't you just tell me that he was even better looking than your ex, that he kept messing with you, and that he invited you for a coffee?"

"Yes, but..."

"No buts. Would you have accepted if you hadn't been scheduled to meet me?" I nodded. "That guy wants you."

"Don't be a pig!"

"I'm not. Do me a favor and take your phone out of your purse so you don't miss it if he calls you. Losing three thousand euros is a bitch, but losing a good fuck? That's a *real* bitch."

That knocked the wind out of me. "He can't call me."

"What do you mean he can't?"

I shook my head, nervous. "I didn't give him my number."

"You're stupid!" She hit the table with the glass of white wine she was holding in her hands. I don't know why it didn't break.

"I didn't think. The rush, the nerves…"

"You didn't think he needed your number to call you? Earth calling Garbiñe. What century do you live in? How did you think he was going to do it, with smoke signals?"

"I didn't think, and he didn't ask me!"

"The poor guy must have been overwhelmed, thinking about what he was going to find under that monstrosity you've put on today." She pointed at my sweatshirt. "You've got clothes, and you go and disguise yourself as a gurney. It's not even Carnival yet!"

"If you think so."

"Well, maybe you had something to gain. You were lucky to be the only woman in the course because in that, it is difficult to distinguish whether you have breasts."

"Not all guys care about boobs."

"Not the *pagafantas*, the nerds, but the hunky ones? I guarantee that they do care. They may like thighs or breasts, but they don't like street lamps with eyes."

"Did you just call me a lamppost?"

Paula made a face, clutching the glass of wine. Sometimes her not having a filter got on my nerves. My cell phone started ringing like crazy, and she took the opportunity to gulp down half a glass of wine.

When I answered the call, she was going to find out. "Yes?" I answered.

"Hello, Navarro."

"What's the matter, Colmenares? Can't you live without me?" My partner seemed very animated on the other end of the line.

"Almost. I'm here with the commissioner, the president of the AUGC, and our course instructors. Did I say instructors in the plural?" My heart started bouncing like a hard-tossed rubber ball. "Sergeant Montoya specifically asked me to call you to ask if you were still on for dinner."

Oh, God, oh, God. Áxel had expressly asked him to call me. That was a sign, wasn't it?

Paula, who was not missing a thing, had put her ear close to the phone. She pinched me to draw my attention to her.

"Garbiñe, are you still there?"

"Yes, sorry, it's just that I'm in a bar and there's some noise. Yes, of course, I'm coming."

"Okay, great. I'll send you the location. I'll meet you there at nine o'clock."

"Perfect. See you there." I hung up, and the "*Yeees*!" my friend let out covered everyone in the room with saliva.

"Tonight you wet yourself!" Paula shouted without caring who heard her.

"Shut up! You're crazy!"

"You're the one who's crazy if you let this opportunity pass you by. Come on upstairs. I'm going to turn this lamppost into a beautiful Broadway marquee that reads, Today it gets wet."

"You're tied up."

"And you're going to be. He'll tie you to his bed. That's what I'm going to take care of personally. Tonight that Mosso is going to give you a good time."

"I don't know if I'm even going to be able to look him in the eye with all the nonsense you're saying to me. You get inside my head, and I say crazy things."

"Well, if I sneak into your head, it will be to do you a favor, or rather, for him to do it for you. Tonight you have to bring out the sex goddess we all have hidden inside, or the only one who's going to get his hands on your slice will be the autopsy guy when *you* kick the bucket."

I rolled my eyes and let myself be pushed out of the bar. According to my friend, this was going to be my big night, not Raphael's.

CHAPTER FOUR

Resilience: The adaptive capacity of a living being in the face of a disturbing agent or an adverse condition.

Áxel

There. It was done. Colmenares had just told me that my sergeant tennis player had accepted and was coming to dinner. The bait had been set. Now all that was needed was for my little fish to bite.

I felt uneasy. In my experience, some women were frightened when they learned about my condition. It was not easy to know you had three months to live. According to her companion, Garbiñe had freaked out when she'd heard about it. That gave me hope since her proposal to join us for dinner had come after she learned about my health. Maybe she didn't care about my death sentence. I hoped she didn't since I was looking forward to knowing her.

I remember the day I was told for the first time that I was sick. Since then, a year and eleven months had passed. I have the date engraved in my mind; it was November 12, 2015. The day that changed my life.

I remember it as if time had not made it distant, perceiving each scene in the same way I lived it.

In November 2015, the doctor walked through the door of the room soon after I had undergone one of those tests that are very complicated for a guy like me, a colonoscopy. Just thinking about the name makes my skin crawl.

I was groggy from the sedation, so I didn't know if the expression on my doctor's face meant things were bad or it was a side effect of the anesthetic. My wife was sitting next to me in a narrow hospital chair that didn't look comfortable.

That I wasn't one hundred percent was a fact. What guy would be happy to have a tube ten or eleven millimeters in diameter with a camera on the tip shoved up his ass? That's an exit, not an entrance. At least, so far, it had been for me. I wasn't so sure anymore. The jokes I'd had to endure at work when I'd told them I was going to take the test. That you're going to like it, that you're going to change sides, that whoever tries it never comes back.

Yes, my colleagues are great.

I smiled, thinking about them. It didn't change the doctor's look when I smiled at her, and that lack of emotion put me on alert. She looked like a judge sentencing a convict to the maximum penalty. The alarm signals were bouncing between my brain and my heart, which was pumping hard. The enemy was in the shape of a woman and wore a white coat that fluttered behind each of those footsteps that echoed in my ear.

"Doctor, don't scare me. I'm going to New York in two weeks to celebrate my birthday," I said cheerfully.

I was known for being the positive one in the group. I used to take things with good humor, an acidic one that made me the parsley in all the sauces. I tended to downplay everything. Where people saw problems, I saw opportunities and new challenges.

Neither my amused tone nor my smile seemed to affect the doctor. She was still without a hint of humor on her face, a wrinkle forming across her forehead as she opened her mouth to address me.

"I'm sorry, but you're not going anywhere," she said categorically. "We just found a tumor eleven centimeters in size, and that's large." She paused for two seconds before dropping the next bombshell. "It's very serious."

Very serious? my brain screamed. The message was so loud and clear that my wife let out all the air she was holding in. It seemed that instead of me getting the slap, she had taken it—a hard one, and right in the face.

"How bad?" was the only thing I felt able to say. I needed to evaluate the problem. To see its dimensions from the outside and not as her bitter words painted it. I was no longer smiling. The defense gears had been activated in my brain.

The doctor folded her arms. Her posture was firm, and her gaze was not hopeful, and that shook me up. Perhaps it was her way of protecting herself when she had to deliver news like that to patients. It couldn't be easy to have a job like hers. Surely, it was a way of keeping her distance and not getting too fond of them. However, at this point, empathy would have pleased me. After weighing my question for five slow seconds, she replied with a raised eyebrow.

"I can't evaluate it."

What the hell did that mean? "What do you mean you can't evaluate it?" Everything that came out of the doctor's mouth increased my concern.

She continued, "Right now, the only thing that is clear is that you are not going anywhere. You better get used to the idea that you will only be able to see New York in a documentary or an action movie. You're going on a different kind of trip. You'd better accept that."

No empathy, no gentleness, no tact, no bullshit. Was that what they taught doctors in medical school? I didn't go to them much. I think it was the first time I'd been since my annual medical checkup at work. The doctor glanced to the right, and a muffled voice spoke from the side. "I'll be right back. I have another patient. I'll be back in two minutes."

She went out a side door she didn't bother to close. In there was a lady in her eighties who had been given the same test as me.

My wife was in shock. Her head was shaking in denial, and she had been unable to open her mouth. I think we both were in shock, and even if we weren't going through the best time of our marriage, the news affected both of us.

In the background echoed the doctor's voice, talking to the other patient. "Congratulations, you have the ass of a newborn."

Really? That lady who had already lived through everything was fucking great, and I, who had a whole world ahead of me, was fucked up? What the hell was going on? I was only thirty-five years old, damn it! I had gone to the doctor because I felt tired, not to have a tumor detected. What kind of macabre joke was this in which my life was hanging by a thread?

I had always been an active man. I took care of myself, I went to the gym, and I was a cop. Not just any cop; I was a Taser trainer. You know, that brand of gun that emits electric shocks to stop bad guys. My life was relatively good. I was married, I had two children, and I had been picked to be the new training manager for Europe. Besides, I was leaving in two weeks to celebrate my birthday on the other side of the Atlantic. No way! It had to be a nightmare or a mix-up. I couldn't have it.

Cancer.

The word burst like thunder in the middle of a storm. That disease you always hope will pass by on tiptoe. That it will not affect the people you love but clings to the hands of friends, relatives, or acquaintances. The disease did not understand age or social status. It did not care about your last name or economic level. Cancer presented itself without warning to finish you off with the stroke of a pen so that the Grim Reaper smiles and takes another soul with him. And then comes the **QUESTION**, in bold capital letters—the one you ask yourself when things go wrong, the one to which no one knows the answer. "Why me?"

The doctor returned with the same look with which she had left the room. The Miss Congeniality sash she had worn in the other room must have been left there with the eighty-year-old's baby butt.

"Excuse me, I'm here again. I have a lot of patients to see today," she told me. "Where was I?"

"Where were you? At the moment when, in addition to sticking a probe up my ass, you just fucked up my life," I wanted to say, but I kept quiet.

"Ah, yes." She clicked her tongue against the roof of her mouth. "I was going to tell you that in two days, you will have an emergency abdominal CAT scan in Barcelona. You have to be prepared in case there is metastasis in any organ. In a case like yours, it would be most probable."

My wife stifled a scream. Every time that woman spoke, things got worse. Metastasis! She had to be kidding, although she didn't look like she belonged to the comedy club. If my alarms had been activated before, now they were screaming. They sounded like the sirens of patrol cars in a full chase. That word, coupled with the "cancer," did not bode well.

My wife was stunned by the information. I could not assimilate the news. Inside, I debated between "Why me?" and "This must be a mistake." My head repeated the words to the syncopated rhythm of my heart. They seemed to have agreed on something

"When you leave, at the counter, you will be given the place and time where the test will be performed, as well as the instructions to follow. You must follow them to the letter."

I nodded, still not believing what was happening.

"I'm sorry. This is not pleasant news to give or receive. Now, you can get dressed. Take as much time as you need."

Without any further gesture of empathy, she bowed her head and walked out. She was in a hurry, as she had already warned us. There were a lot of patients to see today, and it being the private mutual hospital did not seem to change things.

"Áxel." The pleading murmur came from my wife. She had finally broken down, letting the tears flow in an uncontrollable torrent.

I pulled myself together. I was the strong one, the one who went forward. The one who took the bull by the horns regardless of the tonnage. I couldn't collapse in front of her, and even if we weren't doing well, news like that put you in a complex situation.

"Don't worry. I'll get out of this, I promise," I swore, putting my hand on her arm.

Without adding anything else, I got up to face what was going to be the hardest test of my life.

Some days later

"You can't complain," I told myself, looking at the bathroom mirror.

I applied deodorant. Odors had always bothered me. I hated the macho perfumes many of my colleagues seemed to like so much. In a profession where seventy-nine percent were men and body-to-body was a must, it should be grounds for dismissal to not wear deodorant.

I was a *Mosso d'Esquadra* in the Girona town of Blanes, known as "The Gateway to the Costa Brava" because it is the first town on the coast. A tourist place famous for its beaches and coves, surrounded by mountains. There was a week when an important fireworks competition was organized. I was not originally from this coastal town. I came for work and stayed for love.

I had met Claudia on a night out. It had been my first

weekend of partying locally. The guys were determined that I had to get to know the local trendy places and if I could, get a date with a tourist. Instead of picking a Russian, a Frenchwoman, or an Italian, I found the one who was supposed to be my better half. I don't know what to say about that.

It was hard not to notice her. Claudia was not very tall, but she had a beautiful face with huge blue eyes. My grandparents were from a village in the mountains of Huelva, and my parents had emigrated to Mataró, a municipality in Barcelona, in search of a life that matched my father's working aspirations.

My father was a broadcaster. He joined a local radio station, where he grew as a professional, earning a place in the *Cadena Ser*, where he was still working. For my grandmother, her youngest son would always be "the artist." Speaking into a microphone made him one, and she loved to boast about him.

My mother dedicated herself full-time to being a housewife. She took care of the house, our extracurricular activities, shopping, and cooking, and always had our clothes ready. She did it all with a smile on her face.

Three boys, zero girls. Grandpa used to say, "The Montoyas, they only know how to breed dicks." I know. My grandfather was a pig, and he bragged about it.

That night at the disco was the beginning of my new life with Claudia. We ended up sightseeing in every corner of my apartment without stopping. From the wall to the sofa, from the sofa to the bed, from the bed to the shower, and in the morning, on the breakfast table. My hormones were raging. I don't think I had a single corner left untouched. The thirty square meters of the apartment melted under our bodies. It was not a feat, but rather, a matter of dimensions and unleashed sexual energy.

We hit it off right away. She had a hard time smiling, and I always provoked laughter. She told me that was what made her notice me—that everyone around me seemed to be amused. She was serious and responsible, and that night, she decided to take a risk after her friends encouraged her to do something crazy and let go of the restraints she lived under. She gulped down her friend's drink since hers was alcohol-free and came toward me with all the determination she could muster.

"You are new, aren't you?"

She looked so tense that I smiled. "New? What is new? I'm not. I've been used a few times," I answered with my particular humor. I saw her swallow with difficulty, her face concentrated. "And you?"

"Me?"

"Yes. Are you new, or did you come here to be premiered?" I expected a slap, but she surprised me by biting her lip and saying, "Why don't we go somewhere else and check it out?"

That was the riskiest thing I ever saw her do. That daring made us walk out of the place holding hands and end up the way we did.

After our first meeting, we met almost every day, and if the shifts prevented us, we called each other on the phone. After two months, we were living together, and after nine months, we married before her belly showed too much. It wasn't because she was pregnant, or maybe a little, but what mattered was that we were in love. For me, family had always been very important. I was always surrounded by family and friends. Claudia was the natural step.

At the age of twenty-one, I became a father for the first time. Everyone said we were too young and that we should have waited, but we didn't mind. We would have that much more energy to raise our puppy. We were happy. She had been made a permanent employee at the factory, and as I was a civil servant, we had good financial stability. The apartment was too small for us, so, like everyone, we looked for an apartment where we could comfortably fit the three of us and the dog, a German Shepherd puppy that had just been given to me by a colleague at work.

Those years were not bad. We ended up buying a bright

three-bedroom first-floor flat with a small garden in Palafolls, the neighboring town. Why not in Blanes? Well, the new apartment was two streets from her parents' house. Claudia's mother would help us with the child, and that was a great relief.

I had always been competitive and restless, and I wanted to continue to move up and broaden my horizons. I was one hundred percent involved in my work, trying to achieve a better future for everyone. In my house, we never lacked anything. I still remember the time in my childhood when a friend of my father's from the Ser brought me a Superman costume from the United States. My other brothers got the Hulk and Thor. I was the only one who could fly, and that made me feel important.

Toni, my older brother, was annoyed because I kept picking on his green suit, saying that it was a piece of junk. That I could wear the same color with a bellyache and that mine was the most special one. He got fed up with my teasing and told me that if mine was so powerful, I should climb the tree in front of the house and fly.

The result was five stitches in the chin and a slap from my father for being a jerk. The worst of it was the mockery of my brothers and my wounded pride. I remember that I angrily took off my suit as soon as I got back from the hospital and went to my father, very seriously holding it out to him.

He looked at me quizzically. "What is this about?" he asked with a frown.

"You can tell your friend that I don't want it. He's been swindled. This suit doesn't work, and because of him, I've split my chin open." Without listening to his explanations, I left.

From then on, I decided to believe in flesh-and-blood superheroes like firemen, soldiers, and policemen. When I grew up, I would be one of them, and I would no longer need a cape to fly since I would fly in an airplane.

For seven years, we were three, or four, counting the dog. Claudia was not content. She wanted another child, and she had nagged me for three years. I was fine with Christian. I didn't need any more. Children enslave you, and I kept on with my intention to progress.

However, in the end, a pill failed, and little Andrea came into the world, breaking the Montoya curse. She was the first girl child fathered by one of us, which made my grandfather wonder if she was my daughter. That cost him a good scolding from my grandmother, who told him that if he didn't know, he couldn't blame and that his grandson was an improved version. I was always the apple of his eye.

The whirlwind of the house was born crying and spent eighteen months that way, day and night. Her lack of sleep took its toll on our marriage. It is said that at five years, couples usually have a crisis, and we had our first one at seven years when we had not slept for a month. It had been going on for a long time until now.

Arguments became part of our family routine. Claudia and I clashed about everything. She reproached me that my shifts were not compatible with hers, and I said that if she had not forgotten the pill, we would have been fine.

I love my children, but when you argue, it brings out the worst.

She was partly right. We barely saw one another since I had gotten involved with a startup company that was marketing Taser-brand electric shock guns. Either I could jump on the bandwagon at the beginning, or after the system was already in place, I would be at the back of the queue. It was now or never, and that took away a lot of family time, reducing our quality of life. It wasn't all bad since having two jobs increased my checking account, but that didn't seem to matter to Claudia.

She threw herself into everything: the house, her work, the children, and all those entailed. She was president of the AMPA, so she had no time to spare, not even to fuck. I don't reproach her. I know she was tired, but for a man as fiery as me, the lack of sex was a problem. I don't know when she stopped being amused by my jokes or when I stopped making them, but I do know that with me, she stopped smiling, and there came a time when I no longer missed her. That was our life, and I got used to it, even though neither of us was happy.

Working as a trainer in the company meant I had to travel all over Spain to teach courses on my days off. The first place Taser snuck its snout was in the Local Police of Llanera, Asturias, where I spent my first weekend alone.

During the two days I was there, I didn't stop for a minute at the hotel. Between the course, lunches, dinners, and the party we had on Saturday, I arrived home on Monday with my batteries charged and a smile from ear to ear—until I saw Claudia's unfriendly face.

That was the beginning of our real decline. It was my fault. Maybe I did not give her the attention she needed, but I was like that. I didn't want to live regretting what I hadn't done. She knew my aspirations and that I wasn't a comfortable person. I needed to evolve, and she agreed to marry me.

She was the one who had insisted on having another child when I told her that I was fine with one. And now? Now it seemed wrong to her that I was still betting on my profession because, according to her, I owed it to the family.

Our discussions were a loop of throwing shit on each other: what if you do/what if I do, what if you say/what if I say. In short, we ended up drowning in reproaches that made us feel far away while being so close.

Gone were the kisses, the hugs, the confidential glances, and ultimately, the sex. I ended up fucking her in the shower, and after a few months, fed up with the coldness that inhabited my bed, I fell for a stranger who gave me the warmth I lacked at home.

I was not proud of it. A conscience was a difficult burden to bear. I convinced myself that it was a mistake I would not make again. I tried to get closer to my wife, have a romantic dinner, and recover what little we had left, but when what was left was less than a hundred percent, the starting point was too far away.

She had stopped caring that I was staying away from her body. She was relieved that I didn't even try. When I tried to light the embers that night, I found her back littered with ashes that fluttered to the murmur of "I'm so tired."

My relationship had run out of steam. I focused on living, on passing the levels of the video game of the life I had chosen. I might have lost in love, but I wanted to feel proud of my passage through this world. I didn't want to arrive at the day of my death with the feeling that I had left something behind.

For many, it will seem a selfish way of thinking about it, but I did not want to be one of those who could only repeat to themselves, "If I had done that, I would not have stopped doing that."

I opted for a path that had led me to the moment I was in now, about to go to a medical test in Barcelona where they would pass sentence on my future.

Claudia decided to join me and asked for the day off at the factory, forgetting for a moment that our marriage was taking on more water than the *Titanic*.

I hadn't eaten since the night before, which made it easier for me to fast, as the doctor had asked me to do. The children were at school and would stay at my mother-in-law's house. Going to Barcelona was an odyssey. The rush hour traffic jams would take hours to negotiate.

My wife spent those two days crying, away from the watchful eyes of the children. She did it at night against the pillow when she thought I was asleep. During the day, she was taciturn. Seeing her like that undermined my optimism.

I refused to acknowledge that the situation was as bad as she felt it was.

We opted not to say anything to the children until we knew more about what was happening to me. I didn't want to alert them if the problem was less than it seemed.

The palms of my hands were sweating. I suppose that was normal in a situation like mine. On the one hand, I was panicking about what they might find, and on the other, I was convinced that the doctor was going to tell me that it was a misdiagnosis and the doctor from the other day had made a mistake and that the eighty-year-old was the one with the huge tumor in her colon.

Sam Smith's *Stay with Me* was playing on the radio as we arrived at the hospital.

Oh, won't you stay with me? Cause you're all I need. This is not love,
It is easy to see,
But my dear, stay with me.

Why am I so sensitive? No, it doesn't look good,
I gain some self-control,
Inside, I know this never works, but you can sleep with me,
So it doesn't hurt.

The examination was quick and painless. I was put in a gown and asked to remove any personal items.

No metal objects such as jewelry, glasses, dentures, or hair clips. Fortunately, I didn't wear any of that. I just wore my wedding ring, which I took off without difficulty.

The scanner was a large ring-shaped machine with a short tunnel in the center. I was instructed to lie on a narrow examina-tion table that slid in and out of the device.

It only took a few minutes, but the restlessness that plagued me elongated the passage of time.

I had been told that it was usual for a radiologist to supervise and interpret the data. He would analyze the images, send an official report to the doctor who had ordered the exam, and then call me to give me the results.

In my case, it was not like that. As soon as I got dressed, the doctor asked me to enter his office with my wife, who had a frightened look on her face.

He asked us to sit down. It sounded to me like the "Please take a seat" when they are going to give you bad news in case you fall and hit the floor. The doctor was in his fifties. He looked at me with a serious expression, resting his chin on his folded hands.

"Do you play poker, Mr. Montoya?" was the first thing he asked me. What kind of question was that in a moment of uncertainty like mine?

"Sometimes with colleagues. It's not like I'm a professional, but I'm not bad at it."

He gave a slight nod before taking a breath and expelling it with some violence. "Okay, well, then you'll understand me when I tell you that you have a seven-two in Texas Hold 'Em." I swallowed with difficulty. That wasn't good news.

"Same or different?" If they were in the same suit, there was hope.

"Different."

I closed my eyes tightly. It was the second slap I had received in a few days, and this one stung more than the first.

The deuce was the lowest-value card in poker. A pair of deuces lost to a pair of any other denomination. High cards were preferred in the game, and that number was the lowest of all.

Why was a two and a seven so bad? Because if the two was accompanied by a three, four, five, or six, there was a possibility of connecting them in a straight, but with the seven being the other card, there was no way to do it.

If both cards had been the same suit, there would still be a chance that they could collaborate to form a flush, but if not, I would have two lower cards that could not be linked together to form a valuable hand. In other words, I was screwed.

"There are metastases in the liver," the doctor confirmed.

The nurse next to him began to cry. My head was spinning. Claudia was trembling beside me.

"Why are you crying?" I asked without taking my eyes off the girl standing next to the doctor.

"Because you are too young to die."

Boom! That was a full-blown gunshot. I continued to stare at her. The doctor stirred uneasily at the emotion from his assistant. When you ask, you risk getting an answer, and it's not always the most pleasant one.

"I'm not going to die," I told her emphatically.

To which she replied, "It's just that it's so big, and it's so badly positioned!" That was accompanied by a broken cry. If this woman was that affected and she didn't know me, it must be very serious.

Claudia collapsed like a sand castle hit by a treacherous wave. The doctor asked the nurse to go out to the corridor and leave us alone with him. I reached for my wife's hand and clutched it tightly. She could not stop sobbing, yet something inside told me that this couldn't be the end for me.

"Mr. Montoya," Dr. Migueláñez began.

"Áxel, please," I corrected.

He nodded. "Áxel, it doesn't look good."

"I think with the stellar intervention of your assistant, I got the picture."

"I am not going to deceive you. You are in an extreme situation. Having cancer in such opposite areas, the cleanest part of the body and the dirtiest, means we cannot operate on both at the same time. We will have to space the interventions to give you time to recover, and without being able to apply chemotherapy, we run the risk of the cancer continuing to advance. Time is a key factor, and in your case, it is in short supply.

"To give you an idea, this disease is like a fungus that releases small spores that flutter around your body. If they feel comfortable somewhere, they settle, colonize, and take over. In your case, unfortunately, they have already taken over your colon and liver."

My analytical mind allowed me to remove myself from the personal alarm and evaluate the possibilities.

"How much time do I have left?"

The doctor squeezed his eyes shut. "It is very relative. It depends. Each case is different." The doctor was going off on a tangent, and I wanted the truth.

"How much?" I asked flatly.

"Three months."

CHAPTER FIVE

Nakama: A friend so close you consider them family.

<u>Garbiñe, present time</u>

"You look great," Paula said, checking out my appearance.

We had opted for a white linen dress and a blazer in the same color in case it got cooler. It was not that I had many dress-up clothes, but I recognized that the elegant yet casual dress, together with my friend's aid to give some color to my face, brought out the best in me.

"Didn't you go a little overboard with the mascara?" I didn't wear any makeup, so for me, anything was too much.

"Not at all. It's just that you have very long and bushy eyelashes. If you made them up more often, you'd enhance that feline look that you have, and that is your best asset. I just complemented it with a bit of gloss, dark eyeliner, and blush. Add that, and nothing is the same."

"Well, I look very different. I don't want to look like a carnival monkey."

"You're cute. You just keep saying silly things. Besides, that's what it is all about, isn't it? To make you feel different so you could do things you wouldn't normally do."

"We are not going to be alone."

"What difference does it make? The time will come when you can flutter those eyelashes as a weapon of mass destruction. And now that you're ready, I'm leaving too. I'm meeting the hottie doctor, and I still have to go to the body shop."

"Are you meeting the doctor?" I asked, surprised.

"What do you think? After he fondled my tits, he made a joke about my third nipple coming out. It's the least I deserve."

"I'm such a mess. I didn't even ask you about the mammogram." As a friend, I was turning out to be the worst, and Paula was like one of my family.

"In your mind, there is only room for Mr. Deodorant. I don't blame you. It's about time you cared about yourself."

"But did the doctor say anything to you?" Paula didn't seem worried, which reassured me.

"Yes, that I had very fibrous breasts and that the lump he had noticed was not a third nipple, a tumor, or anything else. To celebrate, I made a date with him. You can't help celebrating good news."

"You're amazing," I murmured.

"Oh, come on. You only live once, and you have to learn to enjoy it. Especially after my ex."

Paula was a journalist, and her ex was a university professor. He spent all day teaching and traveled a lot to give lectures, or so he said. One morning when Paula went to the newspaper, she found her boss very upset in the office. She had lost an expensive earring that her husband had given her, and she showed Paula the other one so the two of them could look for it.

It was no use. They didn't find it, and Paula spent the afternoon typing like crazy to finish the next day's article. Hours later, with the work delivered, Paula returned home. She was exhausted, so she collapsed on the couch and felt a searing pain in her butt.

It wouldn't be the sharpest pain she would feel, though. When she looked, she realized it was her boss's missing earring. She was left without a man and without a job at the same time because if there was one thing Paula had, it was too much self-respect to let herself be trampled on.

That had been a turning point in her life. She swore to herself that she would never again give her heart to anyone unless she was dead and donated her organs to science.

"Gabriel was a bastard," I pointed out.

"Yes, baby, but Gabriel taught me to love." I raised my eyebrows. "Don't be surprised. He taught me to love him far away, so much that even if they brought him to me at a bargain price, I wouldn't keep him."

I let out a laugh. Being with her was always refreshing. "You're a fantastic woman, and you'll find a guy who deserves you."

"You too. You just have to let go and let yourself have fun. Life is made up of moments, and only you have the power to decide how you want them to be. I don't want guys who make me shiver. I prefer shagging that makes me shiver, and you should choose the same."

We embraced warmly to say goodbye and wished each other the best of nights.

I picked up my cell phone to look for the message my partner should have sent me. I'd had a text from a number I didn't know an hour ago, and that caught my attention. When I opened it, a huge smile came over my face.

Hello, tennis player. I hope you don't mind me writing to you. I asked your partner for your phone number. I just wanted to thank you for your help in the course. If it hadn't been for you, I wouldn't have been able to present it in such a complete way.

It was the first time I had only one person as a volunteer. Usually, several want to try.

He had written to congratulate me. He had gotten my cell phone number. That had to be a sign. I cleared my throat like an idiot. What was I doing it for if I was just going to type? I sighed, but I wasn't going to leave it unanswered after he'd been so nice to me. It didn't matter if we were going to see each other in a few minutes.

Sorry, I didn't see the message. You don't have to thank me. The course was great, and you were the best instructor I've ever had.

I got nervous when I saw that he was online and the double check came back blue. On my way to the parking lot to get the car, I had a second text from Colmenares in which he sent me the location of the restaurant. He had been there, and he knew the way perfectly.

Montoya was still online, and he was typing. The three dots told me so.

I bit my lip, nervous. I hoped it wouldn't take long. I could not text and drive at the same time.

I'm glad you see it that way, you've been a very rewarding student, and I'd love to get to know you better. I'm off to the restaurant now. Shall I see you there?

Rewarding? What did he mean by that? I wasn't sure, but I wanted to find out.

Of course. I'm going to drive and won't be able to read. It wouldn't be right to be reckless behind the wheel.

God, I was so rusty at flirting. What was I saying? I had never flirted in my life.

No, please don't. Be careful. I wouldn't want you to get hurt on the way.

"How cute!" I sighed. I typed quickly. I didn't want him to think I was oblivious.

I'm usually very cautious, so don't worry. I'm looking forward to chatting with you. I'll be there in ten minutes.

That's it. I had let it out.

Well, we'll solve that quickly because I'm not going to stop doing it all night. Hugs.

Did I want to do it all night? I was getting sweaty.

I had to reread the message to realize that he was talking about chatting. I was somewhere between relieved and disappointed because, for a moment, my Paula-mind had decided to have sex instead of text. I typed quickly so I could get behind the wheel and get there as soon as possible. If he sent me a hug, I wasn't going to leave him without his.

I sent him an emoji and dropped the cell phone into the passenger seat. Mmm, how nice that all sounded. Talk to him and get a hug. I imagined him wrapping me in his arms, and a hot flush covered me. I realized I hadn't recorded his number. I'd better make sure, lest my phone crash and I lose his contact.

When I saw his laughter in response to my goodbye, I stopped to look at what he was laughing about.

Oh, my God! I had sent him a rod emoji. He probably thought I was the female version of Christian Grey.

Sorry, it was autocorrect.

Or so I assumed.

Well, if you're going to be banging around, it's going to be a most instructive dinner, tennis player. See you in no time 😉

He had sent me a winky face, and I didn't know what to say. I didn't want to make the situation worse.

I recorded his number in the contact list as Axe. That private joke made me feel closer to him, which was how I wanted to be—very close.

With my nerves on edge, I started the car, and the radio came on automatically. I let out a laugh that bounced off the roof of my mouth when I heard Raphael singing *Mi Gran Noche* as if it were a divine message, and I started humming.

What will happen? What mystery will there be? It may be my big night.

And when I wake up, my life will already know something it doesn't know.

I will walk embracing my love through the aimless streets.

I'll discover that love is best when everything is dark.

Sometimes I had the impression that I was still the Garbiñe who had come to Tenerife when she was just a teenager, with the same weaknesses and insecurities. Could I become the woman I wanted to be?

I thought about the moment I figured out that my marriage was not going well. How much time had I wasted? How many bad decisions had I made? If that day on the beach, I had dared to stand up to my husband instead of letting him do the usual, maybe I wouldn't be at this point today.

I drove, remembering who I was and trying to forgive myself for the mistakes I'd made. I dreamed of freeing myself from the bonds that had led me to become my own jailer.

CHAPTER SIX

Atelophobia: Fear of not being good enough.

Garbiñe, seventeen years ago

Here it was. "New destination, new life," as Dad used to say.

It was my first time at the airport of Santa Cruz de Tenerife. My father, who was a civil guard, had been assigned to Puerto de la Cruz.

My admiration for him was what made me want to dedicate my life to the *Benemérita*. My mother always said that I was just like my father and the twins were just like her. The adoration I felt for my father knew no bounds. I loved sports as he did, I had his character, and I developed the same passion as he felt for his work. That was why we spent my childhood going back and forth, stumbling from destination to destination, traveling the Spanish geography until we reached a place that smelled of eternal summer, partying, and heat.

To be frank, the abrupt change was not fun for me. First, I had been caught in the middle of the school year. I was going to miss my best friend's birthday party, and a change of residence in the middle of adolescence is a drama for any shy fifteen-year-old girl.

I already felt like a freak when I arrived. We had spent the last four years living in a small town in Léon where everyone knew each other. For me, moving to an island was a radical change that I knew I would never get used to. The fact that the island had a volcano and was surrounded by water on all sides sounded like a doomsday movie to me.

I was sure it was just a matter of arriving and the volcano would start to erupt, and we would die trapped on the island. That was one of my arguments to try to convince my father that we couldn't move, but he didn't listen to me.

And there I was, out of my comfort zone, like a polar bear in the middle of the Caribbean, completely warm and out of place.

The heat was stifling, and humidity caked under my thick wool sweater in the form of sweat. I was whiter than Casper at a foam party, and thick corduroy pants covered my unshaven legs. It was December, and in Léon, it was freezing. When they told me it was hot in the Canary Islands, I thought they were exaggerating. Who would have thought that on December 29th, it would be twenty-four degrees in the shade? I couldn't wait to get to the apartment, take a shower, and change my clothes!

I took a look around. Girls were showing off their toasted skins, and I looked like I had just come back from an Antarctic experience.

"Where do you think that one is going? To the North Pole?" a blonde asked a girl who looked like her clone.

Both were a few meters away. They must have been my age, and they were the opposite of me. Golden hair, dark skin, beautiful, and wearing dresses suitable for that sweltering heat.

"She must have taken the wrong plane or come on an iceberg," the other replied, giggling.

I stared at the ground, embarrassed. At that time, shyness was my middle name. If I could have melted into the ground, I would have gladly done so. They kept chattering as if I were deaf or didn't understand their language.

"Someone should have explained to her that the last great glaciation occurred twenty-one thousand years ago. She reminds me of the squirrel in *Ice Age* with that brown fur."

"Maybe she came here in search of the acorn?" joked the other.

I wished I had the courage of my inner voice, which urged me to throw myself on them and smash their heads against each other to show them that they were the only acorns here.

Something caught my attention. Right behind them was a boy who was also looking at me, laughing. He had long, tousled hair, golden brown, that made me ignore them and notice him. In Léon, there were no boys like that, or if there were, I had not seen them.

"You're going to bake like a potato, *muyaya*," he said in my direction with a deep Canarian accent.

Was he talking to me? I was so nervous I didn't know how to behave. He was very handsome. My cheeks boiled with embarrassment and cowardice.

If you took me out of my environment, I had a hard time relating, and I was completely out of place here. My parents were still at the terminal. They had asked me to wait for them outside since my beastly sisters were threatening to fill the airport with pee, and that was not the plan.

Dad was standing in line to get the rental car, and I had been left in charge of the bags. Because I was so hot, my mother suggested I go outside to get some fresh air. What she gave me was both a shock of heat and a shock of reality. I didn't fit in, and I wasn't going to.

"Dario, don't waste your time. Look at her. Even her tongue has dried up. Let's leave her. I'm not having fun with her anymore. She's a sissy who doesn't answer. Besides, if we don't leave now, we'll be late for the party, and Dani is waiting for us on the beach."

Blonde Number One, an island version of one of Cinderella's stepsisters, stood in front of the boy, trying to get his attention. Unlike the fairy tale, the two girls in front of me had smooth curves that made me, the self-styled Cinderella of the upside-down world, look like a stick bug from the Arctic.

"Be kind, Damaris. Can't you see that she has just arrived?" asked Prince Dario. He was the only one who resembled a character in the story, although instead of riding a horse, he seemed to be riding the waves.

Damaris gave him a "What the hell are you telling me" look that was unmistakable. She didn't give a damn. As a welcoming committee, they were priceless. Now, besides the shower, I wanted to get on the plane and return to my house in Léon.

"Did you come to the island on vacation?"

Dario seemed oblivious to the will of the blonde, who wrinkled her nose and looked at me over her shoulder. He kept trying to make conversation, but my mouth didn't seem to want to cooperate, and neither did my mind.

Where are my grace and wit? Lost like a fart in a hot tub, replied the witty self that was unable to surface. If only I was able to at least overcome shyness and answer the way I felt.

I took a breath, ready to let go once and for all. I was about to do so when my father interrupted me. "Making friends, daughter?"

I was lost as I listened to my mother, the worst of misfortunes for my lack of extroversion.

She was open by nature. She had no trouble socializing and meeting people. She was fascinated by shopping, watching soap operas, cooking, and inviting people she had met in line at the supermarket to have coffee at our house, as well as making friends for me. A paragon of virtue.

I mumbled, "*Mom*" under my breath. I didn't want her to make a fool of me, but she ignored my will as she always did.

"Hi, guys. I'm Amelia, Garbiñe's mother, and you?" she asked affably, leaving me with a face like a bat crushed against a wall. Her wall, that vertical space with which she kept hitting me.

I hated it when she did that! She left me on the sidelines, making me feel like a goddamn five-year-old. All she had to do was say, "Do you want to be friends with my Garbi? Why don't you go play together in the park?" If she went on, I would go straight to the beach and bury myself in the sand until I disappeared.

That was what she had done throughout my childhood, over-shadowing me under the majestic shadow of being a perfect hostess. I always felt insecure in front of strangers. I had the feeling that without her, I could screw up to my heart's content.

My mother was one of those women who captivated everyone. Her attractiveness went beyond beauty. She was magnetically affable. My friends told me how lucky I was to have such a cool mom who threw sleepovers and made lemon tarts to die for. They didn't come to my house because of me but because of her. They would eventually get to know me, though. Worst of all, in her way, she was great. I just felt so little next to her that I was bursting at the seams.

"We are Dario, Damaris, and Elisa," the boy introduced them.

"See? And you were worried about moving and not making new friends! You just stepped on the island and kissed the saint. Look what nice guys they are, and they look like they're your age!" She encouraged me as if they were a mirage and we were chatting alone.

I sank into misery. As if they couldn't hear her! They must have thought I was retarded. I wanted to place my Converse trainers on her shiny high heels and see if that would shut her up.

Dario seemed to be interested in her words since he started a presentation that turned into a one-on-one between him and her.

The two of them laughed, and they seemed to hit it off perfectly, unlike the blondes, who continued to stare at me. My mother gave away everything but my bra size.

In a moment, she had gotten it all out of him. What if he was a serial killer or a rapist? We didn't know anything about him, only that he was very handsome, had a beautiful smile, and I melted under his gaze. And it wasn't the effect of the sun.

I shook myself. Being handsome did not exempt him from being a criminal. My father had taught us that the worst criminals wore expensive suits and brand-name shoes.

It didn't end there. My mother subjected him to the third degree, and we found out that he was our neighbor, that we were the same age and we would go to the same high school, and that they were heading to a party to which I was invited.

"Seriously, Amelia, don't worry. Damaris' mother is taking us to the party. Her father is a pilot, and we've come to the airport to see him off. That's her over there, the one with the red car. If you want, I'll introduce you to her so you can relax," Dario offered solicitously.

It seemed like he had known her all his life, but they had only been talking for five minutes.

She gladly accepted me without asking if I wanted to go. I regretted my inability to stand up to them and tell them that I didn't give a damn about the damn party and I didn't want to go. I just wanted to get to the apartment, take off my filthy clothes, and take a shower. But no. I would never raise my voice in front of her or put my will before hers.

My mother did the whole act. She introduced herself to the mother of this Damaris (of whom her posh daughter was a replica), who kept smiling with those silky lips that looked like blood sausages.

" I don't want to go!" I wanted to shout, but my opinion didn't count.

"Garbi, come and meet Luciana!" she exclaimed.

I hated that nickname. Saying it made my mind travel to a blonde plastic doll with giant pears that I would never have.

My sisters were scampering down the sidewalk. I gave them a sidelong glance to make them realize I was not going to cross and leave them alone. As if my mother had read my mind, she replied, "Leave them to Dario and cross." I strangled her mentally. I didn't know them! Why did she speak to everyone with such familiarity?

I could do nothing to avoid the fatal outcome, which was to ride in the middle of the back seat of Luciana's car, where the evil stepsisters showered me with stomps and loving pinches of welcome.

To top it off, Mom had managed to get Dario, my new neighbor and potential dismemberer, to walk me home after the party.

Maybe, if I had not gone to that party seventeen years ago, that young surfer would not have dazzled me with his jovial character and a stolen kiss while playing the bottle game.

No one had kissed me until then. No one could make me feel special when I was invisible, a girl in the crowd. A wannabe to be swallowed up without anyone noticing me.

That party was followed by others, and that tight-lipped kiss was followed by wetter and more passionate ones.

I got into Dario's game like most of the girls in the high school. We were all dying for his kisses, and we all got some from time to time. He was generous by nature.

The surfer-neighbor began to be part of my daily life. In the mornings as a classmate, and in the afternoons, coming to snack on my mother's delicious lemon cake to get the strength to hunt waves under the watchful eye of his queue of admirers. On weekends, we would party as a group. Sometimes I was lucky enough to hook up with him. Other times, I watched him disappear with someone who allowed him more than kisses.

I never knew what he saw in me. Maybe it was a challenge, a

bet, or just that I was easy for him to be with. I thought I would never find a better-looking, nicer, more attentive guy who would want something with me.

When we had been on the island for a year, something happened that made my world fall apart.

My teacher got sick, and at the last minute, the class was canceled. The twins were at school, and Dad was at the barracks. My mother was supposed to be preparing lunch.

Good old Don Cristóbal, the neighbor, had her naked on the counter, with her legs open and his head buried between her thighs. I will never forget that image of closed eyes and stifled grunts that made me clench my fists and run away.

I was nauseated. I wanted to cry and kick them at the same time. Instead, I went in search of Dario, who had left me on the landing a few moments ago. With any luck, I would catch him before he entered his house. With my heart leaping out of my mouth and tears blurring my vision, I rushed over to him. He was about to turn the key in the lock.

His mother worked at the hospital as a nurse, and her father had left them long ago.

He tried to calm me down and took me to the kitchen to give me a glass of water. Through tears and hiccups, I told him what I had seen. We had been making out for a while, but nothing more than that had happened between us yet.

"Calm down, precious," he murmured in my ear. He kissed the tip of my nose and the tears running down my cheeks. "It's okay. You saw something you shouldn't have, that's all. You shouldn't judge your mother for such a slip. The flesh is weak and very pleasurable."

"What about my father?" I asked, not understanding why he wasn't as horrified as I was.

"These things happen. It's very boring to eat the same dish for years. I'm sure he does the same. Some marriages even agree to it, or do you think your daddy doesn't play in the dungeons?"

I shook my head.

"My father wouldn't ever. He's not like that," I reprimanded him.

"That's what you think. The whorehouses are full. Sex is sex, and when it itches, you need to scratch it. If you've been with someone too long, it gets monotonous, and the flame goes out. Why else do you think there are so many infidelities?"

"It's not true! Sex is love," I burst out innocently.

He chuckled. "No, my girl. Sex is pleasure. You don't need to be in love to get laid. You think so because you're still a virgin and haven't tried it, or am I wrong?"

I shook my head. His eyes were dilated. My mouth went dry when I saw the way he looked at me, like a cat that had just caught a mouse. His hands went from cupping my face to moving smoothly down my chest, which was heaving.

I went to stop him, but he whispered, "Shh. Let me. You can't have an opinion about something you don't know. I'm going to show you what pleasure is, what your mother moaned about. I promise I'll make it special. I'll be careful, and you'll remember it forever. Do you trust me?"

I felt vulnerable. What I had just seen had so upset me that I could only think about running away to somewhere comforting, and Dario had always been that for me. I nodded, earning a kiss.

"That's very good. Now let yourself go. Just as I showed you this island, just as I gave you your first kisses, I'm going to make you a woman and teach you what pleasure is. You'll see how much you like it."

Dario took me to his room and undressed me slowly, kissing every bit of exposed skin. He tried to make it special. He was tender and considerate, and I even caught a glimpse of an orgasm that was tainted by the lacerating loss of my virginity.

When we finished, I stared at the ceiling. He moved sideways, running his index finger along my smooth abdomen to get lost in my navel.

"What did you think?"

I was embarrassed to answer.

"Well…" I hesitated. "I don't know. I don't have anyone to compare it to, as you've already seen," I admitted with a blush.

He rewarded me with a kiss.

"In time, it will get better, and so will you. You'll stop being a starfish and become a mermaid who will raise her song to beg me to do her anywhere, just like your mother. Maybe next time, I'll do you like he did her, on the kitchen counter."

The thought of my mother stung. I went to turn my face, but he wouldn't let me. He kissed me again and took me a second time. It was no better because I felt discomfort, but I let him do it. With him, I felt protected from all evil, and if I was entertained with sex, I did not think about what was happening at home.

I never told anyone what I saw that day, although it was a before and after in my relationship with my mother.

Dario advised me that it was better not to get involved in other couples' stories since one always ends up getting scalded.

Time went by, and our "non-relationship" progressed, turning us into fuck buddies. After my passage through the academy of the Civil Guard, the word "boyfriend" appeared as a link between us. No one was surprised that, in the end, he became my husband. In the end, I got the most sought-after guy in the neighborhood despite the astonished looks of his friends.

I'd like to think my parents' promise to help him fulfill his dream and set up his own surf school if he married me had nothing to do with it, but sometimes I doubted it. There were rumors about my husband's interest in his foreign students. They came to the island to learn how to get on a board and end up lying underneath it, clinging to the instructor's naked body.

Although the gossip made me look like a cuckold, I never found any evidence to make me leave him. I didn't do much to find it, either.

He was the male version of my mother, all light, joviality, good cheer, and disloyalty.

At that time, I was not sure. Now I am convinced that where there's smoke, there's fire. That's how it was with my husband.

What an idiot I was! How unshakable I seemed at work and how minuscule I felt at home. My feelings for my husband were so contradictory that I couldn't see that our marriage was a sham. I don't blame him since I should have realized it instead of letting myself be carried away.

With him, I never stopped being the fearful teenager who showed up one day at the airport in Tenerife, full of insecurities. He knew it, and he used them to subdue the woman eager for affection.

Not that he beat me or mistreated me in any way. I would never have consented to that. But he had a way of turning things around, of making me walk through them, which effortlessly reduced me to a state in which I did not recognize myself as an adult.

I had been through so much with him that I was afraid to be wrong. We had long since broken up but had only recently separated officially. I wasn't ready to face the possibility of bringing someone else into my life. I wanted to find myself and expel the fear of failure forever from my life. But it was so hard and I felt so lost that I didn't know if I was doing the right thing with Áxel.

Just a porn fest, Paula's voice mumbled in my head. *No horizons, no illusions, no love, just sex. Be the protagonist for once, and have fun!*

CHAPTER SEVEN

Mokita: The truth that no one talks about but everyone knows.

<u>Áxel</u>

I grabbed the jacket, grinning like a moron. It had been funny about the stick thing.

I felt my sore abdomen. The last operation was very recent, and the prospects were not good. I was at square one again, carrying that damned prediction. I am tough, but when you are given such a short amount of time, it knocks down a lot of your defenses.

Three months. What would you do if someone told you you had three fucking months left before the switch went off and your name appeared in an obituary?

Knowing the day of your death should be considered a spoiler, or maybe not. I knew better than anyone that we are not eternal. That my moment could come without premeditation, in a chase, or simply by running into the guy I stopped last month with a knife hidden in his back pocket.

No one prepares you to be told a specific day. Maybe, if the fortune teller on duty tells you, you take it as a joke, but when it's an old doctor, things change. I was thirty-five years old, with a lifetime ahead of me, when they told me.

My first thought was, "It's impossible. I have two children to raise, and I haven't been to New York yet. I can't go to the other side without seeing the Statue of Liberty from the plane, climbing the Empire State Building like King Kong, or going for a run in Central Park."

I tried to calm my heart rate. Normally, it was not difficult for me since they had taught us how to deal with stress at the academy. Risky or extremely serious situations were the order of the day. It was necessary to know how to temper your nerves, but nobody prepares you to receive the news of your death, to assimilate that your time is coming to an end and that no one can offer you a solution that guarantees you will get rid of it.

It should be a compulsory subject: how to face the day it all ends. Not that day in particular, but the process and how to digest it. That's the hardest thing of all.

No event in my life had ever caused me so much uncertainty, speculation, and fear at the same time. I was not a coward, never had been, but the bitter aftertaste of that sensation was like rancid almonds.

Extinction, knowing that we are an expired product, was not easy. The realization that we are finite beings and that, in my case, in three months, I would close my eyes to embark on a journey from which I would never return was dizzying.

I had always thought that a good warrior was not the one who won the battle but the one who, when he felt defeat, rose to continue fighting. That day at the doctor's office, I decided I was going to put on my armor and not give up in the face of defeat.

I saw myself again in that office, taking a deep breath, squaring my shoulders and lifting my chin to look at the doctor fixedly. He was waiting for my response to his prediction. I rolled up my shirt sleeves and lashed out forcefully.

"All right, and now that I've almost got a date for a mortician to make me handsome, what are we going to do to fuck the Reaper in the ass and stand him up?"

He could not prevent the corners of his lips from lifting. He uncrossed his hands and rested them on the smooth surface of the table.

"It's not going to be easy to avoid the appointment."

"I have never liked things that are too easy. I accept any proposal. Tell me the strategy, Doctor. I'm not bad at following orders."

We spent more than half an hour in the consultation room. I doubted that Claudia would find out anything. She had enough to do to control her crying and shaking. I opted to tell her that it was better for her to calm down outside. The last thing I needed was the drama of a Venezuelan soap opera. I had to be focused on saving my neck, and I was not here to console anyone, not now. I was not going to die, so I had to concentrate on whatever that man gave me to cling to life until my last breath.

After I insisted a couple of times that she go to the waiting room, she complied. The nurse came in, on the advice of the doctor, to accompany her.

We stood alone, the doctor and I, face to face, both of us frowning, to detail my life minute by minute from now on.

To think that I had only gone to the doctor because I was feeling a little tired. I thought they were going to give me vitamins, not perform an emergency colonoscopy and CT scan and diagnose me with terminal cancer. I was to undergo two operations and several chemotherapy sessions in a fairly short time. The debacle my body was going to suffer would be monumental. I needed to be strong both physically and mentally. I planned to take care of myself as never before, and if it would help, I would pull out all the stops.

"Will my hair fall out?" was a silly question I asked. I already knew the answer. I had seen thousands of reports. Not that I cared too much since I had worn my hair shaved many times. However, the question had come to me as a reflex.

"Most likely."

"On my balls too?"

The laughter came over him without him being able to resist it. I had always used humor, even in my worst moments. Smiling healed everything, and I was convinced of it.

"Sorry," he apologized. "I wasn't expecting that one. You usually lose hair all over your body, but in some cases, you don't. It's still a long way off. We'd better take it one step at a time." He must have thought I was a moron, but that didn't seem to matter. "It's good that you don't lose your humor. Being positive usually helps a lot." I nodded, placing an imaginary medal on my chest. "I will refer you to a specialist, and he will decide where to start. I'm sorry I couldn't have given you better news."

"Don't worry, Doctor. I realize that it is not pleasant for you either. But listen, I'm going to get out of this, I guarantee you. I can't die without seeing New York. I'm going to cure myself for it." I was completely sure that this was going to be the case.

From the disbelief that flickered in his eyes, which he tried to hide, he was not convinced.

"It is good to have objectives, reasons to fight, and hold on to them. Although it is also necessary that we do not ignore the possibility that it can happen, and we must be prepared for it."

We fell into a soothing silence where I started reprogramming my brain while he ran his fingers over the computer's keys.

When I came out, my wife was surrounded by nurses who were trying to calm her down. She was drinking something, probably water, to calm herself. The three pairs of female eyes looked at me with pity. I admit that it was not the kind of feeling I liked to arouse in women. I was always an attractive guy, and the uniform was a bonus, even if I wasn't wearing it today. I planted myself in front of them and gave a nod.

"Shall we go?" I asked uncomfortably.

The nurses helped Claudia sit up, apologizing as if they were to blame for what was happening to me. Claudia needed to hold on to my arm since her knees were not strong enough to support her. I was afraid she would collapse. We didn't start walking until I felt sure she wouldn't faint on the way.

I thanked the nurses for taking care of her, and she leaned her forehead against my shoulder, seeking a hug that I offered her.

We didn't speak until we got to the parking lot and got into the car. Claudia had bloodshot eyes and a red nose.

"Áxel," I heard her murmur, sniffling. I saw her extreme pallor. "You're going to die," she said with a hollow look.

It was a painful statement, not a question.

"We will all die someday. No one is born to stay, but don't worry. You're not dead until you close your eyes, and mine are wide open. See?" I pushed my eyelids with my fingers to give more truth to my assertion.

"Will you promise me?" she whispered shakily.

"Of course, so stop crying." I wiped the tears away with my thumbs. "This has only just begun, and I need you in one piece, okay?" Claudia nodded, and I started the engine. Now came the hardest part: going home and telling the kids.

We did not do it right away. Claudia and I had to talk about how our life was going to change from now on. I did not want to ask for sick leave until the day of my first operation. I had a visit with the surgeon who would operate on me in two days. That was how it was going to be from now on, appointment after appointment. Hospitals would be part of my new reality: the smell of disinfectant, the aseptic walls, the white coats, and green pajamas. I had to get used to it. In my new mission, there was no weapon other than medicine, and the health personnel were the stormtroopers.

We stopped for lunch at a bar and restaurant overlooking the beach in Canet de Mar. We hadn't talked for a long time. We were not ready, and it showed in the form of awkward silences throughout the meal. It was logical that Claudia was scared. I understood her initial shock, but now we had to face the adversity. Overcoming cancer would be our life.

There was more, and the sooner I took it on, the better.

We agreed that I would lead the conversation with the kids. She was not strong enough, and I was afraid that she would magnify the situation by collapsing like she had in the hospital.

"You must keep yourself whole," I whispered, grabbing her hand and running my thumb over her knuckles. She was no longer used to my displays of affection. Our marriage had become so cold that this simple touch made her uncomfortable. I pulled my hand away.

"For someone as unemotional as you, that's easy to say. You've just been told you have three months left, and you look like you've been told it's going to rain tomorrow. I'm amazed at the way you take things!" It sounded like a reproach.

"What do you want me to do? Would you be happier if I were as defeated as you are and crying in corners?"

"No, but it annoys me that you don't see the gravity. All through lunch, you kept telling me that your illness, or "the bug," as you called it, is a new challenge as if it were another challenge in your job and you're going to get out of it unscathed and it's *not*," she replied aggressively. "The nurses told me that a case like yours is terminal! You're going to die, no matter how much you promised me you aren't going to!" She threw the napkin on the table and leaned back in her chair.

"I don't give a shit what those birds of ill omen told you! Look at me, Claudia," I asked her, facing eyes full of anger. "It doesn't count, do you hear me? The only thing that matters is how I feel it, how I perceive it, and I'm not going to let myself be defeated."

"What if you can't handle it? What if you leave us alone?"

"Do you think it would make much difference to your life if I wasn't in it right now?" I asked with the best intentions in the world. Masking our poor relationship was just putting a Band-Aid on a bleeding wound. She looked away. "I may be sick now, but that doesn't cloud my thinking. I left you a long time ago, I admit, but you left me a long time ago too. If the doctor's prediction comes true, your life will not change."

Her blue eyes were filled with resentment. Was that what we had left? This was not the time to bring out the dirty laundry.

"It's never the time to talk. You've been avoiding this conversation for so long. Every time I bring it up, you go off on a tangent."

"And you think *now* is the right time? When you've been told you have hardly any time left?"

"Maybe not, but since it's come up, we should talk the hell out of it. I don't want you to reproach yourself for spending months taking care of a sick person for whom you no longer feel anything but pity. Our relationship has been extinct for a long time, and I doubt very much that it can be recovered."

She shook her head, placing it between her hands.

"I'm going from being the father of your children, the man with whom you share expenses, to the man whose vomit you have to collect in a basin. Imagine what it will be like to go through that."

"We're not that bad!" she exclaimed in self-delusion.

I didn't believe her, even though she believed herself. What was the point of continuing in this false cordiality? "Oh, aren't we? Well, we must live in parallel dimensions because in mine, we have a relationship of sorrow. How long has it been since the last time we did it?"

The question made her uncomfortable, and she shifted in her chair, crossing her arms defensively.

"I don't know. Does it matter that much? It's normal. We're tired. Day-to-day life is swallowing us up, and we've been together for so many years. It's normal that things get cold. It happens to my friends too."

"So, you talk about it with your friends?" It wasn't a reproach, although it might seem so. I just wanted her to admit that she could see that we were not doing well. "Two years," I announced, raising my index finger. "Two years and three months, to be exact."

"Don't fuck with me, Áxel. You've got it written down?"

"No, but almost. It was the night of your birthday. The last time you let me go beyond a simple good night," I murmured thoughtfully. "I think so. It's just that you no longer care about it, and you don't pay attention to it anymore. You've normalized a situation that shouldn't be that way. You're only thirty-three. What happens when you're fifty?"

"But I love you!" she complained, clinging to that statement. "I accept that it is not a passionate love like when we first met, but you are the father of my children. We have lived through many things together and…"

"Close your eyes," I ordered in a calm voice.

"Why?" she asked without understanding my request.

"Close your eyes. It's just to check one thing. Do it, please," I begged gently.

Her eyelids drooped. "Okay, now don't open them and answer one question. It's easy, I promise. What am I wearing today?"

Her fingers twitched as she gripped the edge of the table.

"What kind of question is that?" She kept her eyes closed, struggling to find an answer to my question. "I didn't notice," she finally said, "I had more to worry about than what shirt you're wearing."

"It's not a shirt. I'm wearing a sweatshirt."

Claudia opened her eyes in disbelief. A multitude of emotions welled up in them: anger, frustration, betrayal, and reproach. She grabbed the napkin and threw it hard against the table.

"Why this gratuitous attack now!" Her lip was trembling. She felt hunted, so she fought like a cornered animal.

"It's not an attack. I'm just trying to make you realize that you stopped seeing me a long time ago."

She let out a humorless laugh. "It's funny that you say that. You who forgets about your daughter's judo championships and your son's skating championships. You don't give a damn if it's our anniversary, so you can go off and train with your little pistols because, if you don't, you'll feel like you're not fulfilling yourself.

"And now what? Now your life has stopped. Now nothing matters, as always, because the epicenter of your universe has been your damn selfishness. Neither my children nor I have been able to overcome your love for yourself. Always being the axis of the universe, everyone rotates to the sound of your needs. Even now, you must be the sick one. You, you, you, you, you. Where am I? Where are my goals, my desires, and my wants? Have you ever cared about them?"

"Are you listening to yourself? You're reproaching me for being sick! This is not love, Claudia. This is dependence. I never opposed your goals because you never had any." I should have bitten my tongue, but I did not. She held her breath, hurt, and I tried to make amends. "I'm sorry. I didn't mean that. You did have a goal to be a mother and have a family."

"And that's so terrible? We don't all want to climb the career ladder. I was satisfied with a simple life with you and our children. I didn't need so much, only you." Her eyes filled with tears. She had hurt us so much that she could not turn back.

"Let's split up."

No!" she exclaimed, getting up from the table and coming to me. "I don't want to be separated from you. I just want us to have another chance, but a real one. I want you to be the Áxel I fell in love with again," she begged, holding my face in her hands.

"I never changed. Only the circumstances changed, and that was enough to destroy our relationship."

"Well, let's try, but this time for real. Please, Áxel, please, I don't want to lose you," she begged, seeking my mouth with her lips. It was a sweet and fearful kiss.

Nothing stirred inside me. Nothing throbbed or ignited the flame of desire, but I let myself be carried away by "what if," which is a way of deceiving oneself to postpone any decision too painful to carry out.

"All right," I agreed. "Let's give it a try."

CHAPTER EIGHT

Ilunga: A person who forgives an offense the first time can tolerate a second one but not a third.

Garbiñe, present time

We had arranged to meet at Tasca de Cristian, a restaurant located in the historic center of La Laguna. It was a small place with few tables and a good menu, ideal for a quiet dinner and good service.

When I arrived, I didn't understand what was happening. There was no party, just Áxel and me. Maybe the other people hadn't arrived yet. He was sitting at a single table. So what was going on?

I approached him. He looked gorgeous. It seemed as if we had planned our appearance. He was wearing a white linen shirt, Ibiza style, matching my dress. He stood up smiling and pulled apart the chair right in front of him.

"Hi," I greeted, blushing at his eager gaze.

"Hi there," he replied in a deep voice, leaning closer to me. He rested his lips against my cheek in an intimate gesture that made me want more. When he went to switch sides, the tips of our noses brushed against each other, pulling a smile that did not detract from the intensity of the other kiss he had just planted close to my lips.

I could have melted from that small token of affection, but I decided to ask about the others lest they were about to arrive and find me like that.

"What about the others?" I asked, looking this way and that.

"I hope you don't mind. I just wanted to have dinner with you. I was not willing to have the same thing happen that did at lunch and have them monopolize your time, so I told them I was not feeling well and I was going to stay at the hotel. A white lie. I hope you aren't upset."

His revelation surprised me. Had he concocted the whole thing to have dinner alone with me?

What about Colmenares? That my partner had been part of the deception caught me off guard.

"He agreed to help me out. He said something to the effect that you needed this dinner even more than I did."

My face lit up. "I swear I'm going to twist his balls until I give him the vasectomy his wife wanted so badly. He will no longer need to go to a private doctor."

He made a frightened face. "Fuck, it's no big deal. Is it such a bad idea to have dinner alone with me?"

"It's not about that, it's that he made me look needy in front of you, and that's not the case. Besides, I don't like being cheated. They already did that for too many years."

He ducked his eyes in regret and then turned back to me to try to sort things out.

"He didn't make you sound needy, but rather that you needed to get out more and that he didn't think it was a bad idea for us to have dinner alone. According to him, you prefer one-on-one to mass meetings, so I think he was trying to do us both a favor. Although, if you prefer, I'll call to tell them I'm feeling better, and we'll meet them at the restaurant where they've arranged to meet."

It was my chance to meet him as I had intended. I did not want to spoil it with my sudden attack of dignity.

"It wouldn't be credible if the two of us showed up together. It would be a bit weird. Besides, I'm already here, you have a table ready, and I'm hungry. It wouldn't be good to waste it," I lied.

"So, shall we sit down?"

I nodded, and he smiled, pulling the chair closer to me as I went to get settled.

He gave me one of the two menus on the table.

"If you like, we can order something to share first. I'm not very hungry."

I agreed. "I think that's perfect."

The waiter came to take our order and returned with our drinks. My palms were sweaty, and I was a little thrown. I had not prepared myself to dine with him alone.

"Carnivorous?" he asked to break the awkward silence that plagued us when the waiter stopped to note our choices.

"Today, I'm getting carried away. That's what I was looking forward to most on the menu. It sounds good to get carried away," she murmured.

"You look a little stiff for not wearing a uniform." That he made that remark made me a little angry. "I'd say you're a Civil Guard inside and out. That you have it so deep down inside that you are incapable of not being one, even when you are off duty. Am I wrong?"

"Maybe a little. I'm rusty when it comes to going out."

"Well, you can relax with me. I haven't been going out much either."

"Yeah, but I've been doing it for years."

He looked at me in surprise as he placed the napkin over his legs.

"Years? That sounds like a lot."

"Too much, I'd say. Don't hold it against me if I pass out on the plate."

"Because you suffer from narcolepsy, or do you mean I'm so boring that you go to sleep?"

I started laughing like an idiot. "Neither one. It's more that I didn't sleep much last night, and as I'm not a night owl, maybe I'll end up exhausted."

"Well, we'd better not order soup, lest you choke and I have to give you mouth-to-mouth."

Waiter! One soup! howled my inner she-wolf. "Do you know how to do it?" I provoked him.

"I've never tried it with noodle flavor, but I'm sure I'm not bad at it."

"Well, just in case, we won't order soup, lest you forget the technique, and the night ends before it starts. Right?"

"I agree," he replied with a chuckle.

The waiter came with the appetizers, and we began to nibble. "Are you Basque?" was his next question. Sometimes my name confused people. There were not many Garbiñes on the islands.

"No. Are you an independentist?"

He laughed. "That was a good one," he admitted with shining eyes. "No, my parents were born in Huelva, and so was I. I am Catalan by adoption and Spanish at heart. I don't think the two things go hand in hand. One has to learn to always keep the best."

I was starting to feel comfortable with him. I decided to pick up my pace and answer him the same way I would Paula.

"Well, I'm not Basque either. My parents gave me the name because during a trip to the North, they met a girl with the same name, and they thought it was very pretty. To tell you the truth, I don't consider myself from anywhere. When I was a child, I went from barracks to barracks with my family, depending on where my father was assigned, neither Basque nor Andalusian or Léonese or Tenerife or anything else. I am Spanish," I said proudly.

"Like olives. I hope I don't choke on the stone."

"You won't choke if you don't bite me. Besides, I prefer them stuffed with anchovies."

He guffawed. "I am not Basque either, and my name wasn't because of the independence rant. You'd be surprised if I told you that my mother's platonic love was Axl Rose."

"A heavy metal enthusiast from Huelva?" I asked in amazement.

My mother only brought out her inner heavy when she took off her flip-flops. She would do a drum solo on your ass. If Axl had seen her, I'm sure he would have asked her to be his drummer. In truth, my mother doesn't like that music. She just saw the singer in a video clip and fell in love. My father, who at that time worked in radio, swore to her that if Guns n' Roses ever came to Spain, he would never take her to one of the concerts, lest the one with the roses would take her heart.

"How nice." I sighed, touched by the story.

During dinner, I could not stop smiling. I thought we were going to talk about the course and police experiences, but to my surprise, it was not like that, and I felt very comfortable sharing personal experiences.

I found myself asking him questions about his childhood, and we laughed like crazy people when we realized that we both wanted to be Superman, and neither of us had made a good landing.

It was intimate and special, and I liked feeling listened to by a man who interested me.

The wine loosened my tongue, and I could not stop joking. I was dazzled by that strange joy I was unintentionally unleashing.

How was I able to do that if I had fifteen years left and was already dead inside?

I beg your pardon. Ah, yes, I didn't tell you about my illness. I'm sorry. I told you I don't open up right away, and it's something I still haven't fully assimilated. The sickness.

My age and my failed marriage have been the perfect combination to make me feel like shit.

It started a couple of years ago. I suffered from constant migraines that my husband did not tolerate very well. He always had a very intense social life that was affected by my headaches. And although I tried not to interrupt it, to let him go out while I stayed at home with the baby, anything would cause us to argue.

Playing sports was my escape valve. Now I had to settle for chasing my son Ruben around the park because, as soon as I tried to run, my brain turned to mush.

That year sucked.

With the arrival of summer, Dario immersed himself in the surf school, and a crisis appeared that almost caused us to separate. Parties, rumors of affairs with his students, and the lack of empathy he showed toward my discomfort caused me to kick him out of the apartment for a couple of weeks. But I was soft, and after a few apologies accompanied by a large bouquet of roses, he swore to me that I was the love of his life, and I let it go.

We tiptoed through the summer with subtle conversations where veiled threats could be glimpsed about custody now being given more to fathers.

My world was sinking, and I resigned myself to trying to stay afloat so as not to be shipwrecked in it. I built walls full of pretexts where I felt comfortable. I shielded myself, thinking that things would get better and that nothing and no one could blow up my family.

The year 2015 ended without pain or glory, giving way to a new year where my health was affected.

2016 brought me a second disease as a gift, irritable bowel disease. "Stress," said the doctor. "You have to take care of yourself." The diagnosis made me laugh. With the number of times I had told Dario to go fuck himself, it was only logical that he had finally irritated me.

My attitude toward him changed. I was no longer as tolerant of his comings and goings, which led to an ongoing battle that brought us to the brink of separation for the second time.

How could I not be stressed if my husband was making my blood boil and raising all my defenses? The doctor insisted on referring me to the hematologist, and while I was waiting for an appointment, I got tired of letting him walk all over me.

I stood up in front of my husband to tell him that we couldn't go on like this and we had to separate for the good of the three of us. I couldn't take it anymore. The following week, the scoundrel showed up, tickets in hand for us to take a ten-day cruise in the Mediterranean.

It had always been like that with him. When I made up my mind, he would destabilize me, making me doubt whether breaking up my family was worth it.

I should not have accepted, but I did, falling for it again. I confess that I got my hopes up and believed he was willing to bet on us. My ex planned the cruise as a honeymoon. We parked Ruben with my mother and left, just us. We relaxed and enjoyed ourselves, and let's say that we had a calm interlude until June came, and with it, Dario's high season.

The hematologist had me undergo a bone marrow test, which I attended alone.

Why would my husband come with me? What was the need for him? None, because by now, I knew he didn't give a shit. I felt like an old shoe whose sole kept coming off, so why take me to the cobbler?

When the doctor gave me the diagnosis, I hardly understood. He used terms that sounded like Chinese to me. The only thing I could grasp was that something was wrong with my blood.

"Excuse me, Doctor, but can you explain it to me another

way? What is this polycythemia vera?" I cleared my throat with my pulse racing.

"Your disease is caused by a mutation in an RBC-producing cell. The blood becomes thick because of the considerable increase of red blood cells in it."

"Yeah, but that's not bad, is it? As far as I know, red blood cells are the ones that carry oxygen to the blood. If I have it denser, it will be more oxygenated. Maybe it's because I used to do sports."

He shook his head from side to side. "It's not because of that, Mrs. Navarro, and being dense is not good."

"Okay, then give me a little pill to make it more liquid, and we solve it."

"I wish it were that easy. Your illness cannot be fixed with a 'little pill.' You will have to undergo therapeutic bleedings, take salicylic acid, and maybe radioactive phosphorus."

I tried to assimilate the news.

"Okay. I've always liked drinking sangria, especially with a lot of fruit. I can tolerate aspirin. What I'm going to find worse is the radioactive match. If my son catches it, he'll definitely set the floor on fire." My lip was trembling.

When I was very nervous, I tried to calm down with humor. Sometimes, though, it didn't work out too well.

"Take this seriously. Your disease is serious. There are only four to six cases per million inhabitants, with the average age of diagnosis at the age of sixty. Having this disease before the age of forty is quite rare."

"In other words, I hit the jackpot."

"I am sorry to say that it seems so. The consolation you have left is that, although it is not a curable disease, because of its chronic nature, it can be managed effectively for long periods."

DPM! I wanted to shout. *Come on, ladies. We're on sale today, and they're taking them off our hands.* They say there's no two without three, and I had already made a full house. One migraine, one colon, and for dessert, a fucking chronic disease. The menu was not to be missed.

"I'm never going to be cured." I spoke to myself more than to him.

"No, and there's something else."

"Something else?" I blinked in disbelief.

"I'll try to be tactful. Patients with your disease, well-treated, usually have an average survival rate of fifteen years when they are in their fifties or sixties. In this case, it can be longer. Maybe we can get you to fifty if everything goes well."

Wait a minute, wait a minute.

There it was, the mother of all lotteries, and it had to be me.

"Am I going to die?" I managed to ask.

His head went up and down in the quietest death sentence I had ever witnessed.

"If it's any consolation, we all will."

Oxygen didn't reach my lungs. I was so scared that I hyperventilated. Fifteen years. Fifteen years. In fifteen years, it would all be over for me. If everything went extremely well, I would reach fifty.

Hell, the doctor was only thirty!

I saw him get up to hold my hand. Good morning, Green Sleeves!

"Calm down, ma'am. Please, breathe."

"Breathe? What for? I'm going to die!" The feeling of suffocation increased. It all happened so fast that I barely noticed. I found myself pushed onto a stretcher so I wouldn't collapse in the chair. Between the doctor and the nurse, they managed to get my legs up, and she placed a pill under my tongue.

What was to become of me and my son? Fifteen years was nothing!

From the time I got the news until Paula found out, months passed. I didn't dare tell my family. My father had died two years ago, and I didn't want to upset them. My husband and his mother were the only ones who knew about it because I didn't have the nerve.

How did Paula find out?

I had an anxiety attack in the middle of the night while I was sleeping. Dario was away; he had gone to Fuerteventura for a surfing championship, and my friend was spending the night to keep me company. What a scare she had. She thought I was having a heart attack and drove like crazy to the emergency room.

The doctor discharged me, ordering me to rest and to take things at a different pace, and of course, since she was in front of me at all times, she listened to my history.

The fuss I had to endure from my friend when we arrived at the apartment was epic. Her grief, coupled with the administrative silence I had maintained for months, put her in a really bad mood that only calmed down when I burst into tears, completely undone.

How long had it been since the last time I had collapsed like that? I think since my father's funeral. That was the last day I allowed myself to cry like there was no tomorrow.

I was off work for two weeks until the doctor felt I could return. I asked for a change in my schedule so that my shifts would be more regular and thus help me control the migraine. The commissioner and Colmenares scolded me for having neglected myself so much and made me promise that from now on, I would look after myself more and others less.

The months went by, and the summer of 2017 came into our lives. That was the last year I would live with my husband.

On July 10, Dario came to me with the story that we had to give ourselves some time. I could say that I was caught by surprise, but I would be lying. He was at home less and less. His weekends and comings and goings between islands had become a regular occurrence. He only came to the apartment to have his laundry done. Rumors had reached me that he was seeing

Damaris a lot. When I tried to bring it up, he made a fuss, saying that I was jealous. She was his friend, and it was my imagination. Cheap talk I tried to digest.

My mood got worse. I didn't feel like doing anything. I think, if it hadn't been for Paula, I would have let myself die. It sounds harsh and stupid. I had my son, and that alone was reason enough to live, but I was unable to find myself and have the strength to get out of the hole I had dug myself into.

I hit rock bottom. I lost six kilos and became a bag of skin and bones. My son was whining for me to go to the park, and I was unable to walk. I got scared.

That day I swore to myself that it was going to be the last day, that I was tired of feeling this way, I was being so unfair to my little boy, and he didn't deserve to go through all that. I didn't want his childhood memory to be of a mother who was incapable of smiling.

I was enveloped in a strange melancholy, a feeling of vital failure that was shaking me with such force that it even took away one of the things that made me happiest, going to work.

I wanted to get out, but the well was too dark, too deep, and the rope to climb up was too fragile.

Low anxiety and depression was the new diagnosis.

Months of uncertainty kept me immersed in a strange universe where raising my head was unattainable. Lifting my eyelashes, crawling out of bed, or taking a simple shower was too much for me.

No matter how hard I tried, I was not able to do it, neither with pills nor with the psychologist's talks or with anything else. My world was falling apart, and I was unable to find a way out of the darkness.

Until it happened.

My husband returned home, flicking the switch that brought me out of that vegetative state to which I did not want to return.

It was mid-September. Dario opened the door with his keys

and his tail between his legs. He hugged me, claiming that he had realized that I was the woman of his life and he didn't want to run away anymore. He had had enough.

"Enough? Ha!" I wanted to spit in his face. By this point, I knew who he had been playing house with for months. Damaris was his experimental failure, and now the bastard wanted to come home for me to heal his wounds. Well, it was a no-brainer.

I may have been at my lowest point, but that gave me the push I needed because when all you have left to lose is nothing, you stop being afraid to go for it all. Now I knew what was hurting me and what I didn't want in my life, it was right in front of me, and it had taken me going through all this for me to realize it.

My husband had devastated the woman in me, leaving her in ruins. However, I was not willing to let him undermine what little was left. I was going to rebuild her, recover her, and be proud of who I was.

I looked him in the eyes. He tried to feign a regret he didn't feel, and I ran my hand through his hair to grab it tightly and pull it. Without looking away, I told him, "I'm sorry. You may have now realized what you had, but I have too, and now I know what I want."

"And what is it?"

"Divorce."

That was the best decision I ever made. I'm not going to lie to you. It was not easy. He had a huge tantrum, then made attempts to win me back. He subsequently threatened to get custody of the child.

In the end, it all came to nothing. Dario moved into his mother's apartment, and I put ours up for sale. Now we were just neighbors with a child in common, nothing more. I wanted a new life full of hope, and the farther away from my ex, the better.

I fixed my gaze on the man in front of me. There he was, with a dazzling attitude and a seemingly healthy countenance that stole my breath away. His body was muscular, his arms were three times the size of mine, and those strong hands with elongated fingers made me want to know what it would feel like to have them around my anatomy.

I reached for the glass of wine and took a sip to refresh the image. I was filling myself with expectations that I didn't know if I would have the nerve to carry out. My inner prude was holding me back, and yet I just wanted to get rid of it all at once.

Perhaps if I spent a night with Áxel, his life experience would help me understand what was wrong with mine. Perhaps I could come to understand how he did it and draw on his inner strength to charge me from within.

I just had to let myself go. Dinner was running out, and if I didn't do something about it, I could see myself going home lonelier than before.

I asked, "Would you like to go for a walk on the beach? Today there's a full moon, and I'd like to show you its reflection on the sea."

Had I been too bold? Had I been too obvious? I bit the inside of my cheek and prayed that he would say yes.

"I'd love to," he replied, putting his hand over mine.

CHAPTER NINE

Mangata: The path of light that the moon makes over the water.

Áxel, present time

I walked beside Garbiñe in silence. Since the beginning of the night, we had not stopped talking. I liked the timbre of her voice, her eloquence, the enthusiasm she showed at every memory of her childhood, and the shyness she tried to hide, even though her blush gave it away.

We were barefoot, with the fine sand squeaking between our toes and the fresh foam fluttering under our soles.

"I've always felt like wet sand," she whispered to herself more than to me.

"How is that?"

She shrugged. "I don't know. I guess because I'm used to others acting as waves, covering me until I disappear out to sea. This has never happened to you, of course. You are a wave, it shows."

"Because I am so salty?"

She smiled at me, and her warmth pierced me.

"No, waves can see you coming, and those of us who are sand tend to go unnoticed." She smiled, tucking a short lock of hair behind her ear.

He was thinking of something clever to say about his reflection when she exclaimed, "Look!" Her finger pointed above the water. *Mangata.*

I fixed my eyes on the point where the moon swayed over the water forming a tongue of light that tasted the swell. I had heard the word somewhere. It was becoming very fashionable to know words that lacked a specific term in our language.

"It's beautiful," I admitted.

"It is. Seeing it always calms me down. I usually come here in my lowest moments." The melancholy was taking over my dinner companion, and I longed to make her smile.

Garbiñe pulled out a foot that was engulfed in sand and stumbled, not having taken into account how deep it had been. She bumped into my side, dropping her weight on mine.

A reflex made me grab her and squeeze her against me. Her face was in my armpit. Perfect; the ideal place to get a smile out of her.

"Testing my deodorant?" I asked teasingly against her ear.

She stiffened and pulled away, leaving me with a sense of loss.

"I'm sorry, I got scared. I thought I saw something on the beach, and I didn't want to get bitten by a crab."

"God forbid Sebastian should amputate your finger."

"Sebastian?" she asked, not understanding.

She didn't know who I was talking about. "Yes. You know, the crab from *The Little Mermaid.*"

She gave a nervous chuckle. "I'm not much for Disney. I am more into superhero movies."

"I had no choice but to swallow them all more than once. My oldest son loved princesses, and as for my daughter, it was the only thing that let her sleep at night. There was no way she would sleep if we didn't give her a princess fix. They are about to nominate Disney princesses as the hardest drug. Next to them, heroin is beginner material."

She laughed again, and I found myself thinking I didn't want to stop hearing that sound.

"You are unique. I liked that remark. You have two children, then?"

"It seems so. You know, you can never be sure if you are the father. Just kidding," I corrected. Some women were uncomfortable with that kind of joke. "Christian is sixteen, and Andrea is nine. They have been living with their mother since we separated almost two years ago. And you?"

"I have only one heir to the throne, Ruben. Mine is five years old, and I have joint custody with his father. We separated in September."

"It's very recent," I noted, knowing what that could mean. Separations were not easy, and each person needed time to move on.

"Not really," she said. "The official separation was recent, but we had been unhappy as a married couple for far too long. Since the beginning of July, we no longer live together, so deep down, we hadn't been feeling, or being, what we should have been for a long time."

"I know what you're talking about. Would you like to sit down and continue the conversation?" She nodded. Thank goodness she did, the stitches in my abdomen were pulling, and the pain made it impossible for me to stand much longer.

The course had been very intense, many hours without resting on a chair. The physical demands of the demonstrations made my body ask for rest, even though my heart did not.

We looked for a place a bit away from the water and settled in. Sitting on the ground brought a cold sweat down my spine. The whiplash of pain was imminent. Luckily, Garbiñe did not notice the discomfort that was plaguing me. It was too soon, I needed more rest.

"So, your marital status is separated?" she asked without looking directly at me.

"My status depends on who is asking."

The answer caught her attention. She turned her face to me in disbelief.

"What do you mean?"

"You know, whether I'm interested or not," I answered honestly. "Don't look at me like that. I learned that from women many years ago. If they liked it when they got into it, they were quick to declare themselves single, even if the boyfriend was ordering a drink at the bar. And if that wasn't the case, they pretended to be dykes."

"I doubt very much that they were pretending to be lesbians with you," she muttered, crossing her arms.

"Some of them tried, and that's why we ended up having a threesome." Her eyes widened at my smug look. I burst out laughing. "Just kidding. I'm more of an even-number person."

"You mean you slept with three instead of two?"

"One at a time, and that's how I prefer women." I tapped the tip of her nose with my index finger.

"Are you always joking?"

"Are you always so tense?" I countered.

My back was so stiff that I could have used it as a bow to shoot an arrow.

"I'm not very good at socializing," she confessed. "Although I may seem dull, I have a sense of humor, don't doubt it. It's just that it's hard for me to show it when I'm not confident."

"Well, we'll have to work on that, won't we? I plan to earn your trust until you cry laughing with me. By the way, you don't seem dull to me, just a little reserved. That's not a bad thing. It means you don't give yourself easily to people." Her faint smile grew wider. "Look, there's a beautiful smile emerging."

"That's because you've made me feel so comfortable."

"I'm glad to hear that." I stretched my neck back and stopped looking at her for a moment to lose myself in the sight of the stars. Those who have never been anywhere say that the sky is the same everywhere. In Tenerife, it was beautiful, like the face of a redhead dotted with freckles. Garbiñe had a few freckles I wanted to caress.

"In my opinion, life is too short to be bitter," I reflected aloud. "And grumpiness doesn't get you anywhere good."

"I wish we were all like you and could see life in the same color," she replied. "What color do you usually see it?"

I took a breath, closed my eyes, and released it slowly, then opened them.

"Lately, black, and if I'm having a good day, shades of gray," I said. "A thousand and one things have happened in a short time that I still haven't been able to digest. Besides, I don't feel well."

"You mean healthwise?"

I nodded. "I've been going to the doctor for a while, and it's not nice to be told that you have to be continually checked to see how your disease is progressing. It's quite hard for me."

I did not say it as a reproach but rather as an observation.

"Yet, you are facing life with a smile on your lips that fills me with envy. I don't know how to do that. I wish I did. There are days when getting out of bed becomes a bloody hell."

I reached out, and without asking permission, stroked her cheek, causing her body to twitch involuntarily.

"Everything can be learned in this life. You just have to put a little bit of yourself into it, and if your bed is hell, maybe you haven't found the right devil."

"You make it sound so easy," she whispered tremulously.

My thumb was still on her cheek. I liked to feel it, even if it was with the lightness of a brush.

"It's just as hard to live as it is to decide to stop. If you were to take my advice, I would tell you that it's simply a matter of wiping the slate clean and smiling again. You can't and shouldn't let anything turn you off."

By now, my thumb had moved over her lip, and my body had swayed toward hers. Her eyes dilated at my nearness, waiting for the move I was about to make.

The woman's lips opened to welcome me, and mine were eager to know her taste. Her eyelids veiled what we both already knew, that the spark we lost in our marriages had ignited without our expecting it. They say that the skin belongs to the one who makes it bristle, and if I had to mimic an animal, it would be a porcupine full of quills. That was how the hair on my entire body was.

I descended, driven by the instinct that I was doing the right thing. That the kiss I intended to give her was what we both wanted, and I would have done it if we hadn't been interrupted just before her lips met mine.

"Garbi?"

My companion's arms failed her, and she collapsed on the sand with her eyes wide open like a porcelain doll.

"I told you it was her," said the second voice.

I turned my head to find two blondes who looked alike. Either I had been drinking heavily and was seeing double, or they were twins.

I blinked a few times before I realized it was the second option. If Paris Hilton could double herself, I'd swear she was in front of me.

They were both very blonde, light-eyed, wearing very short dresses, and holding their shoes in their hands.

My companion pulled herself together and looked at them in astonishment. "What are you two doing here?"

"And you? He was going to kiss you!" Paris One burst out.

"What are you talking about, Pili!" Garbiñe exclaimed angrily. *Paris One equals Pili*, I noted mentally.

"Either he was going to give you a halitosis test, or he was going to kiss you," said Paris Two.

"I don't have halitosis!"

Garbiñe was flustered. I assumed they were very close to her, or she wouldn't react that way. I stood up to introduce myself so they could call me by my name instead of using a pronoun. My scar protested the effort. "Hello. I'm Áxel."

They ran their scanners over my entire body. Diving or snogging?

"From Taser," I added.

"What is that, a new way to snog?" asked Pili.

"A police course, you pair of inept women. I don't know what you have in your heads besides hairspray."

Garbiñe had stood up. They looked at her with acrimony. "Well, that didn't look like a police course to me. More like an oral hygiene course where his tongue would end up in your larynx. If only Dario could see you."

Garbiñe was angry. "If Dario saw me, so what? We're not married anymore!"

The Parises snorted. "You two have always been the same. Mom says you're going to come back as soon as you realize you're incapable of living without someone to rule your life. Without him, you're going to be very unhappy. Mom says you won't find anyone else to put up with you."

"Why should I be unhappy? Because I'm not a disheveled mess like you, my sisters? Or because I haven't brought anyone into the house yet like Mom? I'm sick of the three of you judging me because I'm not the same as you! It's true that I don't sleep with a different guy every week, and I haven't exchanged my dead husband for the neighbor, but I have the right to live, to be free, and to do whatever I want without you questioning me."

She looked at them defiantly. I was turned on by this new Garbi.

"And just so you know, I was going to kiss him before you interrupted us! And I'm not going back to that bastard Dario, no matter how much he insists!"

I almost laughed at her belligerence, although it would not

have been the best moment. None of those present would have understood the humor.

Getting the news out loud that my tennis player sergeant was planning to kiss me gave me such a rush that I came close to giving them a live demonstration.

Pili and Paris Two, whose name I did not yet know, looked at me as if I were a paranormal phenomenon.

"He's too good for you," Paris Two stated nonchalantly.

"I'm sorry, what's your name? I didn't understand it before," I interrupted her.

"I didn't say it. My name is Milagros, although everyone calls me Mili."

Oh, boy, Pili and Mili. I was about to burst out laughing, but Garbiñe's face stopped me.

"Well, if I may say so, Mili, I'm perfect for her. If you and your sister will excuse us, we have a kiss pending that I won't miss. It was a pleasure meeting you. See you again."

I turned around without caring whether or not Garbiñe wanted to add anything about it and grabbed her by the hand to drag her off the beach as firmly as my body and the sand would allow.

We got to her car, where she put her hands to her face.

"Sorry," she mumbled against her palms.

"Shame on you!" Two of her fingers flicked open, letting one mint-colored eye sparkle. I wasn't sure if what I read in it was shyness or amusement. It was too dark.

"Shame on them for interrupting us at a moment like that. Fuck, you were going to kiss me!"

She cleared her throat. "You were going to kiss *me*," she clarified.

"What does it matter? The result would have been the same, and I want you panting in my mouth." That cut her. She couldn't hold my gaze, maybe because she knew that what I was saying was true.

She bent without saying anything about it, pretending to try to remove the remains of sand from between her toes and to put on her sandals. Then she straightened, somewhat recovered.

"Thank you. Seriously, they're not bad girls, but sometimes they're terrible. They have no filters. Do you want to go for a drink on a terrace far from here?"

I went to put on my shoes to answer yes when the pain bent me in two. I leaned on the hood, holding my abdomen tightly.

"Áxel! Are you okay?"

I would have given my arm to say yes, but it was hard to speak. I tried to calm down and let the feeling go away without much success.

"No, I am not," I acknowledged. The lies had evaporated in my new life. "I confess that I would like to tell you that I am, but the truth is that my scar has been giving me a hard time for a while. It's only a month since my surgery, and judging by the warning it just gave me, my body has a curfew. I'm sorry."

"You had surgery a month ago, and you've been dancing all night?" she asked, perplexed.

"A certain tennis player abducted me."

"The referee just blew the whistle for the end."

"I think so, too." I exhaled. I didn't want the evening to end like this, but I had to be consistent. I couldn't fool around. Rest was essential for recovery, and today I had overdone it.

"Come on, I'll give you a ride."

During the trip back to the hotel, I was not the best conversationalist. I had not brought my painkillers with me, and I urgently needed to take them.

Garbiñe left the radio on. Leiva's song *Monstruos* accompanied us during the last stretch. I allowed myself to close my eyes and lose myself in the lyrics.

"This is it, isn't it?" My companion had stopped the vehicle in front of the hotel.

"Yes."

"Áxel, it was a pleasure to meet you. I had a good time." That sentence sounded like a farewell and was too dry for my taste. Maybe I wanted to keep my distance.

"Me too. You have been a great discovery and a wonderful pupil. I admit that I was not very inspired, but the pain was killing me and clouding me."

"You are the best teacher."

I squeezed my eyes shut. Another whiplash.

"You're having a terrible time, and I feel awful for not noticing your pain. Forgive me."

"I had fun like I haven't in ages. This is not your fault, so don't beat yourself up about it. I was having such a good time that I didn't want the night to end," I confessed.

How could the evening have been ruined this way? We were doing so well. At the very least, I was planning to kiss her goodbye.

Someone knocked on my window—Carles, my partner. He was also returning from dinner and had seen us. There was no way to say goodbye alone. I cursed my bad luck, feeling my physical condition getting worse by the minute. My abdomen was throbbing.

Before I could add anything, Garbiñe got out of the car and came around.

She opened the door, looking at me with a worried face. "Are you okay? Do you want to go to the hospital?"

"No, don't worry," I whispered, unbuckling my belt and accepting Carles' help to get out. I wouldn't have been able to do it alone. "With the painkillers, it will pass, I'm sure. I just need rest."

"Go upstairs, and if you need anything, call me. My son is with his father. I'm home alone and have nothing to do but sleep," Garbiñe said.

Great! What a chance I had just wasted. I should whip myself, but I couldn't even do that.

"If anything happens, I'll let you know," my partner assured her. "Come on, champ. You've played too much today."

"Just give me a minute, Carles. I want to say goodbye," I begged.

"All right. I'm in the hall."

After he left, I looked at Garbiñe with regret.

"What a party buddy you got, huh? Instead of the prince, you got the fool."

She smiled but still looked worried. "Are you sure you don't want me to take you to the hospital? Maybe the best thing would be to have a doctor see you."

I said no, I just wanted to give her a proper kiss. Was that too much to ask?

Her eyes sparkled. I couldn't wait to kiss her, although my body disagreed. Another whiplash of pain made me have to hold on to the car. It really hurt!

"*Áxel!*" she exclaimed. I breathed hard, trying to quell the abdominal contractions that were knocking me out. "You have to go now to rest. Take your medication. I'm keeping you in a state of tension, and what you need now is to be calm. Let me help you get to the hall."

She slipped my arm over her shoulders. If I had been in my right mind, I would have refused it. We would have ended up in bed with her underneath.

I clung to her slender body. It was true that she had no flesh to spare. However, she had a lot of strength.

"Shouldn't this be the other way around? The prince always saves the princess," I joked, losing myself in her look of determination.

"This is the dark version of the story. Don't you know it?"

"No."

"Well, both are crippled, the monarchy has been abolished, and as they have been left without a kingdom, they had to pass a competitive examination to ensure a salary by becoming civil guards and *Mosso d'Esquadra*. Ah, and in addition, their days are numbered."

"I think this version is much better. I'm sure Disney will buy the rights from you."

She laughed heartily. "By the way, I'd love to know how the story ends. I don't mind spoilers."

"Well, for one thing, the girl leaves the boy in the hotel lobby because he's been trying to be a hero all day, and it's taken its toll on him."

"No kiss?" She shook her head. "What an asshole. I hope it's just a 'to be continued.' Disney wouldn't buy that ending. There's *always* a kiss."

She laughed and added, "I told you I was more into superheroes."

We stepped inside, and Carles came over to take me. She didn't have time to kiss me. If she had, I would have exploded.

I put my mouth next to her ear. "Make yourself beautiful when you get home. Tonight, we have a date in your dreams." I kissed her cheek, thinking it was the most I could aspire to without her rejecting me, although I wanted much more.

I felt her breath catch and swallowed hard. What I would have given to be well and finish what I had started!

"Come on, handsome, let's get you to the room." My partner grabbed me while Garbiñe blushed.

"Rest," she murmured.

"You too," I replied.

"Thank you for everything, Sergeant Navarro," Carles interjected.

"It has been a pleasure and an honor."

Garbiñe raised her hand in farewell, and my friend made us disappear toward the elevator.

CHAPTER TEN

Nunchi: The ability to read the emotional state of other people.

<u>Áxel, present time</u>

I took a breath and let it out slowly. The painkiller was taking effect.

I had only known this woman for a few hours, but it had been enough to alter something in me. An emotion I was unable to revive with my wife, a feeling that was extinguished with the fleetingness of a falling star and that, as much as I tried to recover it, would not return.

Two years had passed since I was given that fateful news. Two years since we'd decided to give each other a second chance, an opportunity to find meaning in our family. We had failed miserably in the attempt.

I turned off the light and closed my eyes, letting myself be carried away by the memory.

<u>Andorra, November 2015</u>

I looked at the snowcapped mountains that welcomed us into the paradise of the Pyrenees.

I have always liked snowy landscapes. They give the impression of being a gigantic piece of candy sprinkled with sugar. I imagined running my tongue over the icy surface and it melting as I passed by, leaving a taste that had nothing to do with reality.

My children were excited in the back seat. Andrea was too excited about her participation in the judo championship to sit still. I could feel her feet tapping on my seat, and no matter how much I called her attention to it, she kept kicking it.

Christian, for his part, had been glued to the window in a posture that would have kept me twisted up for a week. Kids were made of rubber. They could sleep on a tree branch and feel like new when they woke up.

Claudia's eyes were lost in the landscape, and I remembered the moment I told the children I was sick.

I did not hide the truth from them. After dinner on the day I had lunch with my wife, I called them into the living room. As always, they were teasing each other. What if you are the favorite, and I get punished? In short, a festival of reproaches that brought to light how much they cared for each other. They loved each other to death. I don't only mean love, but on some occasions, they would have taken a knife to each other and hidden the body under the bed.

I sat in the side chair, contemplating them as if it were the first time I had seen them. How long had it been since I had sat like that, concentrating on their movements and their words, perceiving them one hundred percent? Surely too long if I didn't even remember. The realization hurt because it reaffirmed Claudia's theory about my familiar absence.

My wife was right. I had been ignoring my family for too long, putting them aside. Maybe that was why life had placed a gigantic stop sign in the middle of the road, forcing me to stop in my tracks and bringing me to a complete halt so I would stop looking at my navel and see who I had become.

It was not a pleasant situation to be faced with, and I would need time to adjust to it. So would my colleagues, to whom I had given the news that afternoon.

The police station almost turned into a funeral home. I say almost because my mood was the only thing that prevented me from being buried with full honors. My superior suggested I take a leave of absence, and I'd replied that I would do so when it was necessary. For the moment, I preferred to have my head occupied rather than turn my life into a countdown.

The long faces, the words of concern, and the discouragement made an impression on me. I asked them to change that. They had me for a while yet, and I was not going to let myself be carried away so easily. The clouded eyes of those I considered my second family recovered, embarrassed, after shedding a tear or two. The defeat changed to hope. It was my war, but I knew I could count on all of them to be on the battlefield with affection and hugs of encouragement.

It was time for the next step, which was to inform my children of what was happening.

"You can stop!" Claudia shouted an octave above her usual tone. Andrea was hitting her brother, and he was defending himself as best he could. My little girl was so fierce. They ignored her. Claudia turned her attention to me. "Are you not going to say anything? Are you going to let them keep fighting?" Her nervousness made my hair stand on end. It wasn't good, even if she tried to hide it.

"Children, please behave yourselves. Respect your mother," I reprimanded them in a firm but low tone, which they ignored. My wife went to the bookshelf, grabbed a copy of *The Pillars of the Earth* with its thousand and forty pages, hardcover edition, and threw it on the parquet floor shouting, "*Silencio!*" We all shut up. Thank goodness she wasn't a policeman. More than one of us would have ended up with a bullet between the eyebrows.

"Now you have their attention," said my wife, picking up the volume, which was undamaged.

My children looked at me with bewilderment. Christian was the first to speak. "What's wrong, Dad? Is everything all right?"

"No, it is not, but it will be." I heard Claudia snort, but their eyes were locked on mine. "I'm going to tell you something, but I don't want you to get scared. Promise?" They both nodded. "I am sick."

"Do you have a tummy ache?" asked Andrea in her thin voice. "If so, Mommy has some syrup in the pantry."

"I have more than just a tummy ache, daughter. It's called cancer, and it's a complex disease."

They both gasped. "That's what people die from!" exclaimed my little girl with wide eyes.

"Yes, but they also die if a donkey kicks them in the head or if one of Mrs. Encarna's flowerpots falls on them while they are walking."

"It's just that those pots are so fat," said my daughter, thinking about our neighbor in the attic.

"Exactly. I don't want you to be nervous, sad, or worried. I'm telling you because of our promise that we would always tell each other the truth. I don't want to break it now. It is not an easy situation. No illness is easy, no matter how insignificant it may seem. That is why I promise you that I will do everything the doctors tell me. I will follow their directions to the letter because I want to be cured. We are not going to let this be the end of me, are we?"

My daughter frowned, stood up, and squared herself in front of me. "We are not. We'll beat that cancer to a pulp with the medicines. It'll be like applying an *osotogari* judo move to your disease."

"A gay bear?" I asked, amused.

"Not a gay bear," she giggled. "An *osotogari* is a judo move, Dad. We'll knock it out!"

I held out my arms, and she didn't think twice about throwing herself into them. "That's my judo princess."

Andrea laughed when I tickled her belly. My son's face was still serious.

"Hey," I called to him, and he swallowed hard. "I'm going to make it."

Christian was older, and things looked different to him. He just nodded and shyly came toward us. "Of course, Dad."

The three of us ended up in an embrace, and Claudia joined us, her eyes shining with tears.

They were my family, and I would fight.

I parked the car in the lot at the Andorra Palace, a three-star hotel that was very centrally located. It wasn't much, but my daughter's judo teacher had chosen it, and we could afford it.

After checking in, we dropped off our bags and met in the hall for a walk through the shopping streets. Andorra was known for its low prices for tobacco, alcohol, and electronics. Many came to the principality, attracted by the cheap products.

The city was nestled between great mountains and surrounded by an intense green landscape, with the blue of the sky as an accompaniment. The city of the Pyrenees, the capital of the state, was located at one thousand twenty-two meters above sea level, which made it the highest in Europe.

Claudia took me by the hand when we arrived at Meritxell Avenue, a real temptation given the variety of display windows and bargain prices offered by its stores. The children wanted to stop everywhere. No wonder, since it was a shopping paradise.

We couldn't say no to everything. Christian ended up with new Nikes at a bargain price and Andrea with a wool hat with two pink pompoms on top.

I was enchanted by Andorran architecture. The city had managed to combine modernity with the ancient buildings of the

Pyrenees style. Centuries of history soaked the stones of the buildings, topped with slate tiles.

The air smelled of forest, altitude, and freedom, concepts that were in harmony, although the streets were full of shoppers crazy to leave their euros in the stores.

The others were chatting without my paying attention to them. My head was miles away in the office of the surgeon who was going to perform the first operation. I cannot say that the man filled me with hope. From the beginning, he warned me that it was not going to be easy. I asked him to tell me the truth. I did not like to go in blind. Fighting in a room with the lights off was much more difficult.

The first thing Dr. Migueláñez told me was that my situation was critical, which did not argue for a recovery, only a patch on the progress of the disease. They were going to operate on my colon in the first instance, and if the recovery went well, in twenty days, I would be back in the operating room for liver surgery. There was no time to lose. They could not give me more time, or the disease would sweep through my body like a tsunami. Twenty days after the second operation, we would start twelve sessions of chemo. My body would not be recovered, but if I wanted to have a chance, that was what I had to do. Take it or leave it. There was no easy path.

After explaining the roadmap to me, he delved into the side effects of the first operation. Those of the second would be less noticeable. So far, I had refused to look on the Internet. I had been told that was a mistake; the best thing was to have a doctor tell me what would happen. I went to the doctor's office as a virgin, not expecting him to tell me he was going to ruin one of life's pleasures.

"So, is the pooping going to stop?" I asked skeptically when he told me they were going to put a bag and a plug into my intestine. Lucky for me, I had a doctor who shared my mindset and wasn't surprised by my off-color humor.

"I'm afraid so. Look on the bright side. You won't leave a trace on your underpants," he countered, smiling.

His lighthearted response made me join in the joke. "My wife will thank you. You don't know how much it annoys her. Okay, so if I'm not going to use my third eye anymore, where am I going to evacuate?"

"What I am going to perform is called a permanent colostomy. This type of operation is usually performed when it is not possible to reconvert the colon because of the characteristics of the disease or because of the segment of the colon that had to be removed.

"Since there is no anal sphincter, whose function is to control the evacuation of feces voluntarily, a stoma or opening is placed in the lower left side. This is where, after the operation, the feces you expel will be collected using a bag like this one."

He pulled out the device and showed it to me.

"From now on, I'll be shitting into a Ziplock."

He laughed again.

"The bag they give me should be big. Do they have different sizes? When I'm in the mood, I'm in the mood."

"Don't worry. There are different lengths and capacities, as well as various formats." He brought out several types for me to see. "Some collection bag systems are open-bottom for easy emptying, while others are closed and are removed when filled.

"The skin adhesive remains on the body while the pouch is removed and washed to be used again. The pouches are made of odor-resistant materials and vary in cost, and can be transparent or opaque."

"My goodness, that box looks like the Cuétara chocolate bag. Well, if there is a variety, yes. I think I'll opt for those closed ones that are removed when full, so I can sell them to the neighbor as fertilizer. What do you think? Can I start a business?"

"You might consider it. I love that you're taking this with so much humor."

"What am I going to do? I'll have to look on the positive side of not sitting on the throne. I can't tell you how much it bugs me to stop being the king, as much as I used to love to squeeze."

"Attitude is fundamental in cases like yours. I encourage you not to lose it. Illness often becomes an uphill battle. You must stay as positive as you can."

"I am a specialist in that, Doctor. Humor has always been my way of looking at life, and I don't intend to lose it now."

"That sounds like a great idea. If it's okay with you, I'm going to explain how you're going to take care of your colostomy."

"Hopefully, it won't require as much care as a Tamagochi. Those critters always died on me. I'm no good with plants either."

"Don't worry, it's much simpler, like taking care of your teeth every day. You should wash the skin around the stoma with warm water, neutral soap, and a natural sponge, using circular movements, and then dry it with a soft towel without rubbing. Once the skin is dry, the pouch is placed like this." He had a medical mannequin on which he showed each step up to the insertion of the pouch. "The sponge and towel must be clean to avoid infection and should only be used on the area. Understood?"

"Loud and clear, don't worry. I'm not going to use that sponge to wash the dishes later."

The man wrinkled his nose. "Your wife and children will thank you."

When the visit was over, he extended his hand to me. "See you on the day of the operation. Don't let me down."

"I won't. I'll be there," I assured him, returning the squeeze.

We had walked quite a ways by the time we got back to the hotel. I wasn't feeling well. I was very constipated. I hadn't been to the bathroom all week. I apologized to everyone and went to lie down for a while before dinner to see if it would give me some relief.

My daughter's judo instructor, who had the room next to ours, rode up with me in the elevator.

"What's wrong with you?" he asked. The news had not yet reached the parents' group, so I summed it up by claiming constipation. He said, "It happens to me every time I go on a trip. If you wait for me for a moment, I'll bring you a little pill that's a godsend. Don't worry, it's natural, the kind they sell in the herbalist's shop. I won't be a minute."

I stayed in the hallway, accepting the offering. Anything would be good if it could get me unblocked.

I went to the bathroom and swallowed the two he had given me with a little water. He had told me that the effect was not immediate; it depended on each body. I went and lay down.

I wasn't aware that I had fallen asleep until Claudia came looking for me to announce that it was dinner time and asked if I wanted to go downstairs or if I preferred to stay and rest.

I did my best and got up. I just hoped that the pill would not get to me in the middle of dinner so I would have to run away.

Fortunately, that didn't happen. We enjoyed the relaxed atmosphere, then went to our room. We needed to get our strength back so Andrea could rest.

The big day had arrived, and the championship my little girl had been longing for was going to take place. She wanted to qualify for the next competition and win the cup. She was as competitive as I was, and that made me very proud of her.

She had already been weighed to place her in the correct category, and I could see the sparkle in her eyes with the anticipation of being the next to fight. The bouts lasted a maximum of three minutes, during which I was sure my heart would jump out of my mouth.

Andrea looked beautiful in her white kimono, with her hair pulled back in a high ponytail.

I gave a loud whistle that made her turn her head and focus

her eyes on me. Her fight was next, and I wanted her to know I was with her, supporting her from the stands.

I raised my fist, and she smiled.

"You've made her happy today," Claudia murmured. "Me too," she added.

I grabbed her hand, offering her a smile, and she rested her head on my shoulder. I felt good to be with them too. I was enjoying it, even if the recovery of my marriage seemed doubtful.

The bout began, and I was mesmerized by the skill displayed by Andrea and her opponent.

"She's doing well, isn't she?" I asked my wife.

"The teacher says she's the best in the class. No doubt about it; she's doing well."

The two girls were spinning and clutching each other on a green and red tatami. They both proudly wore their belts.

Their small feet were set to unbalance the opponent, bending their trunks to propel themselves. Their hands clung to the opponent's jacket, as required by the rules. The objective of judo is to knock down and immobilize the opponent on the ground by taking advantage of their strength and momentum.

A judge was closely watching their movements when my daughter caught her rival off-guard. Andrea's foot caught her in a sweep that had her kissing the floor with her back.

"*Ippon!*" shouted the judge, raising his hand.

"Yes!" I shouted, proudly rising to my feet. I got the long-awaited cramp in my abdomen. Andrea looked up to smile at me, and I smiled back, raising my fist again. The match was over, and my judo princess was the victor. I lowered my face to Claudia and gave her a kiss of joy, and my guts grumbled. "I'm going to the bathroom. I think the pills the teacher gave me last night have taken effect. I just hope there's enough toilet paper. If everything I've accumulated comes out, today's is going to be epic."

My wife took a pack of tissues out of her purse. "Take this just in case, and try not to jam anything. I'd die of embarrassment."

I gave her another kiss and hurried to the bathroom. I barely arrived in time. The toilets were far away in the Polysport. I was right to take the Kleenex with me. As I had guessed, there was no damn toilet paper. I sat down on the bowl, and everything fell into the void. I would miss that feeling. I spent a long time pouring liquid out of my ass. Better diarrhea than nothing, I thought. That won't clog it. When I got up and looked into the bowl, I was shocked. It was full of blood.

CHAPTER ELEVEN

Metanoia: A journey that changes the way you think or feel, the way you live, or your way of being.

<u>Áxel, Andorra, November 2015</u>

Until that moment, I had not felt fear. Death had been an abstract concept. It had now become very real.

With my pulse pounding and feeling mortal, I flushed the toilet in the hope that the terror gripping me would swirl down the drain.

My fingers trembled as I pulled up my underwear, and zipping up my pants seemed like Mission Impossible. "Fuck, what if the doctor was wrong and I die today?" Filling a toilet bowl with blood was not good.

I had been told I was fucked up, but I hadn't been aware of it until now. I had been told I was screwed, but I hadn't realized how serious it was. My life was going down the toilet.

I washed my hands, rubbing them like a man possessed, trying to eliminate something that was impossible to wash away. Fear curdled in every pore of my skin, fear that collapsed my lungs, threatening to leave me without air, fear that flowed uncontrollably, sweeping me away.

I held tightly to the cold stone. I had to calm down. I could not go to my wife and son in that state.

I tried to do some breathing, the kind they teach you in a stress management course in case you have to deal with extreme anxiety. I had never felt it as intensely as I did now. They say that people who suffer from anxiety feel like they are going to die. In my case, it was not a feeling but a reality of which I had just become terribly aware.

What if time had run out? What if I had reached the last level of the video game?

I needed to calm down. The state I was in didn't help; quite the contrary. *Come on, Áxel,* I encouraged myself. *This has to be a preview, not the denouement. Relax. The protagonist never dies at the beginning of the book.* I exhaled loudly, loosening the knot that was pressing on my chest.

Those were the longest fifteen minutes of my life. I searched for images that would allow me to regain control and return to my seat without looking like a spirit from beyond the grave.

The color returned to my face after I refreshed myself for the second time. Some people were leaving the pavilion. Was the competition over?

I saw my wife coming through the door, clutching Christian. I was in her range of vision, so it didn't take her too long to find me.

She came to meet me. "Our son is hungry. I'll get something for him to peck at. Have you had a chance to evacuate?" she asked, wagging her eyebrows. I just nodded. It wasn't the time to tell her what had happened, and I wasn't in the mood to play along.

"I'm glad. If you want, wait for us inside. In fifteen minutes, the awards ceremony will take place, and then we can leave. Unless you want to watch the whole competition."

"No, I'd like to leave as soon as Andrea is done."

"You know I'm not much of a sports fan. If you want, this afternoon, we can go to Caldea as planned. Jesus and Arancha told me they can stay with the kids."

Christian huffed. He didn't like being called a kid. "We'll see, okay?" I answered evasively. I didn't know whether I felt like going to a spa.

"Okay, we'll talk about it later. Sit down. You're a little pale. It must be from overexertion. I hope you didn't clog the toilet." She winked at me and headed for the bar.

I barely remember what happened from the time I sat in the chair until we got to the hotel room. My head was so far gone that I couldn't focus on anything. The deathly cold had seeped into my bones. Not the atmosphere; it was warm in the sports center. The drop in temperature was coming from the irrational anguish that crept through my extremities, turning my blood to ice.

Drops of icy sweat ran down my spine. I couldn't feel any worse. I wanted to cry and scream to the world, "Why me!" I wanted to rip the chairs out of that damned pavilion and make them fly over everyone's heads.

The thought of my children stopped me. Of how they would take my reaction, of their frightened faces full of incomprehension. I couldn't do it. I had to hold on for them. I would never forgive myself if they suffered more than I had already made them suffer with my absence. They deserved to have a father, not the leftovers of the man I had been. I had to live for them. I wanted to fulfill their dream of going to Disneyland Paris, and I couldn't give up now. I wasn't going to let myself be defeated.

When we got to the room, my daughter had not stopped running and jumping, full of joy for the triumph she had obtained. She climbed on the bed and started bouncing as if she was on the trampolines at the fair in summer. Claudia scolded her in case she broke the springs of the mattress and we were made to pay for it. Christian occupied a large part of the sofa, staring at his cell phone, probably texting with his friends.

Another cramp shook my bowels. I went straight to the bathroom, expecting the worst, closed the door, and sat down, then filled the bowl with red for the second time.

I was dying. It was impossible to let all that out and not bleed to death. How many liters could I lose without dying? I didn't want my children to see me die in a hotel room. It was not the time. It could not have been my turn. I was promised three months!

I was shivering with pain and fear. I would miss my daughter's communion, Christian's skating festival, and their first sneaky kisses on the front porch. I wasn't going to be there when they fell in love for the first time, nor would I be there to pick them up if something went wrong.

How could I have been so blind? How could I have missed so much and now have no time left to enjoy myself?

I wanted to smash my fist into the mirror to shatter the guy who was locked in there. Too late; it was too late. The words pounded my brain mercilessly, pushing me into a corner of the ring of my life, unable to defend myself.

Then I heard her. My daughter's laugh brought me back. I might have been half-dead, but I had to face it. I couldn't give up in the first fight. I thought about *Rocky*. It had always been one of my favorite movies. I had seen it hundreds of times. I closed my eyes and thought of one of those mythical moments that stayed with you forever. *"It's not about how hard you hit. It's about how hard you can get hit and keep moving forward. How much you can take and keep moving forward."*

I had to face it. This was my new reality, and I couldn't run away.

I called my wife in terror. I don't even think my voice came out. I pulled up my pants and made her come in, making a gesture of silence so the children would not notice. The blue eyes narrowed without understanding what all the secrecy was about until I opened the door and showed her the porcelain stool flooded with red.

She stifled a scream that bounced against the fingers covering her mouth.

"This is the second bowl I've filled today," I confessed.

"I know you wanted to go to Caldea, but I think we should go to the hospital," I announced with a calmness I didn't feel. Her eyes filled with tears. "Don't cry. Remember, they are out there, and we don't want to worry them." I pointed at the door.

She sniffled and rinsed her eyes.

I stretched out my arms so that she could take refuge in the warmth of an embrace that was unable to reach her. I felt like I was in a bath in the Arctic.

"I'm going to pick everything up," she murmured, breaking off. "Will you take care of the bathroom stuff?"

I nodded.

Nothing more needed to be said. She went out, and I took it upon myself to flush the toilet and get the few items that were left in there.

In two hours and forty-five minutes, we stood in front of the emergency room. Continuing with the tactic of not scaring the children, I told them that the doctor had called me and that I had to go for some tests because of the operation; that they had an opening, and I couldn't say no. I was sorry to lie to them about that, but it was the best thing to do. The poor kids understood and didn't complain when I told them the weekend in Andorra was over.

I asked my wife to take them for a walk and said I would call her on her cell phone if I had to be admitted. At first, she was against it, but she didn't want to argue with our children there. She had no choice but to agree.

I was lucky. My doctor was on call, and it didn't take him long to see me.

"How are you, Áxel?" he asked me when the nurse left after taking my blood pressure. We were inside a cubicle in the emergency room.

"Fucked up. I don't think I'm going to make it to the operation."

"I've been told that you had a little scare. Calm down; it's all right."

"Little scare? Nothing's wrong?" I raised my voice. "I just filled two toilets with blood. I wouldn't call that a little scare. More like Game Over."

His smile grew. Was that doctor crazier than I was?

"I don't think so, not yet. What you had is called tumor hatching. It happens when the tumor collapses. It doesn't happen to everyone. I didn't want to alarm you about something that might not happen. It's more dramatic than serious."

"So, it's normal? I'm not going to die?"

"It's normal. You know we are working on it, but for your peace of mind, you're not going to die today. We will do some tests, but what happened to you is no more than what I have told you. You have emptied."

"Empty? It looked like a gigantic piñata at a vampire party! Dracula would have had a field day with me!"

My muscles were losing the stiffness that had tightened them, and his attitude, so much like my own, soothed me. "Did you come alone?"

"More or less. I drove from Andorra with my wife in the passenger seat and my children in the back. I thought I was dying. If I had known it was normal, I wouldn't have driven so fast."

"I'm sorry. I'll give you my number in case you want to ask me anything in the future." He took a piece of paper and his pen and wrote it down.

"I appreciate it."

"Where are they now? In the waiting room?" He handed me

the paper with his phone number on it, and I put it in my pants pocket.

"No, I sent them out."

"Okay. If you like, we'll do the tests, and when we finish, let them know so that they stay calm. Your wife must be on the verge of a nervous breakdown."

"It sounds like the best idea of the day, Doc. I'm about to throw myself on your mercy."

"We'd better save that for later. I've got a reputation to maintain in here." He adjusted his coat and gave me another smile. "Listen, Áxel. This situation will overwhelm you on many occasions. No matter how well you take things, the word 'cancer' is associated with a sentence of death and pain. This is true for many people but not for all.

"The first reactions to the diagnosis are usually perplexity and fear on the part of the patient and paternalism and overprotection on the part of the closest relatives. However, for you, that was not the case. You decided to opt for a courageous attitude that turned perplexity into motivation and fear into hope. Don't let the disease take that from you. It is the most important thing you have right now. Your courage, your determination, and your faith that everything is going to be okay."

He gave my arm a light squeeze, which I appreciated.

"Thank you. You are the best doctor I could ever have."

"And you are an exceptional patient. Don't forget that."

Half an hour later, I called my wife to tell her everything was okay. Miguelánez was right; it was a tumor hatching. I asked him if we had to do the operation, but according to him, there was no need. I could go home.

I said goodbye with a hug of gratitude and relief. He didn't reject it, no matter how much of a reputation he had to maintain. He held me tightly regardless of the people walking by. He patted my shoulder until I felt ready to leave and return to my family.

"Hey, you're back. I hope the nap was good for you." Those were the first words I heard when I woke up.

The anesthesia was still circulating in my veins, and I had trouble opening my eyes. It was the voice of my guardian angel doctor.

"Hi, honey. I'm glad you're back." That was my wife's voice. She sounded fearful. I couldn't expect anything else after an operation like the one I had just undergone.

"Hello," I greeted them both. There was an unfamiliar aftertaste on my tongue.

"The intervention was a success. I have not left any trace of that bastard. It was a full-fledged extermination. The first bug has been neutralized." The joking tone in which he addressed me was a balm for my nerves. It calmed and amused me in equal parts.

"Thank you, Oscar," I muttered feebly.

Before putting me in the operating room, he made me promise him that when I woke up, it was time to move on to the next phase and to call him by his first name as his friends did. I already considered him one of my friends. Oscar Migubeláñez was giving me my life, and that was only done by friends, even if they were doctors.

"Now you have to promise me that you are going to do everything for your recovery. In twenty days, you will come back here, and we need you to be as well as possible. A balanced diet, rest, and the treatments that we will be explaining to your wife while we have you here. For us to succeed, you must apply yourself."

"You know I'm going for it," I said, unable to fully focus. I seemed to be swimming in a pool of gin.

"That's my warrior! I will leave you to rest. I just wanted you to hear from my mouth that everything went as expected."

"Thank you. You know how important it is for me to have you

by my side. I know some surgeons don't even see the patient after the operations. You standing at the foot of my bed means a lot to me. I appreciate it."

"I'm not doing it for you, but to see your wife smile and for those Taser classes you promised me when you recover."

Claudia blushed. I didn't mind that he alluded to her. It was logical that he had also taken a liking to her.

The doctor's other ambition had always been to be a national policeman, so I swore to him that if he got me out of this alive, I would teach him to shoot a Taser in addition to taking him to a shooting gallery for the day. I wanted him to know what it was like to hold a gun and not a scalpel.

Oscar walked out the door, leaving me alone with my wife. "What about the children?" I asked her with great effort.

I had a hard time putting words together to make sense.

"They went with my parents and yours to the cafeteria just before they brought you to the room. It's been a few hours, and they needed to eat something."

"It's all right." My eyes couldn't stay open any longer.

"Rest. You heard the doctor. You need to recover for the next operation. Sleep will do you good." Her hand squeezed mine.

"Okay, but wake me up when they come up. I want them to see that I'm still alive." My little ones needed to understand that I was not going to let myself be defeated.

She kissed me on the cheek. "Don't worry about that. They'll have plenty of time."

I couldn't stay awake any longer.

CHAPTER TWELVE

Yuanfen: The principle that defines those loves that are predestined.

<u>Garbiñe, present time</u>

I had spent a dog's night, and I'm referring to the dog having a full bladder and not being taken for a walk.

My date didn't show up for the dream. Áxel left me stranded like a cigarette butt. In his place, my adorable sisters showed up, accompanied by Mom and the unspeakable Dario. That happy dream woke me up with a bitter aftertaste and a lot of dried drool.

Great!

I looked at my alarm clock, it was nine in the morning, and all I could think about was our "non-date" and "non-kiss" the night before. That frustrated me, even though the poor guy was not to blame.

As dumb as I was, I hadn't asked him what time his flight was leaving.

I grabbed my cell phone from my bedside table. I didn't have any new messages. I wasn't sure if that was a good or bad sign, but if I didn't call him, he was going to reproach me for my lack of courage for the rest of my life.

I looked up his number in the contact list. There it was—Axe. A goofy grin broke out on my face. I hoped he was okay and that someone up there would answer. With trembling fingers, I pressed the call key and held the handset to my ear.

I matched my breath to the tones echoing in my eardrum, and when he finally responded, my heart gave a definitive thump of joy.

"Good morning, Princess Tennis Player."

"Good morning, Deodorant Prince." I heard him chuckle. "How was your night?"

"It was pretty bad; I'm not going to lie. Someone didn't show up for their rendezvous, and I had to settle for memories of the past. Not a pleasant evening."

"That's because you got the wrong door. I was waiting for you. I thought it was you ringing my doorbell, but since I didn't look through the peephole, I had to put up with the invasion of my sisters, my mother, and, to top it off, my ex-husband. I won't forgive you for this one. You don't know how annoying they can be when I dream about them."

"Oh, trusting woman! That will teach you to look before you open the door."

I enjoyed joking with him. I listened hard, but I didn't hear anything. Maybe he wasn't at the airport yet.

"Are you feeling better?" It wasn't the question I was dying to ask, but I did care about his health.

"Yes, sleeping and getting high is a godsend."

Come on, Garbiñe, ask him! I plucked up my courage. "I'm glad. When does your plane leave?" I crossed my fingers and toes so hard they hurt.

"We don't leave until one o'clock, but we have to be there two hours early for boarding. The president of the AUGC said he would pick us up at half past ten to be on time."

I calculated like crazy. I glanced at the clock—quarter past nine. If I got my wits about me, I'd make it.

"Would you mind if I came to see you off at the airport?" Headfirst and without a lifesaver.

I heard him hold his breath, then, "I'd love that!"

That warmed me. "Okay, then I'm going to get myself together, shower, eat breakfast, and meet you at the airport." My heart rate revved up, and it had nothing to do with an anxiety attack.

"I'm not going to miss that. Hurry up, or you'll be late."

I couldn't stop smiling. Just listening to him, I felt full. The feeling was as strange as it was indescribable. I could only think that Áxel completed me.

I hurried. I wouldn't look as fabulous as last night since I didn't have Paula's hand with makeup, but I'd manage. He'd seen me without makeup and looking like a gym rat.

The time to make a good impression was over. I was already making bad jokes, a clear indication that I was feeling attacked and I was dying to look like the prettiest girl on the planet.

Come on, Garbiñe, calm down. There's no point in attacking your-self when he told you he would love for you to come to the airport. I couldn't deal with myself. I needed Paula's wise words to give me a push, but first, I had to shower.

Fresh out of the shower, I opted to video-call her. The bitch hung up on me the first time and only answered the second time after many rings.

I focused on the screen in disbelief. "Will you please not focus the camera on the ass of the guy you went to bed with last night?" I looked at the perfect male roundness. The camera panned to Paula's dreamy, tousled face.

"What are you doing up so early? And where is yours?" She squinted, trying to see behind my back.

"Don't look for Waldo because you won't find him."

"Waldo? I don't remember the instructor having a name like Waldo."

"He doesn't. His name is Áxel. I was making a joke. You know, Waldo, the guy with the striped shirt that appears in pictures, and you have to find him?"

Her free hand pinched the bridge of her nose.

"Let it go. It's not the point."

"Then why are you talking about him? You know I hate to wake up early, and on top of that, to have to think. What happened with Áxel?"

"He did not come."

"No! But you were his fondest wish! Wait, wait. Don't tell me. You didn't have the guts to take him home. You had him in your sights! I should have given you a couple of tablets of *Vaginaloca* and another two of *Desemputol*. You can't manage on your own even if it's handed to you on a platter."

"Can you stop the soliloquy and listen to me? I didn't need any of those things. Last night we almost kissed, but my sisters' inopportune asses showed up on the beach. Then he got sick, and I had to take him to the hotel because he could hardly stand up."

"What were your sisters doing on the beach?"

"I don't know, but that was the result. My kiss was cut short, and the night went to shit."

"If I had been there, I would have given them what-for."

"Well, that makes two of us. The bad thing is that we don't have a time machine to go back. There's nothing to do about last night."

"What a pain." She snorted.

"That's not why I called. I'm meeting him in an hour to see him off at the airport, and I don't know what to wear."

My friend's face brightened. "Okay, great. Are you in your room?"

"Yes."

"Well, let's not waste time. Focus on the closet, and in the meantime, tell me what you want your outfit to say."

"What do you mean, what do I want my outfit to say?" I asked, panning my cell phone along the hangers.

"You know, what you want to convey. I don't know. We can go for an *'I-want-your-body'* look or maybe *'cancel-your-flight-and-come-with-me.'"*

"I'll settle for *'a-kiss-and-a-peck.'"*

"That's easy. Wear the white ankle jeans, the green tank top with the pushup bra I gave you for Christmas, and the raffia wedges. If he doesn't kiss you dressed like that, he's not worth your time."

"Thank you, Paula. I owe you one." I blew her a kiss and grabbed the clothes.

"More like a hundred, but let's leave it at eating at your house after my doctor gives me a complete checkup and you've gotten the Catalan out of your system."

"Done. Two o'clock?"

"Yes. I'll have squeezed the juice out of it by then. See you later, Garb." She hung up, leaving me with the good doctor's ass as the last image implanted in my retina.

I didn't want to be late. I ate faster than usual and rushed out of the apartment, but after I closed the door, my ex came up the stairs. Great!

"Hi, Garb," he greeted me, giving me the kind of look my private tutor never gave me.

"Dario," I simply answered, putting away my key.

"You look very pretty today." I looked at him in disbelief. I don't think he had ever used that word with me before. "Have you done something differently?"

"If separating from a man who didn't value me counts, then yes, I have done something different."

"Always with the dagger at the ready. I tried to change, and I apologized to you."

"I remember. Right after Damaris slammed the door in your face and kicked you out of her house because she couldn't stand you."

"That wasn't the case," he reprimanded me, annoyed. "We didn't have anything. We were just friends."

"Uh-huh, deep friends who sleep together."

"Jealous?" he asked smugly, moving closer to me.

"More like disgusted. I still don't know how I could have been so blind. No, I'm sorry, I do, because there is no one more blind than she who does not want to see and no one more mute than she who does not want to speak. But you know what? Now I see and speak more than ever."

"Don't be silly. There was nothing to see. That was silly. You know better than anyone that sex is secondary, or don't you remember what was going on in the kitchen of your parents' apartment the day you lost your virginity?"

Thinking about my mother in those circumstances hurt.

"I'll never forget it. You know what it meant to me." I was so close that I could smell his cheap aftershave.

He reached for my face. How different his palm felt now that I could compare.

"Come on, honey. I miss you, and so does Ruben. Just today, he asked me when we're going to be a family again."

That my son adored his father was no mystery. Dario was like a kid, full of laughter and fun. Ruben looked up to him and had fun when Dario paid attention to him and took him to the beach to ride with him on the board. He preferred his father. I scolded him while Dario let him have it all.

His mouth approached mine, fingers pressing against the back of my neck. I rested my hands on his chest and pushed.

"I don't want to have that family again. I'm sorry, but you are no longer part of it. By the way, where is the child?"

He seemed upset that I turned him down. "With your mother, I went down to buy churros for breakfast." I hadn't noticed the intense sweet smell. Dario was carrying a plastic bag. "Why don't you come down to the apartment and join us?" He looked at my cleavage. "Afterwards, we could have some fun. You know, reminisce about old times."

"I can't. I have a date," I answered. I didn't feel like getting entangled in a useless discussion.

"With whom? With the guy from last night?" I looked at him incredulously, although it only took two plus two to find Pili and Mili.

"You don't care."

"That's where you're wrong. I do care because I still love you. Besides, you're my wife."

"I don't even know why you married me when you liked Damaris and Elisa. You always preferred them blonde, busty, and airheaded."

"Girls like them are only for fucking. You were for marriage. There's a big difference. That's why I made you my wife."

"Well, I'm sorry I don't see things the same way you do. I don't think there are two distinct categories. I wanted a two-for-one, to be your wife and for you to fuck me, but it seems that with you, it is impossible to have both," I spat with disdain. "Count me out of your family stereotype. I am no longer your wife, and if necessary, I will go to a lawyer and ask for a divorce to make it clear to you. That is what I should have done when you walked out the door. I don't know why I haven't done it already. I'll make an appointment on Monday."

"Yes, you do," he murmured, cornering me against the wall. "Don't play hurt or naïve. We both know you're very good at those roles. If you haven't asked me for a divorce, it's because deep down, you love me, and you know you'll never find a better one than me." He pressed his mouth against mine, and my knee shot into his balls.

Dario broke away, and the bag in his hand fell to the ground, scattering the churros everywhere.

I snarled at him. "How wrong you are. I don't love you anymore. I only put up with you because you are Ruben's father, nothing more. You'd do well to remember that if you don't want me to hit you so hard next time that you lose your ability for future fatherhood. Goodbye, Dario."

I admit that after saying what I was thinking, I felt great. One of the rocks in my backpack rolled into the river, and the blindfold came off my eyes once and for all. There was no turning back now. He was out of my life, which was the best solution for me.

I had wasted valuable time, and I hurried to my green Ford Fiesta. It wasn't the greatest, but it got me everywhere. I had inherited it from Dad. My sisters still didn't have licenses because they were lazy, and my mother didn't drive either. Dario had kept our car, and I kept my father's, which had sentimental value.

I arrived at the airport in a sweat, parked the car, and rushed to the main gate. It was quarter past eleven. I had wanted to arrive at quarter to eleven to have some time. Even in that, my ex-husband had frustrated me.

My heart was pounding. I had lost some strength due to my disease, and I noticed the weakness. On Monday, I was going to start training. The human body was very ungrateful.

I was afraid I wouldn't find him. Maybe he hadn't been able to wait. I took three more strides and saw him. He looked as handsome as last night, maybe more so. He was wearing blue jeans and a white polo shirt. The color brought out the bronze tone of his skin. His hands were hidden in his front pants pockets, and a suitcase rested by his side. He glanced at his wrist, giving me the time I needed to get close without being seen.

"Are you expecting someone?" I murmured, close enough to make him smile.

The dark gaze scanned me from my feet to the tousled ponytail atop my head. "I don't think I've ever stopped waiting for you."

Could so much be said with so little? Could so much be felt in such a short time? I had just met him, but it didn't seem to matter. The answer thundered through my body, which jerked at the sight of him as if he had shot me with his Taser.

"I'm here," I replied with all the courage I could muster, earning another smile from him.

"I see you. I don't think I have stopped seeing you since yesterday when you came through the door of the meeting room at the barracks with a frightened look on your face. Your image has been with me every minute of the day. Why do you think that is?"

I moistened my lips, and he watched the gesture. I could flinch or behave as I always did by ducking my head, but I wasn't going to do it, not anymore. I cleared my throat and responded, a little startled by my retort. "Your desire is right, but our distance is wrong."

"Ummm, you don't say. Well, we should remedy that, shouldn't we?"

I nodded to him with the same eagerness that had shaken me last night. I came closer and curled my fingers behind his neck to stand on tiptoe so he would not doubt that I intended to collect the kiss he owed me.

Male hands came out to rest on my waist and subtly pull my body against his, encompassing me. God, how good it felt!

"If you don't object, I'm going to kiss you," he warned me.

"Do it, and don't waste any more time. I don't want you to miss your flight because of me," I suggested with determination.

The man's mouth took mine softly, gently, tentatively, and he kissed me with an infinite tenderness that melted my insides. My God, *that* was kissing!

I parted my lips wider and surprised myself by lifting one leg like in the movies. I reached out to meet him with my tongue, and his velvety touch made my dark world light up with color.

The warm palms went down to my buttocks, and for once, I

didn't care where I was or who could see me. Everything had ceased to exist except him and that kiss that was changing my life.

I know it sounds cliché. If someone had said something like that to me before I met Áxel, I would have laughed at them for being on hallucinogens. Now I realize it would have been a big mistake since I hadn't realized that I was dead inside. I hadn't allowed myself to live, and that kiss was the only way I could come back to life.

The seconds turned into minutes. My body demanded more. I never wanted it to end. I could not allow myself to lose it.

A slight throat clearing behind our backs, and "Sorry, Áxel, we have to go," ended the kiss.

It was hard for me to recover. For him too. Without letting go, he answered, "Give me a few minutes. I'm coming, Carles."

"All right, but hurry. We have to check your bag." His companion disappeared.

His lips sought my forehead, and his hands returned to my waist.

"I can't stay, and I swear it's what I want more than anything right now."

"I know." I sighed, losing myself in the hug. "You have to go. You can't miss your flight because of me. I'll call you when you land if that's okay."

He pulled away a little and took my face in his hands.

"Everything you want to give me is a gift. You know what my reality is. You know what the doctors have told me."

I put a finger on his lips. "I also know that if I refused this, whatever it is, I would always regret it." His lips curved. I was nervous because it was hard for me to be so direct. I needed to clear my head, and I relieved the tension I had created with one of my stupid questions. "What is your favorite color?"

That curve I liked so much ended up in a smile, disintegrating me.

"My favorite color is to see you."

"See me?" I asked with a dry mouth.

"I said green," he corrected. "Like your eyes, your car, and that uniform you love so much."

I wanted to die. What an idiot I was. That kiss had melted what few neurons I had left. I could feel the heat on my cheeks when his laughter interrupted the suffocation.

"I was joking. I said just what you heard. Do you know that from today, my eyes will be filled with the desire to see you?"

How do you have someone say something like that to you and not get your panties in a bunch? "Well, my eyes are going to be filled with the same thing, and tonight I'm not going to let you miss the date."

His smile was growing wider by the minute.

"Áxel, last call." We were interrupted by an all-too-familiar voice.

He raised his hand. "I'm coming. Just a minute." His eyes didn't leave mine when he murmured, "This is going to be fast and intense. Hold on tight."

We devoured each other. It was the most epic sixty seconds I had ever lived, where head, heart, and soul joined in a perfect synchrony of moans and caresses.

They usually say that the first kiss marks you forever, but no one warns you that the first kiss has nothing to do with being the first one you get but the first one you *feel.* The one that has the ability to overwhelm each of your cells, to invade you and make you realize that, after receiving it, nothing will ever taste the same.

CHAPTER THIRTEEN

Litost: Surviving that state of stormy spirituality where one realizes their misery.

Áxel

"You've given yourself quite a steak with the sergeant. When I tell you that you're a lucky bastard, I repeat myself. I don't know how you do it, man, but you have it in spades." My friend patted me on the back.

"Don't exaggerate."

"It's the truth! If you had seen how I looked at you last night! Good thing you got sick. Otherwise, I would have given you a hard time."

"Come on, we'll miss the plane."

"*Now* you're worried? In good time."

Carles was one of my best friends. When there was an opening for future trainers at Taser, I was quick to recommend him. He had been my second-in-command and my partner since I joined the police station in Blanes.

I had many friends. I liked to be around people, and they

never let me down. Even when I was going through my worst time in the hospital, they kept me up to date and encouraged me with their visits.

That thought made memories come flooding back.

———

Twenty-four days after the operation in which my colon tumor was removed, it was time to go for the liver.

The hospital had become my second home. An apartment in Ibiza was overrated. Who wanted sun, continuous partying, and turquoise water and beaches when you could have a nice room full of beautiful nurses and views of the city?

I would lie there all day, with those beauties attending to my every need. What if I give you intravenous feeding, what if I change the sheets, what if I am going to increase your medication so that you don't feel that pain and you become unconscious? In short, paradise!

It had been four days since the liver operation. They had removed my left hepatic lobe, in which the second tumor was located. The doctor had said that this organ was capable of growing back like the tail of a lizard, but its functionality would never be the same. From now on, my liver would have to work harder and perform at its best, so good nutrition was vital.

A colleague of my doctor's came to visit me, a nutritionist specializing in cancer. He had treated many patients like me, showing them a different way of eating. Certain foods were best eliminated, and others needed to be introduced into my new nutritional plan.

Organic, low-fat food, and no refined sugars, cow's milk, or processed products. The change was going to be for everyone, my wife announced. What was healthy for me should be healthy for others, although some license would be allowed for my family since everyone else was healthy.

For my children, it was a way to support me, even though I wasn't sure they could give up the chocolate chip cookies they loved so much. Imagining them fighting over cookies made me smile.

"Slow and steady," I told myself. I was reading about what food could do for the disease. In the days leading up to the operation, I had read more books than I had in my entire life. If such a change could help me, I would implement it.

I was already in the second phase. They had been feeding me intravenously, and as soon as I could, I asked them to bring me something solid that I could chew.

You can't believe how much you learn to appreciate those little things. Something as insignificant as sitting on a toilet bowl or the simple pleasure of savoring food. My love for the toilet was an unrequited love story. If I wanted to, I could sit on it and read one of my new books while waiting for the bag to fill up, but I could never again make a perfect, splash-free target shot.

At least I planned to continue enjoying food.

I had drains in the area of the incision, which would help the wound to heal properly. The doctor told me that they would be removed before I left the hospital. I hoped it would hurt less than when they had removed the catheter this morning.

That was one of the worst experiences a man could go through. It should be punishable by law.

I never thought my dick could shrink so much in front of a pretty nurse, but I guarantee you that my dick folded like an accordion after she pulled out that tube. I'd never seen it so small and scared, nestled against my pubis and begging for that brunette not to lay a finger on it.

Some privileged mind, in pursuit of manhood, should think of something else. With the medical advances that had been made, it seemed unusual to have to undergo such torture at the hands of a beautiful girl. I was ashamed to see my member reduced in size by more than half. What was I going to tell the girl? That I'd had a much bigger one, but seeing her with those gloves made it smaller?

An atrocity; that's what it was. And all for what, so as not to pee in my pants? Well, I'd rather wear a diaper than have that infernal tube shoved up the tip of my dick again.

I was given medication to control my pain using a pump connected to a needle inserted into my arm. Anyway, I was a mess. If I was going to impress a twenty-something nurse with my balled-up penis, a bag that sounded like the London Philharmonic every time I let out gas, and my liver that turned to mush, I was in for a rough ride.

There was a knock on the door, and I whispered a "Come in" that got stuck in my throat as I watched my colleagues from the police station walk through the door. Now that was pure excitement.

"Look at him. They've got him in cotton wool!" Tarra exclaimed. They were all there, a total of five uniformed men, wearing wide smiles and taking up the whole room.

"If you want, I'll ask them to put in a bag like mine for you and put you in the next room," I joked, lifting my hospital gown to show him the affected area. "Because of my stoma."

Tarradellas shifted his gaze from my abdomen to my crotch. "If you wanted to show off your dick, you only had to say so. You don't need to use cheap excuses."

I burst out laughing. I had forgotten I had no underwear on.

"I've lived through better times. A while ago, they took out a little tube I peed through. You don't know how much that hurts."

The five scrunched their faces as they imagined it.

"More than being shot by your Taser?" asked Romerales.

"I don't know what to tell you, but I was ashamed to see myself shriveled up like a raisin. The damn nurse had to poke around because she couldn't find it," I exaggerated.

"Well, he had to wrinkle a lot for me not to find that," Olivares noted. "I couldn't complain about the size. Are you sure that with what they took out of your intestines? You didn't ask for a penis enlargement? Can't you see his dick is longer and fatter?" he asked the others, who nodded along with the joke.

"You asshole!" I laughed, unable to avoid the pain that produced.

"Are you in pain?" The commissioner approached with concern.

"Relax. It's just that I'm still too tender to put up with teasing from these guys. I think I've become a bit of a pussy in here. They spoil me too much."

They sat where they could, some on chairs, some on the bed, surrounding me with faces full of affection and camaraderie. "We want you to know that we are all with you. We are very proud of you, and you are an example to follow, Montoya," my superior continued.

"Thank you. Coming from my commissioner, it's an honor."

"My honor to count you among my men. You have taught us a life lesson, and everyone in the police station wants you to come back soon."

"Despite my jokes?" I arched my eyebrows.

"Because of them." He laughed.

Olivares and Romerales chuckled. "I still remember when you called during Jiménez's birthday party, alerting a bomb threat at the police station. You waited until rush hour. We all knew that after coffee and a cigarette, Jiménez would head for the bathroom, and you fucked him up good and proper. The poor guy almost knocked his teeth out, coming out of the bathroom with his pants down to his knees. The look on Sergeant Segovia's face when he bumped into him was priceless."

I had to hold back my laughter at the thought of that epic moment.

"You fuckers!" Jiménez protested, reddening.

"You can't complain," Tarradellas said. "Thanks to that, you're now married. You owe Montoya a favor," he said with a wink.

"A favor? He screwed me over! You don't know what it's like to be married to that woman," said Jiménez, making them all laugh. The door opened, and my favorite nurse came in to add more medicine to the pump.

The brunette with dangerous curves blinded them with a luminous smile. She had a weapon of mass destruction on her face. More than one jaw dropped, and she walked away with a husky "excuse me" that raised more than one flag to half-mast.

"Fuck!" exclaimed Olivares and Romerales in unison. "That chocolate is the kind that melts in the sun," he whispered.

"And the kind that shrinks your crotch, I assure you."

Olivares looked at me incredulously.

"Well, it must be just you since she has made me look like the Rock of Gibraltar."

"If she sticks a cannula up your dick, we'll talk," I said.

"She can stick whatever she wants in me. Did you see the smile on her face and that body? You say the next room is free?" Olivares sighed.

"You can ask her, but I guarantee you that my dick was all curled up."

"Well, I would have asked her to give it mouth-to-mouth to see if it would recover. I think I'm starting to feel sick. Why don't you press the panic button to get her to come back and take care of me?" my partner joked, putting his hand on his abdomen.

"Because I don't want Xena, the princess of the probe, to tube my dick again because of you. Once was enough, thank you. If you want fish, throw yourself into the sea, but leave me alone. I'm not going to help you with her."

"Well, if you'll excuse me," he gestured me, "I'm going to go cast the rod for her."

The visit made the time fly by. I was looking forward to normalcy and getting back to work with my colleagues. When Claudia arrived with the children, she was very happy, almost as happy as I was about the visit.

The expressions of affection, support, and love extended to my family. I was very proud of the men who were part of the police station. They were my clan of warriors, and with them, I always felt at home.

Two weeks later

My life had really changed in forty days, and I had learned from it.

I was looking for a t-shirt to wear. The big day had arrived. Today I had to go back to the hospital to receive my first chemotherapy session, and not knowing how it was going to affect me made me nervous.

I had never complained much. I was used to exhaustive self-defense training, to being hit and thrown to the ground, so pain was part of my daily routine. However, what you feel when you have to undergo surgery twice, in a case like mine, is not the same. Nobody prepares you for something like this.

My body, which until now had looked slender and sinewy, had undergone some changes that made me narrow my eyes at the image I saw in the mirror. On the one hand, there was that square sticker around my stoma, where my new life companion was lodged—a bag. I had to keep an eye on it to make sure it didn't overflow.

I glanced sideways at the half-open bathroom door. Sometimes I found myself staring longingly at the porcelain bowl, and I was not ashamed to say that I had even felt the need to sit on it while waiting for the bag to fill. It may sound ridiculous, but losing that basic function plunged me into a kind of mourning that only subsided when I sat on it. Oscar, my dear doctor and friend, told me that it was logical. It happened to many patients, and I should not feel bad about it. Still, I tried not to let my family see me. I wanted them to think I was coping better than I actually was. I didn't like them to see weaknesses. That made me feel vulnerable.

Failing and declining were part of the disease. Even people who did not suffer from a disease had low moments. It was just my turn.

I ran my finger over the elongated scar that accompanied the colostomy, which crossed my abdomen in a sinister smile. It was still tender and healing. Luckily, it was not inflamed or infected. It was a salubrious pink color that contrasted with the rest of my brown skin.

I was not obsessed with perfection or beauty, although when a beautiful woman crossed my path, I stared at her. Now that my physique had been affected and I was no longer perfect, I realized how disturbing a gesture as simple as taking off a t-shirt on the beach would be.

This was the new me. Whether I liked it or not, I had been transformed, although if I had the choice, I would have preferred to be a Power Ranger, not Frankenstein's little brother. I would never be the same as before. The wounds would decorate me forever.

My body. I closed my eyelids tightly and opened them again. I had no right to pity myself. I was fucking alive! That would have to be enough to get the bullshit out of my head and make me feel good.

Those marks were a sign of survival, of courage, of not giving in. Of looking death in the face and getting out alive.

I put on my t-shirt and stopped staring at myself in the mirror. Acceptance of the new me would eventually come. I was convinced of that. I just had to keep working on the reasons why instead of being horrified, I should love myself as I had never loved myself before.

"Love" was another term I had to work with. The most powerful feeling in the universe for which great deeds were done or the worst atrocities were inflicted. A word so short and so big at the same time. So easy to say but so complex to feel.

Many were those who filled their mouths with it, extolling the love of mother, father, children, friends, family, and partners. It was the same term, but it was very different, depending on the tagline that accompanied it. Passing in one was no guarantee of passing in the others. In my case, marital love was my subject. The failure that had led me to take the exam in September, which I was not convinced I would pass.

My relationship with Claudia had not improved. On the contrary, the disease had added one more stone to her backpack, turning the gap into a chasm that was impossible to cross.

She was no longer just my wife, a tireless mother and worker. Her daily chores had increased, and I had added a moonlighting job as a nurse. She was the one who made sure I didn't skip my medication and took care of my treatments, and if that wasn't enough, she bought the limited list of foods I could eat.

She had developed a kind of psychosis about labels. She read everything to verify it did not contain something that could retard my progress, and the added work put her in a taciturn and stormy mood.

She was making a titanic effort to bear it all with integrity, but she couldn't pull that rickety cart alone, full of reproaches and uncertainty.

Her face was being devoured by fatigue, her weight had plummeted, and she had purplish circles under her eyes that took the shine off her usual beauty. I tried to make it up to her. I wanted to find a way to ignite the flame I had felt when I met her. I longed to warm her with the fire we'd had back then, and I eagerly rummaged through the memories in search of that spark that would ignite us.

I was determined to find that emotion that made me sleep in bursts. I wanted to find my way back to the valley of butterflies that fluttered in my stomach, making me feel capable of anything, no matter how absurd it was. I swear I tried to find her, searching for the sweet taste of her kisses, which now tasted bitter to me. Perhaps the past was too far away, and all that remained of our love was a valley full of broken wings.

When did it happen? When did they stop fluttering?

I was not able to remember and put a date or a place to it, but there was nothing to draw from anymore. It was not fair to put her through my illness, knowing I did not love her as she deserved.

I felt affection and admiration for her fortitude, her strength, for her way of coping with everything, and for so many years dedicated to us. However, I could not stay stuck in what we were and would never be again. It was not fair, neither for her nor for me.

My wife was still young and beautiful, the perfect devoted wife every man longed for. There was still time to rebuild her life. It was time for me to let her go and give her a chance to live.

When she walked through the door of the room to take me to my first chemo session, I knew I couldn't drag it out any longer. The time had come.

"Claudia," I murmured in a low tone full of sadness. She looked so exhausted, so fragile, that my decision hardened. I couldn't keep asking her to sacrifice her life for me.

"Yes? Is something wrong? Do you need me to bring you a painkiller?"

I shook my head, a knot forming in my chest at what I was about to do.

I grabbed her hands, holding that questioning gaze that had so often been my anchor.

I was convinced it was going to hurt. However, the decision had been made, and it was ridiculous to wait any longer. I had had enough of being a selfish fuck. If this disease had taught me anything, it was that there was life beyond my navel, and I had to give her the freedom to live it.

"Sit down. We need to talk."

She looked at me without understanding, but she listened to me. Still looking into her eyes, I told her, "The best thing to do is to separate."

"What?" she asked, unable to believe what I was telling her.

I had caught her off-guard, and my tact was conspicuous for its absence. I was having a hard time being delicate. "It is for the best."

"The best for whom?" she howled, raising her voice. "For you, for the children, for me? Oh, please don't make me laugh! For me? For the children? No, Áxel, no! You mean for yourself!" she countered. "You always put yourself before everyone, even when you're sick. I've taken care of you, I've supported you, I've been your wife, your cook, your cleaner, your babysitter, your errand girl, your nurse, and yet I'm not enough? What do you want, Áxel? What do you need?"

She was crying.

I felt like the meanest guy ever. "To love you as you deserve, and I don't know how to do it, no matter how hard I try."

We sat on the bed.

"I don't need more! I don't want you to strain yourself!"

"Yes, you do. It's just that you've become accustomed to receiving leftovers instead of the full menu, and it's not fair."

"This is enough for me. I don't want more than what we have."

"Listen to me, Claudia. Don't be stubborn. What woman wouldn't want to be loved and adored as if she were the only thing that mattered in life?"

"I don't need that much. Don't you love me?"

"Of course I love you, but not as you need."

"I don't need anything!" she shouted, out of her mind. "Don't blame me for this too, when you're the one who doesn't want to be with me. Is there another one? Is that it?"

I shook my head, trying to get her to calm down.

It was much harder than I thought it would be. The knot in

my chest was the size of a steam roller, and I was having trouble breathing.

"Why have you stopped loving me?" she muttered under her breath with tears rolling down her cheeks. "Haven't I done enough?"

"I repeat, I have not stopped loving you. It's just that my feelings have changed. There is nothing left of that emotion that made the world shake under my feet. I swear I tried to rescue it, but it was too late."

"I don't need to live in an amusement park. I'm not fifteen anymore."

"You aren't a hundred either."

She looked down at her lap. It was hard to see her so dejected. "Is it because you are no longer attracted to me? Don't you see me as beautiful?"

"You *are* beautiful. You always were." I ran my hand over her face, and she pressed against my palm like a kitten lacking love and affection. It fucked me up that I was to blame for her being like this.

"I don't think I deserve the place you gave me. It was too big for me. It's not your fault. You knew how to love me. It was me who failed you. You can't go on with someone who, instead of giving you life, takes it away."

"Let us try. I promise I will try to make you fall in love with me again. I will help you want me again," she insisted, standing up to take a place between my legs.

She kissed me passionately. I let her linger on my mouth in search of a glimmer of hope that I did not find. When her hand descended to my crotch to massage without success, I knew that no matter how hard we tried, it was the end of us.

Claudia detached herself from me worriedly, looked at my inert penis, and searched my gaze for some vestige of fire where only pity was flowing.

She collapsed with a plaintive wail. I wrapped her in my arms to let her vent, but I wasn't able to give her what she needed because I didn't know when I'd lost it.

"Áxel! Hey, Áxel." Carles shook me, bringing me back to reality.

"What?" I was so focused that I didn't realize he was calling me.

"It's our flight. We're the only ones left to board. Are you all right?"

"Yes, I'm sorry. I didn't realize I had been left behind."

"It's logical. Last night, the scar gave you grief. A lot. Do you need me to help you?"

"No, I'm fine," I said, carefully sitting up. I didn't want to hurt myself again. The last episode had been too horrible.

Just when I thought it was over, my nightmare kicked in. It was like going back to square one or even worse because, when the doctors told me that, surprisingly, the cancer had gone, I thought I had won the game.

Then the Grim Reaper came back to bite me again. No one should have to go through that.

CHAPTER FOURTEEN

Mamihlapinatapai: A look that passes between two people, each of whom is waiting for the other to start an action that they both desire but neither is willing to begin.

Garbiñe, one month later

I had a new house, and not just any house. Two weeks after Áxel left, the real estate agent told me that a couple was interested in the apartment. They were both teachers and wanted something in the capital near the institute.

It was so simple that I couldn't believe it. They had a couple of weeks to buy and move, so I couldn't rest on my laurels because I had to find something for Ruben and me.

Guacis. That was the name of the salesperson who told me that she had just found a bargain that she had not yet put in the listings. I didn't want to buy. I preferred to save the money, and when I found the house of my dreams, to invest then. I was looking for something unpretentious to rent close to the sea, with outdoor space for Ruben to play.

Guacis offered me a small house in the Tacoronte area. It

sounded very good. It was far enough away and, at the same time, quite close to the capital. Twenty-one kilometers or seventeen minutes by car, to be precise.

The house had belonged to an elderly couple until a week ago. The wife had just died, and the couple's children realized that the widower, who suffered from Alzheimer's, could not live alone. They urgently needed to rent the property to pay for a woman to take care of him while they worked. His wish was that this little house be a legacy for his grandchildren, so he did not want to sell it.

I loved the photos. Guacis insisted it would be best if we could go see it now, and I don't regret doing so. When I first set foot in the house, I knew I had found the right place. The views were spectacular, and it had a nice yard where Ruben could play.

The house was less than eighty square meters, enough for the two of us, with little to clean. It had a large attached parking space where I was able to leave my car, bikes, and my son's many junk items. One of the things that fascinated me was that through the garage, there was access to an alcove that the owner had converted into a wine cellar because it had the ideal humidity and temperature.

I was definitely going to take it. We went back to the office, and I made the offer. I had two weeks to change it to my liking and make the move.

Guacis prepared the contract, and today, my home was ready.

I had the invaluable help of Paula for the decoration and the purchase of furniture. Colmenares gave me a hand with the painting.

Needless to say, my mom, my sisters, and Dario screamed their heads off, but they couldn't do anything about it. I wasn't going far, so there was no reason for them to hinder me. My mother made it into an epic drama, saying that if I didn't know what I was doing, I would lose my husband, blah, blah, blah, blah, blah, blah. I ended up telling her that it was my life and that, just as she had chosen to take Cristóbal home without asking my opinion, it was her turn to respect my decisions.

I think it was the first time I saw her speechless in front of me. She could not believe that I stood up to her, and she ended by saying, "When it is too late, you will realize what you have lost."

I replied, "Believe me, Mom, I realize, and I feel such relief!"

I sat on the porch rocker, a glass of wine in hand watching the sunset and feeling proud of myself for taking the step and not having my pulse skyrocket. Well, maybe a little bit, but I knew I had done the right thing. Paula, my partner, and Áxel, via telephone, gave me the encouragement I needed.

Thinking about Áxel made that silly smile bloom as the time of our messages and subsequent daily calls approached.

We had established a ritual that we would carry out if my shift allowed it, and if it wasn't in the afternoon, I would have my daily ration of Áxel.

We did not lose contact. Not only that but at the end of each call, I felt he was closer. No matter how many kilometers apart we were, the sound of his voice accelerated my pulse. I had the feeling that I had been waiting for him all my life, and I had finally found him.

He was my last thought every night and the image I woke up with every day. He loved to clown around and send me a daily good morning picture that made me shudder with laughter. All those little details made me long to see him again.

As soon as I had the house ready, I video-called to give him a virtual tour. I dressed in a suit jacket, put my hair in an updo, and showed him how comfortable the place was. From heating a latte in the microwave to uncorking a bottle of wine in the wine cellar to settling on the porch rocker to tempt him with the wonderful sunsets over the cliff to finish on the bed and caress the mattress to show him how comfortable it was.

From that day on, we promised each other that every afternoon, I would go out to the porch, fill a glass, and take a picture to send him and start our daily chat. I admit that, at first, I was embarrassed. I was not much for photos and even less for selfies, but if the reward was the messages that arrived on my cell phone extolling a beauty only he could see, I was more than willing to do it for the rest of my life.

He filled me with infinite tenderness and a desire that became pressing.

The time had come. Feeling more uninhibited than on other occasions, I went a little further, as Paula had suggested, although a few levels below her recommendation. If it was up to her, the photo would have been naked, with a bunch of grapes in my hand and the words, "If you want wine, come and get the grapes." I didn't go that far, but I was emboldened. I undid the buttons of my blouse and separated it a little. I wanted a sensual picture without looking like a slut.

I had the intention of posing, leaving a portion of skin about three centimeters wide uncovered. I'd never done anything like this, and I trembled at the thought of looking unembarrassed. Fuck it! If I didn't do it now, I never would.

I set the timer, got into the right position, and dropped onto the rocker's cushion. I raised my glass and adopted the sexiest look I was capable of offering.

I waited the necessary time, counting the seconds mentally. After one photo a day and sometimes more than ten because I didn't like the first ones, I went to the gallery to see the result.

It wasn't the Venus de Milo, but it wasn't bad.

My lips glistened with red wine, the orange tones of the sky gave a beautiful golden hue to my exposed skin, and my tousled hair made me think of a passionate kiss between two lovers.

I hit send with the text that always opened the banter.

Good afternoon, Sergeant Deodorant.

Good afternoon, Sergeant Tennis Player. Or should I say, "Oh, my God, that's a corps and not the Guardia Civil?" Damn, what a picture you sent me today. That's a step up, or rather down because with my current thoughts, I'm convinced I'd go straight to hell.

Dumb.

I attached a blushing smiley face.

I must be a fool, yes. How could I leave you alone under those circumstances?

Under what circumstances?

The ones that make me think that I would like to be a button to unbutton on your skin.

Ha, ha, ha, ha, ha. I already told you that whenever you wanted, you were invited.

You say these things to make yourself look good, not because you think them.

I don't.

What do you think?

That, if you knew what I was thinking, you wouldn't let me in your house, just the two of us.

I would accept with my eyes closed.

Okay, so close them.

How?

Just close them. If it is true that you are not lying to me, you will trust me enough to play a little game with a good friend. You have nothing to fear. I am thousands of miles away.

But if I close them, I won't find out if you send me a message.

That's what you get for putting it on mute.

But if I close them, I won't find out if you send me a message.

You know that when I talk to you, I don't like to be interrupted.

Nor me. Okay, let's do one thing better. Activate the vibration and place the cell phone right where your heart beats. Open your blouse a little, and feel it on your skin as if it were my palm on you. Let me know when you are going to close your eyes, okay?

Just thinking about it turned me on.

Okay.

I changed the options, agitated. Áxel liked to play games, but I was distrustful of them.

I'm going to close my eyes and put it on my chest.

I opened my shirt a little, checking that no one was around. My house was semidetached. I didn't want an unwelcome neighbor to catch me with my shirt open. I wasn't showing anything, but I was on the verge.

I squeezed my eyes shut, holding the wine glass and feeling the warmth of the screen on my skin.

The salty scent and the billowing wind caressed me like lovers. I had never felt the need to touch myself intimately until I met Áxel. Even though I was ashamed to think about it, at night, in the privacy of my room, I caressed myself while thinking about him. About what it would be like to feel him beyond a simple kiss until I reached orgasm. Believe me, they were much better than the ones Dario gave me. Sad but true.

I was just imagining it, and my body became agitated. I was weak when it came to the sergeant. I moistened my lips and controlled the need to put a hand under the waistband of my pants to give me relief.

The cell phone shook against my skin, and the shock traveled directly to my crotch. I moaned, my altered respiration stifled in response to that simple vibration, and when I opened my eyes, I swear I thought I saw him on me. It was such a shock that I dropped the glass, covering myself with wine. The thin glass hit the floor, shattering into thousands of splinters.

I was so startled that I closed my eyes to assimilate my mistake. He was not there; only the need for him. I went to sit up, but something prevented me. I forced my eyelids open, focused my eyes, and there was Áxel in all his splendor, with a rogue smile and his hands clutching my wrists to prevent me from getting up.

"Hi, Maria," he murmured, making me laugh.

I had told him that when I was young and I went out partying, I had a hard time getting people to understand my name in the discotheque with all the noise in the background. Tired of having to repeat it ad nauseam, I renamed myself Maria, which was much easier and didn't give me headaches.

"Hello, St. Joseph," I answered belligerently, my pulse pounding at two thousand beats per minute.

"Was that the wine from the Last Supper?" he whispered, looking at my blouse soaked in red.

My chest had gotten wet, and my nipples were rising to get

his attention. Luckily, the cell phone had only received some drops on the back, nothing to worry about.

"Why? Are you thirsty?"

"A lot, but all for you."

I smiled. I had not expected the surprise. He had told me that he would be teaching a course on the Costa del Sol at the weekend. I hadn't thought I would have him there in front of me.

"So, in Malaga, huh?" I mumbled flirtily.

"The plane ran out of fuel, and we had to stop in Tenerife. I hope you don't mind. The pilot asked me where he was dropping me off, and I asked him to let me jump from the plane. I told him I had a very beautiful friend on the island, and I was going to take the opportunity to visit her."

I burst out laughing. "As a storyteller, you are unique."

"They're not stories. I knew this would happen," he said seriously. "That's why I asked him for his number, so he could corroborate my story. You can call him if you want."

"Okay, give it to me. Let's see what the pilot has to say."

"Now is not a good time. He's got his phone in airplane mode, and he won't be able to answer. You'd better try it later," he whispered.

I quivered under his caresses.

"You have no idea how much I've looked forward to seeing you again."

"I have a slight idea."

"I don't believe it. So many looks in the world, and the only one that shakes me like a newborn's rattle is yours. Total meltdown mode active." Áxel was unique in expressing emotions. "When you sent me that photo, I almost fainted. I wasn't sure I could control myself. I was close to jumping over the fence and kissing you until the world stopped, ruining the surprise."

"Why don't you do it?" I asked, eager for him to take the first step.

"What?" he asked me.

"Kiss me until the world stops," I encouraged him, eager for it to happen.

"I don't know. I'm afraid you'll evaporate because we're eighty percent water, and it's hot as hell here."

"What if I do it?" I encouraged myself.

"If you do it, I doubt I could resist, even at the risk of you vanishing."

Áxel brought out the flirtatious part of me that had been locked away for too long. I was afraid of taking an unfortunate step, the fears and insecurities were still flickering somewhere in my chest, but he made me believe in that invisible part that I exhibited before his eyes. His time was precious, and he wasn't there for us to waste it. A month had passed, and he had been given three.

I reached for the back of his neck to pull him closer as I saw my reflection in the darkness of his brown eyes, preparing to receive that which I so longed for.

He rested one knee on the rocker and put up no resistance when I pressed for my welcome kiss.

He came toward me in slow-motion, and I watched every angle of his beautiful face until his lips rested on mine, and I could no longer think.

His tongue tangled with mine, making me moan in his throat. I loved how he tasted, how he moved, how he caressed me with soft, deep licks, teeth tugging at my lower lip and slurping it with delight. His knee was between my legs. He did not touch the spot that ached the most, the one that moaned and protested. The one that urged me to slide down to bring his knee into contact with the taut knot that wanted to burst.

I held back. I didn't want him to think I was too eager, even if it was true. I was dying to sleep with him and have him do to me the things he did in my dreams.

We had long daily chats. I had never talked so much to my husband while we were married. Áxel seemed to care about what

I told him. He listened to me giving my opinion about everything, and he gave me his invaluable advice when from my ex, I only got "I'm tired. Don't talk to me about it." I had come to realize that if I had spent all that time with Dario, it was only because, deep down, I was waiting for Áxel.

Sometimes the right person comes along right after the wrong one, and Áxel was my right person. It might sound sappy, even absurd. I had never been one for poetry or pretty words, but he awakened my mischievous and romantic sides. He was the reason I felt that way.

His right hand gently traced the contour of my jaw, and my hands descended down his back, outlining every bump they encountered.

His growl lit a fire in the epicenter of my desire. I just had to wriggle a little more to feel it. I wanted to break free of my mental strings and untie myself once and for all. I think I would have done it if the gathering clouds hadn't released a fierce downpour that soaked us.

"Shall we go inside?" I suggested.

"Don't you like being wet?"

I was going to say something dirty, but I restrained myself. "We'll be better off inside. Besides, if we go on like this, your clothes will get soaked," I pointed out, nodding at his bag.

He sat up, gave me a short kiss, and pulled me up.

My white blouse with reddish spots clung to me like a second skin, as did his blue t-shirt. The water ran down his face so smoothly that I wanted to drink it.

My mind was becoming depraved. Apparently, so was his, judging by the way he was looking at my torso. This was promising. I rubbed my hands together, thinking about how he'd make love to me as soon as we set foot in the house.

A blush dawned on my cheeks. I didn't care if my clothes were transparent with water and wine. I wanted to excite him to the point that he thought of nothing but me. God, I was more like

Paula every day! What a bad influence! With his eyes roaming my anatomy, I felt sweetly perverse.

I tucked my little finger into his to get closer to the door and let him in. It was open, so a push was enough to let us inside. I would clean up the wine mess later. Áxel slipped in behind me, his small bag slung over his shoulder, and kicked the door shut.

We were in the middle of the small living room, with the faint light of dusk filtering through the windows and the sound of the rain clattering in our ears.

I was longing for him, but I was afraid to take the first step toward an intimacy more overwhelming than a simple kiss. I had only slept with Dario, and I had not seen Áxel again until today. We had gone out only once and had a brief farewell at the airport. Was that enough to let me overwhelm him as I wanted? What if he thought I was slutty for acting like that?

It was best that I let him take the first step. Maybe he didn't feel like it, or he had thought better of it, even if his bulging crotch said otherwise. God, I was a mess. I didn't know what to do, and he looked so handsome with his dark hair dripping. Maybe if I took off my blouse like in *Nine and a Half Weeks?*

"I think you should change," he murmured, still caressing me with his eyes. "You'll catch a cold."

I blinked a couple of times before I understood what he was suggesting. He didn't want to undress me? I hadn't moved. Where was the scene in which they come in soaking wet, and he takes her against the wall? I guess that didn't happen in my movie. Maybe his desire was a product of my horny hallucinations.

If I had taken off my shirt, I would have made a fool of myself. I was so confused that the only thing I could answer was, "Yeah, sure. That's Ruben's room. If you want, you can change there and leave your things. There's room in the closet."

Áxel just nodded and disappeared behind the door, leaving me in the middle of the living room with a hollow sense of loss.

I took refuge in the bedroom and leaned against the door for a few moments, debating whether I had done the right thing or if I should have taken control of the situation. For now, it was better for me to calm down and look for more indications that Áxel wanted to go a step further, even if I didn't know how to bring it up or approach it. I was no good at this kind of thing.

I took off my clothes and opted for a loose-fitting spaghetti-strap dress and a cardigan to cover my arms.

I towel-dried my hair and ran the comb through it, looking at myself in the dressing table mirror. My lips were slightly swollen, and my eyes were full of dashed expectations. Maybe I had over-done it, and Áxel wanted to slow down. I didn't understand these things. According to Paula's expertise, the day we met again, the fuck was going to be epic. It was not surprising that her words had influenced me. I needed to calm down and wait until he was ready. There was nothing more to say.

I took a couple of breaths before leaving the room wearing my best smile.

CHAPTER FIFTEEN

Arrebol: When the clouds appear red, illuminated by the sun's rays.

<u>Áxel</u>

I leaned my head against the cool wood of the door to calm down.

I had done a terrible job. I had told myself that with Garbiñe, I would not go in for the kill. I would control what I felt because she deserved a man who would pamper her like no other. One who would be attentive and offer her an encounter that would meet her needs, not one who would drag her by the hair and take her on the floor like a caveman, which was what I would have done if I hadn't thought twice about it.

In my defense, I was not expecting that damn picture with the red sky in the background, turning the clouds into a faithful reflection of her cheeks. The half-open juicy lips were a mortal sin, like the shirt and the intensely green dilated eyes. The excitement she was causing was her fault, completely her own.

She kissed me as the rain fell on her skin, sticking her clothes to that body I was dying to have. It made me wish that the wetness soaking her body was not caused by the storm. To perceive her abandonment was to flip the switch of my determination and make it explode.

Fortunately, heaven took pity on me by giving me a bath of cold water so I could meditate on my intentions.

We had been chatting for a month, and it seemed as if I had known her all my life. I had gotten her, one by one, to show me the insecurities that kept her from being happy. She needed someone who would let her be herself, not a man who would intimidate her. If I did that, it would set her back several squares and ruin her ability to make decisions.

I messed with my hair and snorted. It would be hard to hold on without getting carried away with everything I wanted to do to her.

The important thing was that I had taken the first step, I was in her house, and she had not rejected me. That was a big win.

It's not like we had talked about what we were starting, either. With my life expectancy, it was hard to make plans with someone. I would take whatever she wanted to give me. Pathetic? Maybe, but I preferred something to nothing.

In a month, I would have a checkup, and they would tell me if the beastly treatment I had undergone had worked.

When all you have left is death, you cling to any sliver of possibility, even if it means extreme hardship. The doctor warned me that I could die on the operating table. What they were going to do to me was so grotesque that the chances of coming out of it alive or without consequences were practically nil.

I had promised my children I would fight, and I would submit to anything the doctors wanted to do to me, even if the chances of success were one in a hundred.

Before they put me in the operating room, my children gave

me a t-shirt that said, You will always be our hero. I had failed them for years by ignoring their importance.

I hugged them with my eyes full of tears as the song *Héroe* by Antonio Orozco played on the speaker of my MP3 player.

I think that shot of love was what got me through. That and the promise that I would not fail them again.

I took off my wet shirt, letting my eyes follow the gigantic scar. The one that had not allowed me to kiss Sergeant Tennis Player the first time. The one that had not stopped hurting, and for which the doctor had recommended the use of therapeutic cannabis. Pain and cancer went hand in hand, at least in my case, and it was one of the reasons I realized that something was not right again.

That mark was the biggest one I had, and rightly so. You can't have any idea of the carnage I suffered.

When the cancer returned, my surgeon decided that to eradicate the bug, the best thing to do was to give me an extra bath in chemo. He had deposited my organs in a tray for thorough cleaning after stopping my heart and hooking me up to a machine to keep me alive.

When life tells you *tedejo*—leave, let go—you just have to cross your fingers and say *jódete— fuck off.*

Luckily, I did not stay on that operating table, although I won't forget the postoperative period. The faces of my children as they opened their eyes in the room, looking at me with a mixture of relief and stoicism, and Orozco's song playing again in the background, allowed me to continue clinging to the hope of living. If I had to die, I would do it with my boots on.

I had put up a fight since they activated my countdown. I had opened my arms to life and held on tightly. Even if I had low moments where the pain was so intense that I felt like jumping into the void and disappearing, I did not do it.

Sometimes the need for all the torture to end got the better of me. In moments of weakness, I recognized that I questioned why

I had to struggle. Why was I insisting that even if my sentence was written, it mattered three months later?

That was the question I threw into the universe just before my trip to Tenerife, when the pain was eating away at me, and I had to smoke a joint to be able to sleep. Natural painkiller, as my good friend the doctor used to say. But then I came to this island, and everything changed. The answer I was longing for appeared at a course I gave at the Civil Guard headquarters.

I could not leave this world without knowing her. Without understanding why my heart dedicated its best beats to her and why she made me feel like a rock star in concert.

It was crazy, I know, but who dictates the rules of the game? Who knows how to win or lose? No one teaches us how to live, how to die, or how to love, and even if they tried, we are so egocentric, so self-centered, and selfish that we would not believe it until we experienced what it felt like.

I put my musings aside to search for dry clothes in the bag and change.

I smiled as I gazed at the soft blue cloud effect of the walls and the large Superman logo in the center. That character would always make me feel attached to Garbi.

The room had simple elements and a lot of inventiveness. My sergeant had managed to make it the perfect refuge for a child of Ruben's age. An ideal place to dream and make room for his adventures.

The little house was modest, a typical Canarian one-story building with a white façade and dark wood trim on the door and windows. Simple, like its new tenant.

I smiled, thinking about her. I had changed, so it was time to go out.

She was in the dining room. The light was on, and the sky had changed color.

"I don't know where you want me to put these," I muttered,

spreading out my wet clothes. "If you tell me where, I'll hang them up. I wouldn't want to abuse your hospitality."

"You're not abusing me, don't worry." She approached me to grab the clothes. "I was waiting for you. I was just going to put mine on the clothesline. I have one in the garage in case it rains like today."

"I'll go with you if you let me," I suggested. Garbiñe just nodded.

The garage was long and narrow but quite deep. On one side, there was a metal clothesline where my sergeant hung our clothes. She was uneasy; I could tell by the way she moved. Maybe I had rushed her by showing up unannounced, and she just didn't want to show me the door.

As I thought about her reasons for being so tense, she turned around to glare at me.

"I don't know how to say this. Sorry, I'm a bit of a mess at these things. I'm not trained at all."

Now it was coming. She would tell me she didn't want me to be there. "What?" I asked before I rushed into whatever I was going to say.

"God, how embarrassing!" Her cheeks colored like the reddish sky in the photo.

I approached her, trying to get her to relax. I grabbed her arms, shaking them like a rag doll's.

"What are you doing?"

"Relax! You look like you're going to break. You don't have to be ashamed of anything with me. If you don't want me to stay at your house, just tell me. We're too old not to say things to each other's faces."

She looked incredulous and snorted. "It's not that!"

"Then what is it? If you don't tell me, I can't know what's going on in that head of yours."

"I must seem an idiot to you. Why does a woman in her thirties who carries a gun like other women carry a purse would be terrified to confront someone she likes in a noncontact melee?" she asked, lowering her head.

Her statement made me smile.

"So, you like me, huh?" I inquired naughtily, and she reddened to the roots of her hair.

"You already know that. Do you think I send dirty pictures to everyone?"

I couldn't hold back the laughter. "I hope not, but dirty pictures, really? You only showed a little bit of skin!"

She gave me a warning look. Given her reserved nature, I knew how much effort it had taken for her to share that thought, and I didn't want to belittle it.

"What for you is a little, for me is a lot. I am not one to do these things. However, with you…"

"With me what?" I asked hoarsely. I sensed where this was going.

"I don't know, I don't feel like myself, and I long to do things I wouldn't do with anyone else."

"Wasn't that what you wanted?"

"Yes, but it scares me. I've been this Garbiñe for so long, you see, that I don't know if I'm ready to be the one I want to be," she said in dismay.

She let go of my hands and walked to the back of the room without letting me answer, then turned to the right and disappeared.

"What are you waiting for? Come," she called.

When I got to where she had disappeared, I smiled. She was filling a couple of wine glasses. This was the private bodega she had shown me on the phone.

The reddish stone combined perfectly with the exposed brick and wood structures. There was a rustic table in the center with four stools around it. It was wide and sturdy and appeared to be made from a single piece of wood, a work of craftsmanship in every sense of the word. The light was a simple bulb that swayed and made wobbling shadows. The familiar scent of earth, wood, and dampness wafted to my nostrils.

"This is your little haven. You have a good wine cellar," I observed, passing my eyes over a large collection of dust-covered bottles.

"Mr. Edelmiro said that the wine was for me to enjoy. He didn't want to take any with him. This is one of the places I imagined myself with you," she replied, turning around to take a drink.

I needed one, too, since the image in my mind did not resemble this.

"May I ask what we are doing, or is it top secret?" I encouraged her.

"What were we going to do?" she asked directly, then averted her gaze.

She was hiding something from me, and it piqued my interest. Aha! In a couple of steps, I had her! My butt was resting on the table, and my body was hovering over hers.

"Just that?" I asked naughtily. She drank again. "I have a feeling you imagined us doing more than just drinking wine."

"Maybe it's because you have a cold, and your Mosso's sense of smell is atrophied. What else would we do?"

I almost burst out laughing.

She looked at my mouth a little too fixedly.

"I don't know, you tell me. If my sense of smell is atrophied, I probably won't find the answer," I replied.

"Try," she challenged me, swirling the wine glass.

"Who says that? The blushing Garbiñe, or the Garbiñe who takes dirty pictures to send them to a death row inmate on the phone?"

Her gaze darkened. "Don't say that."

"Sorry. I'm so used to joking about it that I sometimes forget it can be uncomfortable or hurt sensibilities."

"I know you use humor to adjust to what is happening to you, and I understand that. It's just that thinking about it makes my chest tighten." I ran my thumb across her cheek, and she accepted the token of affection without turning away.

"When will you get the results?" she asked.

"The ones from the last operation?"

She nodded, catching her lower lip between her teeth.

"In a few weeks."

"I hope it worked."

"Me too. Now that I've met you, I've got a crazy desire to live. I don't want to scare you or go too fast, but in my situation, I can't stop to overthink things. That's why before…"

"What?" she asked uneasily.

"I rushed. I'm sorry I was a brute. You need us to go slow."

"Who said that?" Her nose wrinkled. "Did you see me complain or hold you back? I only need you. I lied to you."

My eyes flew to hers. Dark pink colored her cheekbones, but there was no shame on her face, only determination.

"To me?"

"Yes. You asked me earlier what I imagined when I thought of you and me in this corner."

"My disease does not affect short-term memory, or not yet," I said jokingly.

"I lied to you," she repeated firmly.

"Really? Very bad, my sergeant. A Mosso should not be lied to when interrogating a suspect. It can make the interrogation much harder."

I took the step that closed the distance between our bodies. The difference in our height forced her to raise her head to look at me.

She set her glass on the table, and I took a sip from mine. I was very hot and thirsty. A multitude of scenarios where we were both protagonists played out in my mind.

I pressed my pelvis against her lower abdomen. I wanted her to feel the excitement she generated in me.

"Is this how you intend to intimidate me into confessing?" She sighed, sticking out the pink tip of her tongue to trace her lower lip.

I had shown her my cards, and I wanted to see hers. "Maybe. I am very persuasive if the confession of the crime is good. How did you imagine us, Sergeant?" I prodded. I was pushing her to a limit she might not be willing to cross, but there was only one way to find out. "Tell me about it."

She cleared her throat. Small beads of sweat dotted the roots of her hair. She was nervous and agitated, but deep down, she wanted to tell me. I was sure of it.

"Me? I pictured us just like this, albeit with fewer clothes, and…oh, God! I don't know if I'm ready for this."

"You were doing very well." I rotated my pelvis to let her understand the effect of her words. "Go on."

Her mouth was probably as dry, if not drier, than mine.

"I imagined myself teasing you, dribbling some wine down my chin for you to lick up with your tongue."

The effect of her words was immediate. My crotch gave a jolt that almost made me climax. "That sounds damn good. Do it," I challenged.

"How?" She hesitated. "It was just a fantasy."

"It's one we can carry out if you wish." She swallowed with difficulty. I was convinced, so I tightened the rope a little more. I wanted to go slowly, but my sergeant had things thought out more clearly than I had guessed.

"Let me take off my sweater," she suggested. The flutter of her fingers on the buttons was the sexiest thing I'd seen in recent times, even when the last one stuck. She solved it by pulling the garment over her head and tossing it to the side.

With her eyes anchored to mine, she reached for the cup, lifted it to her mouth, and let the ruby liquid drip down, soaking her chin, her neck, and her cleavage.

Fuck restraint!

I left my glass next to hers and ran my tongue from bottom to top. I started the movement in the central part of her breasts, following the trail along the neck and chin until I reached her mouth, where I delighted in savoring all the nuances of fruit and passion.

A moan reverberated on the roof of my mouth, and unable to contain myself, I lifted her to sit on the table. I had no intention of abandoning her fevered tongue, which was tangled in mine. Her thighs parted to give me enough space to fit between them. I rubbed my crotch against her forcefully, eliciting the next gasp, which tasted like bliss.

Her fingers had ascended to my hair, and she dug her short nails into my scalp. Her legs clung to my waist despite the swaying of my hips.

"Relax," I hissed. She couldn't hold on. "Put your hands on the table and lean back a little." She did so, her eyes veiled with lust and the need to continue. "Do you give me permission to do whatever I want?" She gave a slight nod.

"Well, if at any time you don't feel comfortable or want me to stop, just say so, understand?"

"Loud and clear. Go on." Her answer made me smile.

"Then let's see what we have here."

I ran my fingers over the thin straps of her dress to make them fall, and her tender breasts rose proudly.

She looked at me with fear in case I didn't like what I saw. What she didn't understand was that my attraction went far beyond the size of her tits. However, I thought they were beautiful.

I grabbed the wine glass and took a long drink. She looked at me expectantly. She didn't know what I was going to do, yet she trusted me enough to give me power over her body.

I let the wine rush from my mouth to her torso, taking her by surprise. When I was empty, I descended like a bird of prey to savor with inclemency.

It was the first time I had heard her scream with pleasure, and I didn't do it by pure miracle. I traced circles with my tongue on the soft nipples to suck them hard, making her arch her back for more.

She wanted it, and I was dying to give it to her.

I pulled up her skirt, then ran my fingertips up the inside of her silky thigh to the soaked fabric of her crotch and pulled it aside to feel her trembling flesh. It was hot and inflamed. I had not yet gotten down to business. The feminine scent mingled with the wine, spurring my intention to please her.

I slid my fingers in and out, pinching the taut knot. Her panting breath escaped through the opening between her luscious lips. My mouth descended the smooth abdomen to worship her navel. When I was satisfied, I went down further, ran my fingers down one side of the lace panties, and tore them with a jerk, making her gasp. She didn't object to me doing the same with the other side. I would buy her more panties like that if that's what she wanted.

I rolled the skirt up to her waist and delighted in contemplating the rosy intimacy laid out for me.

I glanced up to ask, "Do I stop here?"

The tortured green eyes closed with ferocity.

"Don't even think about it," she spat threateningly. "You've started. Now you finish. You can't leave me like before!"

I held back the urge to laugh again. I didn't want to hold back either. "As you order, Sergeant," I growled. "I'll do as you say."

She howled, and it wasn't a pitiful or timid sound. Just the opposite. It sounded fierce, possessive, and hungry, which was how I felt.

I ran my tongue up and down, concentrating on giving her the best experience of her life. I probed the entrance to her vagina with one finger, still stimulating her with my lips.

Her hips were moving forward in search of more, giving me absolute access and offering me everything I wanted to take.

The first finger was followed by the second. It felt so good that I didn't want to stop. Her vaginal muscles contracted as my explorers groped in search of that little bulge that, with skill, I would find. It had to be there, hidden. It was just a matter of insisting.

The gasps were getting louder and more erratic. My tongue increased its speed on her clitoris, pulling it with the occasional suction. I was almost there. I was very close, as the involuntary spasms that gripped my fingers foretold. The clenching and slow, deep strokes gained energy until they became fast and accurate.

I had just stumbled upon what I was looking for, that rough pad that, properly handled, could take her on a journey of no return.

I put all my concentration into it, stimulating that tiny spot of pleasure. But that was not all. My other fingers and my tongue were in charge of inciting the sweet protuberance.

A scream shook the cellar door. Her orgasm sank into my hand, and I drank from her without missing the unbridled pleasure that blanked her features.

When the last convulsion was over, she sought my satisfied gaze.

"Take me. Please, I want it all," she begged.

"I didn't bring any condoms," I admitted.

Not that anything was going to happen. I was very calm. When a guy was given as much chemo as I was, the chances of being a father were much reduced, and I didn't have venereal disease.

"It's all right. I need you, Áxel. I can't stay like this. I *can't.*"

I wasn't going to object. I pulled off my pants and underpants and buried myself in her. "I never do it bareback, you can rest assured. My tests..."

"Shut up and don't stop," she demanded, grabbing the back of my neck. "Didn't you want the other Garbiñe? Well, here she is."

I gave her a delighted smile, and I rammed her mercilessly.

"Yours to command, beautiful."

The stoma limited me in some sexual positions, but not on a table. I didn't have to hold it down. All I needed was to move my hips, and I was damn good at that.

Our mouths sought each other hungrily, tongues entangled as well as her legs. There wasn't a single part that wasn't in contact.

We were a perfect match. I was not surprised to find that underneath the shy Garbiñe, there was another one who had always been there. The one who was passionate about her work and didn't mind being the only volunteer in a room full of men to receive an electric shock.

My grunts, her panting, my coming, my going, her coming—everything combined to make the moment perfect.

Her lips tugged at mine to break the kiss. "I'm going to come again."

"I can't control it if you do," I whispered, lost. "I can't have children because of the chemo."

"I don't think I can either. Dario and I tried after Ruben, and nothing."

"I can come outside."

"No, I want you inside. I want everything from you."

I knew it was irresponsible. Even if neither of us could conceive, it didn't exempt us from the responsibility of having to use protection, but there it was. I don't know how to explain it. It's just that I needed it to be like that too, complete with no restrictions.

Maybe I was back to being a selfish piece of shit, and my primal need to fill her with my seed was what was driving me. I don't know. Whatever it was, I didn't stop, and by the time she started convulsing again, dragging me with her, it was too late for me to consider leaving.

We remained embraced, with our foreheads joined together like our loins, our souls giving each other a bath of caresses that did not let us be fearful about the price of our actions.

CHAPTER SIXTEEN

Schnapsidee: The brilliant ideas that come up when you get drunk.

Garbiñe

The word "sex" had changed its meaning in my personal Wikipedia, going from "Intimate encounter between two people " to "I'm not getting off this train."

"Virgin of orgasm found!" as Luz del Alba, my online yoga teacher, would say. I had signed up for the classes on the doctor's recommendation. She had told me that yoga was a great way to control anxiety, and, given my schedule, the easiest solution was online classes. Her gym broadcast videos she recorded during the week, and the price was very reasonable. I could put them on whenever I wanted, and if the exercise didn't work out, I didn't have to answer to anyone.

The girl was very funny. She had a lot of viral phrases that were hilarious. I think that's why I stayed with her. The sessions with Luz were very enjoyable.

I separated my forehead from Axel's with a smile that came from my soul.

Our breathing was still ragged, and my dress was a mess, but none of that mattered. If I had to give that emotion a name, it would be happiness, without a doubt.

He kissed me tenderly. "Are you all right?"

"Better than ever." I sighed.

"So, have I raised your expectations?"

"I don't think I've ever had one like that in my life," I replied with a laugh.

"What a weight off my shoulders because, for me, it was superb. Argh!"

Áxel let out a laugh and moved slightly to get out of me. Something warm and sticky slid between my legs.

"Argh? Is that a compliment or the mating cry of Yogi Bear?"

"This was, and I quote the marvelous Julio Iglesias, who my mother likes so much, 'a religious experience.'"

"Because you have seen the Virgin?" I joked.

"The Virgin, the Holy Spirit, and all the heavenly court. We'll have to celebrate. Shall we go out to dinner? It's on me. It's enough to let me sleep at your place."

"Okay, but I have to change. The stained dress is not part of my plans. I have an image to preserve."

"If you put it that way, I'm not sure I want to go out. I like this image too much." He fiddled, biting my lips.

"Let me regain my strength with dinner, and I promise you a second round, my sergeant. With two orgasms after so long without having any, I need some time to bounce back."

"It's a deal."

He helped me down from the table and we walked back, stopping every now and then to give each other caresses.

"Where have you brought me?" he asked, intrigued.

"To Mordor."

"To Mordor?"

I nodded playfully. "Uh-huh. According to Tolkien, it means black earth, which is just what we have in front of us," I said, losing myself in the landscape. "Before you say anything. Yes, I'm a *Lord of the Rings* geek, and this is the most Middle Earth place you'll find on the island."

"From today on, I'll be a fan of that movie too. I'm already feeling the influence of Mordor." He pressed me against him. "You are 'my precious.'"

The laughter came out on its own as he nibbled on my neck, tickling me.

"Do you think we should go downstairs?" I asked.

"All right. Let's go for a walk around this place you like so much."

We parked outside the restaurant so I could show him the geography of the area. We were at Benijo, a wild beach on the Costa del Caserío, north of the Anaga district. By day it was a nudist beach with black volcanic sand and gravel from which you could see the Roques de Anaga, some small stone islands that gave character to the landscape and made you imagine that anything could happen in that place.

"This is creepy, isn't it?" Áxel asked, hugging me.

The wind was blowing, lifting the waves and making them hit the rocks hard.

"It's spooky to come in the morning. This is a nudist beach, and you see everything."

"That's not creepy. More like interesting," he countered, giving me small bites on my neck.

I liked the intimacy that had been forged between us. "There are places on the island that are not over-visited. You only know them if someone who lives here shows them to you."

"This is one of them?"

"Well, it was. With the advent of the Internet, special places like this one are becoming more and more visible."

I had my back against his torso. Áxel enveloped me in his warmth, making the drop in temperature imperceptible.

"I recognize that it is shocking," she said. "After dinner, I'll take you to the lookout point. From there, the views are amazing."

"Are you hungry?"

"For you, always."

He turned around, laughing, to feast on my mouth. I didn't know if the new Garbiñe would last too long, but as long as she did, I wanted to make the most of it.

We ordered grilled cheese with honey, a salad, and *arroz caldoso* for two, all washed down with a bottle of white wine, which ended up being two.

After that, driving was not the most prudent thing to do, so we opted to walk to the lookout point and let the fresh night air clear our heads.

The moon rose, bathing the landscape in a festival of light and shadow that made us hold our breath.

"Now it really looks like Mordor," he admitted.

"Doesn't it? If you lived here, I'd take you to places that would astonish you. You would be breathless."

"Just looking at you is enough for that to happen," he whispered, reaching for my earlobe to catch it between his teeth.

A shiver ran from the base of my spine to the back of my neck. "I'm serious."

"Me too."

I turned in his arms to lose myself in that dark gaze. "I'm not the kind to cut off anyone's breath unless it is to stop you."

"It's enough for me if you cut mine, and no need to put me in the dungeon. Or do you need more?"

I shook my head in abstraction at the truthfulness I read in his eyes. "Would you move?"

Áxel narrowed his eyes without losing the link that united us. "Here?"

I nodded.

"Is that a proposition?" he asked.

My mouth had become dry at the same rate my tongue came untied.

"Or is your question the result of alcohol?"

"I know it sounds crazy, and you'll probably say no, but I want you to come live with me."

I had never made a decision that I hadn't thought out, but I was tired of being so restrained about everything. If Áxel had little time left, I wanted him to spend it with me.

"Wow. I didn't expect you to drop something like that on me." We were holding each other around the waist.

"To tell you the truth, neither did I."

His eyes relaxed. "Well, for not thinking about it, you said it very confidently."

"Did I scare you?"

"A little bit."

I bit my lower lip, thinking I had screwed up.

"Sorry. I've been a brute."

"Don't get me wrong. I am willing to accept, but I don't want us to rush into a decision that's driven by wine. Besides, there are my children, the job, and the treatments."

I sighed, pressing my forehead to his chest.

"It was a bad idea. It's just that I feel so good with you that I didn't think about the other things. It's the first time I've done that and just put my desires first. You must think I'm selfish and brainless."

His hand reached for my chin to lift it. "Hey, slow down. I just think that what has happened between us is so intense that it's hard to assimilate. I'm extremely flattered that someone as conscientious as you can make room for me in her life so selflessly, knowing how little time we may have left. Let's not fool ourselves. You know that I'm fighting for life, and I don't have the upper hand."

"Your situation is not the usual one, we agree on that, but I don't want to refuse to live for what time we have. If what we have left is short, I would rather soak up moments by your side. I don't want to count the days; I want the days to count, and I'm convinced that with you, they would. Perhaps if it weren't for your exceptional circumstance, I wouldn't have dared to propose anything so rash. God, I must seem psychotic to you."

"A very lovely and desirable one," he said, kissing the tip of my nose. "You said you never thought about yourself, that you always put the will of others first. In my case, it was the opposite. I was always a selfish shit with my wife, my children, and my family. It was always me before anyone else, and I'm not proud of it. The disease helped me realize who I was so I could change."

"You don't seem selfish to me," I tried to console him.

"I may have gotten better."

I curled up against his torso, leaning my ear against his heart, strong, serene, impregnable. What a paradox. No one who saw Áxel would think his situation was so delicate, yet he kept walking the tightrope.

We opted to go back down to the beach to sit on the sand and wait for our alcohol level to drop.

We lay down and kissed until our lips tasted like promises, immersed in a silence that did not lack words because it said all.

"And where is the sleeping beauty?"

"Don't shout. He'll hear you!" I scolded her.

Paula, coffee in hand, was trying to poke her nose into my room. I pulled her back into the living room.

"If you pull me like that, I'll drop my coffee, and you'll have to mop the floor."

"I wouldn't have to if you'd stop being a damn nuisance."

"I remind you that it was you who invited me to go shopping."

"I didn't think that Áxel was going to show up here."

"We're not in the Wild West, so you couldn't send me a smoke signal. You do have a cell phone! But of course, it was more important to fuck like a rabbit than to send a sad text to your friend so she wouldn't come. **Have girlfriends to trade you for powder.**"

"Áxel is not a powder."

"I've already figured that out. Otherwise, you wouldn't have him sleeping here. Are you sure about what you're doing, Garb? It's one thing to fuck him. It's quite another to let him into your life."

"Too late for that. I asked him to move in with me last night."

"You did what?" she shouted.

"Keep your voice down!" I pulled her outside.

"Have you been abducted by aliens?"

"Yes, ET came down on his bike, trying to put me in the basket to take me home, no shit. No, nobody abducted me."

"That guy is going to die!" she exclaimed, raising her voice again.

"Just like you, me, and everyone else on this planet. I'm sure we're immortal now, and I haven't heard about it."

"Save the sarcasm with me. That's my second last name."

"I don't care if it's your third." I squared my shoulders. "You have no right to judge my actions."

"I'm your friend! The one who pushed you to fuck the instructor, with a small variation! I said fuck, not marry. That's the difference."

"I don't care! I haven't talked about marriage, and it's not fair to bring it into this. I have always supported you, even if you made shitty decisions like walking off the job without getting a dime out of your bitch of a boss."

"I couldn't stand to look at her ass after I found out she was fucking my husband in my house."

"I understand that even if I don't support it. Now it's your turn, and I remind you that until recently, you saw him as perfect for me."

"I saw him as perfect to dust you off or throw him out, but not for him to come and live here, especially without a wedding."

"You're not traditional at all. Why a wedding?"

"So that if you blow it, you'll have something to show for it."

"Take back what you just said," I snapped.

"Okay, I'm sorry. I went too far, but I don't want to see you suffer, and you're talking about love when it should be sex."

"You sound like a bad reggae song."

"And you look like…bah, I don't even know what you look like. But this is a bad idea, a very bad idea."

"He hasn't said yes yet."

"He shouldn't. Maybe he has more sense than you. What would you say to Ruben? If it's hard enough to lose a pet. Imagine losing a man who lives with him."

"Are you comparing Áxel to a dog?"

"I would never dare compare a man to a dog. At least dogs are faithful. I might compare them, if I dare, to a rodent."

I put my right hand over my eyes and rubbed them, feeling fine particles of sand. Talking to Paula could be stressful, especially if you had to talk sense into her.

Last night, we had fallen asleep on the beach, waking up with the first rays of sunlight. Áxel's abdomen was quite sore, so I suggested as soon as we got home that he should go take a shower and lay down on my bed. He took his medication and lay down.

I took the opportunity to get some water, tidy up, and prepare breakfast. There wasn't a part of my body that didn't hurt. It had been too long since I had slept on the beach.

As I was making coffee, Paula knocked on the door.

I had been fantasizing for a week about Áxel living with me, and I hadn't told anyone. I know it sounds like a total freakout, but I couldn't explain my need to be with him.

I would tell Ruben that he was a friend who was coming to spend some time with us, and we would see how we would deal with the issue of his death if that happened. I hoped the doctors had got the treatment right and it would be okay.

"Hello," a man greeted from the doorway.

Paula and I froze in an awkward silence. My friend faced him to inspect him with disdain. When she went into harpy mode, she could be obnoxious.

"Well, well, well. So the sleeping beauty has awakened. I didn't know princes became uninvited squatters."

"Mmm. I've never been royalty, and you're wrong. I was invited. Maybe not for this weekend, but the offer was made."

"Are you thinking of moving to the palace? Are you thinking of moving to another castle?"

"*Paula!*" I shouted in disbelief.

"I haven't accepted yet," he said.

"Well, I hope you refuse, for everyone's sake. You've stirred up her hormones so much that you've caused a neuron leak in her brain."

"*Paula!*" I insisted.

Áxel's hair was disheveled, his eyes looked sleepy, and little wrinkles gathered in the corners of his eyes as if he were trying not to laugh.

"Are you the intrepid, sharp-tongued journalist friend of Garbiñe's behind the blog that has most of the politicians in this country in check?"

"Have you done your homework, or are you speaking from hearsay, Instructor?"

"I don't copy in exams. Before Garbiñe told me about you, I had read your work. I follow you and have even commented on a post. I'm Hero37." Paula's eyes widened, and I smiled. He had just put her in check, and I was glad. "You're very good, and I like that you always hit them where it hurts the most. Your identity is safe, word of a dying Mosso. I'll take your secret to my grave."

She burst out laughing. Deep down, they were in the same mood.

"Sucking up to me and laughing at your death isn't going to make me like you any better," my friend warned.

"Too bad. I wanted us to be good friends. You seem like an intelligent and discerning woman. Besides, Garbiñe adores you."

In one of our conversations, the subject of my friend's blog came up. Her passion for her work was one of the few characteristics we shared, and I was pleasantly surprised to hear that Áxel was following her before I mentioned the Internet site on which she wrote under a pseudonym.

"That's because she knows I always tell her the truth, even if it stings and is usually not what she wants to hear."

I rolled my eyes.

"But I'm sure you mean it with the best of intentions. Friends tend to act as smoke detectors for our most vocal shots." She raised her eyebrows knowingly. "But that doesn't mean we listen to them. Sometimes it's necessary to give yourself a slap, then be there to pick your unconscious friend up off the floor."

"Theory is all very well, Pythagoras, but when you know it is going to be as big as a tsunami, a reinforced concrete wall, and a tax inspector put together, you understand that not even picking up the unconscious is going to overcome it."

It was a duel of two who spoke the same language, and I was the unconscious one they referred to. I had had enough of being ignored. I decided to intervene. "I don't care if I crash! I know how to swim, I have a very hard head, and I have never defrauded the tax authorities. If I get hit, I'll get up without your help."

I pursed my lips and crossed my arms.

"That's my girl," Áxel murmured with a wide smile that made me go to him and take refuge under his arm.

"I'm off. Even if I'm alone, I have to go shopping."

"I'll stay at home and wait for you, or why don't the three of us go?" I suggested. "It's not as if Áxel and I have made plans.

Afterward, we can stop somewhere cool to eat and show him the place."

They both ended up agreeing, and I was happy to enjoy the day with the three of us together. I wanted Paula to get to know him better and understand why Áxel had become a fundamental part of my life.

CHAPTER SEVENTEEN

Irusu: Pretending not to be home when someone knocks on your door.

<u>Garbiñe</u>

I swear, I was on the verge of committing amicide. "If I had known that you were going to behave like an asshole with Áxel, I would have pretended not to be at home when you knocked on the door. I've never been so ashamed. What kind of a nerve do you have to behave like that with him and embarrass me like that?"

We had finished shopping at the mall. Áxel had shown more patience than all the saints during our marathon shopping spree. I ended up buying something special in the lingerie store to surprise a certain person who stayed outside.

Áxel was in the bathroom. It was the first moment Paula and I were alone. In the store, where there were hundreds of people, it was not a good plan to get into an argument with Paula.

But I wasn't going to let her get away with it. I needed to tell her how lousy her behavior had been since it was one thing for her to tell me what she thought as my friend and quite another for her to go for Áxel's jugular.

"I'm sorry. I know you're right and that I'm way out of line." She sighed. "I made a foolish mistake yesterday, and you've both paid for it."

"That doesn't absolve you of responsibility."

"I know, I know. I deserve your reproaches. You can tie me up in the middle of the jungle to be devoured by wild animals who will feast on my entrails. Is that better?"

"No, but it's a start. What kind of mistake do you mean?" I was interested, trying to get over my annoyance.

Paula could act like a dick, but she didn't have a bad heart. She cared about me more than anyone, not like my sisters' sanctimonious dislike. She was adopted family.

Paula looked at me, a little embarrassed. "Last night, I slept with Gabriel."

"With your ex? What about the doctor?"

"The doctor was a one-night stand."

"And Gabriel?"

"Gabriel is an asshole for life, and I am even worse for falling on all fours."

"What happened?"

"Well, what usually happens. He called me yesterday because I still had some of his vinyls. You know how much of a music lover he is."

"Okay. And?"

"As I was telling you, he came for the records. He told me he had broken up with Ursula, and he missed me. I had drunk a few glasses of wine, and I let myself be loved. I'm pathetic, I know." She covered her face with her hands.

"You are not."

"Yes, I am. He came to me whimpering, swearing that he had not stopped loving me or thinking about me. He said he didn't know how to get back with me and that if I gave him a chance, we could start from scratch, and he could live with me again. I said yes. He was always my weak point, that bohemian air and how well we understand each other in bed. Can you believe I accepted?"

I tilted my head to one side since I had forgiven Dario in similar circumstances. I understood her perfectly. Sometimes we're idiots.

Paula continued, "That wasn't the worst of it. At eight o'clock, the doorbell rang. Do you know who it was?"

"The Amazon delivery guy?" Paula was an online shopping addict.

"No! Ursula! She showed up to bring me his stuff. She had kicked him out of the house because the jerk had been hooking up with a student at the university for a couple of months."

"Wow, like the protagonist of *Gabriel's Inferno*."

"Yes, with the difference that my ex does not enjoy the sex appeal of the professor in the book. My ex is less romantic."

"He may be less romantic, but he still takes them by storm."

"It must be because of the morbid curiosity that students have about a university professor. Sleeping with one is a recurring fantasy."

"How did Ursula know he would be at your house?"

"You know him. He's incapable of being alone. He's the typical monkey who won't let go of the branch without having another one to hold on to. Since she kicked him out when she found out about his dalliances, she looked for the asshole on duty, which was me. He couldn't just run to the house of an eighteen-year-old girl who lives with her parents. I need to get my ass kicked. What a fool I am."

"I'm so sorry, baby. You're not a fool. It's just that deep down, you've never gotten over him."

"I guess."

"What did you do?" I asked, holding her hands affectionately.

"Threw his clothes out the window, along with his precious

vinyls, and forced him to go out naked. I swear he's going to go get his fist-fuckin' cousin next time."

"Love to see it."

"Yes, I imagine that from the outside, it may seem funny and that when I look back on it, I will die laughing, but now it stings." I squeezed her hands in understanding. "It hurt me when I found out that Dario had tried to come home to you because Damaris had kicked him out. When you told me you had asked Áxel to live with you, I flipped out. I know it's a very poor excuse, but I saw myself with Gabriel, opening my arms to him beside my bed so he could laugh at me again. I don't learn! I think I'd better move. I have a friend who lives in Barcelona that I met in the race..."

"Wait a minute, wait a minute. What do you mean, move? You're letting things get out of hand."

"I need to get away from Gabriel and this island that smothers me."

"You can't leave me here alone!" I protested.

"You're not going to be alone. He's coming. I know it."

She was referring to Áxel.

"It may take him a while to get things settled, but in the end, he'll come, and you'll end up living together, even though I'm terrified of the idea that he'll die and you'll have a terrible time. I'm not going to lie to you. During the time we've been together, I've liked him a lot. He's an awake, funny, attractive guy, and he seems to be very attentive to you. That's why I'm so scared that you'll fall in love and he'll die. With your history of anxiety and depression, I don't know how you would cope."

"Paula." I sighed, hugging her, feeling her sorrow as my own. She was the closest thing I had to a sister since I had nothing in common with my siblings. It might sound bad, but I didn't feel they and I were part of the same family.

She clung tightly to me and gave me one of those hugs that pulled your soul out of your chest. My friend whimpered a little, and I whimpered too. Tears flowed silently until Áxel's hoarse voice cut the moment short.

"Did I miss something?"

Paula turned away from the hug with tears on her face.

"Yes. I just gave my friend my blessing for your move. You better get it right, champ, because if you sink her, I'll chase you to hell and back."

"I still think the same. I don't want us to rush things. We'll see how we evolve."

"You will evolve with flying colors. You just need to spend some time together for you to see it. I'm so glad you made her smile again, and for that alone, I'm going to take you to a place you're going to be amazed by."

"At the mall?" Áxel's pleading look told us he had had enough for today.

"No, don't worry. We've finished our shopping day."

"Thank goodness. I was about to ask you to drop me off at the mattress store."

I looked at him with concern. "Are you feeling all right?"

He came over and put his arm over my shoulder.

"Yes, relax. It was a joke."

"When it comes to your health, I stop understanding jokes," I said.

"If I feel off, I'll let you know. Besides, I'm on extra medication today." He patted his chest with a mischievous smile.

"What is it? Morphine?" asked Paula.

"Nah, just some therapeutic cigarettes."

"Maria?" asked my interested friend. He nodded, and Paula moved to the other side of him, instigating him to put his free arm around her shoulder. "You don't know how long it's been since I've smoked one of those. I think since college."

"They are for pain!" I protested.

"For a good time, too," Paula said. "Garbi has never smoked a joint, so she has no idea what it feels like. She's a cannabis virgin."

"Stop talking nonsense!" I snarled. Áxel laughed.

"We'll see if she changes her mind today and dares to try one." He hugged me, running his tongue along my neck.

"I warn you, you pair of fools, I am an officer of the law, and I will not be influenced by two members of a sect of Rastafarians."

Áxel and Paula chuckled, enjoying their particular sense of humor. Seeing them together made me happy—another moment to keep in my little jar of unforgettable moments. I intended to fill it to the brim, and when there were no more, to close the lid tightly so none of them would escape.

"By the way, Áxel, forgive me for submitting you to my tribunal of the Holy Inquisition. Sometimes I'm a bit of an asshole and see witches where there are none."

I was deeply proud of my friend. Paula could screw up, but she always recognized her mistakes, and that was to be admired.

"Relax. We all have an inner asshole that we try to silence. Sometimes we are unable to contain it, and what happens is what happens."

She offered him a look of thanks.

The rest of the day went smoothly. We had lunch in *Icod de los Vinos*. Paula wanted to show Áxel the *Drago Milenario*, the dragon tree. Nobody knew exactly how old the tree was, but it was believed to be about eight hundred years. It was the largest and longest-lived of its kind in the world, and it was declared a national monument in 1917.

We strolled through the park, which occupied about three hectares, taking in the different species of flora native to the island. Everything was divided into bioclimatic zones.

We took a few photos of us clowning around. Paula was acting as a guide, telling Áxel the two legends they used to tell the children who visited the park with their school.

The first related the tree to a fierce dragon with a hundred heads that was in charge of protecting the golden apples of the Garden of the Hesperides. The dragon was killed by the Titan Atlas while he assisted Herakles with the eleventh work commissioned by Herodotus. It was said that the blood that flowed from the dragon's wounds and fell on the garden gave rise to the trees known today as dragon trees.

"And the other legend?" Áxel asked without taking his eyes off the trunk.

"The other tells that a merchant disembarked on the beach of Icod in search of '*Sangre de Drago*,' the blood of the dragon, when he found some young native girls taking a bath."

"Mmm, I think I'm going to like this one better. Were they naked?"

I slapped him on the shoulder, which made him smile. "Don't be dirty!"

"It would be the most normal thing. You don't bathe with clothes on."

"That's not a piece of information I was given when I was told the story. You'll have to let your imagination run wild," my friend said mischievously.

"Okay, in mine, they are naked, and the three of them are exactly like Garbiñe."

I reddened to the core. "Go on."

"Well, the merchant went after them and managed to catch one of them." Áxel waggled his eyebrows, and I could only laugh. Paula continued, "The young woman offered him delicacies, and she took the opportunity to escape while the man was enjoying them, thinking that they were the fruits of the Garden of the Hesperides."

"Why did you want to run away?" Áxel murmured in my ear. "Now that the fun was coming and I was thinking of eating you." He ran his nose behind my ear.

My friend, oblivious to our caresses, did not stop. "The girl managed to jump across a ravine and find refuge among the trees. When the merchant went in search of her, he came upon a terrifying tree that wielded its branches like swords and whose trunk twisted like a snake."

"For a snake between my legs. You don't know how you're getting on my nerves, wench," Áxel muttered for just me to hear.

I was very aroused. I wanted to get away to enjoy some alone time.

"Are you listening to me?" asked Paula, causing Áxel to pull away from my neck.

"Yes, yes. You were going for the snake."

She snorted, though she did not abandon the story. "Well, the man tried to defend himself by throwing a sharp weapon at the trunk of the tree, from which a red liquid that looked like blood began to flow. It was then that the merchant fled in panic to his boat, paddling away without looking back."

"What a tragedy! The poor wretch ran away without getting any! Garbiñe's predecessor was a bad woman." He poked me.

"I am not from Tenerife!"

"It's the same thing. You ran away from me," he continued, pressing his erection against my ass.

Paula, looking at us and knowing what was happening, exclaimed, "Time to go back, or you will finish what that pair did not, and this is a public park. I'm not going to be arrested for scandal and end up in a dungeon with a civil guard and a *Mosso d'Esquadra*. It sounds like the start of a joke."

I had no choice but to laugh at her witticism and accept that going back was the best thing to do.

On the way back, I didn't want to bring up the subject of my friend's move. I thought it was only a hot flash. Gabriel was always pushing her out of her comfort zone, and she could do crazy things if he was involved.

When we got home, it was almost nine o'clock. "Will you stay for dinner?"

"No, I'll leave you to dine alone. I've already monopolized you enough," she replied.

"Well, if you're not staying," Áxel took out one of his rolled joints and held it out to her. "Smoke it to my health."

"This is drug trafficking!" I protested, pretending to be offended.

"No way. It's oregano," Áxel clarified, winking at my friend.

Paula kept the present.

"Thanks for everything, guys. I needed a day like this. Áxel, it was a pleasure to meet you, and I apologize for what happened before. You don't know how sorry I am. I wish from the bottom of my heart that everything goes well in your next visit to the doctor. You deserve it."

Her sincerity moistened my eyes. That was my friend!

"There is no need to apologize anymore. Everything has been forgotten. Thank you for your good wishes."

The two gave each other a couple of kisses and said goodbye until the next time.

"I'm grateful that you didn't hold this morning's lousy mood against her. Paula can be overwhelming," I said, snuggling against him.

Together we watched Paula's car fade down the road, honking the horn in farewell.

"She's not a bad person. She's just impulsive. Nothing two law enforcement officers can't control. Are you hungry, Sergeant?" he asked, kissing my hair.

"No way. After our midday meal, I have enough for a year. You?"

"Not yet, but I have something to whet our appetites," he said suggestively.

"What is it?"

"Let's sit on the porch swing, and I'll show you."

We settled in, and Áxel took out one of the cigarettes, wagging his eyebrows.

"I told you I've never smoked one of those."

"There's got to be a first time," he said with a smile, taking a couple of deep puffs. "Try it. Nothing will happen."

Fearing the unknown, I accepted the joint and took such a deep puff that I got dizzy. I started coughing like crazy, and Áxel tried to get all the smoke out of my body by hitting me on the back. Fuck!

"If you do everything so hard, I don't want to imagine a certain part of my anatomy in your mouth. On second thought, I take it back. I'm dying for you to do the same to me. But you animal! Did you think you are a Typhoon Ultra 6000 vacuum cleaner?"

"I don't know what I was thinking. I think I didn't think." My lungs burned from coughing. "I'm going to get something to drink."

"It would be best."

Stumbling a little, I went down to the bodega. I needed to clear my head. That's what I got for going into gardens without being a gardener. There, forgotten on the table, were yesterday's glasses. I looked at them with a tremulous smile, remembering what had happened on the tabletop and wishing that something like that would happen again. I had been crazy with desire all day, and it was Áxel's fault for giving me a taste of something I had never before tasted.

I filled a couple of glasses with one of my favorite wines, an indigenous white that was very smooth and fruity. It would do us good.

Áxel swayed, his puffs much shorter than mine, eyes lost in the immensity of the night. He looked so good that he seemed to be an indisputable part of the place I had made my own.

"What are you looking at so intently?" He glanced away from me.

"Did you know that our galaxy has between two and four hundred thousand stars and that, to the eyes of a giant, the Milky Way would only look like a faint bubble of gas?"

"No, I didn't. Are you interested in astronomy?"

I sat down next to him, offering him the wine.

"I like facts, and I have always been interested in trying to understand the origin of things, even if it is complex. Do you think we go somewhere when we die?"

I snuggled up to him, sipping wine.

"I would like to think that we watch over our loved ones. Of all the theories out there, even if it's the most improbable, it's the one I like the most," he replied.

"Me too. We agree on that. I feel my father watching over me, even though he's not here. I like to think that he is watching over me and Ruben. If you had seen them together! They adored each other."

"I'm sure they did." He held the joint to my lips, and I took a cautious drag.

"That's it. Slowly, just a little. Notice how it goes in gently and relaxes you. How did he die, your father?"

"In his sleep, from a heart attack. Doctors say he did not suffer."

"That's what I'm most afraid of, you know? Dying in pain."

I caressed his face and grabbed the hand with the cigarette to bring it back to my mouth. I wanted to disconnect. Thinking about my father still hurt. I pressed my lips to his fingers in a subtle kiss to lose myself in the liberating sensation that the weed promised.

"I did better this time."

"That's right. Tell me more about the stars."

"Let's see. Experts say that by analyzing the age of the stars and relating them to the time of the Big Bang, it has been proven that the Milky Way is almost as old as the universe. So, we are living in a neighborhood that's about thirteen billion years old."

"My goodness, that's a lot! Can you imagine living that long? How awful! The mortgages and bad decisions we would accumulate. I'll settle for growing old with a green-eyed beauty who loves electric shocks next to me."

A giggle emerged from my mouth. I felt lighter and much more uninhibited.

"By the way, you haven't shown me what you bought at the lingerie store," he suggested hoarsely.

"You want me to show it to you?"

"Of course."

"Live?" That caused his eyes to darken even more.

"This is promising. On with the show, baby."

He approached, took a puff, grabbed the back of my head, and released it between my lips.

I pulled away, embarrassed but eager to please him. "Don't move. I want to surprise you."

"I wouldn't think of it. I'll wait for you," he replied. He hoped it would be good.

CHAPTER EIGHTEEN

Piwkenyeyu: I carry you in my heart.

<u>Áxel</u>

I took the last puffs of the joint, completely serene. Maybe my "therapeutic cigarettes" were what I was looking for.

The doctor had recommended them. The cannabis they prescribe usually comes in bottles with a dropper so that each patient can administer the drops they need. I had one in my backpack, and under normal conditions, I would have taken that, but today was not a normal day.

During my last chemo, I met Florentina, an amazing woman in her seventies who'd had both breasts removed. She grew marijuana at home, "one hundred percent organic," as she used to say. She entertained herself by making creams, oils, and soaps, and she smoked a joint from time to time. As she said, "In this last stage, a cigarette a day brings me joy." Who could contradict her?

She told me that when she was young, she didn't try drugs, but now cannabis brought her relaxation and happiness.

At my last session, she brought me a few buds and made me

promise her that if she died, I would smoke them to her health with whomever I wanted, in a kind of farewell ceremony.

It was her last session because she had metastases throughout her body, and Florentina had decided that she no longer wanted to continue with the treatment. She preferred to last as long as she could without undergoing more chemical processes that left her defeated and wished to die in peace.

Yesterday morning, while I was preparing breakfast, I received a message from her daughter. Florentina had just left with a smile on her lips and a message for me.

"Tell my boy that I'm leaving and to remember what I told him and to go see her. We only have one life, and we have to squeeze the most out of it."

She used to call me her "chemo date," and I would respond by telling her that if I had caught her a few years earlier, she wouldn't have missed it. She would smile with satisfaction, and we would spend the afternoon chatting about things. Not everything is bad during illness. I have met some wonderful people.

I allowed myself to shed a few tears and asked Elisa, her daughter, to give me the address to send flowers to the wake. The funeral was going to be on Monday, and I didn't want to miss it. She kindly gave it to me, and I immediately looked for a plane ticket to fulfill my friend's last wish. While we were having our sessions, I used to talk to her about Garbiñe and her surprise. It made her smile with the wrinkles of a face that had lived. She nodded with shining eyes and sighed, recalling the love she had with her husband, who had left her a widow at the age of forty with four children after suffering an accident at work.

"Love is for the brave," she used to tell me. "It gives you enough energy to fight, to hold on to life tooth and nail. It doesn't matter if it's for a partner, a child, or a family member. It is so powerful that it is the best sword we can raise against the bug. Never forget that."

And there I was, in the place where that blossoming feeling

that moved everything lived. Here was the woman who charged my batteries to face the worst of the battles. I was fulfilling the last will of my "chemo date."

I looked up at the sky to take my last puff. I saw a star twinkle brightly, which made me think of our last conversation. "When I'm gone, look for me on a clear night. When you see a light in the firmament that almost dazzles you, that will be me bidding you my last farewell."

It was silly, but I sensed her there, with the same healing magic she sent me when she held my hand.

"I carry you in my heart," I said to her. "I hope I fulfilled your last wish and that wherever you are, you have reunited with Ramiro." The star twinkled again, and I seemed to see her answer in that wink.

The front door opened softly, and from it came a sweet melody I recognized. It was a song by Camila, *Kiss Me*, which was just what I intended to do to the beautiful woman who came out the door wearing a thigh-length midnight-blue satin robe and an embarrassed smile.

I drained my glass of wine. I got very thirsty when I saw the robe, and I left it on the side table so I wouldn't accidentally drop it.

"You look beautiful," I said, causing the corners of her lips to shoot up. She glanced this way and that as if looking for someone in the dark. "Is something wrong?"

"No. It's just that I'm afraid that a neighbor might see me like this."

"I'm sure they're at home having dinner. Besides, you're not naked. Not at the moment." I raised my eyebrows provocatively.

She positioned herself in front of me, turning my mouth into desert sand. With extreme care, she undid the bow at the waistband to reveal an outfit that drove me crazy. It was a chemise in the same shade as the robe, combining soft lace with a shiny fabric that made it look like a midnight treat.

"I take back what I said before."

Her eyes dimmed a little, and she tried to close the robe. "You don't like it? If I had known that, I told Paula that…"

"No, it's not that!" I stopped her by grabbing her hands. "You misunderstood me, sorry. I meant that you are sublime. Beautiful is an understatement. Come here so I can get a better look at you."

Her eyes lit up again, as did her cheeks. She sat on my legs, spreading her thighs to give me the best view on the island.

I kissed her, as I had been longing to do, with the insatiable hunger I felt, having her close. I kneaded the firm buttocks that wiggled over my erection. I was very hard inside my pants.

Short fingernails raked the back of my head as my mouth descended to taste the erect nipples through the fabric. Garbiñe gasped as the teeth scraped, tugging at them and then flicking my tongue to soothe the itch she must have been feeling. She kept rocking against me, and I couldn't have been stiffer. Her agitated face sought my ear.

"I want us to go inside. I would prefer the bed this time if you don't mind."

"As you wish, precious. We can leave this part out for your neighbors," I murmured.

She gave me a suggestive kiss and picked up the glasses to take them into the kitchen. I followed her closely, and as soon as she deposited them in the sink, I grabbed her from behind to fill her neck with kisses. My hands wandered to the front of her chemise and cupped her breasts.

My crotch dug into her ass, and my fingers tried to hit the combination to the safe.

"Please, Áxel," she begged. "In the bedroom."

I didn't let her cover up. I agreed to leave for that room on the condition that she took off her robe and walked in front of me so I could enjoy myself. She did so, hypnotizing me with the smoothness of her buttocks, which were exposed.

My cock jumped with pleasure.

Garbiñe had taken the trouble to illuminate the room with small blue scented candles that gave off the sweet scent of blackberries.

As soon as we were both inside, she faced me and put her hands on the waistband of my pants, which she unbuttoned with modesty without my hindering her aim.

She lowered them gingerly, taking my boxer shorts with her on the way, then smiled as she got down on her knees, and my budding erection jutted out to greet her.

She licked it before running her tongue over the glans and descending with decadent slowness along the entire shaft.

"God!" I exclaimed, extremely pleased with her attentions.

"Do you like it?" she asked hesitantly.

"Everything you do to me, I like. It's impossible for you to do anything that doesn't please me. I am completely yours."

With renewed confidence, she covered my penis with her mouth, licking it unhurriedly, not stopping until she reached the base.

Her left hand grasped my testicles, caressed them with delight, and compressed them. Garbiñe's mouth opened as she reached the opposite end and gradually engulfed me.

I growled loudly, bringing my hands to her silky hair, controlling the urge to push against the perfect mouth that welcomed me warmly. I gritted my teeth, letting the sweet torture intoxicate me until I wheezed.

"Baby, please stop. I don't think I can go on without coming." She let me go, tasting me for the last time.

"Did you like it?"

"Are you kidding?" I squeezed her tightly and kissed her to show her how much I enjoyed being held in her mouth. "Lie down on the bed, naked. I want to see you."

Her cheeks lit up adorably. She made no excuses and did not oppose my will. She simply obeyed.

I took the opportunity to take off my shoes.

My girl plopped down on the mattress face up with her legs together and her eyes on the ceiling. I was amused. She looked like a virgin on the day of her first time.

I grabbed one of her legs to worship the instep with my lips. There wasn't a single spot where I didn't want to get lost.

Bésame (kiss me),

as if the world would end later. Kiss me,

and kiss by kiss across the sky upside-down. Kiss me,

without reason, because the heart wants it. Kiss me.

Kiss me like this without compassion. Stay in me without condition. Give me just one reason

and I'm staying.

Camila crooned in the background, conveying just what I was feeling at that moment.

I reached her thighs and pulled them apart to feast between them. With each gasp, with each movement that propelled the smooth hips against my tongue, I felt more satisfied.

Garbiñe's twitching fingers tousled my short hair, and her legs wrapped around my shoulders as I delved into the deepest, tastiest place on her anatomy.

"Áxel, stop!"

I didn't listen. I didn't want to. I needed to make her explode, to undo her completely. I wanted to feel her crumple against my lips again.

My forefinger briskly shook the tight knot, and my tongue relentlessly penetrated it until it happened. One last gasp frag-mented everything and filled my mouth with pent-up desire.

I could not afford the luxury of coming since my recovery was more complex, but she could. I did not hesitate. I did not plan to give her fewer orgasms than I could bear. I climbed upward with satisfaction, losing myself in her face to fit myself between her legs and penetrate her with delight.

It was moist, hot, and inflamed.

"Why?" she hissed, the last throes of her orgasm clouding her eyes.

"I needed to taste you because there is nothing more beautiful than your face when you come. Now let's go for the next one."

Trembling legs anchored around my hips, and long fingers ascended to try to unbutton my shirt.

No." I stopped her.

She looked at me blankly. "What do you mean, no?"

"You won't like to see what's underneath. Believe me; it's better this way."

Garbiñe blinked as I rotated her hips and pushed between her thighs. "Better for whom?"

"For both of us," I answered.

I was used to my deformed body. Not that I felt overwhelmed to see what it had become, but where before there had been an athletic torso full of abs, now there was a mass of scars decorated with a bag where my feces went. Granted, I was wearing a girdle, but it didn't make it less grotesque.

"I want to see you." She repeated my phrase from minutes before.

I denied her, grabbing her hands to bring them above her head.

"No," I insisted, still pushing between her legs.

Her eyes filled with disappointment. "Do you think I care about your scars? That I like you for something as superficial as your physique?"

"I know you don't," I agreed without pausing.

"Then why can't I feel you against me as you are, with no barriers between us, with your skin against mine? Do you think I haven't been ashamed to show myself to you naked? That I don't have complexes?"

"You are beautiful just the way you are. You have nothing to be ashamed or embarrassed about."

"Neither do you. I love every cell in your body. Everything

that keeps you alive is perfect for me and a reason to be grateful. Let me undress you, please," she begged.

I closed my eyes tightly, almost panting. After the last operation, things had gotten worse. What if she disliked me? What if she stopped looking at me the way she did? What if she stopped being attracted to me? So many questions for so few answers. I had never been a coward, and I wasn't going to start being one now. In a few seconds, I made a decision that could change everything between us. I released my grip on her.

She reached up with alacrity, unbuttoning the buttons with the utmost delicacy. When the last one opened, firm fingers tried to pull the shirt down, and it wedged against my shoulders. I didn't move. I was frozen, terrified of what I might see when I opened my eyes. Still, I parted my eyelids, masking my gaze under a determination I didn't feel.

"Let me do it. I'll do it," I said.

I finished the work she had begun, hoping that when I met her gaze, she would not perceive the horror within me.

Her legs slipped away from my lower back, filling me with dread. That's it. She had seen the monster under my shirt and no longer wanted to be with me. *Game over, champ,* my brain whispered wearily.

"Lie down," she told me.

I opened my eyes in surprise, looking for a reaction from those green orbs that watched me lovingly.

"What?"

Her smile widened. "I want to get on top. Do you mind?"

I blinked twice in disbelief. "You want to continue?"

She was looking at me skeptically. "Are you serious? Do you think I'm going to let you get out of my bed without keeping your promises?"

I swallowed harshly, and her smile widened. "You're the same man who won me that day at the police course. The one who made me feel what it was like to be kissed with real devotion.

The one who made me feel full for the first time last night, and the one who is just as wonderful as he was with his shirt on. No article of clothing can hide your true beauty or detract from it."

Her words warmed me like nothing else could. Very cautiously, she touched the most visible scar, the one that the girdle did not completely cover. "I want to kiss your body in the same way you did mine. I want to love you all over to thank the doctors and your iron will that today, I can enjoy you completely.

"There is nothing more beautiful than your scars because in them lies your struggle for survival and your immense will to live. I adore them and love them just as I love you. I may overwhelm you, as I did when I suggested you move here, but at the risk of doing so, I need to tell you that I love you and that I can no longer conceive of life without you. I will not stop being in love with you no matter how much you oppose me because I have never felt as alive as I do now."

I hadn't realized I was holding my breath until I felt the need to inhale. "Garbi," I whispered, looking for her mouth and losing myself in it. Then I lay on my back on the bed as she had asked me to do.

It had been so intense, so beautiful that I, who always had words, had been left without the last word. She completed me, and without her, I felt empty.

Sweet lips traced the exposed skin. I let her take all the time in the world, and she lifted my torso and brought her hands to the center of my chest so she could feel my heart pounding.

"This is because of you. You are the one who makes it beat like this. I was in the ICU before I met you. Only my son gave me encouragement to keep it beating, yet now I don't want to stop feeling it like this."

Her nimble hips began a synchronized ascent and descent, allowing me to feel her as the pulsations stopped under my palms. I gazed at her in wonder, the emotions growing until I could no longer contain them.

"I love you too, Sergeant Tennis Player."

She opened her eyes, which had closed in delight.

I had never seen her more beautiful and glowing, with a smile that lit up my life.

We were suspended in that instant where she felt like a horsewoman and I was a wild horse. Where the cicatrices, pain, or sickness no longer mattered, only the purity of two souls who refused to allow each other not to love.

We burst at the same time, abandoning ourselves with the happiness of souls who know true love for the first time. I might have had to fail countless times to find her, but I had finally found my forever love.

I was awakened by knocking on the door.

My girl was still sleeping peacefully. I put on my shirt and pants as quietly as I could. Barefoot and uncombed, I went out to the entrance and opened the door without asking who it was.

Two pairs of eyes stared at me in amazement. I realized who was at the door since the face of the little boy in his father's arms was the one Garbiñe had shown me in one of our many phone messages.

"Who the hell are you?" shouted the father, red with anger.

"I'm a friend," I said, adjusting my shirt so I wouldn't do him more violence than necessary.

He put the child on the floor and he ran straight to his room, where my things were.

"Garb! Garb!" shouted Dario like a madman, entering her house uninvited.

I took a couple of strides to stop him, but it was too late. He flung open the door to find her standing there, disheveled, scared, and naked.

"I can't believe it! You're fucking someone else? Oh, you're fucking him all right!" He scolded her at the top of his lungs, oblivious to the boy who had come out into the living room.

Garbiñe grabbed the sheet and wrapped herself in it, full of shame.

"What are you doing here?" she asked without giving him an answer.

The little boy snuck in from the side to greet his mother, but I stopped him. "Hey, champ, I think Mom and Dad need to have a chat. How about showing me your room?"

"Who are you?" asked Ruben, who did not understand the situation.

"The pig that fucks your mother, son," Dario replied with derision.

"Don't talk like that in front of the child!" Garbiñe scolded him.

"Am I lying?"

I took a few breaths so I wouldn't slam my fist into his mouth.

"He's too little to hear certain things."

"Well, you should have thought of that before you fucked someone else in your house. What an exercise in restraint!"

I would have smashed his mouth right there, but it was the last thing Garbiñe needed.

"Let's go, champ. I'm Áxel," I tried to greet him by offering him my fist. He looked at it without understanding. No one had ever taught him to fist-bump.

"You're not taking my son anywhere," Dario demanded, out of his mind.

"If you'd relax, I wouldn't have to, but in your condition, it's the best thing for everyone, don't you think?"

"Not if it's going to turn out that you're going to the fucking psychologist. Is this the treatment he's recommending? Dick syrup?"

I couldn't take it anymore. He had gone six times too far because three was not enough. I immobilized him and took him out of the game. By applying a little more force, I could dislocate his wrist.

"I'm not a psychologist but a policeman and believe me, it would be syrup you wouldn't like," I whispered in his ear. "So do me a favor and behave with your son in front of you if you don't want me to teach you manners by breaking your wrist so you learn. Understand?"

Dario nodded in pain.

"I'm going to take your son so you can talk quietly, but yell at her just once, and I swear I'll break your knees." I let him go and tapped him on the shoulder with fake camaraderie. "I'm glad we understand each other."

I squatted to the level of Ruben's eyes, which were staring at me in fascination.

"Now that I have Dad's permission, can you show me that cool Superman shield?"

The little boy's face filled with happiness. "Do you like superheroes too?"

"Very much."

"My grandfather was one, you know? Now he's in heaven with Superman."

"Tell me about it."

I turned my head to Garbiñe, who quietly said, "Thank you, I'll be fine." That convinced me.

I offered one last warning glance at the asshole ex and disappeared with the kid into his room, praying the bag wouldn't overflow. I was at my limit, and it was time to change it.

I listened attentively to everything Ruben told me about his grandfather. It was a very intense fifteen minutes, after which I heard the front door close. I imagined that his parents had gone out so we wouldn't hear them. I needed to go to the restroom urgently; I couldn't take it anymore. I grabbed a clean bag from my backpack.

"I'm going to the bathroom for a moment. Look for the dolls you told me about, and I'll be right back to play with you. Don't go outside, okay?"

The boy, who was a clone of his father, nodded.

"Good boy."

It took me five minutes to change the bag, and when I returned to the room, Garbiñe was there with her son.

"Everything all right?" I asked.

She gave me a smile that didn't reach her eyes. "Ruben told me you are going to play with the superheroes," she muttered.

"That's right. You have a very smart and adorable son."

"Thank you, he's a great guy." She sighed. "If you don't mind, I'm going to take a quick shower and get breakfast ready for us."

"Of course, go on. We'll play in the meantime." I was surprised that Dario had not said goodbye to his son, but I didn't want to bring up the subject so as not to upset her more.

The kid was a sweetheart, overflowing with energy and enthusiasm. He reminded me of Christian when he was little. I had shared games before, but very few. How sorry I was about that! Lost time was impossible to recover, so it was best to live in the present as if every day was the last.

When breakfast was ready, Garbiñe came to get us. I told her to start without me. I preferred to wash up first, and after a quick shower, I joined them at the table.

"Your cell phone rang several times, but I didn't want to answer it."

"There's nothing as important as having breakfast with you. The others can wait."

"I don't know. They were insistent. Maybe it's important."

"I'm sure it's someone who wants to sell me something. Let's have breakfast, and then I'll check. I don't think it's that urgent."

I pulled my chair away to sit down, but before I could do so, my cell phone rang again.

Garbiñe looked at me like, "See?" It was better that I answered so we could have breakfast in peace.

I went to the bedroom and grabbed the phone. When I saw the name on the screen, I frowned. It was weird for her to call me. I answered, and when the caller finished speaking, my world split in two.

I rushed out of Garbiñe's room to gather my things and ran to the dining room.

"I have to go."

Garbiñe didn't understand, and I didn't feel strong enough to explain.

"Something has happened, and I have to leave urgently for the airport. I can't wait. I'll call a cab if you can't take me."

"What happened? Are you okay?"

"I don't have time to explain. I need to leave." My heart was racing.

"Okay, take it easy. Let me get the keys and the bag, and I'll take you to the airport. I'll be just a moment."

I nodded, not having the strength to do anything else. God, I couldn't believe it!

CHAPTER NINETEEN

Schadenfreude: The pleasure of another person's pain.

<u>Áxel</u>

I didn't even breathe.

If you ask me what happened from the time we got into Garbiñe's car until I arrived at the hospital, I don't remember.

I kept looping my mother-in-law's curt explanation on the phone.

"Come home, and hurry. Claudia and the children have suffered a terrible accident. We need you. It is very urgent. We still don't know anything about what happened to them, but it's serious. Please come as soon as possible."

"I'm in Tenerife, but don't worry. I'm going to the airport now, and I'll take the first available flight." Teresa burst into tears. "I'm coming, I'm coming," was the last thing I said to her.

I was so shocked, so out of my mind, that I was unable to rationalize the situation. It was one thing to accept your death and quite another to accept the death of people you love. When you add the words "terrible," "serious," and "accident," everything points to a fatal outcome, impossible to avoid.

Okay, Claudia and I were no longer a couple, but I didn't want anything bad to happen to her. For God's sake, she was the mother of my children! My ex-wife had always been good, and if she was teetering between life and death, I wanted to do a body swap. I didn't have much time left, according to the doctors.

Fuck, it was my turn to die, not Claudia's!

On the way to the airport, I told Garbiñe what little I knew. There had been an accident, and my ex-wife and children were seriously injured and in the hospital. She looked horrified and perfectly understood my crazed state. I told her that I would call her when I had more news but that right now, I needed to be with my family. She did not reproach me. She just hugged me, offering me comfort in a farewell I barely felt because of the anxiety gnawing on my insides.

I kissed her on the cheek and disappeared behind the check-in desk, shattered and on edge.

Nothing was known about the condition of the children or my wife, only that they had been urgently transferred to Barcelona. I spent the flight crying like a heartbroken child, unashamed of the sidelong glances people were giving me. I felt terribly guilty since I should have been driving that car.

My daughter had a match close to home, in a small village in Montseny. It was an exhibition match, not very important, so when I told her that I had plans and could not go with her, she wasn't even bothered. I remember her cheeky smile when she told me it didn't matter. She wasn't going to compete for a medal, and she would forgive me if I brought her a souvenir from Tenerife.

I mentally beat myself up. If I had been there, maybe I could have prevented it.

As we walked through the hospital doors, my in-laws and my parents rushed over to join me in a huddle of arms and tears.

"Christian is being operated on. His spleen ruptured, which caused his body to fill with blood," my mother-in-law began.

"What about Claudia and Andrea?"

"Andrea has multiple fractures. An open tibia fracture for which she is undergoing surgery and a break in her arm. My daughter…" Her voice broke.

My father-in-law hugged her to calm her down.

"Claudia is the worst off," my mother confirmed. "She arrived in a coma. The blow was very hard, and the firemen had to help get her out of the car. No legs," she finished, which dealt me a hard blow.

"Oh, my God!" I broke down. I didn't want to imagine what it would be like to face that new reality if Claudia lived. I know that many people live in wheelchairs, but that would be a huge setback for someone like her.

"She's in very bad shape, son. They don't know if she'll survive. She lost a lot of blood, it was very hard to get her out, and the blow to her head was very bad. She might not recover. It might cause a heart attack, and if she survives, she will never be her old self again."

"Come on, Gloria. We don't have to imagine the worst situation." My father-in-law hugged her. "Claudia is a tough woman. I'm sure she'll bounce back."

I collapsed on one of the chairs in the waiting room and cried with the bitterness of one who felt responsible. I had a terrible pain in my chest and the self-condemnation was overwhelming.

My mother sat next to me to comfort me, patting my back, which jerked and lurched.

"I'm sorry, honey. I'm so sorry," she mumbled, clinging to me. We stayed like that until the doctors came out to give us news about each of them.

The least serious was Andrea. She had a cast on her arm, and her tibia was broken. She would need rehabilitation and probably psychological counseling, but nothing more than that.

Christian's operation had been successful. He was stable and would gradually recover. He needed several transfusions, and he would spend the night in the ICU. Once he was out of danger, he would be taken up to a ward.

Claudia was critical. They said that the next few hours would decide if she had any hope of recovery. She was in a coma, and although they had saved her life, it was too early to make an accurate prognosis.

The only one we were allowed to see was Andrea, who had been assigned a room. My son and my wife were sedated and connected to machines that monitored their vital functions.

When we got permission to enter, one at a time, I was the first. When my daughter saw me, she burst into tears and gasped for breath in my arms, asking about her mother and her brother.

I prayed to God to give me the strength to behave like the hero she thought I was. The hero to whom she had given the t-shirt with that word that now felt too big for me. I saw myself as a mere human, hitting rock bottom to try to restrain the impulses that made me want to collapse next to her instead of being her pillar to cling to.

"They'll be all right," I said with a certainty I didn't feel. "The doctors are doing everything they can for them, as they do for me every time I get sick. You'll see that they'll recover, and we'll all be home together much sooner than you think."

Andrea sniffled and wiped away her tears. "Are you sure? All together?" She looked at me hopefully.

I just smiled. "Sure, you'll see."

"The blow was very hard, Dad. The car spun around, and then the truck. Mom screamed, and everything went dark."

"It's over, little one. It's over."

"I was so scared, Daddy, but I tried to be strong. I thought of you, and I knew you would come to save us. Now that you've told me we're all going home together, I know everything will be all right. I'm sure Mom will be very happy when you tell her. She still loves you very much, Dad. She has your picture on her bedside table, and she always kisses you goodnight. If you come home, I'm sure she'll recover soon. Will you tell her? I need us to be a family again and get between the two of you if a nightmare wakes me up."

"Hey, you're a big girl, as well as a very brave one. You don't need to sleep with us anymore."

"But I like it. I always liked it." I sighed against her hair. Right now, my daughter needed comfort and hope. I didn't want to debate with her about our family's future.

"Hold me tight. I don't want to be afraid. When you hold me tight, it disappears, and I stop seeing those images that scare me so much."

I squeezed her in my arms until her breathing relaxed and she fell asleep against my chest.

Fuck! How could I have done things so wrong?

My parents and in-laws had stayed outside, giving us some privacy, but as much as I wanted to keep hugging my daughter, they also had the right to enter. I asked them to come in, begging them to keep quiet and let her rest.

"I'm sleeping here," I announced as they came into the room.

"I'm staying too," Teresa stated.

"It is not necessary. If anything happens, I'll let you know. One person is enough."

"I know, but I want to be by my daughter's side, just as you want to be by yours."

"I'm not here only for my children but also for Claudia. Just because we are separated doesn't mean I don't love her or care about her anymore."

She raised a skeptical eyebrow. "Yes, well, there are ways and ways to love."

"Tere!" her husband warned her. "This is no time for reproaches."

She nodded. "You're right. It's not." She looked at me with red eyes. "I'm staying," she insisted defiantly.

"All right. Do what you think best," I said, not wanting to get on her bad side. I understood her need not to be separated from Claudia.

I spent the night on a chair, clutching Andrea's hand and soothing her demons when she started and screamed in nightmares.

The nurse came in to regulate her medication while I was calming her down. She adjusted the dosage of the drip and waited until she was asleep again to reassure me and explain it was normal that, for a while, she would have difficulty falling asleep and would suffer from night terrors and I should arm myself with patience because what lay ahead of me was not going to be easy.

"Easy." That word had been gone from my vocabulary for two years.

I thanked her for the talk. It had done me good to learn more details. I remembered that I had not said anything to Garbiñe, who was probably worried. It was very late, four o'clock in the morning. I'd better wait for the next day.

When I woke up at seven o'clock, my neck was stiff, and the chair had made my back hurt. I went to the bathroom to wash and change my bag. Andrea was still sleeping peacefully, and I didn't want to wake her.

I looked at my cell phone. I had four texts from Garbiñe from the day before. I went down to the cafeteria to clear my head a little so I could text her while I got a dose of caffeine.

Are you awake?

I waited while they served me coffee and toast. She didn't answer. She was probably sleeping. I wrote her another message.

I'll call you later to explain what happened. Get some rest.

I set the phone down on the counter and took a bite of the slice of bread spread with jam and butter, which was the sweetest thing in my life right now.

Then I went back to flagellating myself. It was not going to be easy to cope with the situation. I was so engrossed in my thoughts about what that accident was going to mean that I didn't notice my mother-in-law's presence until she sat down next to me on the next stool.

"May I?" she asked after she was seated.

"Of course. Sorry, I was so dazed that I didn't even remember you spent the night here."

"I'm not surprised. You spent years without remembering you had two children and a wife. It is logical that you forget me." Teresa's daggers were aimed to hurt.

"I know I was never a model father and husband, and I regret a lot about that time. If I could go back, I would change many things, but I cannot."

"Easy, isn't it? To take refuge in crude excuses that time can't be rewound. With me, you don't need to pretend. You accepted my daughter to be your nurse, to take care of you, and then left her lying around like a cigarette butt."

"I don't blame you for thinking that, but it wasn't like that. We both decided to break up."

"*You* decided to break up," she corrected me.

"If I decided to end our marriage," I said, "it was because neither of us deserved to be tied to a relationship that had been dead for a long time."

"Speak for yourself, not for her. She is not here to defend herself. If my daughter accepted your will, it was because she knew that you no longer loved her, not because she stopped loving you. And look at her now. What good did it do her to love you?"

I pinched the bridge of my nose, overwhelmed by her reproaches. "I'm sorry," I muttered under my breath, unable to add more. I was not in the mood for it.

My phone vibrated, and Garbiñe's name appeared on the screen, announcing that she was awake and that I could call her. My mother-in-law's eyes flew to the cell phone, which was between the two of us, and she let out a hollow laugh. She got up from her stool and gave the phone a push.

"That's why you were in Tenerife while my daughter almost killed herself in that car? You disgust me. My daughter is in the ICU, and your lover is sending you messages. You're deplorable. How little respect you have for her!" she spat disdainfully.

"She didn't..." I tried to excuse myself.

"Save it. You don't owe me any explanations. It is very clear what you were doing in Tenerife."

She got up and walked away, making me feel like shit again. *Fuck, fuck, fuck!*

I looked at my cell phone in disgust and almost threw it on the floor, but that uncontrolled reaction would have gotten me nowhere.

Calling Garbiñe may not have been the best option, but I needed to hear her voice and feel some warmth in my tired soul. The selfish person inside me was the one who hit the dial key and the one who was glad to hear her on the other end of the line.

"Hello! How are you?"

"Fucked," I answered tersely.

"What about them?" she asked fearfully.

"My daughter is recovering from surgery for a broken arm. My son and my wife are in the ICU."

I said it without thinking, and I didn't notice that she held her breath when I referred to Claudia as my wife.

"I'm sorry. I don't know what to say."

"Nothing. You can't say anything. I must have stepped in a pile of shit the size of Brazil."

"Are she and your son very bad?"

"Christian's spleen had to be removed, and he has a couple of broken ribs. Claudia got the worst of it. She's lost her legs, she's in a coma, she has edema in her brain, and they don't know if she's going to make it."

"Oh, my God!" she exclaimed.

"Hey, I'm sorry if I can't get back to you. Right now, I don't know how I'm going to organize myself or what's going to happen to my fucking life or my kids' lives. I don't even know if we are going to leave them orphans. Give me a little time, okay?" I muttered, overwhelmed.

"Of course, of course. I don't want to be in the way. I just want you to know I'm still here. If you need anything, you can call me or text me. I don't know if you need me to come."

"No, thank you," I whispered, not having the strength to continue talking. I didn't need to have Garbiñe there to add to Teresa's wrath, as much as I needed her.

"I'm sorry for what happened, Áxel. I send you lots of encouragement and a big hug. I don't even want to imagine how hard this must be for you."

"It's too much." I exhaled in anguish. "If you'll excuse me, I'm going upstairs to see my daughter. I don't want her to be alone. She's having panic attacks."

"Of course. I won't keep you any longer." She was silent for a second. "Never mind. See you later."

I didn't feel strong enough to find out what she had not said. "See you later."

CHAPTER TWENTY

Yugen: An understanding of the universe that triggers responses too deep and mysterious to put into words.

<u>Áxel, two weeks later</u>

I was at my oncologist's office, and my nerves were on edge. Today they were giving me the results of the last treatment I had undergone. At any other time, I would have been euphoric, hoping Oscar would give me good news to hold on to, but now I was broken. I didn't even feel like breathing. I had been the strong one and had faced adversity with a lot of hope and my peculiar sense of humor. I was unable to be that person now.

My situation left much to be desired. Claudia was still in the ICU. She had complications that made us fear for her life. That deepened the abyss between Teresa and me. They had come to tell us she had hours left. We were thinking about saying good-bye, but my ex had courage, and during that long night, she did not die. She had always been very stubborn.

My son had been moved up to the ward that same day. I was so happy when I got the news that, without thinking, I left

Andrea's room to go to his. No one had prepared me for his reaction.

"Get out! Get out! Get out! You are to blame for everything! I don't want you in my life! Mom is going to die because of you! Do you hear me? Because of you!" he exclaimed, out of his mind.

I was livid. Even so, I tried to reassure him, but he didn't seem to want my explanations. At the foot of the bed was my mother-in-law, her gaze full of venom.

"It was you, wasn't it?" I rebuked her, and she did not look away from me.

"Don't blame Grandma," my son countered. "She had nothing to do with it. She only told me how Mom was, nothing else."

"I don't believe you. I'm sure she's been poisoning you against me."

"Get out!" my son shrieked, forcing the nurse to intervene.

The nurse reluctantly pulled me out of the room, arguing that Christian needed calm right now. It wasn't good for him to get upset like that, even if he was wrong.

She suggested I go with her to an adjoining room where we would have some privacy. The contempt I saw in my son's eyes was a hard blow. The nurse insisted that I should not hold it against him since adolescents tend to blame others for traumatic events like the one he had suffered, and I should be patient. How many times I had heard that word?

She advised me to talk to the psychologist. She would give me guidelines on how to cope with the situation and approach my son in a way that would not be traumatic for either of us.

I accepted because I couldn't do anything else, and I didn't want to make the situation worse. Christian was sixteen years old. It was not so easy to negotiate with him and make him see things. He was as stubborn as his mother, and on top of that, he had always adored her. If he could have exchanged us, I was sure he would have preferred me to be the one in the ICU, and to be frank, I would too.

We spent two weeks in a fruitless tug-of-war.

What worried me most was that he only wanted to be in the company of my mother-in-law, and I was afraid that she would turn his head. Andrea's recovery was going slowly, and the hospital, given the nature of the situation, agreed to keep Christian while he was in therapy and making a recovery.

Coming up from coffee, I found my mother-in-law about to enter my daughter's room. I approached her and asked her to please try to mediate with my son.

"I can't do anything. You know how Christian is when something gets into his head. He blames you for not going with them, and I do too, especially knowing what you were doing when I called you."

"What I was doing had nothing to do with the accident," I said, trying not to add fuel to the fire. "We were separated. I am a free man and have the right to do what I want."

"Of course, it had something to do with it! If you hadn't run off with someone else, my daughter would be fine now. But it was more important to satisfy the flesh than to be with your family."

"My family is the most important thing, as I am demonstrating. The same thing would have happened if I had been in that car. You don't know that I could have avoided it."

"Yes, I know. Christian told me that his mother didn't see the car that ran the stop sign because she didn't remember how to get to the place. She got nervous and wanted to call you on the handsfree to ask you since you had gone there together once. She looked at the buttons on the steering wheel, and the car rammed them into the truck."

I hadn't known that part. That was why my son blamed me. Now I understood.

"You are the cause of it all! Of your separation, of my daughter's sadness, and now, of her more than likely death. I will never forgive you, do you hear me? I don't care if you have a terminal illness. Right now, and may God forgive me, I think that's what you deserve."

"You can't be telling me that you want your grandchildren to become orphans?"

"Yes. If my daughter dies, I'll take care of them because if the choice is having a father like you, it's better not to have one," she spat in anger, leaving me and going into my daughter's room.

I smashed my knuckles against the wall and let out a scream that made the people in the hallway look at me in terror.

The floor nurse came looking for me.

"What's the matter?" she asked, not understanding my state of mind.

"My mother-in-law is a witch."

She smiled. "She is under a lot of strain."

I could feel the vein in my neck throbbing, my lungs were on the verge of collapse, and I had an inhuman need to end it all. She must have seen that I was very bad since she made me accompany her to the other room to give me a tranquilizer.

"I'm a mess. She's right. I'm to blame." I broke down and burst into tears, clutching my hair.

"You're not, and she's *not* right. Any man in your situation would be overwhelmed. You're only human, that's all. Drink some water and let the pill take effect."

"You don't understand. She's right," I insisted.

She frowned. She was up to date on what had happened. Everyone was. "You're not responsible for that car running the stop sign," she said. "Or the truck that ran over the vehicle in which your family was traveling."

"Yes, I am. I should have been there with them."

"Life wanted you to be somewhere else. You pull the cart every day. Believe me, I see many cases here, and very few men spend the whole day at the hospital as you do, even if your son denies you and your mother-in-law behaves badly. Don't give up. You are the pillar for your children, the lighthouse that keeps the light on so they don't get lost in the storm. Sooner or later, Christian will figure it out. Let time put things in place and follow the psychologist's advice. Don't give up." She pressed my forearm to encourage me.

My cell phone rang, and Garbiñe's name reappeared on the screen. The nurse offered me a warm smile and left me alone. Although it wasn't the best time, I picked up the phone. Maybe talking to her would calm me down.

"Hello," I muttered, exhausted by my emotions.

"Hello," she replied. "Did I catch you at a bad time?"

"Every moment has been bad for several days now."

"I'm sorry. If you prefer, I'll call you later."

"No, it's okay." I tried to remember that she was not to blame for my sleepless nights. "I'm sorry; you're not responsible for all this. It's just that I'm in over my head."

"It's understandable. How are they?"

"Andrea is doing better, although the nightmares don't stop. My son doesn't want to see me because he blames me for what happened, and Claudia is still in the ICU. I have to live with my mother-in-law, who is not making things easy for me."

"I can imagine. I'm sorry I can't be there. I wish I could hug you."

"A hug from you would be like touching heaven, but I can't afford to even think about it," I murmured, overwhelmed.

"I'm not asking you for anything, Áxel," she interrupted. "It's just that I'd like to help you and be with you so you don't have to go through all this alone."

"You already are, believe me. Hearing your voice from time to time calms me down," I confessed, and it was true. "Don't think I don't call you much because I don't want to. It's just that I can't." I was at a loss for words.

"With me, you don't need to make excuses. I understand. Your priority now is your family, and you owe it to them."

"Yes!" I exhaled. I couldn't have summed it up better. "I wish things could have been different. I didn't think it could happen like that."

"Neither you nor anyone else. Don't worry about me. We'll have time later."

"Time." Time eluded me, as well as patience.

"In a few days, they'll tell me my results," I muttered.

"Are you nervous?"

"I haven't had time to think about it much," I lied. I was afraid of what the doctor would tell me since if both I and Claudia died, my children would be orphans.

"I'm sure everything will be all right. You have to be more positive than ever. Hold on to your convictions, and we'll see each other sooner than you think. You want to keep seeing me, don't you?" She hesitated.

"Of course! It's just that now..."

"It's okay. I just wanted to be safe and not feel like a phone stalker." She lowered her voice and imitated one of those guys in the movies, which made me smile again.

"You would never be that. Would you like to meet tonight in my dreams?"

"That would be perfect. I'll make myself pretty for you."

"There's no need. You were born beautiful."

Her laughter tinkled. I needed a break, and I allowed myself the license to forget about the present and fool around like a teenager.

When I hung up, I felt bad for Garbiñe. She took the initiative. She texted and called me, and I just answered. I just didn't have the strength, even for someone who made me amazingly happy. I think I was punishing myself, and not talking to her much was my ordeal. I was trying to atone for my sins by pushing her away because, deep down, I thought I didn't deserve to have something good happen to me when all my people were suffering because of me.

It may sound stupid, but at that time, I was not thinking very clearly, and Teresa's reproaches did not make it easy for me.

I hung up after promising that as soon as I had the test results, I would call her.

I felt so fucking bad about the world. Everything I touched was damaged and filled with suffering. Maybe it would be best to be alone.

I couldn't rush. It was one of those low points where you make decisions that you might later regret.

I left the room, shuffling my feet. My life was collapsing by the minute. I no longer felt my soul attached to my body, and where before there was an insurmountable wall behind which I protected all those who mattered to me, now there were ashes and regrets.

I rested my palms on the door of my daughter's room, trembling with rage and helplessness. I was dying to remember the look of pride Christian had given me every time he saw me.

I squeezed my eyes shut in fury, thinking about how a simple decision could screw things up so badly.

I felt like hitting my forehead against the hard wood until I was unconscious so the pain would stop throbbing and suffocate me with its poison. In the haze of my suffering, when guilt played with hope, those green eyes rose to remind me that as long as I had a breath of life left, there was hope.

⁂

"Áxel!" exclaimed Dr. Miguelañez, coming out to meet me.

I stood up and offered him a strained smile.

"Hello, Oscar," I greeted him, holding out my hand.

"And that face?" he asked, shaking my hand.

He did not know what had happened to my family since they were in a different hospital.

"Things have happened."

"Things? What things?"

"Can I tell you inside? I need privacy." I didn't feel like collapsing in the waiting room in front of strangers.

"Forgive my tactlessness. Of course, come in." He extended his hand, and we entered his spacious office.

I told him what had happened. Oscar didn't take his desk chair. As if he sensed I needed it, he sat in the one next to me. I could say that I recounted everything stoically, but I would be lying. I broke down at the word accident and didn't stop until I shattered. He hugged me and let the emotions flow.

He was much more than a doctor or my friend. He was the person to whom I had ceded power over my life. He had fought for my survival. It was ridiculous that I was trying to hide my emotions from him when he offered me the chance to go on living.

"You don't know how sorry I am. If I can do anything…"

"Do you do miracles on demand? Claudia needs one."

"I would say no, but looking at your case, I'm not so sure," he replied, raising his eyebrows.

"What do you mean?" I asked, squinting.

"You're clean," he stated simply.

"Clean. *Clean?*" I asked incredulously. I wasn't prepared for the doctor to tell me the operation had been a success.

"So say the latest tests. Right now, you are as healthy as can be. Congratulations."

"That's impossible, isn't it?"

"Apparently not. I don't know why it turned out so well. I'll be frank. With the treatment, I was just hoping to give you a little more time. In no way did I expect this result."

"So?"

"We are not sure. I have presented your case to the hospital board, and everyone is cross. I had an oncology conference last week. On Friday, to be precise. They emailed me your results, and I had the paper fifteen minutes later, so I decided to present the results in case someone could shed some light on them."

I looked at him hopefully.

"Nobody gave credit, but the most surprising thing was that some American doctors offered to study your case. They want you to be part of a pioneering research project."

"Me?" I questioned, still not believing his words.

"Yes, they study exceptional patients like you. There are very few people who recover 'miraculously,' but you are not the only one. They go in search of these patients. Let's say they are a kind of talent scout for incredible patients. Like the Justice League, but with terminally ill people. Something like that. They are trying to come up with a definitive cure for the disease, and they asked me to suggest you collaborate with them. Only if you feel like it, of course."

"As long as I don't have to travel," I answered after a few moments. I thought about my trip to New York and how much I wanted to cross the Pond. Right now, I wasn't even thinking about it.

"No, don't worry. We'll do everything from here. If anyone travels, it will be them. I just need you to give us your consent to give them your medical history. Sign some authorizations, and let us take some blood samples so we can analyze them. That should be enough."

"Count on it. If I can help other people, you know you can count on me."

"I was almost sure you would accept, but I wanted to make sure before I told you anything. On the one hand, I'm very happy for you, and at the same time, I'm pretty fucked up about the news you've given me. I wish there was something I could do to ease your mind."

We offered each other smiles that couldn't be full, but we couldn't help but melt into another hug, this time of relief.

CHAPTER TWENTY-ONE

Basorexia: Being addicted to kissing.

Garbiñe, a month and a half later

"I don't want to say, 'I told you so.' I swear I don't want to, but..."

"Well, don't then," I said bluntly, still stirring the steaming infusion Paula had prepared for me.

"Fuck! What a fucking shit!"

"Don't swear. If I don't complain, neither can you."

"I just don't understand why you're not pissed off at life, and I don't understand why Áxel is doing so badly."

"I'm more pissed off than you think. However, there's nothing I can do about it. Things have been going like this."

"You can't do anything? I'd go to Barcelona, and I'd hang him by the balls for promising things he can't deliver. Damn you, Áxel!"

"It wasn't his fault. He wasn't driving that car."

"I know he didn't drive that car, but he is guilty of coming into your life, falling in love, and disappearing. That says a lot about him."

"He has not disappeared."

"That's it. You excuse him on top of it."

I snorted. Maybe I *was* defending him, but the life he had to lead now was so absorbing that it barely left any room for me. That didn't mean I wasn't upset or that I didn't have trouble even getting out of bed.

"You look terrible, more like a ghost than my friend. How many kilos have you lost?"

"I don't know. I haven't been on the scales in a while, and food doesn't appeal like it used to. The doctor asked me to get some tests, and I have an appointment tomorrow."

"What's wrong with you is called 'Áxel.' You have to take care of yourself, Garbi, if only for Ruben's sake. You can't throw away your health for someone who just landed in your life and has trouble getting back on track."

"You don't need to remind me. It is for my son that I get up every morning and go to work, even if I don't feel like it."

"Lousy Deodorant Prince! It was a bad day when I advised you to fuck the instructor. I'll tell you again, in case it wasn't clear before. If I were you, I'd go to see him and tell him where to get off. It's true that his ex is in a coma, but he shouldn't have forgotten about you so soon."

"He hasn't forgotten. Or at least, I don't think so. It's just that the situation is very serious and has meant a lot of changes for him. We talk less than I'd like to, but I understand that I cannot demand more from him under the circumstances."

Áxel's ex-wife had been in a serious car accident that fateful Sunday morning when he was at my house. Apparently, she had been on her way to a judo championship with her children in the back seats. Some kids who were returning from a party and were very drunk ran a stop sign and hit her, making the car she was in fly into the oncoming lane, where a truck ran over them.

The firemen could not explain how Claudia had survived the impact. She had lost both legs in the wreckage. They were so badly mangled that there was nothing they could do to save them. The children had fractured several bones, and Christian's spleen had to be removed. Thank God, nothing more serious than that happened to them, but it had been a terrible shock when they could not get out of the car and their mother was unresponsive.

Andrea had to go to rehab every day because of the fracture in her leg, which had left her with a slight limp that had to be treated. Both children had weekly sessions with a psychologist since the accident had left them with trauma and nightmares.

Christian insisted that if his father had been with them, nothing would have happened. He, an experienced driver, would have been able to avoid the hit. I strongly doubted that was the case, but it was difficult to make a teenager who adored his mother understand.

Áxel felt guilty, especially because it had happened while he was spending the weekend with me, enjoying himself and thinking about a new beginning far from his family.

When he said those words, I felt terrible. I knew he wasn't saying it because he regretted our relationship, but somehow he was also holding me responsible, and that didn't let me hold my head up.

However, with life, you know how it goes. Áxel's doctor gave him the good news that, according to him, was inexplicable. There was no trace of the cancer cells that had endangered his life. The doctor could not believe it because even though he had subjected him to aggressive treatment, Oscar had been convinced that the good news was not due to the operation he had performed. He had asked his patient for permission to send his file to a group of American oncologists who were interested in the case.

They were studying Áxel's medical history like a group of

NASA scientists would an extraterrestrial. They took several samples of his blood for study. They had never come across a terminal patient who had been diagnosed twice with three months to live, undergone so many chemotherapy sessions, and was now in complete remission. They believed there was something in Áxel that made him a unique case.

I was very happy for him since if that was true, we had a chance. I was willing to wait for his situation to be resolved so we could pick up where we'd left off.

It was not that Áxel had left me, nor had I left him. He had only told me to be patient because he needed time to redirect his life. He was at a very complex point. Right now, his children needed him, and he could not fail them again.

It was understandable, but that didn't mean it hurt any less. I missed him so much, and I didn't want to press. I had to give him time. Any call or message brightened my day, even if it was very brief.

He was overwhelmed, and I didn't want to get in the way. My relationship with Dario was more controlled after the run-in at my house. I think he wasn't prepared to be dethroned, and seeing someone other than him with me had spun him out of control. The next time we'd met, when it was his turn to drive Ruben, he'd apologized to me. He'd brought me a bouquet of my favorite flowers, saying that he had not behaved well. He was very sorry for his behavior, and he recognized that I was free to see whoever I wanted. He had been jealous and lost his temper, he said, but he had realized that he had made a terrible mistake and would try to make up for all the mistakes of the past.

I didn't want to go back to him, but I wanted us to get along for Ruben's sake. The three of us agreed to do things from time to time so our son would be happy.

My phone rang, interrupting my thoughts. Hats off to the king of Rome.

"Hello, Dario."

Paula made a face of disgust, but he couldn't see her. "Hello, sweetie. Your son and I are at the beach," he said. "He wants you to come to Las Teresitas to show you how he has conquered the waves."

"I don't feel like going to the beach. Besides, I'm with Paula."

"Well, tell her to come too. Come on, woman, don't be like that. If you saw how he's enjoying himself! You have to see him. I think we have a promising surfing star. I'm sure we do. Having a father like me, it was inevitable for him to have a passion for the sea. To finish convincing you, I'll tell you that Dani is preparing paella at the beach bar. We could eat here and watch the sunset. You know how much you like her paella."

I couldn't help but smile.

"All right, I'll be there in a little while. It wouldn't hurt me to get some rest."

"That's my Garb. I love you, beautiful," he said before hanging up. I couldn't add anything to that.

"He convinced you, huh?" my friend asked grumpily.

"It's not what you think. We just get along."

"Yeah, sure, tell that story to a wolf who hasn't eaten Granny. Your ex is like Gabriel, cut from the same cloth, neither with you nor without you, and when they see the chance, wham, they've already gobbled you up again."

"I don't feel anything for Dario. It's over between us."

"And so did I with Gabriel and look. I ended up falling like the idiot I am."

I got up from the table and gave her a huge hug.

"It won't happen to me. I learned my lesson, don't worry."

"Okay, fine, I'll have faith in miracles. But tomorrow I'm going with you to the doctor, and I'm going to tell him off if he doesn't give you something to make you better. At this rate, you're only going to be good for throwing yourself to the dogs, and very skinny ones at that."

"What would I do without you? See how you can't move to Barcelona? I need you here."

"I haven't ruled it out yet. We'll see what I do. Will you pick me up tomorrow?"

"Yes, the doctor is closer to here. I have an appointment at half past four, so I'll pick you up at four." She hugged me again.

"Very good. And don't let that fool Dario soften you up. Raise the memory shield and think of all the bad things he put you through. If you have doubts, call me to refresh your memory, and I'll be happy to do it. You and he are just a pair of pronouns. Don't forget."

"I won't. Come on, crazy woman, let me go, or I'll be late."

I felt sorry for myself. I was not looking forward to spending the rest of the day with Dario, but it was better than wallowing in grief. I told myself I was doing it for my son, who loved those times of pretended normalcy.

I looked at the cell phone screen for a message that did not exist.

Damn my addiction to his kisses! If I was in my right mind, I would turn the page. It would be very difficult for Áxel's wife to recover, and if she did, she would depend on his care. Knowing him, he would not leave her in such a delicate circumstance, and then what would become of me?

I wished I could resist the drug of seeing him. Now I could understand drug addicts. I was addicted to his mouth, his smell, his skin on mine, his smiles, and the way he made me believe I was the most precious thing to him, even if it was a gross lie.

I was clinging like crazy to his one "I love you," which now tasted like gall to me.

Tears fell silently during the whole journey. I was immersed in a strange melancholy that was difficult to overcome when emotions for Áxel filled me.

When someone makes you feel like their universe, it's hard to go back to feeling like the last shit on the planet.

I arrived at the beach under a blazing sun. Dario was grinning from ear to ear and wearing a swimsuit. For him, it was no problem. He wore one of the ones he sold in the surf store.

Watching my son enjoy himself always recharged my batteries. Ruben played like crazy while his father encouraged him to ride the waves. I just watched them, thinking about how different things would have been if Dario was like Áxel.

Comparing them was inevitable, and my ex always lost. What an injustice, given how easy everything would have been if I could have exchanged them. However, that only happens in the movies.

We ate at Dani's beach bar and watched the sunset while drinking mojitos, warming ourselves under the last rays of the day. My son insisted he wanted to show me his room in the new apartment Dario had rented.

I ended up having dinner with them. When Ruben fell asleep curled up on my lap, I carried him to his room, which was a replica of the one at home.

"I hope you don't mind," his father murmured behind my back. "I thought that if I decorated it the same way, it would be like not moving."

"It's a nice touch," I whispered, kissing my son's head after tucking him in. Hearing him breathe made me feel a little less unhappy.

I told Dario that I was leaving since I had to work the next day.

"It's late. Why don't you stay? I can sleep on the couch and…"

"Brake. Dario, there's nothing left between us. I don't want you to think the cordiality we have now is for anything other than our son."

"Is it because of the Mosso?"

I shook my head, and he relaxed his shoulders.

"No, it's because we don't work as a married couple. We tried several times, and it was a disaster every time."

"The disaster was me," he admitted. "I never knew how to value you or give you the place you deserved."

"And now you do?"

"Yes!" he exclaimed, grabbing my face. "I promise you, precious, I am a new man, one who loves you madly and is not willing to lose you."

His lips fell on mine in a kiss that tasted like the past. I pushed him away.

"I'm sorry. I'm no longer the woman you married, and you would do well to stop thinking of us as a couple." I made Paula's words my own. "You and I are just pronouns and Ruben's parents, nothing more. Now, excuse me, it's very late, and I'm working tomorrow."

He walked me to the door, and I went downstairs, knowing I had done what was best for everyone.

"You're green," Colmenares remarked, looking at me as I rounded the bend.

We were in pursuit of a car that had exceeded the speed limit just at the point where we were strategically hidden.

We stopped him, but instead of stopping, he accelerated. I put my foot down, and we got involved in a chase like the ones in the movies.

"It must be the reflection from my uniform," I said, not admitting that the turkey and cheese mini I had gobbled down for breakfast seemed to want to spill out of my mouth at any moment.

"Well, judging by the look on your face, I'd say you're either turning into the Hulk or you're going to redecorate the dashboard."

I took the curve hard, and my stomach bounced.

"Open the windows. It's the heat." My partner pushed the button to lower the window, and I pushed mine.

"We'd better stop. I've got the license plate number written down. The fine will come to him anyway."

"I'm not going to stop until we get that bastard. What if he runs away because he's a killer or has a corpse in the trunk?"

"You watch too much TV. On this island, those things never happen, or if they do, we never see it."

"There's always a first time." I raised my eyebrows. "Besides, he's heading straight for the road that's cut off. When he realizes it, he'll have no choice but to stop if he doesn't want to crash into the rock that has fallen down the mountain, and that's only a kilometer away."

We had been warned that morning that a gigantic boulder occupied the entire road, so we were checking that people were going at a prudent speed down the hillside to avoid accidents.

In no time, we would reach the point I was talking about. When we rounded the next bend, we would be there.

We heard braking, and fortunately, no impact. The kamikaze had realized just in time but left skid marks on the asphalt. I turned our car to block his path. If he thought about leaving, he would find our vehicle forming a barrier. We got out to confront the fugitive.

"Civil Guard, please get out of the vehicle!" I announced without getting an answer.

"Navarro, be careful," my partner warned me.

I nodded, reaching for my gun.

"Civil Guard, please get out of the vehicle!" I repeated, approaching the driver's window.

He looked like he was in his forties. He refused to look our way. Next to him was a young girl with a frightened look on her face. I hit the glass hard.

"Don't make me tell you again, or you'll spend the night in jail!"

The man turned his face, and as soon as he did, I knew why he had fled. He rolled down the window with a shy smile and a dismayed expression.

"Gabriel?" I questioned, surprised that Paula's ex was our target.

"Hello, Garbiñe."

The nausea that came over me was impossible to control. I found myself clinging to the bodywork and throwing up my breakfast on him. The girl let out a startled squeal, and he yelled, "Fuck!"

The girl got out of the car in a panic.

"You puked on Gabriel this morning?" Paula asked incredulously as we sat in the waiting room.

I had saved what had happened to tell her while we were waiting for my turn.

"I swear, you should have seen his face and that busty brunette getting out of the car in disgust. He had a little piece of turkey hanging from his nose."

"Fuck him! I'm sure it was that student who was screwing him behind Ursula's back."

"It seems so. He wanted to act cocky in front of her, driving his new BMW at top speed without thinking that we were checking the curve. He had pretended to be sick to miss his class. That was why he accelerated when we flashed our lights to stop him. He got nervous, and because of the area he was in, he assumed it was me. Well, that and the girl is a minor."

My friend's eyes widened. "Minor?"

"Yes, sixteen. She goes to college because she is an advanced student."

"Well, she may be very intelligent, but she has terrible taste in men. Screw him. I'm sorry you were unwell, but I'm glad he got the consequences of your illness. Let's see if he'll learn for once."

The nurse called me.

"I'm coming in with you, and I won't take no for an answer. After they tell you what's wrong, we'll go shopping. I want to give you a nice present for what you did today."

"For throwing up on your ex?"

"Exactly. I never got to do that, and not because I didn't feel like it. We have to celebrate."

I smiled at Paula, who gave me some of the joy I was missing these days.

We went into the room, and the doctor asked us to sit down. He was looking at the blood test results so seriously that it made me scared.

What if I had not given enough importance to what was happening to me? What if my illness had worsened because I had not taken care of myself, and now I had less time to live?

I glanced at Paula, who looked as scared as I was. She grabbed my hand and spoke before anyone else.

"What's wrong with my friend, Doctor?"

CHAPTER TWENTY-TWO

Facepalm: The action of holding the palm of one's hand to the face as a sign of bewilderment, despair, or embarrassment.

<u>Garbiñe</u>

"Impossible. It must be a mistake." I exhaled and brought my hands to my face in disbelief.

"Nothing is impossible, Mrs. Navarro. Unlikely, yes, but impossible? No," my doctor commented emphatically, still holding the blood tests.

"But it can't be! I'm serious!"

He shrugged. "So am I. I am referring you to a specialist. You understand this is not my field. In a couple of weeks, you will see with your own eyes that the tests do not lie, and neither did I."

Paula was staring at us silently.

"Oh, my God!" I covered my face with my hands.

What the hell was I going to do? How was I going to tell Áxel that I was pregnant with his child? It had to be a mistake. Carrying his baby was crazy! He was doing chemo, and I had been trying for years without success! He had assured me that his spermatozoa were fried! How could a weekend with him be enough to bring them back to life and get me pregnant? It was like something out of the Bible, where virgins get pregnant, men part the seas, and paralyzed men walk.

We left the doctor's office with news that had left me breathless and a prescription to buy iron to control the anemia.

"Let's go to the pharmacy," Paula said cautiously, clinging to me. "Don't worry. Everything will be fine."

"Everything will be all right? Are you kidding me?" I shouted hysterically.

I was like my neighbor's cat, who, as soon as she goes into heat, slips away and comes back with a new litter. I glared at Paula in disgust.

"Don't look at me like that. You can't reason because of your hormones, which have taken command of the mother ship, but to make sure and resolve your doubts, I'm going to buy one of those tests that tell you the minute the zygote was conceived," she said firmly.

We both looked down. My abdomen was flat, yet the doctor was sure there was more there than my intestines in there. Instinctively, I put my hands to my belly as we entered the elevator.

"Oh, my God. What have I done!" I muttered, realizing that if it was true, I was in big trouble.

"Basically, fucking and not using a rubber makes your tummy swell up."

A lady entering with a preteen girl gave us a dirty look. I looked down at the floor of the elevator, muttering, "Paula, please," and nodded at them. She frowned.

"What? I haven't told any lies, and the sooner you know, the better. Prevention is the answer. You have to be responsible to avoid unwanted situations."

"You are just as responsible for this as I am," I argued, pointing at her.

"Me?"

I shot her a warning look. "As far as I know, I didn't put the tip of his dick at the entrance to your cave," she said, not using the kind of words she would have used if that girl wasn't there with her mother.

"No, but you prompted me to..." I had to look for the right words.

"I encouraged you to enjoy yourself, not to be oblivious."

I bit my tongue before I blurted anything I might regret so the lady across the room could stop covering the kid's ears and condemning us to hell with her gaze.

We remained silent until we arrived at the pharmacy. We ordered the iron pills, and Paula bought three pregnancy tests.

"Can you tell me why you bought so many?"

"Because they are ninety-something-percent effective. If all three are positive, I don't think it will be necessary to go to an analyst or have the gynecologist attest."

"That's what notaries do," I told her.

"It's the same thing. Let's go over there and find out." She pointed at the coffee shop on the corner.

"Do you expect me to pee in that hole to find out if I'm expecting a baby?"

"No. I was thinking about the tree," she answered with disdain. "What difference does it make where? Is your pee selective and wants a terrace overlooking the sea?"

"I don't know! I'm nervous, and you're not helping!"

"I'm not helping? I've bought you three gadgets with cutting-edge technology, and I've found you a place where you can sit your royal ass so we can satisfy our doubts. Go on, get going. You're not thinking coherently today."

"I don't feel like it now. It won't come out," I complained.

"We have a half-liter of water or a full liter if necessary. I'm not letting you go anywhere until you pee."

Half an hour later, we had the answer: three positives.

Paula gave me that smug look that made me want to shove the tests down her throat one by one. She was leaning against the sink with her arms crossed. I had two choices. I could flip out or go under, and I didn't know which one to choose.

"What do I do now?" I protested more to myself than to her.

"Well, it's easy. Either you put your heart into it and have it, or we ask for an hour to terminate the pregnancy, and we get rid of the zygote before it has hands and feet."

"What about Áxel?"

"He is a guest cameo in this film. He didn't even know he could be a father, and he can continue to be ignorant. You told me he wasn't a good father to his children, so there's no need for him to be a father to this one."

"But he's fixing it now. Maybe he should know."

"Yeah, but coldly analyzing the situation, he's going through quite a lot. I know you'll tell me it's because of his circumstances and so on, but what can I say? It's too important a decision to leave it in the hands of a guy who is thousands of miles away. You don't know if he's ever going to come back."

"You are unique in your encouragement."

"I wasn't trying to cheer you up, just to give you a reality check. If you want a pat on the back and an 'Everything will be great, you'll live happily ever after,' find someone else. I'm practical."

"You're a catastrophist."

"Realist," she corrected me. "That man doesn't have the headroom to be thinking about a baby right now, and neither do you. I don't know if you want to give Ruben a little brother or sister, knowing all that raising a child entails, plus the absence of a father."

"I'm not sure what to do."

"Well, flip a coin. If it comes up heads, you don't tell him, and if it comes up tails, you tell him. What do you want me to say?"

Paula took a euro out of her purse and threw it in the air.

"Wait! I didn't say I was willing to let a coin decide my future!" The euro fell on her palm, and Paula covered it with her other hand so I couldn't see the result. "Is it heads or tails?" I asked when she didn't uncover it.

"I thought you said you didn't want the coin to decide."

"I don't," I replied, biting my lip. "It's simple curiosity, like when a gypsy reads your palm. You know it won't happen, but you still want to hear."

She raised her hand, and we both stared.

"It's a bird, so you'd better take flight. That's your gypsy prediction."

"Bird?"

"Yes, don't you see? This is a harrier hawk. Is it heads or tails?"

"I don't know. This was much easier when the king's face came up. Taking into account that on the other side, there is a number, and the bird has a face. I would say beak."

"Let it go! I told you I wasn't going to let a coin decide it." I turned on the tap and washed my face with cold water.

"You say that because the result is not what you expected."

"I don't know what I expected. Don't you understand?"

"What I understand is that I don't know if I'm going to have the patience to put up with you for nine months. I'm moving."

I turned to her with my face dripping.

"You can't do that to me. This baby is yours too."

"Mine? It will turn out that in the absence of the father, you're looking for another one. Are you trying to blackmail me emotionally?"

"I pray you won't leave. I need you more than ever, Paula. I do." I shook off the water and let out a whimper.

"Don't start crying on me. You know I can't stand to see you in a bad way. It's the only thing that softens me."

The whine turned into a pout, and the pout turned into a full-blown bout of tears that caused me to end up in my friend's arms, soaking her t-shirt.

"Everything will work out. You'll see. Whatever you decide, you can count on me. If I have to move later, so be it. What a fix."

When I got home, I felt the need to call Áxel. I didn't want to say anything to him yet, but I needed to hear his voice.

Ruben was with his father, which gave me the privacy I needed.

On the fifth ring, he answered. He sounded tired.

"Hello. How's it going? We haven't talked for days."

"Yes, I'm sorry. It's just that all this is not easy. I know I've been neglecting you, and you have every right to get angry or stop talking to me."

"It's okay. I understand."

"If you told me right now that you're not going to call me anymore because you're fed up with the situation, I'd understand. I don't know how you put up with me."

His response made me cringe. "Do you want me to stop calling you?" I asked, afraid of what he would answer.

"No," he said hastily. "Believe it or not, the selfish part of me refuses to let you go."

I was relieved. "I'm glad to hear that since I don't feel like giving up stalking you." I tried, without much success, to sound amused. All I managed to do was sound higher-pitched, and he sighed instead of smiling.

"You don't harass me. Sometimes I think that I should never have taken that flight to visit you. Maybe then the accident wouldn't have happened and..."

"And you and I would never have been together," I finished for him, sinking into misery.

"No! Don't get me wrong. It wouldn't change anything that happened between us, but it would have changed what happened to them."

"Haven't you ever thought that the same thing would have happened, only instead of Claudia being in the ICU, you would both be? Maybe it happened this way so your children could count on you."

He waited a few seconds in silence.

"I've thought it all through. I don't think there's a damn theory that hasn't crossed my mind. This is much harder than my illness. Claudia is not getting better, Christian is living with his grandmother because he doesn't even want to see me, and Andrea is sad because she doesn't know if she will be able to do judo again, her mother will die, or her brother will ever come home.

"There are times when I curse the moment I decided to become a father. Not everyone is cut out for it, and it is clear to me that I did a terrible job. If I could turn back the clock, I don't know if I'd have them again."

I clutched my belly, feeling a deep sadness. "Don't say that. You're thinking like that because the situation is not good, but as soon as it changes and your children understand everything you're doing for them, you'll see things in a different color."

"Remember when I told you my favorite color was to see you? I was making fun of your remark about seeing life in a different color, but it didn't come out. I've even lost my humor," he reflected.

"I remember." I sighed. "There's nothing I don't remember about what happened between us," I acknowledged, at risk of sounding like an idiot in love.

"Well, that's still my favorite color, even if you don't send me our daily sunset photo anymore."

I held my breath. "Is that a request?"

"It is an observation. I've always liked to see you, although I know I can't ask you for more than you give me since I hardly give you anything."

"Áxel," I muttered.

"I have to go. It's family therapy time, the only part of the day when Christian allows me to see him. If you want, I'll call you later, and we'll continue talking."

"I would very much like you to," I admitted.

"Done. I'll call you tonight, and we'll have a long talk," he promised.

"All right."

"See you later, Sergeant Tennis Player."

I hung up, not knowing what to expect.

If Áxel was thinking about fatherhood and was devastated by the problems he was having, all he lacked was me with a pregnancy that he neither wanted nor expected. To be fair, we weren't even in a relationship. We were not a couple. We had only been together for three days, and although we had not lost contact during this time, having a child was a step farther down the road.

That was what my rational mind was telling me, yet, I felt an infinite joy inside me.

Paula was right. The hormones were turning me into a bipolar madwoman. Who could plan to bring a child into the world under these circumstances?

I decided to lie down and let my mind go blank for a while. I was emotionally drained and needed to rest. I thought about my life, how I had gotten to this point, and how things could go wrong in a single second.

I fell asleep, and when I opened my eyes, the alarm clock read three in the morning.

Why hadn't I heard Áxel's call? Easy; I had slept like a log.

I felt on the bedside table for my cell phone and sent a message of apology to Áxel. The poor guy must have thought I hadn't wanted to answer. When I looked at the screen, I came face to face with reality. I hadn't woken up because he hadn't called.

That infuriated me. I threw the phone on the floor and cried like the hormonal mess I was. I was trying something that was nonsense. I didn't want to accept reality, which was that I was in fifth place in his life, or maybe tenth.

Maybe when I called him, he felt the need to tell me things he didn't feel. Maybe he felt trapped by my presence and didn't want to tell me over the phone, or maybe he was driven by memories, not because he wanted to keep something going with me. I was a fool, an idiot who couldn't see beyond my hopes. That was what it all boiled down to—Áxel was my hope. What a fool I was.

"What if it's not? What if something happened to him and you just blew up the phone?" asked an unwelcome little voice.

I got up like a bolt of lightning and realized that my phone was dead, and I was unable to resuscitate it. Shit! *Garbiñe, breathe. I'm sure you have your old phone. The one you decided to change for the latest model because it was no longer good enough that it only makes calls.* It's a good thing the light bulb came on sometimes.

I searched until I found it. There, disdained, without battery, with the screen covered with dust and the memory full of memories from another time, was my salvation.

I plugged it into the charger, trying to revive it while fighting with the one I had broken.

Who the hell had come up with the brilliant idea of changing the size of the sim cards?

After I got my way with eyebrow tweezers, I looked for the adapter that the company gives you to use with any cell phone and inserted it into the old one.

It turned on, much to my relief, and the battery appeared to be charged to fifty percent, a sure sign that it was on its last legs, and that was why it was charging so fast. I remembered why I had changed it.

I updated and looked around to make sure I hadn't missed a message. The result was the same as a few minutes before: nothing.

I wanted to cry so badly that I ended up doing it. I had forgotten how sensitive women get when they're pregnant. That you can go from being Carrie the phone killer to a fucking waterfall in tenths of a second.

I couldn't sleep, and at six o'clock, my alarm was going to go off for work. Hiccuping and sobbing uncontrollably, I did what any pregnant woman with two fingers in front of her would have done.

Call my mother? Don't kid yourself; that would never have been a good option. I didn't call Paula or the proximal cause of my fragile emotional state, either. I was more direct. I went to the kitchen, opened the freezer, and armed myself with a half-liter of salted caramel ice cream and a soup spoon, then went to the dining room. Once there, I selected a movie on the hard drive I had hooked up to the TV that was tearjerking enough to make me slit my wrists and let go to my heart's content. That was a good therapy session, not the one with the psychologist who charged me sixty euros.

When I got into the shower at five o'clock, my eyes looked like billiard balls, and my nose looked like a clown's.

Slightly calmer and feeling like my brain was numb, I went in search of my cell phone.

If I couldn't get out of bed this afternoon because of the coming migraine, I would be solely responsible for it.

I made a decision. I was not going to insist anymore. I was ready to let him leave my life no matter how much it hurt me because, with my attitude, the only thing he was doing was hurting me more than I deserved.

I grabbed the phone, and an incoming message flashed on the screen.

I held my breath as I read.

I'm sorry I didn't call you. It's not an excuse. I couldn't do it. I spent the night in the hospital with my children. During the meeting with the psychologist, they called us to come urgently. Claudia died an hour ago.

My heart stopped in its tracks.

I'm sorry for breaking my word again and not being able to call to talk. I'm broken, and I have so many things to take care of. I know I keep asking you the same thing, but give me time. Please don't push me away. I need you.

I squeezed my eyes shut because, apparently, despite having gone to the tear fest, I still had some left in the chamber.

I cried for Claudia, who I did not know but who did not deserve that ending. I cried for the mothers who cannot see their children grow up and miss the most beautiful moments of the people they love the most in their lives.

I cried for the children who grow up without the affection of their mothers, without listening to their advice, their scolding, and without receiving those hugs, sometimes so necessary.

I cried for Áxel, for all that the loss of the woman who had been his companion, the mother of his children, and for all that would come to him with that fatal outcome.

And I cried for myself since I did not know where that event was going to take us.

I left the house. Some stars were still visible in the sky. Soon the sun would rise.

I saw one star shining brightly, and right next to it, another. I smiled at them.

"Take care of her, Father. She needs you. Tell her to be calm. I will do what I can for the man she loved most and for her children. Let her forgive me for falling in love with him if that causes her pain. Tell her I will try to help her little ones, not usurping her place but seeking the best for them. I will fight tooth and nail to build a family where she will always be included. I will make sure she is always present."

The two stars twinkled, offering me the calm I needed and a determination I had not felt before. I had made a decision, and nothing could stop me.

CHAPTER TWENTY-THREE

Backpfeifengesicht: A face that asks for shouts and blows.

Garbiñe

"I don't know if we were right to show up unannounced," I said, glancing at Paula, who looked like something out of an episode of *Falcon Crest*. "Do you think that black Pamela hat is going to make you go unnoticed?"

"I don't want to go unnoticed. Nobody knows us except Áxel, and you never know who you might meet, even at a wake. You should have listened to me and bought one like it at the airport store."

"You know I don't like to draw attention to myself, and you look like a flying saucer landed on your head!" I protested.

"I don't know why I'm wasting my time trying to instruct you, Grasshopper. This gives you glamour, while the outfit you've chosen makes me want to go to confession and not for having lewd thoughts."

We were at Sancho de Avila, the funeral home where a mass

was to be held in Claudia's memory. There were a lot of people gathered. It looked more like a gypsy wedding than a wake. I stopped counting when I reached a hundred.

"She must have been very well-liked," my friend remarked, looking at the people piling up everywhere.

"It seems so. Áxel always said his ex was a very good person, but their love ran out."

"From using it so much," she finished for me. "You sound like a Jurado song."

"I sound like reality. These things happen. Look at me and Dario."

"I don't agree with you there. Yours was not because of use but because the bank where Dario deposited was in purple numbers."

"You mean red?"

"No, purple. He smothered you until it changed color."

"You and your witticisms. You should write a humorous book instead of running a journalistic blog. With a bit of luck, you'd make a fortune."

"Sure. Hey, have you noticed how hot those Mossos over there are? The dark-haired guy in the corner is fucking hot."

"Please control yourself. We're at a funeral," I scolded.

"What's that got to do with it? I didn't wear this for the dead." She pointed at her outfit. "Besides, we're not going to be at the funeral all day. At these events, you also socialize, believe it or not."

"Paula." I sighed.

"Paula, my ass. A lot of guys get turned on by these circumstances." She clicked her tongue.

I snorted.

"What? Being so close to death makes you want to caress life, and I'm going to caress it all over him if he'll let me. Oh, wish me luck. He's just been left alone."

"Don't even think about it," I warned. I was not here to watch my friend flirt but to be with Áxel in his pain.

She winked at me.

I don't know how she could take a step in that dress and the stiletto heels. She was wearing celebrity sunglasses that covered half her face, and her lips were painted bright red. Her coppery hair fell below her shoulder blades. How could anyone not notice her?

The poor Mosso's eyes rolled when he saw her approaching like the predator she was.

Luckily for us, the funeral was held when I had four days off, and Ruben was with his father.

I called Paula to tell her what had happened and explain the decision I had made regarding Áxel. She suggested that before deciding whether to fight for us and tell him about the pregnancy, it would be better to travel to Barcelona and see how he reacted. Since the idea had already been in my mind to travel to Barcelona to see him, her suggestion to accompany me was a blessing.

In less than half an hour, Paula had acquired two plane tickets and was urging me to pack my bags. If it didn't work out, I could go sightseeing in the city if I had any strength left. I hoped in my heart that nothing would derail my plans, but perhaps that was too much to ask.

I looked around, trying to find Áxel in the crowd. I had not seen him yet, but that was not surprising, given the size of the place and the number of people.

I had dressed discreetly, unlike my friend, who had no decency. Her dress was missing fabric everywhere, both in the generous neckline and in the slit of the skirt. She was like an actress out of a movie from the fifties, only missing the elbow-length gloves and a cigarette in a long holder.

I looked down. Maybe I had gone too far with my modesty,

and Paula was right. I had opted for a pair of black pleated pants, ballerinas in the same color, my hair slicked back, and a shirt buttoned to my throat. Going over my attire mentally in the absence of a mirror, I recognized that my friend wasn't wrong. I looked like a novice about to enter a convent. Maybe if I loosened a couple of buttons…

I put my hands to my neck and heard a scream. I saw a bunch of people milling around in a corner.

My help-your-neighbor radar activated, and without realizing it, I was in the middle of the whole thing.

"Let her breathe," said one woman. Another woman dressed the same way ordered. "Pull her legs up."

A third shouted, "Someone call a doctor."

A fourth one took a flask out of her purse to put it to the stricken woman's mouth, claiming it was a little bit of water from Carmen.

I made my way over and crouched next to the woman to take her pulse. "Are you a doctor?" asked a member of the quartet.

"No, civil guard, but I know how to take care of people when they get sick. Don't worry; she has a pulse. It looks like a drop in blood pressure." The four pairs of eyes looked at me with relief. "Give her room to breathe."

Four fans were opened to wave over the woman. "I don't even know how she can stand up," said the woman with the flask. "The poor thing has suffered so much. She hasn't even slept. Losing a child is unnatural, and with how good Claudia was, even more so."

"So young and leaving two children." added the one holding her legs.

So, the woman whose head she was holding was Claudia's mother. It was logical that she would have collapsed with what she must have been going through. I didn't even want to imagine it.

"What's her name?" I asked.

Áxel always referred to her as "my mother-in-law." I didn't remember him ever telling me her first name.

"Teresa. Her name is Teresa."

I nodded and patted her exhausted face lightly.

"Teresa, Teresa, wake up. Are you all right?" I murmured. "Come on, Teresa, answer me."

The woman shuddered and opened her eyelids to fix her dull blue eyes on mine.

"Where am I?" she asked.

"At the funeral home. We were about to enter the chapel, and you fainted," the woman who had given me her name told her. "This nice girl helped us take care of you."

Teresa blinked feebly, unable to offer me a smile. In her state, I couldn't have either.

"Do you have any pain? Your head?" I felt it carefully in case it had been bumped.

She denied it.

"She was holding onto my arm. That's why it wasn't worse. But with my little strength, I couldn't prevent her from falling," explained the woman who had asked for a doctor.

"It's fine, much better this way. Blows to the head can bring complications. Do you think you can stand up?" I asked. She nodded, "Then come on. I'll help you. Hold on to me."

"What a sweet accent you have, girl, and how nice. Are you Argentinean?" one of the women asked. "I have a neighbor who is from there, and she is as beautiful and kind as you are."

"No, I'm Spanish, but I've been living in Tenerife for many years. I imagine the accent has rubbed off on me. Many people confuse it."

"Tenerife. How nice. My daughter went there on her honeymoon with her first husband. What's your name?"

"Garbiñe." I said my name, and Teresa gave me a push that threw me on my ass on the floor. I have to say in my defense that

I wasn't expecting it since the strength of the woman I had just picked up off the floor wasn't much.

"Get out! Get out of here! What the hell are you doing at my daughter's wake? You've come here to laugh at her! Is that it? It wasn't enough to steal her husband. You have to come here to strut around while her body is still warm! I didn't know who you were, so I let you help me, but you are the one to blame for everything! The one who slept with my son-in-law while my daughter was having the accident that cost her her life!"

Her screams echoed above the sepulchral silence that had fallen.

I felt the heat rising in my face without understanding how that woman knew who I was.

The ones with the mantillas crossed themselves as if they had just seen Satan reincarnated, and I was so shocked that I was unable to defend myself or open my mouth.

"What's going on? What's all this shouting?" The masculine voice made people open a path, and Áxel's eyes met mine, which were about to overflow.

"You're a scoundrel, do you hear me? It takes courage to bring your lover here on a day like this! In front of me and your children! You scoundrel!"

He clenched his jaw and right hand where there was a little girl about nine years old with a slight limp, looking at me, scared and crying.

Like a gale and emulating the Tasmanian devil making one of his characteristic hurricanes, Paula stood in front of me to extend a hand that no one had offered me and lifted me off the ground giving a warning look that only I could intuit under her sunglasses.

"Are you all right?" she asked quietly.

"Get me out of here, please," I murmured, wanting to teleport to the shelter of my home.

It was not the time to confront a wounded mother and tell

her that her daughter was separated and Áxel was a free man. Picking a fight, confronting her, and getting my boy in more trouble than he was already in was not my intention. I gave him an "I'm sorry" look I hoped would communicate that, and I was dragged away by Paula, who was about to plant one of her heels between Teresa's eyebrows.

She kept screaming, but I could no longer hear anything but my sobs. We went outside, and I leaned against a wall. My friend hurriedly lit a cigarette and offered it to me.

"I don't smoke, and I'm pregnant," I told her between hiccups.

"I know, but it will calm you down."

I declined.

"It's up to you. I'll either smoke, or I'll smash that woman's face in. She's an asshole and a busybody. She said all those things in front of everybody and threw you on the ground after you went to help her."

"I didn't know who she was or that she knew of my existence. I was just trying to help her," I whimpered.

"Mothers-in-law know everything. They are women with supernatural powers descended from the most ancient witches. You would do well to remember that. Gabriel's mother knew he was screwing Ursula long before I did, even though she'd never seen her in her fucking life, and he'd never told her about it," she grumbled. "Next time you want to give a mother-in-law a hand, let it be around her neck, and make sure there are no witnesses and she doesn't breathe when you leave her."

"Don't be a savage!" I protested.

"If you want, I'll come in and invite her to join us, along with her coven of crows, who are eager to peck."

"Ooh." I put my hands to my face. "Why do I always screw up?"

"You don't screw up. It was your kind nature that prevented you from seeing the enemy disguised as a lovely old woman. Believe me, that woman is the enemy."

"She just lost her daughter. She doesn't know what she's saying. She's not in charge of her actions," I tried to excuse her.

Paula took a deep puff.

"She's gone straight out to do harm. If she was a good woman, she would have thanked you and kept quiet, even if it burned her. But no, she identified you. She gave the tipoff to all those present so they could attack you, and she didn't care that Áxel came, clutching his daughter, to hear her spout her venom. That woman wants you out of her life. She slapped you with an open hand, and you make excuses for her?"

"You think that way because you don't have children."

Paula's gaze turned icy. "Of course, O great goddess of fertility! Because only those of you who are parents know what it feels like when something happens to one of your offspring. The rest of us don't have a say because, according to you, we are not up to the task. We don't know what it feels like. Bringing a child into the world gives you elevated wisdom that we poor mortals who have no offspring are not able to grasp."

She snapped her fingers at me. "I know what pain is, even if no baby has come from between my thighs. I know what it is to worry about others, even if I have no children. I know what it is to want to die of grief because, in case you've forgotten, I didn't give birth to my little sister. It was as if I had."

"I'm sorry, I didn't think."

"Of course, you never think. Why think? The only important thing here is to be a mother in order to have an opinion."

I had hurt her, and I felt terrible. Paula was the only one who had lent me a hand in there, and I was repaying her like this.

"Paula." I grabbed her arm, knowing I had hit the wrong key. "I wasn't thinking clearly. I'm sorry. I didn't mean to remind you about Betina."

She nodded and leaned against the wall next to me. She took off her glasses and put them in her purse.

The Mosso she had been talking to appeared before us.

"Are you all right?" he asked.

"Yes, we love dramatic entrances." Paula took the last puff of her cigarette and threw the butt to the ground.

"Lucas Lozano, this is my friend Garbiñe Navarro. Sergeant Garbiñe Navarro."

The Mosso gave me two kisses just before Paula included the word "sergeant" when repeating my name, in case it had not been clear. He looked at me admiringly. "From what force?"

"Yours, the one you have insisted on covering as if you were going to enter a cloistered convent."

"From the *Guardia Civil*," I corrected, rolling my eyes.

Paula shrugged. Lucas lifted the corners of his lips without offering a full smile. "He's a friend of Áxel's. He's not on the enemy's side," she said.

"He was my Taser instructor, and we ended up with a good friendship."

"Mine too." He looked at me with curiosity.

"I'm glad you agree on something, even if he taught you more than just how to give electric shocks, and the friendship he offered you is much deeper."

"Otherwise, we wouldn't be here," Paula added, making me blush.

Lucas cleared his throat.

"Yes, well, there have been rumors about it," he said with restraint.

"Let's not go back in there," I warned, wanting to be alone with Paula.

"That's a good decision," he said. "Don't think I'm judging you. It's just that, given Claudia's mother's condition..."

"They were separated when we met," I said to justify myself.

"I know, and so do most people. Don't worry too much. We all know what a wounded mother is capable of saying."

It did me good to hear his words and to understand that not

everyone wanted to let me loose in the Plaza Mayor to decapitate me.

"Thank you."

"You're welcome."

"Are we still on for tonight?" asked Paula.

Lucas melted her with a honeyed gaze. He was a very attractive man. "Of course."

"Well then, let's text each other later, shall we?"

He nodded and dismissed us with a slight nod. "See you later. Nice to meet you, Sergeant Navarro."

"Garbiñe, please."

He nodded again and turned around to go inside.

"There seems to be chemistry between you two," I said as Paula watched the Mosso's hindquarters.

"I'll tell you that after I've tasted that brown body. I just hope it provokes in me the same reaction as when you throw a handful of Mentos into a glass of Coke."

"Shall we go to the apartment?" I asked. I didn't want to stay there a minute longer.

"Without you talking to Áxel?"

"I don't think he's coming out, and we're not going to go in, so. We'll find a time to do it. We'll be here for four days."

"That is true. Even I see that staying here is not the wisest thing to do. This way, we can rest for a while because catching the 6:30 a.m. flight and showing up at a funeral at noon is exhausting for anyone."

If I expected Áxel to call me immediately, I would have been disappointed. It didn't happen. I didn't want to burden him, and I wasn't sure if he had taken my foray into the funeral home well. I had caused him a lot of embarrassment, so instead of comforting him with my presence, which had been my brilliant idea, I had burdened him even more. I didn't even want to think about the mother-in-law's big show in front of the child or how my meddling affected his relationship with his son. Maybe after today, he wouldn't even want to see me.

At five o'clock, I typed **I'm sorry** with trembling fingers and hit send. I stared at the screen and got silence.

Great. My idea of coming to Barcelona had been brutal so far.

Paula insisted that we go out for a walk. The apartment was close to Paseo de Gracia, only a few streets away, and I needed to clear my head a little. She engaged in a bout of shopping, which left us exhausted.

At seven o'clock, we sat down on a terrace to have an ice cream and regain our strength. My feet were in tatters, and my morale was at rock bottom. It didn't matter what Paula said or that she insisted that I go out with her and Lucas. I just wanted to get into bed and cry about my misfortune.

At half past eight, the Mosso came to pick up my friend, and after insisting ad nauseam that I couldn't stay alone and I should accompany them, I decided to accept, even though I felt like a third wheel.

Paula asked Lucas to wait for us on the couch while she went with me to the bedroom to put on one of her dresses, which was loose all over but was better than one of the sweaters I had packed in my suitcase.

The Mosso turned out to be a great conversationalist. He was friendly and personable, and we had quite a bit in common. Dinner went better than expected, and we ended up at a music bar to have a drink after dinner since Paula insisted that it was too early to go back to the apartment and the night was young.

They were on the dance floor, dancing to one of the hits of the moment, *Échame la culpa*, by Luis Fonsi and Demi Lovato, when my cell phone vibrated.

There it was, several hours later—the first message from Áxel.

Where are you?

As if I was going to tell him. Now I was the one who didn't want to talk. I was hurt, grumpy, and had had a drink or two too many.

What? I know! Pregnant women should not drink alcohol. So what if I had had a glass of wine at dinner and a gin and tonic now? I needed to escape. To stop thinking about him and his hours of no response.

I was not as rude as Áxel. I decided to respond.

In a bar

Which bar?

In one where they serve drinks. Does it matter?

We need to talk.

Ha! Now we had to talk when it suited him. I didn't feel like it. I didn't like the tone of the message. I was sure he would tell me off for having gone to the funeral and reprimand me for having taken that damned plane and for making a fool of him in front of everyone. He would tell me that after today's little stunt, he didn't want to see me again. That I shouldn't bother him anymore and that I should stop harassing him by phone. Yes! That was all he wanted to tell me, but since I already knew, I didn't need to hear it from his mouth and feel even worse.

**No need for that. Relax, I got the message. I'll leave you alone.
It's over. I hope you're doing great. It was nice while it lasted.
So long, Áxel.**

I dropped the handset into the bag. It vibrated again, but I ignored it. I thought about drowning my sorrows in alcohol. It would be a bad decision, but Lucas and Paula were having a great time, and I had to settle for looking at other people's kisses, so it was better to make the night less painful. I would take the first flight to Tenerife to start my new life without him.

What was the point of wanting to throw everything I had into the fire if Áxel didn't even want to see me?

I gulped my drink and went to the bar for another.

CHAPTER TWENTY-FOUR

Aiyana: Eternal flower.

<u>Áxel</u>

I tried to normalize my breathing.

The day had been fucking hard. I was prepared for it to be. I knew Teresa was not going to make it easy for me, and neither was my son, but I did not expect to come face-to-face with Garbiñe. She was there while my ex-mother-in-law threw venom on us in front of my daughter. It was devastating.

I was taken by surprise. First, because I had not expected her to travel to be with me. I had not asked her to do so, thinking that would be going too far. Second, she showed up at Claudia's funeral. I knew it was not to claim her place since Garbiñe was not like that.

I was convinced that she had acted out of affection, so it hurt me even more that she had suffered the wrath of Teresa, who had gone straight for the jugular.

Luckily, my girl was not alone. Paula had intervened to get her out of there before my ex-mother-in-law tore her to shreds.

If she hadn't, I would have been morally obliged to intervene since she didn't deserve to have all that venom poured on her.

As soon as she got up, I tried letting go of my daughter and going after her, but the warning look Teresa gave me made me stay in place. If I did, the situation would get worse, and Claudia did not deserve a farewell wreathed in scandal.

The hive of harpies made up of Teresa's sisters and friends did not give Garbiñe the benefit of the doubt. I had to be thankful that my ex-father-in-law was with Christian, waiting for the mass and not witnessing the mess.

My friend Carles grabbed my shoulder. I confess that as soon as I saw Teresa enter the chapel, I wanted to go talk to Garbiñe, offer her my apologies for the bad time, and ask her to see me later.

"Now is not the time," he warned me in a calm voice, looking at my daughter. "You owe it to Claudia. You'll have time to be together and clear things up later."

"But…"

"She'll understand. Garbiñe is not stupid. She'll know why you haven't gone after her. Listen to me. You'll have time."

Andrea tugged on my hand.

"Daddy, who was that woman, and why did Grandma insult her?" she asked, not understanding Teresa's rudeness.

Carles shot my daughter a smile and squatted to be at her eye level.

"Your grandmother is very upset and is saying things she doesn't mean. You shouldn't pay much attention to her. Sometimes, when ugly things happen, sadness speaks through the mouths of your elders, and they act on it. Do you understand?"

"Yes. It's like when I get sad in judo class because I can't do the exercise, and I get upset with Nerea, even though it's not her fault."

"That's right. See? You're a very smart girl."

"Thank you, Grandfather." She smiled impishly.

"Now, the important thing is to say goodbye to your mommy and be strong so she knows that even though she is not here, we will not stop carrying her in our hearts. Claudia would not want to see us sad. Prepare your best smile so she can be calm when she sees you from heaven."

"Dad told me that she will be the star that shines the brightest."

"Without a doubt. The most beautiful of all, and it will shine for you every night so you can look at her and tell her everything that happens to you."

My little girl sniffled through her nose. Her eyelids were swollen because even though she had tried to hold back, she hadn't been able to stop crying the whole day.

"I will. I'll smile to make Mom happy."

"Of course. And now let's go in. Without us, they won't start the mass."

I moved my lips to thank him, and he responded with a second squeeze. I glanced at the door leading into the enclosure, but it was impossible to see anything with so many people there.

We entered the chapel and occupied the first-row seats.

The ceremony was very emotional. Many people wanted to dedicate a few words to Claudia. There were our friends, relatives, the parents of the children who went to school with us, the judo and skating students, my Taser students, my colleagues from the police station, and her colleagues from the factory. In short, all those who appreciated us. There were so many of us that many were left at the gates. Wreaths of flowers, farewell ribbons, and messages of affection and mourning filled the corners.

My son Christian, broken by the loss, was the last to speak, hands shaking and eyes red-rimmed.

"Mom, you always took care of me and understood me. You were my branch to hold on to, the one who supported me in my crazy ideas. You were the best mother I could have ever dreamed of, beautiful, kind, brave, and with an eternal smile that never faded, no matter how big my stumbling block was.

"You were always there. You taught me the beauty of being different and how to face those who made fun of me for not understanding that skating is not only a girls' sport. You tried to instill in me that the important thing was to pursue dreams, even if they weren't everyone's. You never bothered me because my grades were more Cs than As, and if I faltered, you were there to try to help me solve the trigonometry problems you did not understand.

"I may not have been the best son or the best at anything, but however insignificant I am, you made me feel like I was your star, the most important thing in your life next to my sister. That was enough for me, even if sometimes I wished the dwarf didn't exist.

"Now that you are gone, where your love was, there is only emptiness. I will never see you again, and I know that I will never be the same. You don't know how much I miss you and need you.

"Goodbye, Mom. I wake up thinking it was all a nightmare and I will find you in the kitchen making breakfast. I don't think I will ever stop missing you, and I'm really afraid that someday your face will no longer be clear in my mind, and I won't remember your scent or the way you stroked my hair when I was anxious about exams. I sense that right now, you would like me to smile. I swear I'll try, but I can't because you took my last smile with you.

"If you could talk, you'd tell me to be strong since you'll be up there to take care of me like grandma says. Sooner or later, we'll meet again, and we'll make up for lost time. I dream of that day, Mom, because until then, it will be impossible for me to be happy.

"I love you, and I will always love you. Don't forget me. I will do my best not to forget you until you embrace me again and I can feel at home. You will always be my eternal flower."

Everyone was silent. Tears streamed down the faces of those present, including mine.

Christian folded the paper and walked down the stairs and into Teresa's arms.

That was the worst thing, seeing my son broken and not being able to hold him in my arms. Not being able to offer him the comfort he needed because he didn't want me to touch him.

Christian and Teresa were the angriest. They had joined forces and pronounced judgment: guilty on all counts. If they had had the choice, it would have been my body that rested in that coffin today. That was how it should have been, but destiny and the Grim Reaper were playing this game of dice, keeping me on the board and leaving my wife in a box.

I wanted to stand up, go to Christian, and hug him like when he was little and he saw me as a role model instead of a defendant. I wanted to kneel before him, beg his forgiveness for having failed him, and tell him that, if I could, I would have exchanged myself for his mother if it meant he would stop looking at me the way he did. But I couldn't. As soon as I tried to get close to him, I was met with the cruelty of his accusations. Worse was the hatred I saw in his eyes and the indifference he showed when we were in the same room.

I controlled the urge to go to him and burned when Teresa whispered words of encouragement and congratulated him for his beautiful words. She sheltered him by giving him the affection I wanted to give him. She was breaking my soul, showing the world my failure as a father.

I had a hollow chest and pain cracking me because if it is sad to lose someone you love in an accident, it is sadder to know they are still alive and don't want to see you.

My parents and Carles tried to encourage me. My siblings also supported me, speaking words of affection, but it didn't matter. I felt like a failure. I had failed Claudia, my family, and my children, damaging them in an irreparable way.

At the end of the ceremony, we went to the cemetery. I looked for Garbiñe on the way out, but I didn't see her. How could she be waiting there after the reception she'd had? It would have been crazy. I'm sure she had left, tired of waiting. It pained me to think that she could imagine that I had belittled her visit when it was quite the opposite. Seeing her face was the highlight of my day.

My mother clung to my waist. Andrea kept her fingers braided around mine; she hadn't let go the whole time. I focused on what I had to do rather than what I wanted to do. If I had been ruled by my emotions, I would have run away. I would have run until I felt my lungs burning to end up jumping into the void so that it would all be over.

Running away is cowardly, I reminded myself. I had to face my new life, no matter how fucked up it was. As Carles said, time would put things in their place, like an efficient majordomo tidying up the cutlery. I had no choice but to think that way because, no matter how bad things were, Christian and Andrea didn't deserve to lose me too.

My parents insisted that we all eat together in their apartment in Mataró, and that included Teresa, my ex-father-in-law, and my son. According to my mother, I had to smooth things over with Teresa. Let her perceive that I was not the enemy. Even if she was not focused, I had to do it to get Christian back. He had refused to come home with me.

He had just turned sixteen. He was no longer a child, and I didn't want to pressure him or go to court to claim my rights and make him hate me even more. If I did that, I would lose him forever, and in a couple of years, he would be of age to do whatever he wanted. Experience had taught me that adolescence is a delicate crossroads where one wrong step can lead you to decisions you will regret for the rest of your life. I preferred to give him time and approach him little by little, at his pace, without letting him forget I cared about him.

We had been away from home for hours. My cell phone had run out of battery, and no one there had a compatible charger. I could have run out to buy one, but it didn't seem the wisest thing to do.

I went to the kitchen to get the glass of water Andrea had asked me for.

When I was about to return, my mother came in. Let Andrea spend the night here and go talk to her, she suggested with a beatific smile on her face.

"To her?" I asked without understanding who she was referring to.

"You know, the woman Teresa threw out. She was responsible for making your eyes sparkle a few months ago. Am I wrong?"

Mother's wisdom. I admit I was caught off-guard. "No, you aren't," I acknowledged, feeling bad for not telling her about Garbiñe.

"I'm old, but I'm not stupid. Just because I don't talk about it doesn't mean I don't know it exists. I don't think it's wrong for you to rebuild your life. You deserve to be happy after all you've struggled with. You've had it bad enough. It's time for you to stop living half-heartedly and do it completely."

"I don't know, Mom. It's all so complex," I whispered.

"Teresa is impossible. She's hurt, and she's spiteful, but she'll get over it, just like Christian. If you let this girl get away from you, you may never get her back. Teresa and Christian love you. They just don't know how to handle what happened."

"Oh, yes. Teresa loves me, but dead and underground."

"Don't say that. She may be taking it badly, but she adored you and saw no better husband for her daughter than you. That's why she's taking it so hard. That doesn't mean she's acting right or that you should stop living because your ex-wife did. Son, you were not to blame."

"I wish I could see it so clearly." I sighed. "I think I *am* partly to blame."

"No, you are not," she reproached me, grabbing my face firmly. "Her time had come, and you of all people know how that is. When it is not someone's time, it is not, no matter how dark things look. God wanted her by his side for a reason we don't know, and neither you nor anyone else could have prevented it. Look at me, Áxel."

I looked into her serene eyes.

"I need you to fight for your happiness. You fought for your health, which is the most important thing. Once you have it, the second step is happiness since if you lose your intention to be happy, life withers away. I cannot tolerate that happening, just as you would not allow it to happen to your children. Every mother wants her little ones to be happy, and I want the same for mine."

"I'm a big boy, Mom."

"You will always be my child. You will understand that over the years. No matter how much time passes, for a mother, her child is always that helpless being she carried in her womb. The one she gave birth to with fear in her heart and for whom she never stops suffering for a moment. Children give you many joys, but they also give you many worries that are reflected in the times you open your wallet at the hairdresser's to have your gray hair covered."

I smiled. My mother could get a smile out of me, no matter how bad things were.

"Go talk to her."

"Garbiñe. Her name is Garbiñe, Mom."

"A very lovely name. The same as that of the Basque Miss Spain of '83. A beautiful woman with character."

"My Garbi is too."

"Well, you owe her. She came all this way and had the balls to face Teresa's fury for supporting you! That girl took all that without batting an eyelash, and it says a lot about her that she did not stand up to the harpy your ex-mother-in-law has become.

Meet with her. Clear things up, and tell her she has my blessing for returning the light to your eyes."

"Mom." I held her in my arms, grateful to have a mother like her.

Her words and affection were always a balm. In moments like this, I understood Christian's pain since my mother was very dear to me.

The tension on the trip back to my ex-in-laws' house could have been cut with a knife. They had come with me in the car that morning, so I had to drive them home. Luckily, they were quiet most of the way. Teresa rode in the back with Christian, and her husband was beside me. Andrea had stayed with my mother.

I just drove and thought about what I was going to say to Garbiñe. I had to do it damned well if I didn't want her to slam the door in my face.

The farewell was sullen. My son looked at me suspiciously. I was sure Teresa had talked his head off, and he had listened to her. I tried to kiss him, but he rejected me, making me feel like a stinker. He went straight to the door without looking back, provoking in me an intense need to shake him so he could see the damage he was doing to me. I didn't; I just looked at him with the pity of a scorned father.

"He's my son," I said through my teeth.

"And he just buried his mother, while you brought your new love to the wake. What a lack of respect! I don't understand why you haven't covered your face in shame."

"I don't have to give you explanations. Claudia was my ex-wife. We no longer had any connection. We could each make our life with whoever we wanted."

"Do you think I'm not aware that your mother has stayed with Andrea so that you can get your fill of fornicating with that slut?"

"Teresa!" her husband exclaimed.

"I don't have to bite my tongue when he did not know how to respect the holy sacrament he made before God!"

"Nowadays, marriages are not for life. Love ends," I told her.

"Yes, it's over when fresh meat is shoved down your throat, and you can't zip your fly."

"Teresa, stop it!" Antonio told her.

"Thank goodness your son didn't go with you. He's the only one with decent feelings."

"If I let him stay with you," I said in a warning tone, "and I put up with your insults, it's because deep down, you're not well. You don't think half the things you say, but I won't tolerate you filling Christian's head with nonsense. Do me a favor and behave like his grandmother, not like one of those busybodies on those shows you like so much."

Her palm slammed against my cheek, silencing me.

"Enough!" Antonio interceded, embarrassed by his wife's behavior.

I clenched my fists since my mother had never hit me, no matter how big the problem was.

"That was the first and last time you'll slap me. I'm not slapping you back because you are my *ex-mother-in-law*, not because I don't think you deserve one in return. If I find out that you laid a hand on my son or you spoke ill of me, you will be sorry."

"Are you threatening me? Don't make me laugh. It's you he doesn't want to see. You've dug your own grave. I'm not the reason he won't tolerate seeing you."

"Christian may be resentful, but he'll get over it. Nevertheless, I'll move heaven and earth to get him back home. Now I'm leaving. I've had enough for today. I'd like to say the company has been pleasant, but you'll understand if I don't. I am sorry for your loss. Antonio," I told my ex-father-in-law by way of farewell. He nodded as he pushed his wife toward home.

I was seething with rage at Teresa's irrational behavior. I knew that everything she was saying was fallacious, yet I kept whipping myself, wondering if I wasn't getting what I deserved.

My thoughts intertwined with my mother's advice, my son's reproaches, and the look of regret and shame Garbiñe had offered me from the floor.

The first thing I did when I got home was put my cell phone on the charger. I needed to talk to her. It was dark, and I'm sure she didn't understand what had gone on. With the phone charging, I undressed and jumped straight into the shower. I needed to feel the warmth of the water on my cold skin, dragging with it all the regret I was carrying. I thoroughly rinsed, and when I was clean, I wrapped up in a fluffy towel. I ran my palm across the mirror and looked at my lifeless, reddened eyes.

I had cried a lot. I felt no shame about it. My parents never told us that bullshit about men not crying. On the contrary, they taught us that it was a way of channeling emotions and that it was sometimes necessary to let tears flow to avoid collapse.

I mentally drew Claudia's face and thought, "I'm sorry." Her benevolent blue eyes would have accepted without hesitation. In my memory, she was always ready to forgive and accept my apology and exonerate me, no matter how great the grievance was.

I looked for something to wear, and once I was dressed, I picked up the phone. I had a single message from Garbiñe. "I'm sorry."

It had been many hours since I should have answered her. I could imagine her waiting for an answer that never came, and it hurt because I was convinced that I had saddened her.

I had no appetite. It was late, and I should have had dinner by now, but I didn't care. My stomach was tight, and if I had tried, I wouldn't have been able to get a single bite in.

Armed with a courage I didn't feel, I sent her a message to test the waters, but I didn't want our conversation to be limited to an exchange of texts. I needed to see her. I was terse and direct. I limited myself to asking her where she was. The pleas would come later.

From her response, which was not long in coming, she was upset. I tried to get her location, but she stopped answering, and I was forced to ask for her location as a favor. Sometimes it was worth it to have been a Mosso and have many colleagues owing you favors.

In forty minutes, I was at the door of the bar. I crossed my fingers, hoping she was still here.

There was a side bar into which people crowded to get their alcohol fix. In Barcelona, no matter what day of the week it was, there were always people ready to party, especially on Thursdays, which was the university students' day.

Tables dotted the sides, leaving a central space for the daring to dance.

I looked at the soft benches, but I saw no trace of Garbiñe. Maybe she was in the bathroom since I didn't see her dancing. I looked at the other bodies and thought I saw my friend Lucas Lozano clinging to a copper-haired woman. Paula! If she was there, Garbi would not be far away.

I pushed through the crowd in search of her, not an easy task given that many people had had a few drinks too many.

A jerk elbowed me and threw half a glass on the floor. Luckily, it didn't stain my clothes. I would have only needed to stink of liquor.

I didn't feel like an argument. I was just interested in finding Garbiñe.

I arrived to find Paula and Lozano kissing. Dancing had been put on the back burner. I looked away to give them a privacy they didn't seem to care about and patiently waited until they surfaced to breathe.

"Hello," I greeted them, interrupting the lascivious looks they were giving each other. They both looked away from me with eyes filled with desire.

"Hello." Paula smiled, raising her eyebrows. "We thought you weren't coming."

"It's been a complicated day," I told her without letting her get her claws out. "Where is Garbiñe?"

"I don't know. Just having fun, I guess. I think she got tired of waiting for an answer that wasn't coming and decided it was time to move on."

There it was. If I thought that the claw would not come, I would have been wrong. Restraint was too much to ask from a woman like Paula.

"She's over there on the dance floor, dancing with that guy in blue," Lucas said, lending me a hand.

Paula sent him one of her annihilating looks.

"Thank you," I told Lucas. Before I could go, the redhead grabbed my arm.

"Not so fast, cowboy. It's okay that you're screwed. That it's a bit of a pill for you to swallow, but she hasn't had it easy either. She put a lot of courage into showing up here when you'd almost stopped calling her, and it's all been to offer you her support. So far, all she's gotten is insults and silent indifference from you. Get it right. Don't fuck up anymore, or I'll bust your balls, no matter how sad you are."

I smiled at her, knowing that Paula's anger was a façade and she was only trying to protect Garbiñe from me.

"If I hurt her, I will serve them to you on a tray so that you can make earrings from them."

She looked at me with disgust.

"I'd never wear your balls in my ears, but I appreciate the thought. Don't fuck up, Mr. Deodorant, or you know who the next Nutcracker will be."

"I won't. I promise." I winked and went in search of my girl. I just hoped she was still my girl.

When I looked at the guy Lozano had pointed out, I realized it was the guy from the spilled drink. I had not associated the blonde with Garbiñe. First, because her back was turned. Second, because she was wearing a dress so short and loose that it looked like a wide t-shirt. It wasn't her style, even though it looked great on her. And third, because she was dancing as if her life depended on it. Her hands were raised, and the octopus guy's hands were all over her.

I had never been jealous, but that fondling was too much for me.

I planted myself behind him and tapped his shoulder, and when he turned around, I pushed him away, claiming it was my turn. Brazenly and with a lot of nerve, I stepped in to hold her against my body.

She didn't notice the change of partners. She just laughed and hummed the song that was playing, *Will Thoughts*, by Rihanna and DJ Khaled. Her hips jerked against mine, and I involuntarily responded to her closeness. That sweet, fruity scent that drove me crazy stung my nostrils, prompting me to drop my chin into the hollow of her neck.

"Hey, you! Find someone else. This bitch is mine," the guy who had been dancing with her a moment ago shouted behind my back. "Didn't you hear me? Get out!"

I turned my head without letting go.

"You are wrong. She was waiting for me. She was just spending time with you. She is *mine*," I emphasized in a warning tone.

The boy, who was under twenty-five and had more testosterone than a bunch of bodybuilders training for a competition, frowned.

"She told me she was alone."

"Well, she's not," I corrected.

He grinned, and the next thing I saw was his fist coming at my face.

Luckily, my reflexes had not been impaired by alcohol or narcotics, and the guy was smashed. If my sense of smell didn't fail me, which it seldom did, that guy was not on top of his game. It wasn't difficult to intercept his blow and put him in a headlock.

Garbiñe turned around to see what was going on. "What are you doing?" she reproached me, staggering.

"I came looking for you. We have some unfinished business to talk about."

"Not now. Too late. I was having fun with my new dance partner." She swayed from side to side, making me worry that she would fall.

"You see, man? I told you she preferred me. Let go of me," growled the guy I was holding.

"I'm going to let you go, but go straight home." He snorted, and I moved closer to his ear so he could hear me without difficulty. "In case you didn't know, she's a Civil Guard from the vice squad, and I'm a Mosso d'Esquadra. It's true that we're not on duty today, but it wouldn't cost me anything to call one of my colleagues and have him search you. He'd probably find traces of the substance you've taken to be in this state. I could even tell him that you are a drug dealer and you will spend the night in jail."

"That's a lie!" he protested.

"Yeah, but who are they going to believe? Think about it. Either you leave, or I'll get you a room with full board at the police station."

"Let go of me, asshole!" he shouted. "All right, she's all yours! Besides, she's not that hot."

"You're wrong about that, but you'll never know," I said, pushing him away from us. "Honey is not for an ass's mouth," I spat.

Garbiñe looked at me with her arms in the air and a sad face. "Not even for the mouth of a Catalan Mosso," she added, pushing my chest with her index finger and stumbling away. I grabbed her and pulled her tight against my body with a smile.

I was so smug that she frowned at me. Even drunk and angry, she was the most delicious woman in the world. "Sergeant Tennis Player, you don't know how much I've missed you."

We had to talk, but first things first. I kissed her mouth as I longed to. As I did every night in my dreams when I allowed myself to meet her and forget the shit I was swimming in.

I might not have deserved her surrender and that gasp, her body pressing mine with abandon and her tongue curling with delight, yet that was what I got.

Her fingers swirled against the nape of my neck, taut breasts anchored to my torso, making me remember how much I had longed to taste them. My hands descended to her ass and kneaded it desperately.

I felt her trembling, and I let myself drift in that sea of doubt and desire. I have no idea how long we sailed adrift, drinking each other, letting our desire whip us, need in every movement. Then I stopped to lose myself in the green of her eyes, which claimed the place that had always been hers.

CHAPTER TWENTY-FIVE

Nankurunaisa: Time orders everything.

Garbiñe

The world orbited at breakneck speed as Áxel kissed me.

Okay, maybe I made a fool of myself and saw monsters where there was only the need for time to sort things out, but what can we do? We are not born perfect. In my defense, I will say that my reasoning capacity was altered lately. Besides, I hadn't slept much from anxiety, I had been attacked by an old woman out of her mind with grief in front of Áxel, who didn't lift a finger, and then I got no response from him even though I had sent him an "I'm sorry" message.

Yes, it had been a very hard day for him, but had he had a single moment to answer me, even if it was "I'll talk to you later?"

However, when I looked into his eyes, I saw what I wanted to see, my place in the world. My insecurities didn't matter, only what I felt with him.

"I'm sorry," I murmured, causing his lips to curve into a

resigned smile. I was aware of the spectacle I was surely putting on. I wasn't like that. I was just trying to forget everything.

"I'm the one who's sorry. The day got complicated, I ran out of battery, and I couldn't answer your message."

I felt even worse. "No, it's not your fault. Argh. You don't have to apologize for anything. I'm an idiot."

"Are we going to get into an argument over who is the guiltier or dumber of the two of us? I guarantee you that I have medals and hold first place on the podium. They're even thinking of naming a street after me that used to be called the 'fool of the day.'" He put his hands to my face.

I pretended to smile, but my eyes were full of worry. "I was out of my mind," I tried to justify myself. "I should have been more patient. I should have…"

"The only thing we owe each other is a long conversation. Do you think you can hold it in your condition?"

I looked at him with a frightened look. Did I *look* pregnant? I had lost weight! "What state do you mean?"

"Which one do you think? It's more than obvious that a certain sergeant wouldn't pass a breathalyzer test. I've never seen you dance like that before. I seem to remember you telling me you never danced."

Somewhere between relieved and embarrassed, I shrugged. "I just tried to forget."

"Forget me?" he asked with a black look in his eyes.

"Maybe," I confessed contritely. "Although it would have been impossible."

"I'm glad to hear that since I don't want you to do it. I wouldn't blame you for it because I'm not a paragon of virtue right now. However, I'm not going to push you into it, and I'm not going to make it easy for you."

His hands descended to my lower back and pulled me against him. His erection pressed against my abdomen, making me aware of his throbbing desire. The same desire that flowed through my loins, making me feel alive again.

I boldly breathed, "What if I told you that I want you to push me, not out of your life, but between my legs?" I purred, rubbing against him.

He growled, then grabbed my ass eagerly and devoured my mouth again.

How good he tasted! How well he kissed and how nicely he moved! Or was it me doing it against his knee?

I realized I had spread my thighs and sought relief by rubbing against him, not caring that we were in the middle of the dance floor. If a Latin song had been playing, I might have disguised it, but no, it was pop. It lit me up like the street lighting on the days before Christmas. God, I was rubbing myself like a cat in heat, and he wasn't slowing me down. Rather, he was spurring me on.

He bit my lower lip and tugged hard. They were not sweet kisses but stark hunger. I gasped and almost came against his thigh in one of my movements. Áxel's bent leg was the right place for me to act like a reggaeton diva.

He separated from me, his breathing erratic, but a need to satisfy the urgency spurred us on. I didn't question it when he pulled me with him, and after a maneuver that was unfair to those in line, he pushed me into the handicapped restroom, which was the only private place to finish what we had started.

We ignored the reproaches and booing behind our backs. He said it was a health emergency. To be honest, it *was* an emergency. If we had stayed on the dance floor, we would have set the place on fire with our flames.

As soon as we were in, he slammed me against the door and slid off the shoulders of my dress. It swirled around my feet.

"I knew it!" he exclaimed, taking my naked breasts into his mouth. Fingers tangled greedily in my hair.

I felt my body boiling. I wanted it everywhere, but especially inside, deep inside.

He had not shaved. The two-day stubble scratched my skin,

activating every cell, which responded by bristling. My gasps echoed, dulling the music that crept under the door. The pinkish marks of his teeth dotted my torso, etching the descent to the apex of my legs.

He removed my thong and knelt on the floor, leaving only my sandals on, to lift my leg over his shoulder and plunge his mouth between my folds.

I was unable to do anything but stare into those dark, searching eyes that watched my face.

"Touch yourself for me," he asked, running his tongue up and down.

"Is that an order, Sergeant?" I sighed, catching my lip between my teeth to silence the moan that was building in my throat.

"I'll say," he replied, quirking his lips in a roguish smile.

I had never touched myself in front of Dario, let alone been naked while he remained clothed and stared at me, but I felt like a porn actress or a dancer in a live sex show. I felt like doing it and making him as horny as I was. Would I be able to?

I brought one hand to my breasts and the other to the place from which he had removed his tongue.

"That's it, beautiful. Touch yourself for me." His mouth was glistening with my juices. He watched every movement, greedily absorbing it, and I, encouraged by the delight I saw in his eyes, grew bolder with every caress.

I pinched my nipple and inserted two fingers into my soaked sex, panting and curving my back, seeking greater friction with the underside of my palm.

"Don't close your eyes, Garbi. Look at me. I want to see how you offer me your pleasure. I want you to come for me."

That wasn't going to be difficult. I was so horny that any friction, no matter how slight, could catapult me to orgasm. "I want you for that."

"And you'll have me, but first, show me how much you missed

me. Show me how you touched yourself while thinking of me every night. You did, didn't you?"

I nodded, earning a wonderful smile from him.

"Well, because I used to touch myself too and come, dreaming of all the things I wanted to do to your beautiful body. You were my favorite time of the day because when night fell…"

My body was burning, my fingers were digging into me, and my nipples couldn't have been tighter. My hips were shooting up in front of my spectator, who was still holding my thigh over his shoulder so as not to miss any detail.

"That's it, beautiful. Move, and give yourself pleasure. Move for me."

I did. I squealed, letting myself go full out, howling loudly, noticing how he stood up to pull down his pants with alacrity, put on a condom, and take advantage of the last few throes of release to wedge himself between my legs.

It was like spreading butter on hot toast. He held my leg against my waist and pumped without letting my orgasm die. Oxygen barely filled my lungs from the intensity of what I was feeling. It mattered little if I died of love in his arms. It would have been a great death.

"Let's go for another one, beautiful. Tell me you're ready," he murmured in my ear, putting his free hand between our bodies to stimulate the sensitive, swollen knot.

I could not respond; I was too overwhelmed by the sensations. My vagina was contracting, squeezing him hard. I couldn't explain it, but the pleasure kept me chained to him, growing, expanding, making me gasp like a fish out of water.

"It's coming, I'm coming," I announced as the world fragmented and Áxel fragmented with it.

***

I caressed his bare chest on the bed.

The headboard in the other room was still banging loudly. I looked at Áxel, and he raised his eyebrows.

"Tomorrow, Paula won't be able to move. I hope you won't either," he murmured, pinching one of my breasts.

"I'll be happy," I confessed, rubbing my nose through the dark hair on his torso. Not that he had much hair, just enough. Soft dark streaks that made my skin tingle as I rode his hips and caressed him with my bare breasts.

After the episode in the bathroom, we decided the best thing to do was to go to the apartment. Lucas and Paula were thinking the same thing and didn't put up much of a fight.

We made love again in my room, this time more peacefully, while in the next room, a sex war broke out. I just hoped they didn't break anything, or we would forfeit the bond we had posted.

Our friends shouted so loudly that the crystals of the lamp above our heads threatened to shatter. I held back my laughter, and Áxel's chest heaved. Then there was silence.

"They have succeeded in crushing the enemy," remarked my bedmate.

"Rather, I think they crushed each other. Way to make the springs creak." I laughed.

"You're no slouch yourself. If you saw how you bounce on my hips when you ride me, you'd have a completely different opinion of yourself."

"Are you saying I'm a savage?"

"I'm saying that I love the way you ride me and those sweet tits fling themselves over my eyes." He pinched me again, and I smiled.

"As long as you like it, I'm satisfied."

"Are you kidding?" he asked, looking up at me. "If you need me to show you again how you turn me on, I guarantee it won't cost me anything to prove it to you."

"I believe you. Besides, you've left me completely satisfied for today." I sighed, a little bruised by the intensity of our desire.

"I'm glad. Do you think the time has come for you and me to talk?"

"I'm all ears," I proclaimed, fiddling with his flat nipple.

"If you do that, I won't be able to talk."

I smiled, gave it a playful lick, and put on a caring face. "All right, I'll stop now, my sergeant."

His fingers moved lazily up and down my arm. "There are too many things, but I want to start with one I think is fundamental. That is to apologize to you on behalf of Teresa."

"In her name or yours?"

"It doesn't matter. What she said was unfair."

"We all know that. You don't have to apologize on behalf of anyone. It wasn't your fault," I replied.

"Yes, I do. Claudia would have disowned her mother's performance. Teresa is angry at me. She blames me, and that's why she attacked you. Indirectly, I had a lot to do with what happened this morning."

"What I don't understand is how she knew who I was."

"That was my fault, too. She saw one of your messages while she was eating breakfast at the bar and figured it out. She doesn't hate you; she hates what you mean to me." Pain tightened his muscles, and I wanted to ease it.

"But you and Claudia had been separated for two years."

"For Teresa, that has nothing to do with it. She's always been a traditional woman. She goes to mass every Sunday," he clarified, "and for her, there is only the sacred bond of marriage. You know, what God has joined together, let no man put asunder."

"I understand that she is a believer. However, you told me Claudia was not happy either."

"She wasn't, but she idealized us, and I don't think she ever forgot about me. When they had the accident, Andrea confessed to me that she had a picture of us on her bedside table, and she kissed it every night. I swear I would have loved for her to have found another man who would have made her as happy as you make me."

"Oh," I said in a small voice.

"I had no idea that this was going on. Otherwise, I would have discussed it with her. From all the information I have been gathering, I think that, deep down, both Teresa and Claudia were hoping I would come back."

"And I came on the scene just in time to make things worse."

"You didn't make anything worse. Life can be a bitch sometimes. You don't need to say it. That woman is going to hate me for the rest of my life."

"My mother thinks she'll get over it eventually. By the way, my mother sends you her regards and wants you to know that she is very happy that my eyes are shining again, thanks to you."

I lifted my chin to look at him and chuckled. "You're making that up."

"Not at all. She insisted on staying with my daughter so I could look for you. Don't be scared, but she wants to meet you." he declared, which left me with my mouth open.

"Meet me?"

"I don't see another woman around here." He looked left and right. "Do you?"

I frowned. "Don't tease me."

"I'm not. I know we have been together for only a week or so, but I don't know how to explain it. I know it's you. I don't need anyone but you and my two children to make me happy."

I looked at him with a worried face as I thought of the baby growing in my belly. Where did he fit in that equation? And Ruben?

"I have a son, too," I blubbered.

"Excuse me. Ruben is also in the equation. Where there's room for two, there's room for three."

"What about four?" I muttered to myself.

"I'm overwhelming you," he remarked as he contemplated me.

"No, no, it's okay. I also think about a life with you. Remember, I was the first to propose that you come live in Tenerife."

"The offer still stands?"

"Of course."

"I'm glad, but I've been thinking about it, and I think the best thing would be for you to move here. Barcelona has many more possibilities. We could look for a house near here so you could gradually enter my children's lives and I, Ruben's. For the kids, this offers more possibilities than an island, and you can ask to be stationed here."

"What am I supposed to do with my son? I have joint custody."

"You might be granted full custody by your ex. Then my mother could lend a hand as a babysitter, and I could too."

"I don't want to take custody away from Dario. He may have been a terrible husband, but he adores our son. There are also his grandmothers and my sisters. I don't want them to stop seeing him, and my son wouldn't want to either."

We were both silent, immersed in our own thoughts. It was late, and my soul ached as much as my eyelids.

"We don't need to decide now. We just need to think about it. It's an idea we can't rush. We have time," he said, kissing my hair.

"I'm exhausted, and you must be too. What do you say we continue talking tomorrow? Maybe the pillow will whisper the answer."

"I'm fine with that," he murmured, kissing the crown of my head again. He pulled the sheet and blanket over us, and I snuggled in with the lullaby that echoed in my ear from his heart. "Rest."

That was the last thing I heard.

"Come on, sleepyheads. Get up at once!"

Someone was pounding on the bedroom door, and I knew from her voice that it was Paula.

"Leave them alone!" a man thundered, accompanied by her giggles. "Maybe they'd rather stay locked up in there. I think I'd prefer that too."

More giggles.

I blinked a couple of times and watched my sleeping beauty's eyelids open sluggishly.

"Hello, handsome."

"Hello, my Sergeant Tennis Player. Did you have a good rest?" I nodded and received a succulent good morning kiss. "I have to go to the bathroom to change my bag."

"Well, you'd better put something on. Paula and your friend are awake and eager for us to go out with them. They almost broke the door down."

"What do you want?" he asked suggestively, licking one of my nipples.

"If you do that to me, I can't make a coherent decision."

"What if I don't want you to make one?" He repeated the operation.

"Didn't you have to go to the bathroom?" I interrupted. If he kept lavishing that kind of attention on me, we would not get out of the room.

"Uh-huh, but I have time for a quick one."

I narrowed my eyes. "How fast?" Just looking at him, I was aroused. That fast. He turned me around, put me on all fours and penetrated me with an accurate thrust that stabbed me to the cervix.

His right hand rubbed my clitoris very hard. I had a terrible urge to pee and I think that increased my sensitivity because in two minutes, I burst on his hand, and he burst seconds later.

He kissed the bottom of my spine as he came out of me.

I could get used to this. "Me too," I mumbled, dropping down on the bed.

"Shit, I didn't wear a condom! I'm sorry."

"It's okay. I can't get pregnant anymore." I wasn't lying.

He laughed.

"Much better. A pregnancy at this point is what you and I were missing. I love that we can fuck as much as we want without worrying. You know my wigglers are inoperative, and I love doing it without a rubber separating us."

He bit one of my buttocks and sat up. I felt his seed flowing down my leg, and I wrapped myself in the sheet, not knowing what to say. I was about to tell him that he was wrong, that his sperm were more effective than those of an eighteen-year-old and my eggs were in full bloom, but I chose to remain silent. I was afraid of his reaction, so I swallowed my words and let the occasion pass. I wasn't sure I was ready to hear from his lips that he didn't want that child, and I had to abort.

Áxel put on a t-shirt and underwear, grabbed the bag with the spare clothes and winked at me. He told me he was going to take a shower.

I heard him greet Paula and Lozano.

My friend slipped into the room, adjusting the door without closing it. "I had to go out on the landing to reassure the neighbor that, if they were killing you, it was to get laid and that we had two Mossos and a civil guard inside. Not to worry, it was just sex, and good sex at that."

"Pig!" I insulted her by throwing a cushion at her, which hit her smiling face. "If the neighbor came, it's because you almost knocked down the building last night, and no one had hired a demolition company."

Paula threw herself on the bed, laughing.

"Why deny it? Lozano fucks with fear. These Mossos should be given a course on how to use the truncheon in depth."

I burst out laughing, and Paula turned sideways, looking at me suspiciously. "Everything all right between you two?"

I nodded.

"Well, I don't think so. Your eyes are a bit cloudy, and that wrinkle on your forehead says you've been thinking too much. What's wrong? Is he upset about the news? Hasn't he taken it well?"

"I didn't tell him."

"Why?"

"I still can't. He has a lot of problems with his son and ex-mother-in-law. The last thing he needs is for me to come to him with an unwanted pregnancy."

"How do you know if he wants it or not?"

"I know, and he doesn't need it now."

"It's not about what he needs. That baby is a fact, and the father has something to say about it."

"What if he doesn't want us to have it? Everything is very new, and the situation is not the best. I'm very afraid that he will ask me to have an abortion."

"You should have thought about it before. A pregnancy is a matter for two. He can't hide his head under his wing. If he doesn't want it and you do, we'll see to it that the baby lacks nothing."

"He's not the one hiding it!" I complained. "I don't have the nerve to drop a bombshell like that. What if I lose him forever when I tell him? I love the baby, but I love him too."

"Yeah, well, let's wait. You can always tell him that it's gas, and when he is born, you can tell him that he must be a descendant of Patufet."

"'Patufet?'"

"Yes. It's a traditional Catalan tale like *Tom Thumb*, only this boy is eaten by a cow because he hides in a cabbage and ends up getting out of the animal when it farts."

"You slut!"

"And you are a fool. Do what you want, but lies have very short legs."

"I have not lied."

"No, you've left out something that could change your lives, but you go about your business," she replied.

I snorted, and she gave me a more relaxed look. "We've come all this way so that you can clear things up and tell him things, not to spend four days fucking like rabbits and go back without telling him about his future paternity. Wake up, or I'm going to tell him."

"The one who tells what to whom?" asked Áxel's voice from the door.

I was startled to think he might have heard us, but from his relaxed face, he hadn't heard anything. Paula sat up, and I feared she might open her big mouth.

"It's not nice to listen to other people's conversations." She stood and looked at him defiantly.

"And the little secrets whispered in the ear are old-lady stuff."

"We were not whispering in each other's ears, and as you can see, there is not a single wrinkle in my complexion."

"But you were telling each other secrets."

"No, we were just knocking you down a peg for your lack of sexual libido. We hardly heard you last night."

He raised his eyebrows in amusement. "That's because you were screaming louder than Tarzan clinging to his vine."

"Stop with the swinging and make your Jane get up and take a shower. She needs it."

Áxel laughed. "All right. Meanwhile, entertain Cheetah before he peels the banana all by himself. He told me he's waiting for you in the room. How hard Tarzan's life is in the jungle! We'll give you twenty minutes. Then we'll leave. Understood?"

Paula looked at both of us. In her eyes was a warning. *Either you do it, or I do it.* I was convinced that this time, she was bluffing.

CHAPTER TWENTY-SIX

Hygge: Feeling of happiness in a cozy place.

Áxel

Pregnant. Garbiñe was pregnant.

I remained frozen for a few minutes, not knowing whether to enter or stay put. What should I do? What could I say to her? It's not that I wanted to spy. It's just that the door wasn't closed, and they weren't exactly softspoken.

I had arrived as Garbi told Paula that she hadn't told me because my wife had just died, and I couldn't get out of my stupor. The doctors had assured me that it was impossible for me to have any more children.

I had almost died from the amount of chemo I'd had, so having more offspring was the most improbable thing in the world. It was like expecting an anthill to survive a fire. But of course, the doctor didn't count on my abnormality within this disease. Weren't they studying my blood in the United States?

A father again! My God! I didn't know how to take the news, since I understood Garbiñe's fears. Fuck! How would I tell my children, who had just lost their mother? I would have been right in telling her that with the ones we had, we had enough.

Don't look at me with that face. I had no idea. The idea of her conceiving didn't even cross my mind. If I had used a condom, it would have been more for Garbi—to reassure her. It was done. A baby of hers and mine was growing in there.

Thousands of emotions circulated through my mind, from absolute fear to extreme happiness. Our child!

I was not a believer, but I thought life sent you things for a reason. If in this raffle I had a baby, I was not going to reject it. I had thought about it once with Andrea, and I couldn't be more sorry that the idea had crossed my mind. I adored my daughter, and I wouldn't want her not to exist, not for anything in the world.

I almost burst out laughing when Paula referred to the Patufet story. I found it funny that a Canary Islander knew that story. The best part was when she told Garbi that she would pass the pregnancy off as flatulence. That girl had wit. I smiled.

I understood that I hadn't made it easy for my sergeant to tell me, but I was going to do everything in my power to make her trust me enough to confide so important a thing. I did not want her to doubt my decision on the matter. It would be complicated but not impossible to achieve.

When I came in, Garbiñe was livid, and even more so with the question I asked since her character prevented her from telling me the good news point-blank. Paula left us alone. My pulse raced with excitement as I watched Garbiñe stand up, rolled up in the sheet, to get some clothes and take the shower she so urgently needed.

Surprisingly, I was excited. I didn't want to run away, just the opposite. I wanted to hug her and whisper that everything was going to be okay. I pressed her against me from behind, smelling the scent of sex still lingering on her smooth skin. She offered me a feeling of bliss in a cozy place.

"If you keep touching me like that, I'm not going to make it to the shower," she murmured as my hands reached for her breasts while she was reaching for a reindeer sweater.

"Is it Christmas?" I joked, admiring the garment she had chosen.

"Don't even think of laughing. In the Canary Islands, it's always hot, and the only warm clothes I have is my collection of Christmas sweaters, which my mother insists on adding to every year. I've been getting the same gift since I was thirteen."

He chuckled under his breath. "And does she give Pili and Mili the same?"

"No, they are more into makeup."

"I see. I think you're going to look beautiful with that pair of reindeer and their red noses, especially since what they cover is wonderful." My hands went to her belly.

She shrank back, and I was able to keep my hands on that special place where our son was growing. She didn't say anything. She just stood very still, holding her breath.

I kissed her neck and pulled away.

"I'll be quick, I promise," she whispered, turning around with trembling lips.

Banging came from the next room, followed by gasps.

"The banana and Cheetah have given you a twenty-minute head start. Take advantage of it." We smiled in complicity and kissed before she disappeared through the door.

We strolled around Barcelona, knowing how Paula was dying to ask questions. She insisted on posing the four of us for crazy selfies.

We stopped at a terrace for breakfast, and although it was cold because it was winter, we were very comfortable, thanks to the outdoor stoves. Paula didn't have to go outside to smoke, and we could chat quietly while watching the passersby.

The girls ordered hot chocolate and sponge cake, and Lozano and I ordered long coffees and sandwiches. After so much wear and tear, I was hungry.

"Since when do you order chocolate?" Paula questioned her friend. "As far as I know, it's not too good for your migraine."

"I don't know. I just feel like it today."

"Maybe you're craving it," I encouraged, watching with amusement when they opened their eyes like saucers.

"Or maybe you've given her such bad sex that she's looking for a substitute in her cup," Paula scolded.

"I didn't hear any complaints last night or this morning," I boasted.

"It's just that I feel like something sweet. There's no need to make a big deal out of it," Garbi protested irritably.

I reached for her neck and kissed her. "Relax, honey. We're just kidding."

"You say you have headaches?" Lucas asked.

"Yes, they are terrible. When I get migraines, I'm not a person. I've been locked up in the dark for almost a week."

He narrowed his eyes. "You've never thought of wearing an earring?"

"I already wear two." She stroked her pierced earlobes. "But only on special occasions."

"I don't mean those but a special one for migraines. My mother had the same problem as you, and since she got them, she hasn't had one. It's called a daith piercing, and it's placed in the inner cartilage of the pinna. Here." Lucas gestured at his ear.

Garbiñe made a pained face. "There? I'm not a big fan of piercings."

"You don't know what you're missing. I just tried one that made me crazy." Paula licked her lips.

Lucas repositioned himself in the chair, and I laughed because

I knew what kind of earring my friend was wearing in her intimate area.

"As I was saying," Lucas continued, "she's been using it for a few months, although it's a new method. My mother was very reluctant, but the pain was so severe that she finally gave in. She doesn't regret her decision."

"Do you know where to have it done?" asked my sergeant, curious.

"They do it in the same place I got mine done. They are very professional. Do you want me to call and ask them if they have any openings?"

Garbi shrugged and looked at me sideways. "What do you think?"

"Well, if it can help you, you don't lose anything, and if it doesn't work, just take the earring off, and that's it. It's not like a tattoo either. Those are forever. However, it is your ear, and no one should decide for you or make decisions that involve your body. You will always have the last word in everything, and I will respect your decisions."

Paula looked at me suspiciously. I had a feeling the redhead suspected I knew.

"All right, call," Garbi told Lucas, lacing her fingers through mine.

"If she gets an appointment to get her ear pierced, try to get an appointment for me, too," Paula suggested. "I think I'm going to get that nipple piercing you suggested."

"You're going to pierce your nipple?" howled Garbiñe, slamming her hand on the table, which made the crockery shake.

"Yes. Lucas says that it greatly increases sensitivity. After having played with the one he has, Cheetah trusts her banana."

"'Cheetah?' He said that before." Garbi was amused.

"Uh-huh. He's Tarzan, you're Jane, and that's my banana over there."

Garbiñe rolled her eyes, and I laughed.

"I don't know how you can say such things in public," my sergeant reprimanded Paula.

"Because I'm not a prude like you, who does dirty things and doesn't speak of them. The walls of the apartment howl by themselves, and you looked like a vacuum cleaner."

Garbi turned red. Lucas took out his cell phone and got ready to call. A few minutes later, he told us that they both had an appointment in four and a half minutes, so could we get a move on?

We finished breakfast with alacrity and headed for the piercing place, which was not exactly around the corner.

<hr>

The place looked clean, and the man looked professional. I was thankful that he wasn't a rough, dirty-looking guy with tattoos up to his eyebrows. I know tattoos don't mean anything, but I'd seen too many guys in jail flaunting them.

"I'm going to put a banana on you," said the guy, who was no more than thirty years old.

"No, no, I don't want a banana. I want one of those migraine piercings. He's the one with the banana," Garbiñe muttered, pointing at Lucas. Her hands were sweating, and she was very agitated.

The tattoo artist laughed. "Yes, I know he's the one with the banana, I put it on him too, but I was referring to the type of piercing. I can't put an earring in at the moment. I'll put one of these on you," he showed her the object, "which is called a banana because of its curved shape."

Garbiñe reddened to the roots of her hair, and Paula laughed like crazy.

"I'm sorry. I'm very nervous."

"It's all right. Everyone here knows what your friend has in her nethers by now," I clarified.

"Don't worry. It won't hurt, I promise. You're in good hands," the man reassured Garbi.

It took one minute for the guy to pierce her ear with a kind of cannula and emplace a curved bar with two small balls at the ends. "I've left it a little long and loose so it doesn't bother you or swell. In a month, you will be able to change it for another one. There are some beautiful designs out there. However, this one suits you very well, doesn't it?"

The man looked at me, and I admitted that I thought it was a very sexy earring.

"Now we're going to get mine," Paula announced.

"Are you sure you want to get a boob pierced?" Garbi taunted.

"I'm very sure, and if I like the result, I may have it done on the other."

"Well, let's get to it because I have another customer coming in."

"We're going out to give you privacy," I announced, going to the front of the store with Garbi.

"Did it hurt?" I asked, pressing her body against mine.

"No, it was a little annoying, but nothing that couldn't be endured. I'll keep my fingers crossed that it works. Paula is brave. Look at her nipple piercing."

"She's a little crazy. She excites him."

"I don't?"

I provoked her by biting her lip. "You excite me, that's for sure. You don't know how glad I am to be here and know that we are well. I was beating my head on the wall. I know you weren't there to explain, but the ideas that one can come up with are the worst. That's why it's best to say things and not keep them inside. Shared sorrows are less painful, and the joys are much better," I murmured, squeezing her tighter. "I don't want you not to tell me things for fear of my reactions or carry worries on your shoulders that I could alleviate with a simple reply."

She hesitated.

Tell me, I begged inwardly.

"That's it. Do you want to see it?" Paula shouted, sticking her head out from behind the curtain. That put an end to the possibility of a confession.

"I think we can live without it," Garbiñe said.

"Maybe you can, but I can't." I went to open the curtain, but she stopped me.

"Don't even think about it. I don't want Áxel to have nightmares about your twin balloons."

"I agree, but keep them inside. You'll show them to me when we're alone."

"You're old-fashioned. I always go topless on the beach. I don't think Áxel will be very surprised."

"Maybe not, but I'd rather not think of your tits every time I look at your face."

Paula burst out laughing. "Okay, fine, but you should get one too. I'm sure he'd love it." She nodded at me.

"For the time being, he'll have to settle for this one." She pointed at her ear.

"You're missing out."

"Thank goodness your father won't see it. Lord Carrington would have a stroke if he saw your pierced tit."

Paula rolled her eyes. "I'm too old to be affected by that kind of thing. Besides, my father threw in the towel with me many years ago. He knows I'm not into being a lady. I'm coming out now. You can go on shooting your mouths off."

Garbi had touched a sore point her friend did not like.

"Lady?" I asked once she had disappeared.

"Uh-huh. Although it may not seem so, her father is an English nobleman. On a trip to the Canaries, he fell in love with Paula's mother, and they married. He built a hotel empire. He doesn't have to lift a finger if he doesn't want to. He could live off the proceeds."

"A Paris Hilton in the making."

"Don't tell her that. She can't stand the blonde, even though they have more in common than she admits. They are both rebels without a cause."

"Well, knowing what she might be, I'd rather your friend be an unscrupulous journalist than a spoiled little girl from the English gentry obsessed with teatime."

"I see her more as the Red Queen in *Alice in Wonderland*. Paula loves that movie, especially when she exclaims, 'Off with their heads!'" She came back to my lips to kiss me again.

Once we left the store, we approached the port area. My friend Carles called me asking permission to take Andrea to L'Aquàrium. He thought it would distract her and make her sadness more bearable.

I would not have enough lives to give thanks to the friends who had helped me.

Yesterday, while I was on my way to the bar, I called him from the car to tell him I intended to go talk to Garbiñe and that my mother was staying with my daughter. He encouraged me to do so, reminding me that my relationship with Claudia had been dead for more than two years and that it was over long before that. According to him, I could be sad because she had been a very important woman in my life, but the sorrow I felt should not limit my actions or thoughts about Garbi.

Of course, I gave him permission. He was the girl's godfather, and they adored each other.

We agreed that he would take her out to lunch and then to look at the fish that fascinated her so much. We would meet at the door of L'Aquàrium at seven in the evening to pick her up.

On the promenade, they had set up craft stalls that the girls wanted to look at. Sausages, clothes, toys, and handmade jewelry were a delight to the senses.

I stopped at one that sold pendants for pregnant women. It was a little ball with an object inside that made it chime. The chain was long, so it would fall to the mother's abdomen and it could be adjusted depending on the stage of gestation. It was silver. According to the explanation on the sign, that chime would soothe the baby in the womb, along with the voice of his parents. Once born, it could be put on him or her and be a familiar sound that would calm him or her.

Garbi had gone ahead, stopping at a stop where they sold handmade handbags.

"Would you like one?" the sales clerk asked, snapping me out of my reverie. I had my eye on a pendant with a green stone. I glanced sideways at Garbiñe, who was still interested in handbags.

"Yes, give me that one, please."

"It's beautiful, isn't it? Your wife will love it. The stone is chrysoberyl. It brings tranquility and helps us to believe in ourselves by increasing our confidence. In addition, it attracts optimism and hope; hence it is the ideal stone to wear when starting something new."

"If there was any doubt in my mind that it was the perfect one, you just cleared it up. I want it."

"I'm glad. Shall I gift wrap it for you?"

I smiled to myself, thinking of Garbiñe's face when she opened my surprise. "Yes, please, and do it quickly before I get caught." I winked at her, and she laughed.

"It won't take long."

"Buying a necklace for a pregnant woman? Have you gotten one of them pregnant and didn't tell us about it?" The female voice that reached my ear shook me from head to toe. I turned around to find Paula staring at me with suspicion. If I had thought she suspected I was up to date, there was no longer any doubt in my mind.

"I just liked it. I think the color is perfect for Garbi, don't you?"

"Ummm. How long have you known?"

I shrugged. "Since I heard you this morning."

"Wow. You never cease to amaze me."

"I hope for the best."

"I hope so, too. So far, you're on the right track, Sergeant Deodorant. I hope you're the kind that lasts and not the kind that quits when you get a little sweaty."

"What do you think?" Her viper's tongue amused me.

"With you, I'd rather not risk it. What's at stake is the happiness of my friend, and even if I like you, I will always be on her side and look out for her happiness. I know life has been a bitch to you, and I'm sorry, but for me, that's no excuse for you to hurt her. Think about what you are going to do and act accordingly. Garbi doesn't deserve to have a bad time again, and she's too caught up in you."

"I will not fail you or her."

"I hope not. Now pay. I approached you to alibi you and make sure you understand the importance of the decision you make in this regard."

"Completely, and I love that you are so protective of her. I guarantee you that you don't have to be. I want her to be happy too."

"We'll see about that. For now, I'll give you the benefit of the doubt, but I'll keep an eye on you."

I paid, and we walked away. It was not the only purchase I made. With Paula's help, I bought a cuddly stuffed animal and a tiny Superman onesie, perfect for our little boy.

Paula packed everything into her gigantic purse. Good thing she was one of those women who carried an XXL bag.

With so much walking, we got hungry and went to eat at Hotel Front Maritim, a beautiful restaurant located on the sea. The views were spectacular, and although we preferred to go inside because it was cold, the panoramic windows offered a delightful landscape.

We ordered some starters to share, and for the main course, black rice with cuttlefish and scallops.

The four of us seemed to fit together perfectly because, even though Paula seemed like a difficult woman, I found her funny and knew her background was good.

We spent the meal joking and telling anecdotes, and for the first time in many days, I felt calm. I looked at Garbi, who was laughing. Her eyes were shining, and she seemed to be happy. I would have liked to freeze time and for us to have stayed there forever, calm and relaxed, in a bubble of smiles and good warmth.

We were having coffee when I told her. "I want you to sleep in my apartment tonight."

She gasped. "What about your daughter?"

"I will tell her that you are a friend."

"I don't think she'll buy it. She saw and heard everything your ex-mother-in-law told me."

"Children are simpler than we think, and Andrea is on my side. I want you to come with me. I need to make the most of these days, and I need us to get to know each other. I need you to be as sure of me as I am of you. I need you to know that I'm serious, and I can't think of a better way to do it than asking you to come home with me," I confessed, stroking her hand.

"I don't know what to say."

"Say yes. Just let yourself go. We will find the best way for all of us to be together. I don't plan to leave you, abandon you, or end this relationship. I want you in my life now and always."

I had said it without hesitation, not caring that our friends were spectators to the intimate moment. She hesitated, but in the end, she nodded. I sought her sweet mouth to seal our pact.

"Tonight, you, me, and a good sex marathon, Lozano," Paula burst out.

"You bet, even if I have to go to work without sleep."

"Don't worry about it. I'm going to keep your flagpole up all night. I'm an expert at it."

The two of them laughed in complicity and kissed each other.

We paid the bill and went back to the apartment to pick up Garbi's stuff.

"Pack your suitcase and take it all with you. See you at the airport in two days at eleven o'clock. Don't be late," Paula warned, taking Garbiñe's clothes out of the closet.

"Two days to myself?" I asked, raising my eyebrows and looking at the redhead. "Are you sure?"

"Don't make me regret it, Montoya. Today you made points. I give my girl permission to spend the time we have left with you, but take care of her, and don't fail me," she said, wrinkling her nose.

"Are you sure?" Garbi asked, not believing her friend's words. "We came here together, and I feel bad about leaving you behind."

"You're not letting me down, and I'm sure. You have a lot of things to talk about. You should resolve them before you go back to the island. Besides, I plan to have a great time with Lucas, and when he's not around, I have plans on the side. You know I wanted to go visit my friend and see some of the sights of the city. Don't worry about me. I can take care of and entertain myself."

"I have no doubt. Thank you for being such a good friend."

Garbi squeezed her.

My phone rang, interrupting the show of affection. It was my mother, who invited us to dinner. I decided not to say anything to Garbi. I went to the living room to talk to her so it would be a surprise for my girl. I had no doubt that she would fit right in with my family.

CHAPTER TWENTY-SEVEN

Cafuné: Stroking someone's hair with affection.

<u>Garbiñe</u>

"Are you sure your daughter is going to take this well?" Áxel was looking for a parking space in the lot closest to L'Aquàrium. I was distressed, thinking about how rough it must have been for that little girl to have me cross her path.

Maybe I had been too hasty in saying yes, and the most practical thing would have been for me to stay in Barcelona while he went back to the apartment with the child.

"Andrea is not like her brother. She is a very open child. She won't make things difficult for you, you'll see. My little girl adores me."

"I don't mean that. I don't question her adoration for you, but she just lost her mother, and that's a terrible tragedy. It makes the most sense for her to grieve with you and not for me to be there."

Áxel stopped the engine once he parked the vehicle. "I understand what you are telling me and it may be hasty, but either you come with us, or I won't be able to go down to Barcelona for these two days. I live seventy-five kilometers away. It's not exactly around the corner. My daughter has to go to school tomorrow, and I don't know how it is in Tenerife, but here they go from nine to one and three to five. Besides that, she has extracurricular activities."

"I don't know if your daughter will be well enough to go to class."

"According to my mother, she is sad, yes, but she needs to get back to normal. At home, she will only sink deeper. Being entertained and with her friends will do her good. Andrea is a tough girl like me. She's not the typical kid who gets upset about everything. She has a lot of emotional maturity. Sometimes I think she and Christian live in opposite bodies."

"Every child is different," I chided him.

"Of course. It's not that I don't love my son, don't get me wrong. It's just that sometimes his immaturity and excessive sensitivity overwhelm me."

I stroked his arm. "Give him time."

"I'm doing it. I confess I've been thinking all morning about the best option, and if I thought inviting you home would have been bad for Andrea, I wouldn't have done it." He offered her a shy smile.

"I'm not going to object. You're her father, so you know what she's like. If I have said this to you, it is because I don't want you to have a harder time or a rift to open up between you."

"I thank you, but it won't happen, don't worry. Tell me something, is it for another reason? Don't you like the idea?"

"The idea of spending time with you delights me. There is nothing but my concern that this is not the right thing to do."

Áxel looked at me tenderly and squeezed my thigh. "Relax. If I thought your presence would be a problem for her, I wouldn't have asked you to come. I need you by my side. You don't know how much."

I smiled at him. I needed him too, even if I didn't tell him as often as he told me.

His thumb caressed my cheek, and then he pulled me close for a kiss.

Áxel's kisses were like soft and sweet summer rain, the kind that soaks your clothes and skin without you realizing it. When you do realize it, it's too late since the fine drops have turned into an agonizing storm that sweeps you inside.

My tongue craved his, and my moans were enveloped by his. We were an accumulation of fingers and braided need that did not seek to unravel.

At the tattoo store, I had come close to confessing to him that I was pregnant. If Paula hadn't interrupted us, I would have. I'm sure by now you're thinking I'm a screwup, and in a way, you're right. I'm not denying it. In my defense, I can only say that I'm terrified of losing him, and although I had to tell him, I needed to find the right moment. I'm not like Paula, who would have stood up to him and thrown the pregnancy tests in his face as soon as she saw him.

"Ready?" he asked me, distancing himself from my eager mouth.

"Let's get to it," I replied, pulling the handle to get out. If he saw this as the right thing, who was I to contradict him? You have to take life as it comes, even if it's not easy.

We arrived outside of L'Aquàrium, a gigantic circular building located in Port Vell, right next to the Maremagnum.

The smell of salt was in my nostrils, and we were surrounded by water, yet the smell of the sea did not remind me of Tenerife. Maybe it was due to the environmental pollution. I don't know; it was just different.

People strolled distractedly, chatting and smiling. Couples, friends, and entire families that made me remember how I had felt at points in my life when my father was still alive, and my sisters were little. Now it was different. My distance from my mother and sisters hurt me.

Many times I got upset, thinking that I was a bad daughter for being so different. I didn't visit them much, and when I did, it was more out of commitment than because I wanted to.

Pilar and Milagros had teased me since they had learned how to do it, and when I ignored them, they teased me more. They found in me the perfect target. They were popular, and I was not. We looked like the daughters of different fathers. Who knows, maybe we were? Since I'd discovered my mother cheating on my father, I couldn't get it out of my head that maybe Cristóbal was not the only one. I had never talked to her about that incident, not even when my father died. Maybe it was never the right time to do it, or maybe I thought dirty laundry should stay where it is.

My breathing had quickened, and my palms were sweating, even though it was cold. We were getting closer, and I could see Áxel's friend in the distance.

We walked together without touching. I didn't think it was appropriate to arrive in front of Andrea like a couple in love. He didn't make any attempt to touch me either, and I was grateful for that since it would have made me more nervous than I was.

We met Carles, who was wearing a black wool coat and a smile that was not reflected in his eyes. He looked distressed, although he tried to hide it with a carefree manner.

Next to him, Andrea was hugging a stuffed dolphin that looked new. He must have bought it for her as a gift.

Áxel's daughter gave us a full scan. Her expression was not cheerful, and my spine felt like it was about to snap in two since I was so tense. No one would blame her for looking at me like Snow White's hated stepmother. She had met me at her mother's funeral in shattering circumstances.

"Hello, princess," her father greeted her as we approached. He bent to her level to kiss her cheeks lovingly.

"Hello," she replied, accepting the gesture.

Carles looked at each of us serenely, hugged his friend to greet him, and gave me a couple of kisses.

"I want to introduce you to someone," Áxel continued in a neutral tone.

She turned her clear eyes toward him. They were beautiful, almost crystal blue like her grandmother's.

"I know her. She's the one who was there when we buried Mom. The one grandma kept shouting at, saying she was your lover." Áxel held his breath at the term, and so did I. "Is she your girlfriend? Vicky's father had one of those, and her mother got very angry. Vicky explained to me that's why her mother threw her father's clothes out the window. After that, her father never came back."

God, how direct. I was afraid of something like that.

"Andrea, your mother and I have been separated for two years. It's not the same."

"Yes, I know that. Is she your girlfriend or not?"

Áxel swallowed hard. I was about to tell her I was a friend, but he stepped forward.

"Yes, she is. Garbiñe and I started a relationship before the accident happened. Neither of us knew what was going to happen to Mom."

"I don't like that name. It's weird and ugly. I also don't like that you lied to me when I asked you if we were going to be a family again, and you said yes."

"It wasn't the time to tell you. It's not that I wanted you to think I was going back to Mom. It's just that I didn't want to add to your worries. I could have cut you off when you asked me if we were going to be a family again, but I didn't feel I should. I'm sorry, daughter."

Andrea nodded.

"Yeah, adults lie a lot. Vicky told me not to get my hopes up when I went back to school and told her you were going back to Mom. She didn't believe you, and I didn't either."

"I…"

"Let it go, Dad. It's always the same. You parents think that because we are children, we don't know anything and don't understand things. You got tired of Mom just like I got tired of my whale stuffed animal, the one we gave to Cousin Susana when she was born two weeks ago. Now my godfather has given me this dolphin."

"Honey, I didn't exchange your mother for Garbiñe. Our relationship ended because we only loved each the way you love Vicky, as friends."

"She didn't. She always said it was you, and that's why she kissed your picture every night. But whatever. You have a new dolphin now."

I was having a terrible time. What reasoning that baby had!

"I love you very much, Daddy, but I didn't like it when you lied to me. You don't like lies, and neither do I. If she's your new cuddly toy, just tell me, and that's it."

The two of us were speechless. The girl snorted and came straight to me.

"Hi, I'm Andrea."

"I am Garbiñe, the dolphin," I joked without much success. I was too nervous to get the words right. "I'm sorry about your Mom, and I want you to know that I'm not going to lie to you. I have no intention of replacing your mother, but I love your father, and I would like you to give me a chance to make him happy. We'll go slowly, and I'll try to get to know you if you'll let me. It's a very difficult time right now. We'll go at your pace, okay?"

"What a farce," she said.

"If you have trouble with my name, you can call me Garbi."

"I prefer Dolphin." She was testing me. I could see it in her eyes.

"That's good. I love dolphins. In Tenerife, there are many. If you come, we can go out to the open sea to see them in the wild."

The little girl's eyes widened. "Are there wild dolphins?"

"Yes, it is wonderful to see them."

Andrea looked up at her father. "Can we go? They are my favorite animals."

I had hit the right note. And having her call me by the name of her favorite animal rather than disappointing me cheered me up a little.

"We'll see. If everything goes well, maybe we can plan a getaway at Easter if Garbiñe feels like it and you two understand each other. It would be good to start by learning her name if you want her to invite you."

Andrea shifted her gaze from her father to me. "That seems fair."

Áxel smiled at the little girl, and I felt we had cleared a hurdle.

After the first uncertain feelings, Carles lightened the situation by telling us everything they had seen inside the aquarium. He and Andrea took turns relating what they had read about the species that swam in the aquarium.

Áxel thanked him for making his daughter's day more bearable, and we said goodbye in the parking lot. He had left his car there, too.

Once we were in our vehicle, Áxel blurted the news. "Grandma asked us to come to dinner with her."

I hadn't known. He had told me his mother wanted to meet me, but not today when I was wearing the damn reindeer sweater. If I had known, I would have asked him to stop at the mall to buy something more suitable.

"Okay. Then I can show the stuffed animal to Grandma."

I looked at Áxel questioningly. I wasn't going to get on his case in front of his daughter. His eyes shone with amusement. What a bastard he was. He knew I wouldn't make a spectacle of myself in front of the little girl.

"Garbi will be here for two days. I told her she could come to the apartment with us and sleep in Chris' room. That way, you can get to know each other. What do you think?"

Andrea looked at him. She reminded me so much of him in her expressions and the way she faced him. "Do you want me to come?"

"Yes, of course," he answered.

"Well, that's it. Let's go. I'm hungry. I haven't had a snack."

Andrea ended the conversation by curling up in the back seat. She hadn't let go of the stuffed animal, which she squeezed as if her life depended on it. I felt sorry for her, so small and without her mother. Happiness had been taken away from both of them. It was not fair.

Even though I had lost my father when I was older, I felt his absence the same way—that lack of someone who had been everything to me. If Andrea had let me, I would have sat with her, let her rest her head on my shoulder, run my hand through her beautiful hair, and filled it with caresses. Even if in mourning, there was no comfort, I wanted to infuse her with the warmth she lacked. We were so close and so far away at the same time that it made me angry to see her and not be able to do anything to lighten her burden.

No one deserves the pain of losing a loved one, especially when you are a child. Such situations undermine innocence and make you leave a world wrapped in rainbows and glitter and show you the ugliest and darkest parts. If only we could always live wrapped in that halo of protection and keep that belief that nothing bad would ever happen to us.

I continued to watch her in the mirror. She pressed her forehead to the window and raised her eyes to the sky, searching for the brightest star in the firmament.

A tear hung on her rounded cheek, and her shoulders shook. I had to keep myself from wiping her face and hugging her, even if she pushed me away. Andrea was suffering silently behind that tough-girl pose.

I looked away, giving her space. I didn't like to be seen crying either. I tried to do it as she did, in silence if there were people who could notice. I felt bad for having imposed my presence on her and not thinking that my arrival in Barcelona could lead her to discover a part of her father's life she was not ready for. I should have thought things through and done them differently.

Now there was no turning back, neither for my pregnancy nor for my inclusion in Áxel's family. I only hoped things would gradually get better.

If I'd thought the dinner was going to be uncomfortable, I would have been dead wrong. Áxel's mother Gloria turned out to be a delight. Her jovial and carefree manner reminded me very much of her son's. She was tremendously nice, and her husband was also.

She did not prepare a pretentious dinner. Quite the contrary. On a floral tablecloth, she placed bread with sliced tomatoes, cold meats, some salads, and snacks. What a difference from my mother, who always pretended to be on top with her sophisticated French casseroles.

At no time did she refuse to let me help her. She invited me to take an active part in the kitchen, and that was a great relief. Feeling integrated from the beginning, that I was part of something, that they opened their arms to me without question, was a balm in every sense of the word.

Gloria was a vital woman who went out of her way for her children. She was a laugher. She loved jokes, and between her and her husband, I noticed that there was still love, the kind I thought my parents had for each other, full of tenderness and respect.

Now, seeing them so close, you could perceive the signs. Those complicit glances, their shared smiles, those looks. Not to mention the way she caressed him whenever she could without hiding, the veiled communication their glances offered each other, or the affection with which they spoke to each other.

Yes, Gloria and Martin had the kind of marriage I coveted. The kind that every girl dreams of and very few achieve.

Andrea was still reticent, but as the couple kept asking me questions, she listened with interest to everything I said about my island. She even questioned me on a couple of occasions. Bless childish curiosity.

"So, you live on a volcano? she asked, interrupting my story about the marvelous views from the top of Mount Teide.

"On an island that has a volcano, yes."

"And it doesn't scare you?"

"No." I smiled.

"But it can explode, and you can die!"

The child was very sensitive on the subject of death, so I responded tactfully.

"It has been one hundred and eleven years since the volcano erupted. That gives me peace of mind. Besides, death is part of life. We never know where we are going to find it or at what moment. We have to learn that it is part of us, and everything has a beginning and an end. At the end of the day, our essence and the beautiful things we did in this world will remain. Like you and my son Ruben."

"My father was about to die, and my mother…" She fell silent. "Well, you know."

"Yes, I know." Everyone was listening to our conversation. I didn't want to make a mistake. It was a good moment for both of us. "My father also died a few years ago, and I had a very hard time, as you are going through now. Losing someone feels like nothing else."

She kept holding my gaze.

"Oh, I'm sorry," Gloria murmured apologetically.

"Thank you. The worst thing was that I couldn't say goodbye.

It was sudden, and I didn't have time to get used to the idea, although he knew I loved him very much." My eyes watered whenever I thought of him. "In the afternoon, we went to see him. My son was there as usual, crawling around, while Dad told him anecdotes about me as a child. My son loved it, and the next morning, he was gone."

"What happened to him?" Andrea asked, resting her chin on her hands.

"Andrea," her father scolded, "it's not polite to ask such questions."

"It's all right," I replied calmly. "He had a heart attack. No one expected it since he had no coronary disease."

"What is coronary? Does it have to do with a crown? Was your father a king?"

"No." She seemed so grownup in her reasoning that I forgot there were terms she might not yet have mastered. "Coronary refers to the heart. My father was the king of his house. He was a civil guard, like me."

Andrea narrowed her gaze.

"Do you know what the *Guardia Civil* is?"

"Yes. They wear a weird hat called a unicorn, even though it's black. My father gives them Taser lessons."

"The hat is a tricorn," Áxel corrected with a hint of a smile. "People don't usually wear unicorns on their heads. Tell us what your father told your son about when you were little."

I looked at him sideways. "Well, when I was a little girl, I was given a Superman costume. At that time, we lived in Léon, in a small apartment with a window overlooking a courtyard."

Oh, God, I could see it. Gloria crossed herself, and I smiled and went on with the story.

"My neighbor's child, who was a piece of junk a couple of years older than me, told me that if I put on the suit, I could fly out the window and wave to all the neighbors who were looking out."

"For God's sake!" Gloria exclaimed. "Don't tell me you jumped, just like my son from the tree."

I nodded, showing them the lower part of my chin, where there was a barely noticeable mark. At the time, it was worse than the slaughter of a pig.

"You see, Mom?" Áxel raised one fisted hand and put the other on his waist. "We are predestined by Superman."

"It seems so. I can imagine your parents' distress. How awful! When my Áxel threw himself from that tree, I wanted to die. At the wrong time, they brought him that suit from the United States. I still remember him bringing it back with a serious look on his face and asking for it to be returned because it didn't work. That anecdote haunts him like the ghost of Christmas."

We all burst out laughing. Even Andrea raised the corners of her mouth.

"I'm sorry to interrupt, but it's late. My daughter has to go to school tomorrow, and we have a long way to go."

"That's right, son. I'm sorry. It's just that I was having such a nice time that I forgot about the time and that it's the middle of the week."

"Let me help your mother clear the table, and we'll be on our way."

"No, daughter, no. There are four plates. Martin and I will pick them up. We have nothing else to do. You've done enough. I'll settle for you stopping by on the way to the airport."

"I don't know if we'll have time, Mom," Áxel warned.

"If we have time, I promise I will come," I said, eager to see her again. "It was a pleasure dining with you," I added, rising from my chair.

"For us too. Thank you for accepting our invitation, but above all, for coming now. It means much more than you think."

Her confession made me feel good. It lightened the feeling that I had done something wrong. We looked at each other fondly, and I gladly accepted the embrace in which I was enveloped.

An hour later, we entered Áxel's house.

It was no big deal—a simple four-room apartment, austere and masculine. Andrea was asleep in the arms of her father, who took her to her room and tucked her in next to the dolphin.

I stood in the hallway and stared at them.

He covered her with the blanket, making sure she wouldn't get cold. Then he stroked and kissed her hair lovingly.

Without sitting up, she brought her lips close to his ear and whispered something so softly and intimately that it almost made me cry to watch them.

With a last kiss on her temple, he sat up, walked on his toes so he didn't make noise, and closed the door behind him so as not to disturb her with the sound of our voices. He grabbed me by the waist, and I put my arms around his neck.

"You have a wonderful child."

"I'm glad you think so. I must admit that at L'Aquàrium, I doubted whether I had done the right thing when I saw her reaction, but you handled it in a masterful way. I'm going to give you the medal of merit for knowing how to deal with a little girl who's a bit of a tomboy." He kissed me sweetly.

"I tried to put myself in her place. I've done nothing more than that. It's not an easy situation for her."

"That's why I'm going to award you two medals instead of one. No, three, because you've got my parents in your pocket too. If Andrea hadn't had school, they wouldn't have let us leave."

"Your parents are great. The credit goes to them. You have an enviable family."

"I'm not going to contradict you on that. I have wonderful parents. Are you tired?" he asked, putting his hands on my back to hold me close to him.

"It's been an intense day," I acknowledged. "And you?"

"Well, I thought I'd show you my room, the place in which I've had a date with you every night for the past few months. What do you say?" His eyebrows rose mischievously.

"Wasn't I going to sleep in Christian's room?"

"Who said anything about sleeping? I was thinking of something much more active, like a sightseeing tour before I take you to your room to sleep like a good little girl."

"Oh, I see. Well, you know what? I really want you to give me a tour of your bed. Mmm, I'm going to do a tour of your body, blondie," I said. "Andrea won't wake up?"

"She sleeps like a log," he muttered hoarsely.

"I'm feeling the log right in my belly."

He smiled. "Let's see if you chain yourself to it like that weird woman."

"I don't see myself chained to your trunk, shouting, "No logging!"

Áxel burst out laughing.

"Have I ever told you that I love you?"

"Not enough," I replied, turning up my nose.

"Well, let me prove it to you." He kissed me in a way that tasted like forever.

CHAPTER TWENTY-EIGHT

Emuná: Being calm despite not having all the answers.

<u>Áxel</u>

"Dad, what's this?" Andrea asked, emptying the contents of the bag that I swore I had left safely out of sight.

The pendant was wrapped. The stuffed animal too, but the Superman onesie had no wrapping because the stall was full when I bought it, and I didn't want Garbiñe coming up on me. I just paid for it and put it in the bag I had hidden in Paula's purse, thinking I would find the time to wrap it in the apartment. I didn't count on Andrea's curiosity making her open the bag.

"They are gifts. Leave them in their place."

"I know they're gifts. They're wrapped, except for this. Who are they for?"

I had promised her that I would not lie to her again. However, Garbi had not yet told me the news, and telling my daughter without talking to her seemed wrong.

I did something I was great at: distraction. I had to focus my daughter's attention elsewhere.

"We're going to be late for school. It's enough for you to know that they're not for you, Miss I-want-to-know-it-all," I said, putting everything back and taking the bag to leave it in my room before Garbi came out of the bathroom and caught us. "Have you finished breakfast?" I asked, returning to the living room.

"I didn't have much of an appetite, so I drank some orange juice and ate a couple of cookies."

"They're the dinosaur ones, your favorite!" She shrugged as I returned to her side. "I'm not going to force you, but you have to promise me that at recess, you'll eat the snack. It's your favorite sausage. It's important that you eat, or you won't have strength. Is your backpack ready?"

"Yes."

"Garbi, I'm going to take my daughter to school. I'll be right back. I left your breakfast in the kitchen." I shouted loud enough for her to hear me. She responded with an "Okay" that made me smile as I was grabbing my keys.

That simple scene could become commonplace for us. I would love for it to be so. I'd make breakfast in the mornings while she showered and I took the kids to school.

I thought about how we had loved each other the night before, slowly, unhurriedly, making love with both body and soul until we joined skins.

I didn't have the heart to ask her to change rooms. Her rhythmic breathing told me she had fallen asleep while my hands caressed her back. I may not have had all the answers, but my state of calm as she touched my body made me think it didn't matter what happened as long as I had her with me.

I set the alarm on my cell phone for an hour before Andrea would wake up so I would have enough time to arouse Garbi up with my kisses and cuddling. We ended up loving each other again like two hormonal teenagers trying not to get caught in their parents' bed.

I cleaned up and went to Andrea's room. For her, getting up was an odyssey. I prepared breakfast and gave her time to get dressed without a fuss. Afterward, I pretended I was going to wake Garbiñe up so as not to cause suspicion.

She got up with a smile on her lips. She was under the sheet in case my daughter got a fright and came in. I winked at her and kissed those lips, which were owed thousands of "I love yous."

Garbi got up and said good morning to Andrea, who responded without grumbling and went straight to the shower.

We had made progress. My daughter did not look at her with as much reticence. The adaptability of children had fascinated me, and I was sure Garbiñe would find a place in my little girl's life more easily than we expected.

I drove her to school. Andrea kept hugging the stuffed animal, which she didn't want to part with. It reminded me of when she was a little girl, and I gave her a bunny that she carried everywhere. She couldn't fall asleep without it. Mr. Carrots was present at many family events. We could say that he became one of the family, and he was like that until about a year ago when my daughter accompanied me to a talk I was giving in the children's oncology ward. Oscar, my doctor, had asked me to come dressed in my uniform as a favor and give a talk to the children about safety, the work we were doing in the commissary, and as a finale, a demonstration by my friends from the Canine Unit, showing how dogs can find missing people or people buried under rubble.

Andrea noticed a little boy no more than five years old with a shaved head, deep circles under his eyes, and a perennial smile. She didn't take her eyes off him for the duration of my presentation and that of the dogs. The little boy, oblivious to my daughter, enjoyed everything. Everyone on that floor was a little warrior with a zest for life that would make anyone's heart swell.

When we finished, my daughter went over to him and handed him Mr. Carrots, telling him that she wanted to give it to him and the bunny would surely bring him luck and keep him company while he was in the hospital. The little boy's face lit up, and he promised him that when he got out, he would return the rabbit.

Three months later, Einar died of acute lymphoblastic leukemia. Oscar called me to come and pick up the stuffed animal, which had not left the child during that time. He told me the little boy stopped breathing while hugging that bunny that had brought him so much joy.

When I told Andrea what had happened, she asked me to tell the boy's mother that Mr. Carrots was now Einar's and would be with him forever, wherever he went. I passed the message on to Oscar, who in turn passed it to the family. His mother decided to bury the little boy with the stuffed animal and give a photo to my doctor to give to Andrea. It was from a week before her son died. It showed Einar with his big smile, posing next to Mr. Carrots. The little boy had asked his mother to take that picture to show Andrea how well he was taking care of the stuffed animal.

My daughter, who was not prone to easy tears, had pressed it to her chest and put it in her jewelry box, where she deposited everything she thought was indispensable.

Now, seeing her clinging so tightly to the dolphin, I couldn't help but think of Mr. Carrots and Andrea's kindness. She had a huge heart, and I was sure that sooner or later, she would make room for Garbi and the baby.

"Are you all right?" I asked, opening the door for her to get out.

She took one last look at the dolphin and left it on the seat. "I don't feel like walking into class and being asked by everyone."

Seeing the sadness that enveloped her, the pain stabbed me to my toes.

"It is logical that your friends want to know how you are feeling, but you have the right to have your space. If you don't feel like talking about it, tell them you'd rather they talk to you about other things."

"Then they will think that I don't want to talk about my mother. That I don't want to remember her, and that's not it!"

"They won't believe you don't want to remember your mother. It's not an easy situation for you or for them. No one knows how to behave in the face of death, especially when you are small. If they ask you, it is because they care about you, nothing more."

"I know, I just miss her so much, and I get sad when I think about her." She ended up buried in my arms.

"I know, honey, I know. We all get sad, and we will all miss her."

"Not all of us," she murmured, pressed against me.

When I heard that, I crouched to observe her fixedly. "If you mean me, you're wrong."

"Now you have Garbiñe. Mom doesn't matter to you anymore."

"Your mother will always matter. It makes no difference if I'm in a relationship with someone else. She was one of the most important and incredible women in my life. Do you know why?" She shook her head with tears running down her cheeks.

"Because she gave me the greatest gift in the world: two children I adore and for whom I would give my life. I am very proud of you both. Your mother and I may not have been good for each other, but we did very well raising our children. We both adored you and continue to do so, me from here and her from heaven, because the love with which we made you takes precedence over anything else."

I gave her a huge hug, and we stayed like that until she calmed down enough to reassure me that she was okay and wanted to go in. Once I saw her go in the door, I asked the secretary to let me talk to the principal for a few moments.

With kindness, she took me to the office, where a woman with dark hair and a solemn face gave me her condolences. She spoke kindly, allowing me to sit down for a few minutes to collect myself. I told her about my daughter's fears and concerns and how she was affected by what might happen at school, and she told me to calm down.

The teacher had spoken to Andrea's classmates in anticipation of her return to the classroom. She assured me that the children had understood that they should act normally and with special sensitivity toward her. She assured me that my daughter was very well-liked among her classmates, as she was always ready to lend a hand to anyone who needed it, and she doubted that any of them would do anything to upset her.

She also offered me the services of the school's psychologist. He would make sure that everything was going well, and if I authorized it, he wanted me to visit once a week to help her cope with her new reality.

I thanked her for her support and signed the consent for my daughter to receive that weekly hour to adjust to life without her mother. Any help was welcome.

I said goodbye, again received her condolences, and headed for the apartment.

When I arrived, I was surprised not to see Garbi in the living room. I glanced into all the rooms until I found her. She was sitting on the bed, on the quilt. The damn bag had fallen open, leaving the baby's garment exposed.

I swallowed hard, not knowing what to say. With my daughter, it had been easy. Garbiñe was another matter. With her, there was no point in distraction. I would find out why that piece was there.

"Did Paula tell you?" she asked without looking at me, running her index finger over the shield.

"No. I heard you talking yesterday."

She nodded. "I don't know what to say. I promise I didn't mean to pry. I sat on the bed to put on my shoes, and the bag tipped over."

I approached her gently and sat down next to her to take the tiny garment between my fingers.

"Do you like it? I thought it was funny, ideal for our baby." Her eyes poured the concern she felt into mine. "I didn't know how to tell you. I wanted to. Part of the reason I came here was to tell you about it, but then everything got complicated, and I thought..." Her voice cut off.

"That I wouldn't want the baby."

She nodded.

"I heard you say that, and while I would have liked to have found out differently, I admit I didn't make it easy for you to come clean. I understand that you had doubts and didn't know how to approach the subject. Now it's done, and I know we're going to be parents," I proclaimed, lacing my fingers through hers.

"Yesterday, in the piercing store, I was going to confess it to you, but Paula interrupted us, and then I couldn't find the time. Maybe I'm a coward."

I reached up to stroke her cheek.

"It's all right; don't worry. I'm not angry, not even upset. Things come as they come, and what's in here?" I put my hand on her belly. "It took two."

"I'm sorry." She started crying, and I held her to my chest.

"I'm not. It's the best gift you could give me. I love this baby almost as much as I love you. I want anything that's from you, and I feel so lucky to have you both."

I urged her to get up and settled her on my knees to calm her down. "I love you, Garbiñe, and I love this little miracle in here. I don't want you to doubt my feelings or commitment to you. You are as important to me as my children are, and I will fight the odds to bring our family together. It will not be easy or perfect, but it will be ours.

"Life has taught me that the most important thing is not what I have but who I have. That is the true value, the meaning of everything, the place where everything begins and nothing ends."

Her body was shaking from the tension and nerves she had built up by keeping the secret.

"Are you really not upset?" she asked, hiccupping against my neck.

"Not a bit, and if you stop crying, I'll show you the other gifts. Do you feel like it?"

She nodded without moving. "I don't deserve you."

"Of course you deserve me, and I deserve you. Don't ever forget that." I took the first package and let her unwrap it. It was the stuffed puppy. She had once told me she wanted to have a dog.

"It's adorable." She sighed.

I offered her the smallest package, the one that meant the most to me.

When she saw the pendant, she swung it in front of bright eyes. "It's beautiful! I love it! I always wanted to have one of these with Ruben, but Dario told me it was nonsense. You don't know how much it means to me," she burst out excitedly.

"So, you know what it is?"

"Of course. A pendant that pregnant women wear that makes a sound the baby can hear."

"You're a very smart girl. However, what you don't know is that I bought it for the green stone since it reminded me that my favorite color is still seeing you."

She smiled at our joke, then, "Being with you is like receiving the caress of the sun in the middle of winter. It is the breeze that blows to clear a gray day. It helps me understand that sometimes, to find the north, you have to get lost in the south and arm yourself with crazy things that offer opportunities. Until I met you, I didn't know what it was to love with a full soul. You complete me, complement me, and make me feel perfect, even though I make mistakes and bad decisions."

"I love you too, precious," I murmured, clinging to her mouth, love oozing from every pore of my skin.

I undressed her slowly, exploring every nook and cranny of her skin and filling it with my breath. I wanted to make her feel how my feelings overflowed, filling her from the outside as well as from the inside.

I took her, savoring every gasp, every muffled moan of pleasure.

We looked at each other without ceasing, exposing our unanswered doubts, delving into each of the scars that held our souls, melting between questions, promises, and kisses.

Love is battle. It is storm. It is calm and crisis. It is learning to forgive offenses even when they have not been committed. It is believing in "us" when all else fails. It is finding your place on the path when no one marked it for you.

She was all that, and I wasn't about to give up.

"You're going to suck me dry," I joked, half-dressed.

She laughed and put away all the presents except the pendant, which was lying on her belly.

"Are we going to see something other than your bed? I think I know it well enough."

I tugged on my lower lip provocatively.

"Never say you have enough. There are places in it you still don't know. Tonight, I'll show you how wrong you are."

"We've just got out of bed, and you're already thinking about tonight?"

"I just can't stop wanting you. I don't know what you've done to me, but I just want to be with you in my balls."

She laughed. "We could move to one of those nudist towns so

I could fuck you in any corner, and it wouldn't be necessary to dress up all the time. I'm sure they need security forces."

"Uh-huh, and instead of a gun, you would always have a baton at the ready."

"Don't tell me you don't like the idea." I waggled my eyebrows.

"Oh, yes, I'm excited. Your phrase would be, 'Hands up, or I'll beat you up!'"

I laughed and pulled her over to kiss her. "That's just for you, beautiful. To the others, I would offer an electric shock."

"You'd better since if you're offering downloads to the others, you're going to have more children than in *Gremlins*."

"Mmm, jealous?"

"No, realistic. If you got me pregnant in one weekend, think about what you could do in a year."

"All my weekends are yours. Do you want me to make you more children?" I whispered, biting her earlobe.

"I think four is enough."

"We'd better go for a drink. I'm thirsty. And stop looking at me like that, or we won't get out of here today."

"All right, but tonight we're going to Cuenca. And Zamora," she added.

"To Zamora?"

"Uh-huh, because we'll need more than an hour. Do you know where I want to live forever?" Her tone was serious.

"Where?"

"In your smile. That seems to me the ideal place to live." The corners of my lips turned up because if I had taught Garbi anything, it was to smile again. She planted another kiss on me, and we walked out the door, laughing.

The two days went by in a blur. When I took Garbi to the airport, I did it with regret in my heart. We promised that we would find a way to make our lives fit together, and until Easter, we would make it a point to see each other daily. We would set up our afternoon video call again if our shifts allowed it.

We would look forward to Holy Week, which ran from March 25 to April 1 this year. We were already in mid-February, so it wasn't far off.

It was going to work out, and we were both going to do our part to make it happen.

CHAPTER TWENTY-NINE

Iktsuarpok: Go out to see if anyone is coming.

Garbiñe, Easter 2018

"Will you stop peeking out the door! You're getting on my nerves!" Paula spat, finishing hanging the garland that decorated the living room.

"What do you want me to tell you? I can't help it."

"You're attacking me every time you open it. The adhesive tape comes off, and I have to climb back up the ladder. If I break my neck and fall to my death, it will weigh on your conscience."

"Will you stop inventing deaths that are not included in the Penal Code?" I snorted, between amused and uneasy. Áxel had told me a while ago that they were picking up the luggage and they wouldn't be late.

I hadn't seen him for a month, and it felt like a year. Even though we saw each other daily on video calls, it wasn't the same as feeling his touch. Besides, he was coming with Andrea. It would be our litmus test, one I hoped to pass for everyone's sake.

Paula had brought me an inflatable mattress so the girl could

343

sleep with Ruben, who was running around the living room after the puppy I had finally decided to adopt.

A couple of weeks ago, my partner and I had received a call about a possible case of animal abuse. We followed protocol and called the shelter, and when the owner of the dogs refused to take care of them, they asked us to accompany them. Apparently, it was not just someone who was not taking good care of his animals. It seemed to be a much more serious case that required a search warrant, as the man they were reporting was a violent guy who was involved in the despicable world of clandestine dog fighting.

The guy was a real piece of work, and after showing him the document authorizing us to search his home, he had to agree to let the shelter take the dogs. After that, we gathered information about what was going on there.

We entered the house and searched until we found what we needed to arrest the asshole, who had a long list of priors. With a little luck, he would be in prison for a long time. The guy was breeding and training dogs for a clandestine network that was profiting by organizing dog fights for a national fighting circuit. Seeing the high profitability of the business, he had opted to organize meetings on the same farm for unscrupulous islanders and foreigners he recruited through social networks. We found a file on the computer named "Animal Vacations," in which he included a long list of names, origins, and money spent.

It didn't end there. In a cabinet, we found syringes and anabolic steroids that were given to the dogs to enhance their strength and aggressiveness. A local veterinarian and a pharmaceutical company appeared in the file. From the quantities and the shortcut on the screen, I would say that, in addition to medicating them, he was dealing those drugs on the Internet. It looked like he had another niche market there.

The iceberg was gigantic. I hoped that, given the information we seized, our forensic colleagues would be able to put an end to his damned web.

While Colmenares placed the PC in the trunk and the suspect was isolated in the back of the patrol car, I walked around the grounds of the house.

The farm was grotesque, having huge numbers of dogs locked up in maximum security cages in conditions that made your soul ache.

The dogs were all irritable. Some were violent and others devastated, at the limit of their strength.

Many bore scars, amputated legs, bloody claws, nicked ears, or open wounds that oozed the scent of putrefaction. The smell was nauseating, and the enclosure where he kept them was full of tiny, filthy cages.

Flies swarmed over feces and urine in a repulsive olfactory festival that almost made me vomit.

How could people do that to animals? I could hardly contain the urge to cry. Not that I was an animal activist, but I was respectful of wildlife and the environment, and what was happening there was horrifying.

At the back of the room was a bitch who had just given birth. The puppies were huddled together, trying to survive in that world of man's imposed violence. There was a very small one that was not allowed space at the teats and was cornered, whimpering to reach the food his brothers were enjoying.

What a paradox. It was like life itself, where the masses corner the fragile, and the strongest prevails. Knowing was not the same as seeing it, and I had felt like that puppy.

"He's the weakest," said the girl from the shelter, seeing that he kept an eye on her. "In a litter, that can happen."

"You mean he is rejected by the mother and siblings?"

"Yes."

"What do you do in such cases?" I asked with interest.

"You can't force things. When it happens, it is better to integrate him into another litter or keep him with other dogs. It is usually better than leaving him in a place where he will always be rejected."

I couldn't control my need to give him shelter and a place in the world, and I talked to Susana, the girl from the shelter, to start the paperwork to adopt him.

That was how Oreo came into our lives. He was a beautiful white American Staffordshire terrier with a chocolate face, paws, and tail.

Needless to say, Ruben was delighted with the puppy. Susana had told me that, although it was a potentially dangerous breed, it was one of the best with children. "There are no dangerous dogs, only ignorant humans," she told me to convince me.

With good training and a loving home, Oreo would become one of the family.

"I hear a car," I warned Paula excitedly. "I think they're coming." I opened the door again, and the garland fell.

"That's not the way to do it," she grumbled in exasperation.

I did not pay attention to her since I was right. Colmenares's car was peeking around the curve of the street. My partner had offered to pick them up while we prepared the house to receive them.

When I saw them get out of the vehicle, I could not control my desire to go to the access gate.

"Welcome!"

Andrea seemed taller and a little less sad. She carried her dolphin in her arms and wore a curious look as she tried to absorb everything. She glanced at me, raising the corners of her mouth a little, not too much. It wasn't bad for a start.

Colmenares was at the back of the vehicle to open the trunk and help a smiling Áxel, who was taking out a suitcase.

"Hello," his daughter greeted me as she came up to me.

"How was your flight?"

"Slow."

Áxel, who was now next to me, rolled his eyes. "This girl doesn't understand how many kilometers there are from Barcelona to here. She thinks that going by plane is like teleporting," he said, looking at Andrea from the corner of his eye.

I wanted to jump on him so badly that holding back was an ordeal.

"It's logical. The same thing happened to me the first time my parents brought me here," I said, turning my attention to Andrea. "Come in. In the house are my friend Paula, my son Ruben, and Oreo."

"I'm not hungry, thank you," replied the child, her eyes fixed on the front door.

I burst out laughing. "My Oreo is not for eating. It's not a cookie, although he looks like one, but a puppy we recently adopted."

Her eyes widened, and interest flickered in her blue eyes. "You have a puppy?"

"Uh-huh. Come in and see him. He loves to be scratched behind the ears. If you do it, you'll win him over in no time. Besides, pretty girls are his weak point," I whispered confidently.

She nodded and stepped inside the house.

Áxel turned to me, and I was able to receive him as I wished by trapping his lips until my companion cleared her throat.

"If you're going to set up a porno, let me know. I'll call the partners and charge them admission for the show."

"You'd like to make money at my expense," I joked. "But for the moment, it won't be possible. We'll put on the show when no one sees us."

Áxel and I reluctantly parted, but not before he fondled my belly. "You still don't show," he murmured in my ear.

"That's because you haven't seen me without a bra. I've never had such big tits. With Ruben, they didn't get that way," I murmured so my partner wouldn't hear us.

Áxel let out a sound that made me tremble. "I'm going to

make up for it tonight. I'm sick of you being so narrow-minded on our nightly dates. Lately, you don't finish anything you start in my dreams."

"Why is that?"

"I don't know. I think it's an alliance between the alarm clock and my sheets. They have decided to eradicate my nocturnal emissions, and you've got me all charged up."

"We'll have to remedy that, won't we?" I inquired as confidently as I could.

"Find a bed!" Colmenares exclaimed, snorting as he passed.

We both chuckled.

"Don't be jealous. You have Martina every day, and I have Áxel less than I would like."

"That will change at some point," my partner proclaimed. "From the way he looks at you, I'd swear that before the chickpea is born, he will become a Tenerife resident."

We looked for each other without speaking. Áxel knew I was not going to move since it was difficult for me because of shared custody. If anyone took a step in that direction, it would have to be him. We both wanted to start a family; we had talked about it continuously for the last month. We just hadn't come up with the best formula yet. We had to find a common ground that would reconcile our realities.

"Slow and steady," I said to myself.

When we entered the living room, the three of us burst out laughing. Paula was sitting on a chair, wrapped in the garland of flowers. Andrea scampered around her, pursued by Ruben and Oreo, who threatened her with the unbridled wrath of the Cookie Monster. My friend had a strong dramatic streak. According to her, at the boarding school she'd attended, she was always cast as the lead in the plays they performed.

Paula's background is hard to match. Some call her the Paris Hilton of Tenerife, and it's true she belongs to a wealthy family with a title. Her father sent her to boarding school in Switzerland until she was old enough to go to university. We met after she had finished her degree and was trying her luck as an intern at a newspaper in the capital.

I remember that first meeting as if it were today. I was in the middle of an intervention by the *Guardia Civil*. She was looking for news, and my mistake, or my success, was to let her ask. I had her hounding me for a week in search of an article that, according to her, would get her promoted from intern to columnist.

I don't know whether it was those golden eyes, the face dotted with freckles, the genuine smile, or her biting humor, but something made me want to help her, even though it could get me in trouble. Maybe it was the mix of everything or that she was so different from me that I was drawn to her like a moth to a flame. Paula reminded me of a lion with that copper hair and the strength she exuded. Her perseverance, her boldness, and her inexhaustible vitality pushed me to give her more clues than I should have.

She got her promotion, and I got a loyal friend who, even if she was a loudmouth at times, would give her life for me without hesitation.

Paula made you think she didn't like children, only the manufacturing process, but nothing could be further from the truth. She was an enthusiastic nanny, so functionally being an only child and being raised at a boarding school must have had an influence. If she hadn't had children with Gabriel, it was because they were both too focused on their careers.

He kept telling her that they were still too young, that they should live more, but he was already in his forties, and my friend was in her thirties. He repeated it so much that she internalized Gabriel's words and made them her own. If you asked Paula, she would tell you she didn't want children. She had enough to put up with, that they were a nuisance full of responsibilities, and that she never wanted to be a mother.

Cheap talk. The reality was that every time she saw a child, her eyes lit up.

May she one day find a man who would do her justice and make her as happy as she deserves.

If Colmenares had not been so good with his wife, I would have encouraged him to throw himself at Paula.

"I beg your pardon. Where is Lozano? No way! When I arrived at the airport, there was no sign of the Mosso." I asked about him, and Paula told me that they were only compatible in bed. For four days, it was fine, but she didn't want anything serious with the Catalan.

I didn't want to interfere since, when it came to matters of the heart, she was very much her own person. If she said no, it was no, no matter how much it seemed to me that he was more than her match in bed.

"Are you law enforcement officers not going to do anything?" she shrieked, looking at us from her captivity. "They're holding me hostage. They tied me up and are threatening me. Somebody do something! They're trying to take away my French fries!"

Andrea stopped in front of her, grabbed the weapon of mass destruction that was Oreo, and placed the puppy on Paula's legs for him to lick.

"Oh, my God! In addition to leaving me without food, they're trying to make the beast devour me! It wants to eat me! Help, agents! In a few seconds, there won't be anything left of me. Get it off me before it's too late and it licks me to death!"

"No, Aunt Paula, no. *Oreo* is not a beast. He only kisses you because he loves you very much. Just like me."

Paula looked at Ruben with adoration, and my little boy threw himself on her neck to kiss her and give weight to his words. My friend's face was buried between Oreo's licks and Ruben's kisses.

"Do you love me very much?"

He nodded vehemently without letting go.

"Well, it doesn't show. You were the instigator when the garland fell. You wanted to tie me to the chair."

"No! It was her idea!" He pointed stiffly at Andrea, who was smiling in amusement.

"Mine? No way!" she exclaimed slyly.

My son looked at her sternly since we had taught him from an early age that it was not good to lie but that it was also not good to tattle if he wanted to make friends. He was experiencing a moral conflict.

"I think we're dealing with two very dangerous criminals, comrades," said Áxel, drawing the attention of the little ones. He had adopted a police attitude and looked at the pair of rogues suspiciously.

"I swear it wasn't me, Daddy." Andrea raised her hands in innocence.

My little boy's eyes widened in glee as he looked at me. "Me neither, Mommy!"

"So, it's clear. Our main suspects are *his* victims." Colmenares added, pointing his finger at the puppy. "This was all Oreo's idea. He's trying to erase the redhead's freckles."

We all looked at the puppy, who was still worshipping Paula's face.

"Let's go get him, and I'll take him into custody!" my companion said, rushing toward the dog.

The children shouted no, Andrea grabbed the dog in her arms, and Ruben pulled her into his room. The three of them barricaded the door, but their laughter could be heard from outside.

"Good start," I murmured in the ear of my sergeant, who seemed pleased by the camaraderie of the children.

"It seems so."

Paula joined in, assisted by Colmenares. "If you want, I can finish what the hound started," he suggested, waggling his eyebrows.

"Try it, and your wife will castrate you like a dog." They were always joking.

"Want a beer?" Paula nudged him with her elbow.

We all nodded.

"I need to get the dog taste out of my mouth. I think your Oreo likes redheads."

"Well, I didn't see you resisting. Maybe you're into zoophilia," Áxel taunted.

"I think that he detected that deep down, Paula is a bitch," I harassed, knowing she wouldn't mind the joke.

"Are you saying that because she likes to get down on all fours?" Colmenares, who was up for anything, joined in the collective joke.

"Police brutality! What's the matter with you? Do you have so little to do that you need to mess with this poor journalist? And you'd *like* to see me on all fours, but you'll have to wait for another life. Martina would play pool with your balls, and you know how well she plays."

"You don't know how skilled she is at putting my cue in the hole."

"Pig!" she rebuked him.

"You started it, redhead."

"Are they always like this?" Áxel questioned, grabbing me around the waist.

"Almost always. When they are together, they are like children but without the charm."

"Good to know."

"Come on, little ones. Let's stop it and drink a toast. To reunions." I raised my bottle, which was nonalcoholic.

"Here's to reunions!" they agreed, almost as happy as I was.

Áxel and Andrea spent five days with me and Ruben. Five days full of bittersweet emotions where we explored the possibility of forming a family.

The first night, after dinner, we made a small campfire on the front porch, toasted marshmallows, and drank chocolate while gazing at the stars.

Áxel distracted the children by telling stories about the stars. "This year, on the night of April 22-23, there will be a shower known as the Lyrids. There could be as many as eighteen shooting stars per hour."

"Could we pick them up like shells, Mommy? Maybe Grandpa will come one of those times," my son asked enthusiastically.

"No, honey. Grandpa's star is not the kind that falls," I told him, which made him lose his enthusiasm. "If Grandpa fell, he would no longer be able to protect us from up there. Besides, it's a figure of speech. Stars don't fall to the ground. You just see them glide, like you or Daddy on the waves."

"Oh." He sighed and took a bite of his s'more.

"Eighteen stars falling an hour is a lot, isn't it?" Andrea asked, looking sideways at Ruben.

"Well, it's nothing compared to the Perseids, which fall in August and reach one hundred fifty per hour," Áxel told the girl.

"That's outrageous!" she burst out enthusiastically.

"And beautiful," I interjected. "I've never seen so many falling stars as in Tenerife. I do not know if it is because of the clean sky or because, according to ufologists, this island is magical, and aliens love it. The point is, the meteor showers are spectacular."

"I want to see them!" The girl looked at the sky in case one suddenly fell.

"You'll have to come back in August," I encouraged her. She looked at her father.

"Can we, Dad?" She whirled excitedly and got to her feet to approach him.

I crossed my fingers since I wanted them to move here in August. I didn't want my son to be born without his father.

"If you want." He exhaled, his hopes rising because of her smile.

My chest warmed with the possibility of getting closer to the girl. I had faith that my island would conquer her as it had the frightened teenager who had never lived surrounded by water.

I had planned many activities that she would have a lot of fun with, hoping to fascinate her so much that she wouldn't want to leave.

To begin, I told the children Indian stories, which used to be my father's favorites, as we ate marshmallows and downed the sweet drinks. When we finished, I set up a tent in the living room, in which I placed mats and sleeping bags.

Ruben was enthusiastic about Andrea. She was very affectionate with my son, and Oreo was their tireless companion. We listened to them laugh until twelve o'clock. Then silence fell, and we were finally allowed to have the reunion we deserved.

Exhausted and sated, Áxel told me that he had not expected Andrea to make it so easy for us. He had had some reticence during the flight, but he had only had to set foot in the house and take hold of me to lose it.

I kissed his bare chest. "Do you think we'll make it?"

"I believe that if I could cheat death twice, I am capable of anything."

"Aren't you afraid of how your children will react when they find out they are going to have a new brother or sister?"

"I have faith in them. They've taken a big hit, but they're good guys. In other circumstances, the news might have gone unnoticed if it meant I was happy."

"The situation changed with Claudia's death."

"It did. That's why I can only wait and give them time and trust."

"I don't want things to get worse for them. They deserve every good thing that can happen to them."

"So do we. Your statement says a lot about you, and I can't tell you how glad I am that my children's happiness matters so much to you. It is essential for them to grow up in a loving environment, and we can provide that for them."

"And Christian?"

Áxel sighed. "It will cost us, but in the end, he'll back down. Trust me. I'm good at conflict resolution."

"How can I not? I feel like you've stolen my soul, and I can't even file a complaint."

His smile widened. "You don't know how glad I am to hear that, my sergeant, because now that I know you're not going to report me, I'm going to give you an encore that will take your breath away. Those breasts," he said, placing his mouth on them, "deserve a tribute."

He feasted on my sensitive nipples, hardening them into taut peaks.

The kisses, accompanied by sweet licks, wandered until I begged him to change course lest I come. A wolfish grin appeared. He claimed it was too soon for that. He amused himself by walking his fingers around my belly, depositing whispered words of affection to our future child. In addition to igniting my body, they did the same to my soul.

Just when I thought I couldn't feel any more bliss, he thrust his head between my legs to make me explode with delight. As I was swept away by the orgasm, he took me very gently, taking away my insecurities for the future and making me cling to his mute vow that we would make it as a family.

His orgasm reverberated between my thighs, filling me completely.

I wanted nothing less than forever with him. Áxel was the one battle I wasn't going to allow myself to lose.

CHAPTER THIRTY

Schadenfreude: Pleasure derived from another person's misfortune.

Garbiñe

The next morning, our adventure began—an excursion to an animal farm in the south of the island.

Our children were thrilled until the woman at the ticket booth praised how much the little girl looked like me.

Andrea tensed at the comparison and responded, "She's not my mother."

The poor embarrassed ticket agent apologized, claiming that since we were both blonde and light-eyed, she had taken it for granted that we were related. Áxel and I played it down and didn't let her make a big deal of it.

The animals seemed tired of having to take tourists around the farm, but they looked well cared for. The children didn't notice. They had an immense desire to get on the dromedary.

The animals had chairs hanging over the sides of the hump.

My motherly streak came out when I saw them, and I asked if they were safe for children. The trainer made it clear that the little ones were given extra safety restraints, that I should be calm, and nothing could happen to them.

Áxel's condescending smile made me blush. They took a souvenir photo of the four of us before we climbed onto the platform to take our seats.

The dromedaries were tied together to form a caravan, which reminded me of desert movies in which we saw nomads traveling on their backs. At the head of the line was Áxel with my son, and we were in second position. Andrea surprised me by not objecting to riding with me. She sat in her seat and let the man put the safety straps on her. I felt the need to talk to her and make it clear that I did not intend to usurp her mother's place, only to help her and offer her all my love.

"Andrea," I murmured once we were secured. She looked at me with eyes that had stolen the color from the sky. "I won't pretend to be your mother. I know you already have one and that she was wonderful. What the woman at the entrance said…"

"It was a mistake, I know."

"Yes, it was a mistake. However, I understand that it upset you," I suggested tentatively. "It's not an easy situation, and I'm very proud of how you're coping."

"I'm small, but I'm not stupid. I know what's going on, even if you don't tell me."

"What's going on? You mean your father and I being together?"

"No! I knew that since the day of the funeral. I mean, what you don't tell me."

"What didn't we tell you?"

Her gaze descended to my stomach. "I know there's a baby in your belly."

I went white in the face of her annihilating look. I swallowed hard.

"Don't lie to me. You promised you would not."

I thought about the conversation we'd had at L'Aquàrium with her father and decided the best thing to do was to face reality. "Yes, I am pregnant by your father. We didn't expect it. He came into being without warning. We both thought we couldn't have children."

"But you can," she countered.

I nodded, looking for a trace of what might be going through her mind.

"Does it bother you?" I asked.

"It's up to you."

"That's true, but I would like to know your opinion. It's very important to me."

Andrea shrugged and stared at Ruben's back.

"Luly's parents—she's one of my best friends—separated too. Her father's new girlfriend is also having a baby. Her mother says that's what men usually do when they leave their wives. Find a younger one, who is usually uglier, and blow up her belly like a balloon. According to her, men get bored with eating the same dish and need to spread their seed around the world, branding the new one as if she were a cow or something."

"Your father does not need to spread seeds. He is not a farmer or a cattle rancher, to go around marking cattle."

"You're younger than he is, aren't you?"

"Yes, but…"

"Your belly will swell, even if it's not noticeable at the moment, right?"

"Yes."

"Well then." She crossed her arms. "He did the same thing as Luly's father."

Andrea was too smart to disagree with me.

"Sometimes we older people say things to children that are better kept to ourselves. What your friend's mother said to you came out of resentment. When something happens to us that we don't like, we attack, but that should not be done because we lose all credibility. Do you understand?"

"What I know is that Luly was as sad as I was when her father left them."

My heart shrank at her confession. "I can imagine. You want your parents to stay together forever, but the reality is that many things happen in life that change us, and it would be very selfish to try to hold on to someone if that person no longer feels the same way about you."

"Is that what happened to you with Ruben's father?"

"Yes. We tried many times, but we wanted very different things. Instead of making each other happy, we were hurting each other, and that wasn't good for us or for Ruben."

"Does your ex-husband follow Luly's mother's theory?"

"As far as I know, no. He has been with other women, but he doesn't have a steady girlfriend whose belly he has swollen."

"He must be an exception."

"I'm sure. By the way, may I ask how you found out about my pregnancy?"

She locked her gaze with mine.

"As the grownups say, by putting two and two together. I saw the onesie with the Superman logo the day you came home to sleep over. Dad told me it was a gift, and then I saw the bag in your suitcase next to a stuffed animal. I know I'm not supposed to snoop, but you had it open, and I needed a piece of blank paper that my brother keeps in his room."

"It could have been a gift for a friend your father and I had in common."

She clicked her tongue. "Oh, come on. I was paying attention when you told the Superman story. Dad had one about the super-hero, too, so I figured it was something like that. We girls are naturally smart. My grandmother says I should be CNI since I don't usually miss anything."

"I see."

"You'll see when my brother finds out. Are you going to tell him?"

"I'd rather your dad do it."

"Do you know what it is?"

"No, not yet. I have a new ultrasound this week. Would you like to come and see your future brother or sister?"

"Will Dad and Ruben go?"

"My son doesn't know anything. It's early. The first three months are the most complicated in a pregnancy. I wanted to make sure everything was okay before we told you."

"Don't worry about me. I'm not a snitch like those other bumblers."

"Bumblers?"

"You know, the ones who come to class one day to tell you that the Three Wise Men are not magicians, nor do they come from the East, nor do they follow a star or bring gifts to all the children in the world in a single night. Parents tease us, just like they tease us about the Tooth Fairy or that if we tell lies, our noses will grow. I don't see the point of lying to us. It's absurd! Do you know how disappointed you are when they do that?"

"I was a child too, even if you don't think so."

"Weren't you upset when you found out?"

"I think I was fine, but since I had two little sisters, we kept the traditions. Maybe it's a disappointment, but it's also nice to believe in magic and enjoy the parade. To think that for one night, any wish you make can come true. I don't know. I don't see it as being so bad, although I understand and respect your point of view."

Andrea scrutinized me with a look that seemed to pierce my soul. "You're nice. You're not as pretty as my mother, but you're not bad."

"Thank you for your compliment. I trust that, given your aversion to lies, it is sincere."

Andrea nodded. "I'm not lying."

"I'm glad to hear it. And you know what?"

"What?"

"No one will be as beautiful as your mother or smarter or give you better advice than her. Your mother was unique and unrepeatable, a being of light who is now next to my father in the sky, watching over you. Life smiles on you, and you will become a great woman like she was. I'm sure my dad takes care of her. I asked him to. You know that?"

"Why?"

"Because even if you don't believe it and everything is too recent, I care about you. Just like your father and your brother. I will not replace her, but I would love for you and Christian to accept me so we can start a family. I promise that if you give me the opportunity, I will help you in any way I can. I probably won't do as well as she did, but I will do my best to earn your trust and make as few mistakes as possible.

"I want you to know that I will always be there for whatever you need, help you achieve your dreams, and give you a hug when you are having a bad day. I'll listen to you if you feel like telling me things and give you advice if you want it. Whatever happens, you can count on my support even if things go wrong or if you make bad decisions. It doesn't matter. You can always count on me. I say that from my heart."

"So, you won't be angry if one day I try to make you a cake and I get the salt mixed up?"

"No, because the important thing will be that you made a mistake trying to do something nice for me."

"Okay." She was thoughtful.

"What are you thinking about?"

"Luly was Snow White's stepmother, the one who kept looking at herself in the mirror, wanting to be the prettiest, and I was Cinderella's Fairy Godmother."

I could only smile at the remark. "And that pleases you?"

"I think so." She looked away as the dromedary broke into a trot.

It hadn't gone as badly as I thought, and I felt much closer to the girl. Andrea was a coherent and well-rounded child. She had traits I could relate to. I was convinced that everything was going to be all right.

As if he sensed that we had finished our conversation, Áxel turned his head and mouthed, "Everything okay?" I didn't want to break the truce with Andrea. I responded by raising my thumb. He winked at me and diverted his attention to my son, who was asking him a question.

The swaying of the chairs was pronounced, but fortunately, we had no incidents beyond Cupid's intervention in the middle of the ride.

We were riding a dromedary in heat that sensed the possibility of love.

Andrea died of laughter when our sexy lady of the desert approached her father and poured her love breath on him. Áxel watched her nervously since the yellow, uneven teeth seemed to want to nibble him.

The guide joked about his success with the best camel in the bunch. That was why they called her "Princess."

At the end of the forty-five-minute walk, the children toured the animal farm. Rabbits, goats, and chickens all passed through their hands. The attendants told them stories until it was time for lunch, and I took the opportunity to tell Áxel about my conversation with his daughter.

Áxel

"So, she's aware of everything, and she doesn't think it's wrong? It seems to me that she's pretty much on top of it."

I couldn't keep from smiling. "She's a little witch. She hasn't said anything to me all this time."

"I imagine she was looking for someone to corroborate her theory. That's why she asked you. She's a little bit of a liar." I pinched the bridge of my nose.

"It's my fault. I told her I would never lie to her, and in a short time, she has caught me in two. I don't want to lose Andrea. I couldn't bear it."

"You're not going to lose her." Garbi came closer to me and put her arm around my waist. "Your daughter loves you very much. You're very important to her."

"Christian is still very elusive. He only wanted to come home to see his sister and has taken every opportunity to tell me how happy he would be if I failed with you and you slammed the door in my face. According to him, that's what I deserve for what I did to his mother," I confessed desolately. Having my son drift away made me sad.

"But you didn't do anything!"

"In his eyes, I am still to blame for not avoiding the accident, and my ex-mother-in-law doesn't help."

"That woman is like the plague."

The corners of my lips turned up at the comparison. "What have I done to deserve someone like you?"

Garbiñe's eyes lit up. "I was never the prettiest or smartest in the class, nor did I have anything to make others envious. That never mattered to me, and now less than ever. Being who I am, I have you by my side. No matter how many difficulties we have, you are betting on us."

"That's because I was lucky that no one saw you with my eyes. I want my hugs to excite you and my kisses to heal the tears you once shed and be your means of transportation to happiness."

"You say such beautiful things that you leave me speechless. I want you like this, silent, so I can cover your lips with mine."

I sought the relief she gave me, the calm that flooded my chest every time our mouths met in a palpable dream. I sucked in her breath, sensing it in every part of my anatomy. She would always be my favorite color, the one with which I would paint the walls of my life and build the foundations of our future.

After lunch, we took the car to the cliffs at Los Gigantes.

Andrea was amazed by the landscape and the black sand. She ran around the beach with Ruben, and they ended up taking a dip in front of our amused eyes.

They built castles that were devastated by the waves. They trapped a crab that they finally released. We stayed until dusk, when the breeze raised the hairs on our bodies.

When we got home, we washed off the sand. I asked Garbi to leave me alone with my daughter for a while, and we took Oreo for a walk while she bathed Ruben.

"Are you having a good time?" I asked.

"Today was not bad. I'm looking forward to tomorrow, though. Garbi told me that we will go dolphin-watching in the ocean, and in the afternoon, we will go up the volcano. I hope we see a lot of them."

"Volcanoes?"

"No, dolphins!" she snapped in annoyance.

"I know. I was just teasing you. Garbi told me you know about the baby. Why didn't you ask me?"

"I knew when I saw the little Superman suit, and as far as I remember, you didn't tell me the truth."

I sighed. "You're right. You must understand that it wasn't the right time. Your mother had just died, and you had just met Garbi. I felt I couldn't hit you with something like that. Does that make sense?"

Andrea stopped dead. She stood in front of me with that gaze of hers that penetrated deeply.

"You didn't tell me the truth. *Again*," she scolded, pursing her lips.

I let out the air I had been holding in. "I didn't lie to you either. I told you it was a gift, and that was true. I simply omitted for whom."

She was unconvinced. You could see it in the posture of that little body that was growing every day.

"Dad, I'm not as dumb as you think. I miss Mom a lot, but I would have understood if you'd told me you were with another girl and were expecting a baby."

"I didn't know about the baby. I found out just before you did. Garbiñe was afraid I didn't want it because I had told her I had enough with you and Christian and I didn't want any more children."

"Don't you want the baby?" she sputtered in horror.

"Yes, of course I do, but at the time, I didn't know I was pregnant, and we thought we couldn't be parents. I meant the ones we had were enough, and we didn't need any more to be happy."

"Does she make you happy?"

I smiled. There was no reproach in her question. "Very happy."

"I want you to be happy, so if she makes you happy, that's fine with me. Besides, I want a little sister to teach her judo. I'll make her a champion. If it is a boy, it wouldn't be fair because it would be three against one. It has to be a girl. Shall we come and live here?"

"I can't guarantee the sex of the baby," I admitted with amusement. "Would you like to live here?"

"I don't know yet. The place is cool, but I'd lose all my friends. Do you mind if I answer you after we're home and I've made up my mind?"

"No, honey, take your time. It's a decision that shouldn't be made lightly."

"And you will take my opinion into account when you decide whether to move?"

"Of course."

"All right, then. I'll sleep on it like you grownups do," she said conscientiously, resuming her walk.

Dinner was quiet. The little ones were exhausted. It didn't take them long to say they were sleepy and wanted to go to bed. Garbiñe told them a story, and I stood watching them from the door. I could imagine our life like that, tucking the children in after a full day of activities to end up in bed, dedicating ourselves to each other.

Garbi would snuggle on my chest, and I would repeat a thousand times that I wanted to live in her smile. There would never be a lack of laughter in our home.

I closed my eyes, thinking about Christian. I had offered for him to come with us to meet Garbi, but he had refused. I regretted that he was so far away. I had to find a way to get him back, but how?

Christian

I slid angrily across the pavement, preparing to perform a triple Salchow. I picked up speed, launched, and spun three times in the air, projecting my father's face instead of where I wanted to land.

I hate it, hate it, hate it, I thought at every turn, getting ready for the landing. I saw the wheels hit the ground, but my skate was out of position, and I fell.

My chin hit hard and split. It hurt, but not as much as the empty hole that had deepened in my chest since I lost my mother.

I heard my trainer rushing toward me, shouting my name as blood stained the polished gray floor.

Anger, pain, grief, and defeat. How was it possible that I hated him but missed him almost as much as I missed my mother?

It was crazy, I know, but that accident had taken away a part of me my father didn't know about. I couldn't help but blame him for taking away the chance to be who I really was. Only my mother knew my secret. She was my rock, and now I had nothing left, not even myself.

I had always been the weirdo. At school, they made fun of me because I didn't like what the other kids liked. In front of my father, I didn't say anything. He was the prototypical handsome *Mosso d'Esquadra*, with people skills. They looked at me sideways and whispered behind his back.

Was it my fault that I liked my classmates' blouses more than the skater suit? When my mother discovered me in my room, trying on one I had stolen from one of the girls and wearing her padded bra, she didn't say anything. She just looked at me.

I felt the need to give her an explanation. I approached her, crestfallen, to excuse myself, but she said, "It's okay. People can wear what they want." I broke down in front of her. They say transsexuals are born, and they feel that way from a young age. I didn't think I was one. In short, while I didn't feel good about my body, I didn't think my anatomy lacked anything. I was just curious.

I liked the girls' breasts, their beauty, and their clothes, but I didn't want to become or date one. I saw them as friends.

Mom promised me she would help me find out who I was and that if I liked boys, there would be no problem. I told her Dad would object. He had been confused when I'd told him I wanted to take up skating. I didn't want to imagine how he would be when I told him my girlfriend's name was Manuel.

It would have been better if the accident had taken me with her. Maybe then I could have chosen another father who would understand and accept me. I had been thinking for days about throwing myself on the train tracks or slitting my wrists with a razor. I wanted to die.

Then I could feel my mother's arms around me again, and she would tell me that everything was okay. It didn't matter what my sexual orientation was. The important thing was my happiness.

Life was unfair. First, my father got terminal cancer that almost killed him twice. Then my parents separated, and to top it all off, the accident cut Mom's life short.

The Monday after the accident, I had an appointment to visit an LGTBQ counselor, but I didn't go. Mom had insisted that it was for the best. She wanted me to feel good about whatever decision I made and to know that other people had had the same thing happen to them as me. I was not alone.

She insisted I tell Dad, but I begged her not to. I needed to get more information first and not feel so bad about being different.

My mother took with her the secret and the possibility of my going to the association for counseling.

I didn't feel able to tell my grandmother. As much as she loved me, she would have thrown her hands up. She would have said I was a deviant or worse. She was very Catholic, and according to her, homosexuals were devils. How could I tell her I was one? She was capable of taking me to church for an exorcism to get the demon out of me.

Now what was I going to do?

I had built walls around myself because I did not feel safe. Dad had suggested that I accompany him to meet his new girlfriend, who lived in Tenerife, but I was not capable of being close to him. I was terrified that he would be disgusted by my preferences and disown me. I would rather he thought I was a hateful adolescent, incapable of doing anything but blame him, than find out what I was hiding.

My trainer's hands lifted my face.

"This is going to need stitches. Don't worry. Girls like men with scars. It will give you an irresistible look. I'm going to take you to the hospital. I'll call your grandmother."

"I don't want you to worry her."

"I have to call her, or would you prefer I call your father?"

"He's traveling."

"Well then, no more talk. I'll call her. Every great skater has multiple fractures and scars. Let's go. The next triple won't escape you; you'll see. It was a near-perfect performance, and if you master it, the championship will be yours."

I offered him a tremulous smile and continued to think about how shitty my life was.

CHAPTER THIRTY-ONE

Nodus tollens: Realizing that your life is not understandable and you tend not to understand anything.

<u>Áxel, Lloret de Mar, three weeks later</u>

Having my ex-father-in-law call me to talk was not a usual thing, but my world had ceased to be predictable years ago.

We had arranged to meet at a bar away from the tourist bustle, a place that looked more like Mary Poppins would have tea with her colleagues, the magical nannies, there than a retired bricklayer and a Mosso retired from the service.

It smelled of homemade sweets and syrupy fruits. The décor was soft, weathered wood dotted with pastel armchairs covered with fluffy cushions and set in front of low refurbished tables.

The place made me think of the word "home," maybe because during the days we had been on the island, Garbiñe had baked butter cookies and muffins with the kids.

It was afternoon, and we'd celebrated because the visit to the gynecologist had gone very well. Remembering the ultrasound made me feel a pinch in my chest. Hearing our son's heartbeat for the first time when we had been told that it was impossible. Life had proved it *was* possible, a little piece of heaven, a ray of hope, a new opportunity to do things right from the beginning. This time, I wouldn't mess it up.

Sometimes you realize your life is not understandable, and you really don't understand anything. Who would have thought we would be blessed with a child when science said it was impossible?

We had our fingers twisted together, and my thumb traced circles on the inside of her wrist as my daughter stared at the monitor with her mouth open.

"Is that my daughter?" Garbiñe asked, turning to the doctor.

"Or son. We still don't know the sex," he corrected her.

The clinic had recently opened in Tenerife, Garbi had told me. The doctor was from Barcelona, and he came to consult one week a month. The rest of the time, his team was in charge of the patients while he worked in Barcelona. He was too handsome to sniff around women's legs. They were happy, but I doubted the future fathers felt the same way, given the danger from the white coat, light eyes, and dark skin.

"Don't you know the sex, Dr. Ulloa?" asked Garbiñe, her cheeks on fire as the doctor's expert hands ran the device across her belly.

"It's early. Besides, the baby's legs are crossed, and the cord is between them. Maybe on the next visit, we'll see it clearer. Mind you, it's a perfectly healthy and well-formed baby, which is what matters."

"Yes, I am very relieved. Thank you, Dr. Ulloa. It seems like this is the first and not the second."

"Every pregnancy is different. Logically, you are a little nervous, given your medical background, but you are in the best hands. I guarantee you we will do what is best for both of you at all times."

Garbi nodded.

"And I told you to call me Mino, not Doctor Ulloa. That's my father," he chided, winking at her and flashing his even white teeth. As if he hadn't said enough, the handsome man added, "It is essential that you feel comfortable with me if you want me to be at your side on the day of the birth."

Garbi nodded complacently.

"I'll be there too!" I interrupted to make my presence known.

He turned his head toward me. "I would expect nothing less. We will both be there with our favorite pregnant woman to make sure everything goes according to plan."

Favorite pregnant woman? She was *my* favorite pregnant woman. For him, she was just another patient. I felt like shaking him to make it clear. That guy brought out the most primitive part of me. He was the typical man a woman was unable to resist. A handsome young doctor and confessor of vaginas. He had read more lips than I had in my entire life.

"Are you married, Doctor?" I asked. I saw how his gestures contracted as if he was annoyed by the question.

"No. Why?"

"Because my wife and I have a friend you would enjoy."

Garbiñe opened her eyes in surprise. I had never addressed her as my wife. I didn't even think about Andrea being with us in the office. I was just trying to keep my distance and feel safe, I admit it.

"Áxel," Garbi reprimanded me.

"What? He's the perfect man for Paula. I'm sure they would like each other."

"I appreciate that, but I'm not interested in dating. I'm focused on my work and my patients. For me, that's the priority."

"You leave Mino alone! I don't know why you've suddenly got a matchmaking streak." Garbiñe laughed.

The doctor wiped the gel from her belly and urged her to adjust her clothes. "No problem. I thank you for your concern, and if at some point I was to look for a partner, I would let you know so you could give me a hand. I'm a little rusty in that regard, and you have done a very good job," he noted, looking at Garbiñe.

Again I felt jealousy gnawing on my insides. It was all my imagination, and Dr. I've-got-pussy had no other intention than to bring my son into the world safe and sound, but I had not been able to restrain myself.

We said goodbye to the doctor, or rather, Garbi did. I was really pissed that I couldn't be at the next visit, which was in a month's time. I was nervous about Dr. Ulloa's hands on her, and also, we might find out the sex of the baby, and I didn't want to miss it. However, it was impossible for me to return on that date since it coincided with a course I had to teach.

Also, it was during the week, and Andrea had school. I would have to put up with it, whether I liked it or not. Garbi seemed very comfortable with the doctor, and I could not tell her to change doctors because I was jealous.

We left the office with the most beautiful ultrasound in the world, the one that made my girls put their heads together to find similarities to that gray spot and forget about what would happen in thirty days.

"It's a girl, and she looks just like me," said Andrea, squinting at the image. "Look at her profile!"

"Well, if it's a girl and she looks like you, she'll be beautiful."

My daughter smiled with pleasure, as did Garbiñe. I couldn't have chosen a better life partner.

The next day, we left. We had done so many activities that if my daughter hadn't fallen in love with the island and her future stepmother by that point, she wasn't going to.

"Dad," Andrea whispered, pulling me out of my reverie.

"What, honey?"

"I want to move," she said flatly, leaving me speechless. Garbi and I looked at each other, unable to believe her words. "What? Wasn't that what you wanted?"

"Yes, but only if you really want to. That's what we agreed, remember?"

"Of course I remember. I told you, and I have a long memory. How can I not?"

"Don't you want to think about it?"

"No, I am determined. I don't want my little sister to grow up without me. She needs me. I have to teach her too many things, and from home. Even if we have Internet, it will be very difficult. Besides, here you can go to the beach all year round, see dolphins in the sea, climb volcanoes without them exploding, and roast marshmallows on the porch. We can't do that at home."

"No, we can't," I agreed. "Well, that's it. We'll move whenever you want. What about your friends?"

"They can come on vacation, and I'll see them when we go to see the grandparents. You just need to convince Christian because you're not going to leave him with Teresa, are you?"

"I don't want to leave him behind. Your brother is part of the family."

"I thought so. You'll have to come up with a strategy. If Christian was more into surfing than skating, you'd have an easier time. If he'd wanted to come with us, he might have been as enthusiastic about the island as I am. I don't know how we would have slept, though. That house only has two bedrooms. Now that there will be four of us, you will have to think about moving to a bigger place. With you two and Oreo, there will be seven of us, and that's a big number for such a small place."

"We can put bunk beds in Ruben's room," I offered.

"No way. Christian's feet smell terrible, and Ruben, for such a little boy, farts like a terror. I need my space, and the baby can't sleep in a polluted place. It would spoil her sense of smell for sure."

Garbiñe's lower lip trembled, and she burst out laughing.

"Well, Garbi and I will have to talk about that. She just moved in."

"I think it's a very well-thought-out and well-founded idea. Andrea is right. I thought about it when I found out I was pregnant. We need something bigger, and now that Andrea is convinced, that's all the more reason. Anyway, this is a rental house. Many boxes are still untouched in the garage. I don't think the move will be difficult if we find something we all like."

"That would be great! And look near the sea, which I love, and Ruben loves, too."

"On an island, the sea is always near," I observed.

"Yeah, but I want to see it from the window. Since I'm moving, I want to be able to see dolphins."

Garbi and I burst out laughing. "We'll do what we can. Now that we know everything is going well, I think it's time for Garbi to tell Ruben, so you and I will go for a walk while she goes to Paula's house and talks to him, okay?"

"Okay. I'm sure Ruben likes the idea, Dad. Last night he told me that you were very cool, he liked me a lot, and he had wanted a little brother for a long time. He told me that last year, he asked the Three Kings, but they didn't listen to him. I explained that sometimes they are late and some orders get lost. I created the perfect scenario for Garbiñe to be able to tell him that, in the end, the Kings did listen to him. That would be cool. She likes to keep the magic of Christmas," said my daughter, pointing her thumb at her.

"Thank you for your concern for Ruben. I think your idea is great. I'm sure he would love it if I gave him that kind of news. Thank you very much," said Garbiñe, excited.

"There's no need. That's what we older sisters are here for—to maintain traditions and keep the little ones' hopes alive," she said solemnly. "I'm not a Christmas bummer. Ruben is safe with me."

"I'm glad to hear that. You're going to be the best big sister in the world." I squeezed her.

"I will do what I can."

My daughter moved toward Garbi's belly. "Did you hear that?

You're in luck, little girl. You're going to be in the care of the best." She lifted her face to my sergeant, who could barely hold in her excitement. "May I?" she asked, looking at the softly rounded belly.

"Of course," Garbiñe agreed happily.

Andrea placed her hands on the little belly and slid them in an affectionate gesture that melted the mother-to-be. Garbiñe's hands rose tremulously to the girl's back, and she ended up hugging her with her ear placed on the curvature.

Tears rolled down Garbiñe's cheeks. She raised her eyes to the sky, murmuring a "Thank you" that burned in my chest. I reached out to engage them in a three-way embrace.

The bells the owner of the cafeteria had placed over the door tinkled, announcing the entrance of a new customer. Antonio, my ex-father-in-law, had entered the premises.

When he reached the table, the girl came to take our order. "Two black coffees, please," I told the waitress.

She withdrew and within two minutes, came back with two cups accompanied by two freshly baked blueberry mini-muffins.

"Watch out. I just took them out of the oven. I hope you like them."

"Sure, thank you very much."

"You're welcome."

She withdrew, leaving us alone.

"I didn't think of you as a regular at a place like this."

"I am not. You know I like Juan's bar and my morning *carajillo* better. Some habits are ingrained," he confessed.

"So?"

"So I was looking for a place where Tere and her friends couldn't poke their noses in. Those women have eyes everywhere. They wouldn't look for you or me here."

"True, but I wouldn't mind being seen with you. Although I imagine that if you do, it's because you have to tell me something complex. Am I wrong?"

"No. That's why you are such a good Mosso. You've always been sharp. You know I've never gotten too involved. My daughter wanted to marry you, and I accepted that. Then you separated, and I didn't say anything. For me, your happiness comes before the church. I don't think like my wife. The idea that marriage is forever is obsolete."

He poured sugar and stirred carefully. "When my grandson wanted to live with us, I didn't like the idea. I believe children should be with their parents, but I understood that you needed time, so I didn't oppose it. However, sometimes you have to show your face and speak."

"I don't understand."

"I imagine not. I delayed this conversation too long. The time has come for us to have it and for me to tell you what I know. Before I do, I have to say that I don't blame you for my daughter's death. I think that if it happened this way, it was because it had to. I do not see Teresa's attitude as being right. My wife was not fair to you or the girl you are with. You have every right in the world to rebuild your life, and my daughter also. In fact, she had started to do it."

"How?" I didn't know what he was talking about.

"My daughter had started something with someone, but nobody knew anything about it. It was all very recent. You know how Teresa is. She would not allow Claudia to rebuild her life with someone other than you. For her, marriage is sacred, and she had faith that you would reconcile. Claudia was very influenced by the upbringing her mother gave her. I just worked my backside off and didn't get involved. That's why it was so hard for my daughter to turn the page. It's not easy to do so with a mother like hers. However, she had."

"How do you know that?"

"Because I saw them. She left the kids with us and said she was having dinner with the girls from work, but it wasn't true. I had run out of cigarettes, so I went to Juan's bar to buy a pack, and I stayed longer than I should have. They were kissing in the street, unseen by anyone but me, who wasn't supposed to be there. I thought that since it was your friend, you would know about it, but the way you acted, I'd say he hasn't told you yet."

"My friend? What friend?"

My head was spinning. It wasn't that my ex-wife shouldn't get her life back together. Of course she should! But it was news to me, and if what Antonio said was true, maybe I could get Christian back and put my ex-mother-in-law in her place.

"I don't know if I should say his name, but the evil is already done, and I'm not one to throw a stone and hide my hand." He was silent for several seconds, and I waited for him to speak. "Tarradellas, Andrea's godfather, was the man who kissed her."

Carles hooked up with Claudia? I would never have thought it. They got along well, but only to a point. He had always praised her beauty and sympathy. It never crossed my mind that he was attracted to her.

Why didn't Carles say anything? Why didn't he speak in my favor with Christian or Teresa at the funeral? What if my ex-father-in-law was confused? Maybe Antonio had been drunk and had gotten mixed up about seeing them.

"Are you sure it was him?"

"They were under a lamppost. My close-up eyesight is gone, but my long-distance vision is as sharp as a bat's eye. Besides, he brought her in his car, and he had the emergency lights on. I waited for them to finish and gave Claudia a five-minute head start when I saw her leave."

"How do you know they hadn't been together long?"

"Because my daughter wasn't in a hurry to leave. You know, lovey-dovey stuff. He was texting her on his cell phone, and she was grinning like a fool in the doorway. It was a strange moment.

We both tried to disguise it, but we knew each other too well. My daughter ended up confessing, and I supported her.

"She told me that it had started a few weeks ago over coffee to organize the party she wanted to give my granddaughter for her victory in the interschool judo championship. He had been looking at her for a long time, but he hadn't dared to take the step. That afternoon bore fruit, igniting a spark that hadn't existed before."

"Wow." I sighed. "I had no idea. If it's as you say, Carles must have had a terrible time."

"He is a good man. His intentions were serious. He just didn't have time to carry them out."

"I have to think, and I have to talk to him."

"I can imagine. I took this step because I appreciate you. You will always be the father of my grandchildren."

"Christian is not doing good, spending so much time with Teresa. As one gets older, one's faults become more pronounced. She has always been very closed and very believable. I love her, and we've been together for many years. Don't misunderstand me; it's just that she says things that..." He clicked his tongue. "Children are for parents to raise and grandparents to spoil. If I have to speak for you to get your son back, I will. I just wanted you to know."

"Thank you, Antonio, you're a good man," I murmured, taking a sip of coffee. "It's on me. I have to go talk to Carles."

"Go. I'll stay a little longer and enjoy the muffins. Now I am at peace because I know I have done the right thing."

"I will always be grateful to you for that. Thank you again."

I shook his hand and went in search of my best friend. I needed to talk to him and have him clarify things for me. I didn't want to lose him. Carles was very important to me, even though he hadn't come forward knowing what he knew, and that hurt me.

I had to find out why and try to resolve it.

CHAPTER THIRTY-TWO

Fernweh: Feeling homesick for a place you have never been.

Áxel

I had no trouble getting Carles to agree to meet for a chat.

Since my return, we had not seen each other, and I sensed that he thought I had summoned him to update him on what had happened in Tenerife. We met at a restaurant where we used to go to eat. Andrea was eating at the school, so we would have enough peace and quiet to talk openly.

When he saw me, his smile widened.

"What's up, man? You're looking good!" he greeted me.

I looked at his slightly thinner, haggard face. How had I missed the signs? Had I been so blinded by navel-gazing that I hadn't noticed what was happening to my best friend?

"You, on the other hand, look exhausted."

"Yes, well, it's just that Carbajal has taken sick leave, and I had to take a double shift this week. You look great. The trip was good for you."

"Let's say things are falling into place."

"And my goddaughter?"

"She wants to move and for us to buy a bigger house."

Carles laughed.

"That girl is unique. I knew that Garbiñe would eventually win her over. Are you going to do it? Are you going to move?"

"Yes. Having a long-distance family is not in my plans."

"What about Chris? How did he take it?"

"I haven't said anything to my son yet. You know our relationship is still very strained."

"I thought maybe Andrea had smoothed things over between the two of you."

"To smooth out our differences, I would need a very large file. I asked her to stay out of it. I don't want them to fight because of me. Besides, Andrea is excited about the arrival of her future sister."

"Is it a girl?"

"We don't know yet, but she insists it's a girl because it wouldn't be fair for it to be three against one."

"I can imagine. Did you get along well with Garbi's son?"

"Very well."

"So, you're doing it."

"Christian is missing from the equation, as you said. I'm not leaving without him."

"Of course not! Have you thought about how to bring him around?" He leaned forward, fixing his eyes on mine.

"I thought about you."

"Me?" My answer made him pull back. "I don't know how I could help you, but you know you can count on me for anything."

"Anything?"

Carles nodded.

"Well, start by being honest. Why you didn't tell me you were with Claudia?"

He went pale, and the cup he was going to put to his lips did not reach its destination.

"You don't have to pretend, not with me. I thought we were friends and we told each other everything. What did you think, that I would oppose you? That it would make me uncomfortable or upset me? For God's sake, Carles, you're my best friend, and Claudia is the mother of my children! I would never have opposed your happiness!"

Carles pinched the bridge of his nose and looked at the table-cloth, shaking his head. "I knew you wouldn't have objected. I wanted to tell you, but Claudia didn't feel ready. She had been too engrossed in your relationship to jump lightly into ours.

"I always told you that I thought she was very pretty and I liked her very much. I don't want to make excuses. I just want you to understand me. I always liked her, even if I didn't say anything. That night you got involved with her, you screwed up my plan! Although, if she preferred you to me, it had to be that way."

"I had no idea. Why didn't you tell me?" He shrugged.

"What was I going to tell you?"

"Well, that you liked her. If I had known that, I wouldn't have started anything with her."

"But she liked you. Otherwise, she wouldn't have hooked up with you. It was written. I just respected it. As long as she was your wife, I never said anything to her. When you left her, I tried to be her support. You know what I mean—to bring her closure. Fuck, I'm not made of stone!" His voice broke.

"You liked her a lot."

"I loved her! I had adored her for years. Seeing her was like being nostalgic for a place you've never been, like you've always been with New York. Claudia was very stubborn. She was impervious to my advances and kept slamming the door in my face. Then one day, something changed."

I didn't want to interrupt him. I needed to understand why my best friend had kept something so important from me for so long. "It was three weeks before the accident. I met Claudia to give her a hand with Andrea's party. She had barely eaten, and I insisted on ordering beer instead of coffee. You know Claudia wasn't much of a drinker, and I played dirty, I confess. I needed her to loosen up and not just see me as Andrea's godfather or your friend. I wanted her to see *me*, the man she always overlooked."

"And she saw you."

"Yes, she saw me. For the first time, a different light flashed in those beautiful eyes, the color of the sky. I thought I could touch it with my fingers," he murmured regretfully. "I didn't have enough time to make her the woman in my life. She left before I could tell her what I wanted, that I had always loved her and I had been waiting for her because she was the engine of my life. I didn't make it in time. I had planned a romantic weekend the following week when it was your turn with the children, but Fate cut her life short."

A bitter laugh passed between his lips. "That fucking accident took away the only chance I had with her, and worst of all, I couldn't tell you anything because I promised her we'd keep it a secret until she felt ready. I am a man of my word, Áxel; you know me. You know I would never betray a person who placed her trust in me, especially when it meant so much."

"Is that why you didn't tell me?"

Carles nodded. "I'm sorry I kept you in the dark about what was going on. I really am. And I'm sorry I couldn't comfort you the way you deserved."

"I'm sorry I took the woman of your life away from you, and I'm very sorry for your loss. You would have made a great couple," I told him seriously.

Carles broke down and cried like a child. Seeing a brave man break down in a public place was not easy. My friend buried his face in his hands, trying to hide it. I pulled the chair closer and put my arm around his shoulders. He tried unsuccessfully to hold back his sobs, then cried on my shoulder.

His grief lasted for several minutes, then, "It is too late to make memories with her. I watched her struggle between life and death for days without letting her know I was there. I may not have been there as much as you, but no one was supposed to suspect anything. You don't know what it was like not to be able to say goodbye. To know she was on the other side of the lifeless glass and not to be able to approach her to kiss her one last time. In that instant, my soul left me to be by her side."

Hearing that confession hurt me. I did not like to see my friend in that condition, broken by grief over the loss of Claudia. I didn't even want to imagine what it had meant for him. If, instead of my ex-wife, Garbiñe had been in that situation, I would be the same or worse than Carles. I felt the need to tell him something that would give him hope.

"She knew it. She knew it for sure, and that's why she fought tooth and nail until the end. She felt you were waiting for her."

"It was not enough."

"No, it wasn't. Sometimes even the strongest love is not enough, but you gave her the best three weeks of her life. She was never fully happy with me. She surely was with you. Come to think of it, you were made for each other. I don't know how I could have been so blind."

"Sometimes I console myself by thinking that she needed to leave you to notice me. I don't know. Maybe it's bullshit. There are times when I break down and think I am just a Band-Aid, a substitute. That the one she really loved was you and not me."

"Don't talk nonsense. We were together for many years, and we had children. That, whether you like it or not, brought us together. However, it doesn't mean I was the ideal person for her. I feel much closer to Garbiñe than I ever felt to Claudia in all the time we were together.

"Now, I am going to tell you something. If she hadn't loved you, if she hadn't fallen in love with you, she would never have let you into her life. Claudia was extremely strict about those things.

She loved you, Carles. You can be sure of that. We no longer had anything, only our love for our children and a special affection from having been together for so many years. It was you who occupied her heart at the end."

His body jerked against mine, and he pressed his face into my shoulder again. "Thank you for your comfort and for your words. They mean a lot to me. You don't know what a weight it is off my mind that you finally know. I could hardly look at your face without feeling guilty."

"Now it's all cleared up."

"May I ask how you found out?"

"Antonio knew."

My friend broke away from me, blinking in surprise. "Your ex-father-in-law knew?"

I nodded. "He saw you kissing one day."

"As careful as we were." He exhaled.

"We can all make mistakes. Besides, when Claudia met him on the landing, she confessed."

"He didn't say anything to me."

"You see? You were much more important than you imagined."

"Maybe you're right." His eyes recovered a bit of the hope he had lost. "Now I understand. That's why, before you arrived at the funeral home the day we buried her, he made me come in to say goodbye and left me alone with her for a few minutes."

"Antonio is a great man. He is nothing like Teresa."

"Claudia was terrified that her mother would find out. She said Teresa would never admit a man other than you into her life."

"My ex-mother-in-law is a very difficult woman with strong convictions, even if they are often not the right ones."

"I understand that your plan to bring your son closer to you is to tell him about us so you and Garbiñe's relationship don't seem so bad in his eyes."

"That was the idea, although, given your promise, I understand that you don't want to do it. I know you are a man of your word. I'm not going to ask you to tell Christian. On second thought, that's not a good option anyway. He adored his mother, and I want to keep it that way. I'll have to find another way to bring us closer together. However, I don't want you to misunderstand me. You and she were nothing to be ashamed of."

"I understand your position, and I share it. If there was no other way and your happiness depended on my talking to your son and telling him the truth, I would do it. I would rather break a promise than see you two estranged if I could help it."

"I appreciate it, but I'm sure there's something else I can do. Let me think about it."

"I'll think about it too. I'm sure that between the two of us, we'll think of something."

Garbiñe

"You haven't got a brain in your head, daughter! Getting knocked up by a man you've just met is despicable!" My mother was giving me the sermon in her Sunday best, with a steaming cup of tea in her hands. "On top of that, I had to find out from Dario. If it were up to you, I would have taken communion, and I wouldn't have known you had another child."

"Oh, please, Mom. I'm telling you, aren't I?"

Maybe she was right. If my ex hadn't opened his mouth, I would have delayed the conversation. Facing my mother made me crazy, and I knew she would take Dario's side. Dario had been quick to disapprove of my pregnancy. When Ruben was up to date with my state, it was only a matter of days before his father found out. He ran into the arms of my mother, his protector, to cry about his miseries.

"If your father was here, you don't know how disappointed he would be."

That was it. I would not tolerate that. After years of silence, for her to come out with that now! Well, no more. I was tired, and I didn't want to keep silent any longer. The time had come to have the conversation we'd never had.

"In me or you?"

She looked at me with wide eyes. "Praise the Lord, you mean because of Cristóbal?"

"I'm saying it for you. I haven't done anything wrong. I just fell in love and got my life together. You were screwing Cristóbal when Dad was at work. I never said anything, and I could have. Your behavior was despicable."

That was it. I had let it out.

My mother looked like she was about to explode. "What are you talking about, you fool? Are the pregnancy hormones getting to your head?"

I looked at her blankly. She wouldn't dare to deny it, or maybe she would.

"I saw you, Mom! One day, coming back from class, on top of the kitchen counter, while you were supposed to be making lunch, he was having *you* for lunch."

"I won't tolerate you talking to me like that."

"I don't care what you will tolerate. I don't even know why I kept quiet. Well, maybe I do—because I didn't want to hurt Dad. He didn't deserve to know what a sneaky liar you are."

"Liar? Don't make me laugh. If I slept with Cristóbal, it was because your father was always tired, and I needed more than he gave me. And as for the lies, I could accuse you of the same thing! You never told me about your illness. Dario did."

"You know I'm sick?" I didn't see that coming.

She folded her arms and looked at me smugly. "Of course. He told me about it as soon as he found out. Who do you think comforted him when you had those crises when you would lock yourself in your room and not let him touch you?"

"I can't believe it." I snorted. "Did you expect me to eat it when

I was sick? I was suffering from hellish migraines that made me unable to do anything."

"It is proven that headaches go away with sex. Your husband is a young, vital, fiery man, and you were not up to it. Even in that, you were like your father. It's logical that he had to seek comfort in the arms of others. What was he going to do, settle for you?"

"How about being by his wife's side when she needed him the most instead of partying with others? How can you side with him instead of me? Where did you leave your maternal instincts, at the municipal dump?"

"You don't understand. You're not warm-blooded like us."

"Ask Áxel about that. He thinks otherwise."

"That's the name of the substitute?"

"That's the name of the man in my life, and I'm ashamed that you are my mother. And to think there was a time when I felt inferior to you. Now I feel sorry for you. I don't know how you can be so hollow and empty of feelings."

"*Hollow?*"

"Yes, hollow. You live for your image, for what others think of you. For your parties and for what people will say, but inside, you are empty and selfish. Knowing I was sick, you never came to ask how I was, and you recommended that my husband should have fun with other women without taking into account the damage it would do to me. You deceived my father, and you made me believe I was less than you because I didn't have your self-confidence, your poise, and that innate energy that attracted everyone. What I didn't realize was that you are no supernova but a black hole that sucks the light out of everyone who comes near and tries to love you."

"Are you an astronomer now?" She scoffed.

"No, I just dropped the blindfold. You will always be my mother, even if the title is too good for you. I will let you see your grandchildren because, whether I like it or not, you are their grandmother, but you and I will limit ourselves to something you know how to do perfectly: pretend a cordial relationship. I won't expect anything from you, and don't expect anything from me either. You will have no say in my life, and I will stay out of yours. If you like Dario so much, leave Cristóbal and marry him. I'm sure you'll be very happy fucking each other," I said, getting up from the sofa.

"You're ungrateful. How can you talk to me like that?"

"Because you deserve it. I may be ungrateful, but you are a bad mother. We are at an impasse, and if you'll excuse me, I'm leaving. I'm meeting Áxel for a video call."

"That's right, go away. You're an expert at leaving when you don't like something."

"Of course I'm leaving. I don't like you, and I don't have to put up with you anymore. I hope life gives you everything you deserve, Mom."

"Are you wishing me something bad?"

"God forbid! I do not believe in an eye for an eye because, in the end, the world would be full of blind people."

It was the last thing I said loud enough for her to hear me since I was walking down the hall.

CHAPTER THIRTY-THREE

Kumorebi: Light filtering through the leaves of the trees.

<u>Garbiñe</u>

I settled comfortably on the rocking chair on the back porch, glass of grape juice in hand. I had relegated wine to the background.

The evening light filtered through the branches of the neighbors' fruit trees, warming my skin.

The sun tinted the sky with red, blue, and orange, which made me think of Áxel and the kisses we gave each other in this place that felt empty without him.

The pregnancy was progressing well, although I was worried about the time of delivery. It was still months away, but given my illness, complications could arise. Dr. Ulloa had told me that I had to take good care of myself, especially my diet. I should also walk or swim to keep in shape and keep my circulation in its optimum state.

I asked him not to talk to Áxel about the risks that a person like me could suffer. I did not want to worry him. There was a small possibility that things might not go well, but maybe nothing would happen to me. It was better to stay positive and trust Mino's professionalism. He was one of the best in his field, which was why I wanted him as my gynecologist. He had been recommended by my doctor when I told him I was expecting a child.

The familiar ringing of the phone ended my musings.

Áxel's face appeared on the screen, and my smile widened. I pushed all my worries out of my mind. Nothing was going to go wrong; we deserved only good things. Life had been hard enough on us without more things going wrong.

"Hello, Sergeant," I greeted him as his incredible dark eyes greedily swept over me.

"Jesus, Garbi! Have you grown, or did you put on one of those pushup bras?" he exclaimed, eyes on my cleavage.

I had imagined his reaction since my blouse barely covered my new friends. "I water them every night. I've already gained two sizes."

"I want to see them. I don't believe all that's yours."

"Are you asking me to show you my tits, Sergeant?"

"It's not a request but a plea and a need. Come on, baby, let me see them."

I blushed and moistened my lips. I had my hands free to move as I pleased since I had become an expert at making video calls. My cell phone was on a table so I could gesticulate without restraint, and today, I was less restrained than usual. I needed an outlet, and Áxel's proposal didn't seem so bad.

I looked this way and that to make sure there were no prying eyes. Feeling kinky, I reached back to unclasp my bra, pull it off without showing anything, and put it in front of the cell phone camera so Áxel could check the size of the cups with his own eyes. I then placed the label in front of the lens.

"A hundred?" He sounded flabbergasted.

"Uh-huh," I admitted, putting the garment aside.

"I'm on the verge of a heart attack. My pulse is racing, and my need for an ocular inspection is dire. Be good and show me what I so badly want to see. Have pity on this poor, needy man." He pouted

I laughed. "I will, but only because I haven't done my good deed for the day yet."

I slowly ran my fingers down the skin of my cleavage and undid the buttons one by one. If a neighbor saw me, it was easier to cover myself than if I pulled it over my head.

"A little faster, please. I need you."

I wanted to provoke him. Feeling desired was a new experience, and I was enjoying it. I licked my lips, which were much more swollen than usual. A pregnant woman's body undergoes many changes, most of them due to fluid retention. That had done me a favor. The enlarged body parts felt great. A little more breast and hip and much more sensitive lips that I kept attending to with my tongue and teeth.

"Woman, you're killing me," he muttered when I reached the last button. I unfastened it, revealing a vertical line of flesh. "Today is one of those days when I'd like to give you one of those hugs that make you lose your underwear."

I laughed under my breath. "Are you ready?"

"I've been ready for weeks. You don't know how much I miss you."

"I have an idea," I replied, opening my shirt.

The coolness of the breeze caressed the same spot as his eyes. It felt as if *he* were brushing me instead of the wind. My nipples puckered with longing.

"God, baby! What I would give to be there, to be able to kiss them, lick them, and shower them with attention. Caress them for me, please."

"You're asking a lot of me. Someone might come," I replied.

"Well, go in the house. I want to see all of you."

"Are you proposing phone sex?"

"You're getting it. I have to unload my sperm, or I'm going to end up with hot ideas in my brain."

I chuckled at his nonsense.

"We can relieve ourselves together. I'd rather do it that way than bang it against the shower tiles. Do you feel like it?" he asked slyly.

"With you, there is nothing I don't feel like. I'm looking forward to one of those nights where everything hurts the next day, although given our distance, it's not possible," I tempted him.

"Okay, we'd better leave it here. I'll go to the airport and hijack a plane that will bring me straight to your house."

I was walking while listening to him, then placed the cell phone on the sideboard and stood in front of it, leaning on the table.

Without being asked, I took off my shirt, letting him stare at me openly. I swear I didn't see him blink once, which made me want to be the sin he would never regret.

I was determined to be bold enough to leave him open-mouthed. From the way he was hyperventilating, I was succeeding. That, or he was in the throes of an asthma attack. The corners of my lips turned up at my quip. Desire flowed through my bloodstream, demanding that I continue.

I was barefoot, which meant I was able to get rid of my pants and reveal the panties Paula had given me. It was from a popular underwear brand with funny messages. Maybe my subconscious had thought of Áxel when I chose it after the shower; I don't know. He held his breath when he read the message. *I'm the six that's missing from your nine.*

"You are perverse. You get off because I'm thousands of miles away."

"Who says I want to get out of it?" I ran my thumb under the elastic. I was empowered and wet and horny, a bad combination when my guy was so far away.

My left hand was gripping the table, and my right hand had

set a course south to a wetter, warmer destination. I ran my fingers over my clitoris, which responded by hardening, and let out a gasp that made him grunt.

"Take that off! I want to see the whole picture. It's like watching an evening movie on Canal Plus when it was pay per view, and you had to imagine what was going on behind the lines."

"You watched those movies? You were just a kid!"

"It's never too early when it comes to sex!"

"I'll remind you of that when Andrea's time comes." His expression changed, but he refocused, expelling the image. Most fathers act that way when they hear that their daughters might become involved in relationships.

"You are bad."

"If you want to watch, I want to watch too. Strip for me. Don't be stingy."

In five seconds he was naked, locked in the bathroom, and jumping up and down to finish getting rid of the pants that were still tangled in his underwear.

"Where's your daughter?" I asked when he finally got rid of the fiendish garment.

"Now you're worried about whether I'm alone?" He clicked his tongue. "Relax; she's at judo, I just locked myself in here as a precaution. I'd hate for there to be an unforeseen event and get caught with a naked pervert looking at me on my cell phone while she demands I do dirty things with her."

"Me, a pervert?"

"Very kinky, and you know what? I love to see you so uninhibited with my pendant on. Look how you have me!" His hand went up and down his taut member, which made me salivate. "My turn has come. I've fulfilled my part of the bargain."

All right," I agreed, fiddling with the cotton piece. I stood with my back to him, butt in the air and head turned so as not to miss his expressions. With my free hand, I pulled down my panties and rubbed my legs together so they fell to the floor, causing a shock in my sex that brought out a small whimper.

The other hand continued with caresses Áxel could not see but could perceive.

"Fuck, your ass has grown too. It's much tighter and rounder! You're going to give me a stroke! I want to lick you like an ice cream cone without forgetting any part."

"I'd love for you to do that. I'll remind you the next time we meet. By the way, I think that's the first time a man has ever told me that my ass has grown as a positive thing."

"Well, you can keep it for me so I can turn into a wolf and howl at that appetizing full moon. As soon as I get there, I'm going to lock you up so no one will bother us, then binge on you. I need to fill my tank. I've been on reserve for weeks."

"Exaggerated," I taunted, feeling the same way he did.

I spread my legs and looked for a good angle so the target could see how I was being penetrated. I wanted him to see how the flow was soaking my fingers.

I came with force, the lust of the moment sweeping me away. I had to lean against the table to relieve the heaviness of my new breasts, which were painfully tense.

"Keep going, honey! Don't stop. God, you're squirting! Remember me thanking the guy at the cell phone store when he recommended these for video calls? I can almost feel it going in you!"

I had to laugh. I needed to see it, and although I was embarrassed about what I was about to do, Áxel clearly enjoyed the boldness of the new Garbi.

I turned around, rested my hands on the table, and with a little jump, sat on it, putting my ass on the edge. I spread my thighs wide and put the fingers that had penetrated me into my mouth.

"Oh, my God, baby! I'm going to come!"

"You can't do it yet," I said, slipping my fingers in and out as if they were his member, the salty taste bursting on my taste buds. When I had my fingers wet, I anointed my nipples, then pinched and pulled them, feeling thousands of shocks in my vagina.

"You are a feast for all the senses. Look how I am! This is all because of you."

I had closed my eyes without realizing it, the mist of passion veiling his handsome face. He was rigid, the head of his member swollen and shiny.

"Tell me what you want me to do, and I will do it," I suggested.

"I want you to finger-fuck yourself as if it were my dick. Make it hard, intense, slow, hot, until you come screaming my name. I want you to be so horny that you wet the floor." Those words spoken in a hoarse voice made me go crazy. "Let me get a good look at you. Put your feet up on the table and show me how I make you feel when I'm inside you."

I did it. I liberated myself completely, feeling every thrust, every gesture, as if it were his, from the man who made me give myself without reserve, with whom I grew, expanded, and exploded, feeling the joy of being alive.

My hips rose, intoxicated by his hot gaze, when I saw him stimulating himself without taking his eyes off the spectacle I was offering him. My hands were his, and my gasps matched his grunts. It was him I was surrendering to, even if I was rubbing myself.

I didn't hold on long, and neither did he. We were both on the edge. When I shouted his name, he yelled mine. It had never sounded so good. So beautiful and so full.

Unhinged and breathing erratically, I looked at him and saw nothing I didn't like. Áxel, for all his flaws and scars, was the most handsome man I had ever seen.

"It was brutal," he admitted, turning on the faucet to clean himself.

"It was," I replied, trying to get off the table without falling. Underneath me was the proof that I had come abundantly.

"Did you wet the floor?" he asked, soaping himself.

"I think I saw a couple of ducks swimming by. I'm getting off the table with care so I don't slip."

"If there are ducks, hunt them. If you don't do it, the Chinese restaurant in your town will."

"I doubt he'll come now, and I'm not going to open the door for him. If you'll excuse me, I'm going to the bathroom too."

"Okay, but take a shower with the curtain open. I need more images so I have something to think about when this wears off."

"Who's the pervert now?" I questioned, going into the bathroom to turn the water to lukewarm.

"I've always been. The one who was prudish was you, and you've never been prudish with me."

"That's because you turn me on so much."

"And you me. Now, be a good girl and get in there and soap up. I'm going to tape you."

"Don't even think about it. You can watch me but don't record it, or no more private functions."

"That's the only thing that will help me resist until I can touch you again. I want you to come for the May 1st long weekend."

"You know I'd love to. Let's see if things have improved with your son by then. Maybe I can win him over."

"I hope so. Teresa and Antonio scheduled a trip to Lourdes, so he'll be with me."

"Great. I hope we don't miss it this time," I admitted, grabbing the bottle of gel to squirt it on my skin.

"You know what you're doing to me? I've got a boner again!"

"Don't say it, or I'll never look at this soap the same way. Okay, rub yourself and keep looking at me. We're going for a second round."

CHAPTER THIRTY-FOUR

Alexithymia: Inability to identify and express emotions.

Garbiñe, one week later

"Thank you very much for changing the time and agreeing to broadcast the ultrasound live. Not many doctors would have agreed to my folly."

"I'm not like most doctors, and you're not just any patient," he replied cheerfully. "Besides, the person you should be thanking is the patient who agreed to change the time as soon as I told her what it was for."

"Thank her for me."

"I already did," he replied. Paula had accompanied me to the consultation room and was sitting next to me, quieter than usual. How handsome Mino was had freaked her out. Maybe it was better that way since every time she spoke, she started something. "Before we start and you call Áxel, how do you feel?"

I had been more exhausted than usual for a few days, which I attributed to the walks I was taking with Ruben and Orco. When Dr. Ulloa told me that walking would improve my circulation, I took him at his word. I told him that I was more fatigued than usual. It could be the pregnancy or that I was anemic, but to be on the safe side, he had scheduled tests to see how I was doing.

"Headaches?"

"I haven't suffered from migraines since before the pregnancy, so they seem to be under control."

"You must follow all my instructions. Given your condition, we had to eliminate practically all the medications you were taking to control your disease. I need you to tell me everything, no matter how small it may seem to you, to ensure your good health and that of the fetus."

"I am very strict in all facets of my life, but on that one, I border on obsession. I guarantee I follow every guideline. I don't want anything to happen to me or my son."

Paula, who was sitting next to me ogling the doctor, agreed with me. "She is not lying to you. I can attest that she is complying with every measure you gave her."

"I'm glad to hear that." Mino seemed immune to the charms of my friend, who was unsettled.

It was strange that her physique did not make the man nervous. Paula had an animal magnetism toward the opposite sex that was usually activated by her mere presence. However, Dr. Ulloa was not affected. He was much more attentive to me than to her.

You may think it's normal since I was the pregnant one, but with Paula, it was never like that.

"Go to the gurney and pull down your pants."

They used to ask her that before me. I laughed, contemplating my friend's dumbfounded face.

"Paula, are you ready to call Áxel?"

"Of course. You know I can't wait to see what he says when we find out the sex of the baby. I'm sure he'll be excited no matter what."

"I think so too. This little one is a miracle. All we want is for everything to go well."

"It will be fine, you'll see. And now listen to the doctor and show us that belly so we can find out if it will be a mini Áxel or a beautiful Garbi."

I walked to the gurney, eager to find out.

Paula took advantage of the moment to ask Mino for a checkup. He told her that he had a full schedule but that if she wanted to be seen at the clinic, any doctor on his team would be happy to see her, and she could make an appointment when she left.

My friend's expression must have been epic. She was never rejected by the opposite sex, but she was relegated to the status of "just another patient." It was gratifying. Don't get me wrong, but I thought it was funny to find a man who didn't want to get his hands on her crotch, even professionally.

I climbed onto the gurney, pulled my pants down to pubic level, and waited for both of them to appear.

Paula did so with a frown and Mino with his usual affable expression.

Paula took out her cell phone to call while the doctor put cold gel on my belly and moved the ultrasound wand, tracing circles. I had asked him to do me the favor of changing the time because at two o'clock, Andrea was usually home. Áxel and I had planned a surprise I hoped she would be excited about.

"Hello!" the voices of my man and his daughter said in unison.

"Hello," Paula replied affectionately.

"Have they told her yet that the baby is a girl?" It was my future stepdaughter.

"I'm with her, but we still don't know anything. Look where we called you from."

Paula changed the camera position to focus on me, the sonographer, and Mino, who waved at the camera with his free hand.

She let out a shriek that almost deafened us.

"She's at the doctor's, Dad! We got a call from the doctor's office!"

Áxel exuded happiness. "Yes, honey. It was a surprise for you."

"Did you know?" she asked, squinting at him.

"Garbi thought you'd be thrilled if we all found out together."

Andrea put her hands to her mouth and looked at the cell phone with moist eyes. "Thank you, I'm so excited! I don't know what to say!"

That made my heart swell.

"Garbiñe unveils the mystery she is hiding," Mino muttered. "Look, those are the arms, the fingers."

"Does it have all of them? I've heard that some babies are born without some of them."

Mino squinted at the image with total seriousness.

"I think so. He's not missing any."

"That's great!" Andrea murmured. "It's better to have them all. Each one has its use, you know, Doctor? The fat one is to say that everything is fine, the index finger to point or to get rid of snot that is bothering you—using a handkerchief, of course. The middle one is for combing the hair of bullies, the ring finger for getting married, and the little finger is for scratching your ear when it itches inside."

We all laughed at her explanation.

"I can see that you are very knowledgeable, and the baby has all its fingers. Can I go on?" asked Mino, lowering the device to the legs.

"Yes, please."

"Very good. So, here we have the legs, the feet with their corresponding toes, and here! Let's see if it doesn't resist this time." He shook the device and pressed it to my belly. The baby was annoyed and changed its position, positioning itself sideways and offering us a perfect view. It was a neonatal "fuck you." I held my breath because I was sure what I was seeing. It was not the first time I had seen it.

"Well, it looks like it's a boy. These here are his testicles."

"That can't be testicles!" Andrea shouted. "I'm sure it's her ovaries. They've come out."

"What are you talking about, daughter? You don't even know what ovaries are," Áxel scolded.

"Of course I know! Mom said that it's something we women have inside, and they're big, round, and fat. They swell up when men do things that upset us or say silly things. I'm sure my little sister was upset because you said she has a penis. She's a girl!"

Mino laughed under his breath. "Your mother's theory about ovaries is true, but this little guy hasn't grown any because he's a boy," the gynecologist confirmed. "I hope that won't be a setback for you. Being the only girl does have its advantages. I'm sure your brothers will be very concerned about you, and you'll be the princess of the house."

"I don't need you to worry about me, and I don't like princesses," she protested in disgust.

"Why not?" Mino asked.

"Because they're lazy."

"That's not true. Look at Rapunzel, Merida, and Mulan. They were all very brave princesses," Paula argued. "Haven't you seen the movies?"

"No, I got tired of Snow White's foolishness. She choked on an apple. Didn't anyone tell that little girl not to eat things given to her by a stranger? I prefer the Avengers. No one takes the piss out of them."

"Well, I'll see to it that you change your mind. Not all princesses are like Snow White or Aurora. I'll show them all to you so you can learn a very valuable lesson," Paula told her. "Not all princesses are stupid, and not all warriors are good. Since you are a smart girl, I know you will take care of your little brother just as you did with Ruben when you were in Tenerife. You will teach him to fight like he was a girl, and you will fill him with love because, in the end, whether he is a boy or a girl is not important. The important thing is that he is part of you and yours. Right?"

Andrea raised her shoulders. "You're right about one thing. I'll have to teach him to fight since boys get picked on too. If my brother had done judo instead of skating, he wouldn't have come home the other day with a black eye and a split lip."

"What do you mean, a black eye and a split lip?" asked Áxel, who didn't seem to be aware of the event.

Andrea made a face. "Oops, it slipped out. I shouldn't have said anything. I'm sorry, Dad."

He was agitated, and who could blame him? Christian was being a tough nut to crack.

"What happened to him, Andrea?"

Paula, Mino, and I kept our eyes on the girl, who didn't know how to get out of the mess. The ultrasound was on the back burner. She stood up and, lifting her chin, told her father, "Ask him. I'm not your snitch!"

"Andrea!" Áxel snapped.

"I don't know what happened. Chris didn't tell me. I only know that he came home and locked himself in his room afterward. If you want to know anything else, you'll have to ask him directly."

"As if that is so easy," her father chided.

"I have to go to school now. Saved by the bell," Andrea muttered.

"Don't think you're going to get away from this interrogation, young lady. On the way to school, you're going to tell me everything you know. I can't believe that's it, as smart as you are."

Andrea let out a snort, then looked at me. "Here's a big kiss, Garbi, and one for you too, Paula. Give another one to Ruben and Oreo, and…what are you going to call him?

"I have no idea. Your father and I have to decide, but suggestions are welcome."

"I will think about it, I promise."

Andrea pressed her hands against her mouth, air-kissed us, and disappeared.

Áxel had a worried look on his face. I knew the wrinkle that crossed his forehead well and felt the need to relieve him. Fucking distance. If I had been here, I would be hugging him now.

"Honey, I'm sure it was just kid stuff," I tried to reassure him.

"I don't know how to respond to that since I don't know if it's just kid stuff. To be frank, I have no idea what's going on in my son's life, but that's over. He's going to have to explain himself, whether he likes it or not, and I swear to God, he's coming home," he said grimly.

"Don't say anything you'll regret. I'm sure you were a pain in the ass when you were his age. Uncontrolled testosterone is very bad. Maybe it's a flirtation or a misunderstanding with a friend. If it was important, your ex-mother-in-law would have told you," Paula interceded. "Don't let some silly thing tarnish the moment."

"My son coming home with a black eye and a split lip is not silly, but I admit that you're right, and now is not the time."

Áxel's eyes searched mine. "I'm sorry, honey. I didn't mean to."

"I understand your concern. It's best that you take Andrea to school and try to talk to him."

"I'm sure I will. I will listen to both of you, and I don't want you to doubt that I am very happy. We are going to have a beautiful baby."

I offered him a wide smile, and he returned it without it reaching his eyes. He couldn't give me any more since he was concerned for Christian.

Watching his relationship with his son eat him up hurt me terribly. I wish I had been there to intercede and smooth things over.

I just hoped Áxel would be able to get close to him and not push him farther away. We had to win Chris's acceptance. Otherwise, we would never be a family.

. . .

<u>Áxel</u>

I asked Andrea to stay with Luly's mother until dinner time.

It was seven o'clock. Christian would be leaving training, and I needed to see him. I waited for him outside. I didn't want to confront him and make him uncomfortable inside.

That my son was upset with me was one thing. That I didn't know what was going on in his life was quite another.

Before I went to the sports center, I went to see Teresa. I wanted her to explain why she hadn't told me about the incident.

She opened the door suspiciously. Antonio was not there. She must have been aware of Garbiñe's pregnancy, and I expected her to throw it in my face. She just asked me what I wanted and told me she was in a hurry because she was expected at the neighborhood association meeting. I told her it wouldn't take long. I simply wanted to know what had happened to my son and why she hadn't told me.

According to her, there was nothing wrong with Christian but my irresponsibility. The boy had told his grandmother that he had slipped and hit his head on the edge of one of the lockers in the gym because the floor was wet. He was knocked off-balance by the blow and kissed the floor, splitting his lip. She believed him and didn't assign it much importance, so she hadn't told me.

I didn't believe that version of events, although I didn't want to seem upset. I would talk to my son and draw my own conclusions. However, I made it clear to her that she had to tell me what happened to Chris, even if it was a simple cut on his finger. I would assess the importance of the event since I was his father.

After the talk, which did not last more than fifteen minutes, I walked to the sports center. In a short time, Christian would come out, and I would face him. I would try not to sink even deeper into the mud.

I walked nervously down the sidewalk. Since my illness, nothing had unsettled me as much as the situation with my son. It wasn't cold, yet I shivered. It was the terror of losing him. Of doing or saying something that would distance him even more from me. I didn't know how to act. If it had been a police intervention, I would have no doubt about how to proceed. However, with Christian, it was like handling a barrel full of flammable products with a lit torch in my hand. If I missed and he got too close to the flame, he could set it off, sending everything to hell.

I leaned against one of the lampposts and saw him appear with Lena, his skating partner. The two seemed to be sharing confidences. She laughed and tousled his hair, and he responded by grabbing her shoulders to plant a gentle peck.

Wow. I'd had no idea they shared anything more than friendship. The kiss had lacked the sexual impetus of their age, which made me think that they were just starting out. Adolescence was a time of discovery, after all.

I waited for Lena to walk away, waving goodbye to him, before I made him aware of my presence.

Hello, son," I greeted him cautiously.

He looked at me in surprise and turned his face to hide the damaged eye. It wasn't fast enough for me not to see the trail of what, judging by the trajectory, had been a blunt punch. Anger boiled up inside me as I imagined someone hitting my son, but I tried not to let him notice. I didn't want to go for the throat.

"What are you doing here? Where's Andrea?" he asked suspiciously.

He approached me with his hands in his pockets and his bag slung over his shoulder. He did not come to kiss me but kept a prudent distance. I couldn't make physical contact.

"She's with Lily. They're going to stay together until dinner. I came to see how you were doing since I haven't heard from you for days."

"That's what the phone is for. You didn't need to come. Technology connects us to the world. All you had to do was make a phone call."

"I didn't want to call you. I wanted to see you and have a drink and a talk like before. I'd like to know how you are, and I'd like you to tell me about it while looking me in the eyes."

"Do you care?"

"Of course! I have never stopped caring about what happens to you. It is you who insists on keeping away from me. If it were up to me, you would be in the apartment with Andrea and me."

"There must be a reason," he mumbled.

It wasn't going well, and he was getting defensive. I had to find another topic that would bring us closer together instead of pushing us apart.

"I didn't know you were dating Lena."

His stunned face made me wonder if I had hit the wrong note again.

"Are you saying that because you saw that I gave her a peck? I can't believe you spied on us. You're the worst, Dad."

"I wasn't spying on you. I was just waiting for you, and I saw you. It's okay. At your age, it's normal to want to kiss a girl."

"What do you know about what is normal and what is not?"

"I was your age too once, oddly enough. I also liked kissing girls." I smiled, trying to get closer.

"You still like it. I doubt you've ever gotten the woman you're going with pregnant without kissing her first. But with me, you're wrong. What you saw doesn't mean anything, just that we like each other. Everyone greets each other with kisses. It's the fashion, and that's it. I don't go out with her, and I never would. She's not my crush."

"It's okay. I didn't mean to upset you with my remark. She's pretty and nice, and you've been skating together for years. It wouldn't be strange if you ended up dating."

"I told you there's nothing." He snorted. "Let it go."

"Okay, I got it. What's with the eye? What happened to you?"

"I fell while skating."

"That's not what your grandmother told me."

Christian's eyes widened. "You went to see Yaya?"

"I was worried about you. We can't go on like this. You are my son, and I miss you. Since the mountain was not coming to Mohammed, I thought I would go to the mountain. I want you to come home and tell me what's happening with you."

"You don't want that."

"I do."

"You took it upon yourself to impregnate another to find a substitute for me. Since I am not good enough, it is better to make a son to your measure. One who does not give you problems and you can mold to your liking."

His words stung since there is no greater pain than losing a child you love with all your heart when there are no real reasons. There was nothing to separate us, but he had put a chasm between us. I had to find a bridge to cross it and reunite with him.

"What you say is not true. I love you, Chris. Just because you are going to have a new brother doesn't mean I want to displace you. I want to form a family in which you are included, as well as Garbi, your sister, Ruben, and your future little brother. Andrea is thrilled with the idea. I don't know what to do to make you like it too. I want you back. Tell me what you need me to do, and I swear I will do it."

"Do you have a time machine that can bring my mother back to me?"

"You know I can't do that," I admitted with resignation.

"Then I don't want anything. I don't need you, Dad."

"Well, I need you very much. Please let me be your father, Christian. Let me fill the void left by your mother."

"You are incapable of doing that, and you know it. In case your memory fails you, I did, and you screwed it up. I admired you a lot. You were everything to me, even if I was invisible to you. Even if your work took up everything.

"You changed during your illness. Finally, the invisibility cloak that covered me fell off, but it didn't last long since you decided to separate from Mom, from the woman who loved you the most in this world, to run off with another woman and start a new family. Don't give me that. You took my mother! I can't be near you. You took her away from me."

"I didn't take anything from you. It was an accident."

"No! It was you! I hate you! Don't come after me anymore. I want nothing to do with your ideal family plan! Leave me alone, and get the hell out of here. Go be with the other one."

Christian was screaming at me, out of his mind. I wanted to grab him, shake him, and carry him like when he was little and threw a tantrum. I'd take him home and hug him until he realized that was his place.

My son ran away, ignoring my cries. It didn't matter how loud I called or how much his contempt hurt me. He had built an impregnable prison of reproaches, and he was no longer a child. I could not take him in my arms and make him see reason. I hit the lamppost hard, hurting my knuckles.

Fuck! Had I done so badly? If only I could find a crack, a little hole where I could shine enough light to make him come to his senses.

CHAPTER THIRTY-FIVE

Hanyauku: Walking on tiptoes on hot sand.

<u>Garbiñe, May 1st long weekend</u>

It hurt me to see him so worried and out of place. I wasn't used to his brown eyes being sad. He almost always had that glow that gave me more energy than a dose of caffeine.

He arrived on Friday night with a frankly angry Christian and a delighted Andrea. So that Ruben's room would not be over-crowded, and following Paula's advice, we improvised a room for Chris in the cellar.

I just hoped he wouldn't uncork the bottles and finish off the reserved wine. According to Áxel, he had come reluctantly, and when a teenager is angry, they are capable of any act of rebellion.

He came close to not getting on the plane. The only thing that pushed him to do so was Andrea's tears. She was not going to let him ruin her weekend, and Christian couldn't tolerate seeing his sister sad, not that he had a choice. He gave in, warning his father not to make plans with him because he wasn't going to leave his room.

They were staying until Tuesday. We had to make Christian act human and want to see the island.

"We'll introduce him to Kyle. I'm sure they'll hit it off since they're about the same age," Paula suggested.

Kyle was an expert surfer who had been living on the island for months. He was sponsored by Paula's parents' hotel chain and had been training and studying in Tenerife since September. I knew him through Dario. We had spoken on occasion, and he seemed like a nice guy, although his world and Christian's were far apart.

"I don't know. I don't see that they have much in common."

"It doesn't matter. Kyle is gorgeous, and he's very successful since everyone wants to look like him. I'm sure he'll introduce some pretty girl to Chris, and with a bit of luck, he'll get a crush on an islander. That's our best bet—that he falls in love with some girl, and that pushes him to come here."

"In three days?"

"You fell in love with his father in one. If he has the same sex appeal as Áxel, he won't have a hard time."

"I can't refute that. We'll have to light a candle to some saint. As Luz, my yoga teacher, would say, "Come on, Saint Cyprian. Give us a hand.""

"More than one. You'll need a whole package of candles. I hope you don't mind. I brought Kyle up to speed, and he's happy to help."

"Do you think including a teenage surfer in our plans is the best thing?"

Paula shrugged. "That boy is very mature for his age. I have an eye for these things, and Kyle is our best asset. You'll see."

"Okay, but don't tell Áxel. I don't think he'll be amused that you explained Chris' life and our plans to a stranger."

"My lips are sealed."

412

The doorbell rang, and I knew who it was: Kyle Andrews.

The boy was originally from Hawaii. He had a Samoan mother and an American father. He was handsome, to say the least, with exotic features, cinnamon skin, and sea-colored eyes.

"Hello, Mrs. Navarro. How are you?"

"Come in, don't stay at the door. And call me Garbiñe, please."

Andrea was with Ruben, eating breakfast at the table. Oreo lurked at their feet to capture any debris they dropped on the floor.

Áxel was taking a shower, and Christian had ignored his father's call to eat with us instead of staying in his room. I knew he was awake, but he had isolated himself as he had promised, refusing to come out.

"Come with me, and I'll introduce you to Chris. I hope you'll hit it off."

"I like everyone, so it won't be hard for him to like me."

We went down to the cellar. It had no door, and I just blurted, "Christian, are you decent?" That got no response.

I crossed my fingers that I wouldn't find him naked and jerking off. At his age, it would have been normal. Luckily, he was dressed.

Christian was wearing headphones, looking at a magazine, and moving his feet to the music. He was humming Demi Lovato's latest hit, *Tell Me You Love Me*. He wasn't bad; he had a good voice and a sense of rhythm.

"Christian," I called unsuccessfully. Raising my voice, I repeated, "*Christian!*" The high-pitched tone caught his attention, and he turned around, but it wasn't me he noticed. It was the boy standing next to me with his eyes on him.

Kyle stood unmoving, his bare arms sinewy and crossed over a chest sculpted by exercise. He wore a baggy tank top and print Rip Curl pants. His tangled black hair curled at the ends. He was smiling.

Áxel's son jumped up like a spring, bright red, his mouth half-open.

Not that I was good at detecting when two people connected, but the energy flowing between them was so electric and strong that it reminded me of the first time I saw Áxel. I didn't understand what was going on.

The way Kyle was looking at Chris didn't seem to be a simple evaluation between two guys. Chris was looking at him the same way.

Wait a minute. That couldn't be happening, could it? Could it? Áxel had never told me that his son was gay, but given his reaction to Kyle, I'd swear he was.

"What are you doing here?" Chris asked me in a disgusted tone, looking away from Kyle and swallowing hard. He pulled his shirt down to cover the part of his skin that had been exposed.

"I came to introduce you to Kyle. Kyle, this is Chris." They glared at each other, and I smiled on the inside. I couldn't be that lucky. If those guys connected, I was going to kiss Paula. "He'll be your guide on the island, and he's in charge of making sure you have a good time. I figured you wouldn't want to spend the morning looking at houses with us."

"I don't want to do anything with you. I told you that," he replied sullenly.

"Then you'll do it with me. Get up, man. I'm going to teach you how to catch waves," Kyle announced.

"I don't surf. I just skate." Christian lifted his chin and sat up in bed.

"Then you're in good shape, and I'm sure you have good balance. Sliding on concrete must be like sliding on the sea. It can't be much different. Get up! The beach gets crowded, and the sea is waiting."

The dark-haired man held out his hand to my stepson to help him up.

Chris was still nervous, and his eyes darted from me to Kyle hesitantly. Then he took the hand that was much darker than his. I held my breath as their skins brushed. While they didn't hold each other for very long, I could tell the chemistry was flowing.

Kyle spoke Spanish well, although with an accent that said he was not from Tenerife.

"First I have to change," Christian announced.

"I'll leave you. I'm going to continue making breakfast. When you're ready, come upstairs and eat. It's not good to do sports with an empty belly."

"Don't worry, Garbiñe. I have food on the bike, and the boards are waiting for us on the beach. We'll have breakfast there. If it's okay with Chris, of course."

"Anywhere that's not this house will be fine."

I repressed the urge to roll my eyes.

"We'll have lunch at the beach bar with my friends. Don't wait for us at noon."

"Okay, but Christian, keep your cell phone handy in case your father wants to call you or we need to reach you for anything." He stared at me but gave a slight nod, which I took for a yes. "Have a good time, guys."

"We will," Kyle replied without taking his eyes off Chris.

When I told Áxel that his son was going to spend the day with a group of boys his age and that he was going to learn to surf with the current champion of Tenerife, he could not believe his ears. I told him Paula had thought it was a good idea to introduce him to someone who would make him appreciate the idea of staying in Tenerife, and neither he nor I were good candidates for the job.

"Remind me that I owe Paula a beer. If she's gotten Chris to agree to meet new people and get out of the room, that's quite an accomplishment."

"Hey, I had something to do with it too," I complained, pouting.

"Then I'll have to thank you as well," he said, moving close to me. "I will be thanking you for eternity, vertically, horizontally, and diagonally."

I laughed. "Seriously, it's a great idea. The only thing that can make a kid his age want to change his life is finding a good enough motivation to do it. Finding friends and other things that catch his attention could be the push he needs."

If he had seen how Kyle and Chris looked at each other, he would have been even more hopeful. I preferred to keep that part to myself in case it was a hallucination.

He grabbed me by the waist. He was hooked on the droplets hanging from my freshly washed hair. When his mouth eagerly moved over mine, I gave back the desire that intoxicated us. The night before had not been enough to sate our appetite for each other. I didn't think I could ever get enough.

"You don't know how badly I want this to work," he murmured against my lips.

"And me. My intuition tells me that Kyle will be a good companion for Chris. Now, finish your breakfast. My kisses will feed your heart but not your stomach," I pointed out. "We have to go see the houses Guacis found for us to see if it's the one we're looking for."

"I live to serve, Sergeant!"

We spent the whole day outside. We saw a few properties that looked good, but none of them were right. They either had fewer rooms than we needed or lacked sufficient outdoor space.

My feet were swollen, and my morale was shaken.

Áxel offered to give me a massage, and I couldn't resist. Andrea and Ruben were playing on the porch with Oreo. That pair got along wonderfully. Chris didn't call. It was eight o'clock, and it was only logical that he was fine. I knew nothing had happened to him because, being in the *Guardia Civil*, they would have told me. Áxel sent him a text asking simply, **Everything ok?** The answer came immediately. A short message said that he would have dinner with Kyle, and then they were going to a beach party.

Since Áxel wanted to keep his son safe, he agreed, telling him not to drink and not to come back later than three. We would leave the garage door ajar so he could enter without disturbing anyone.

"Kyle is a good person," I told him after Áxel put the phone down.

"You told me that twenty times today. I'm not worried about my son's safety. I've raised a boy who knows how to take care of himself, and he's not a troublemaker, I trust his good judgment to stay out of trouble. He has never given me any problems in that sense. He is at a difficult age, and we have to give him space. I have always thought you should allow, not limit, as long as they respect the rules. Do you think that's wrong?"

"On the contrary, I think like you. We should give freedom, according to behavior. If Chris shows us he is responsible, I have no problem with him going out if we know who he is with and he lets us know where he is."

"I like that we talk about these things, and we agree on how we want to raise our children. If there is something we don't agree on, I prefer to discuss it with you privately. In front of them, I would like us to be unanimous."

I sighed with joy. I loved the concept of family that he was describing.

"It couldn't be better. Let's go out with the kids, it's going to get dark soon, and now that I have you here, I don't want to miss seeing the sunset with you."

Christian

I tiptoed over the hot sand. It no longer burned as it had that morning when I first stepped on it, as dark and fiery as lava. It had retained the heat of the first rays, which had warmed the tiny black grains.

We were in Callao, near Punta Hidalgo.

Kyle had told me the place belonged to the islanders. The *Tinerfeños,* natives of Tenerife, didn't take kindly to outsiders coming to steal their waves. He would have been considered an outsider, except that they had adopted him and had a lot of admiration for him because of his triumphs as a surfer.

He declared himself in love with the island, and although he missed his native Hawaii, he had no intention of returning.

He had told me all this while I was changing. He didn't leave the room, and I didn't ask him to. He didn't look at me directly. He amused himself by contemplating the dusty labels on the wine bottles to give me some privacy.

If he had been looking at me, I don't know what would have happened. Kyle seemed to be watching me with different eyes. Very different from Diego, the boy I liked in high school and who was the cause of my black eye.

It was my fault. I had been late in the shower, alone with him. In the locker room, the showers were open. I made an effort not to look, though I wanted to see his slender body covered in water. However, that day I took a look—just one. That was enough for me to get a hard-on and for him to catch me in that shameful state. When he realized my condition was for him, he came for me. The split lip had been a side effect of the soap. I'd slipped and hit the floor.

Luckily, no one else was there. Otherwise, it would have been much worse. I put up with his insults when he called me a fucking faggot. I didn't move from the floor when he spat at me or when he kicked me in my ribs, warning me that if I said anything, he would make my life miserable and tell everyone what I was.

Being gay wasn't as frowned upon as it used to be, but in

small towns like mine, it wasn't cool, especially when your grandmother forced you to go to mass on Sundays. I told her a story that she swallowed with no problem, but when my father came to pick me up at the sports center, I feared the worst. He has a built-in lie detector. It was practically impossible to lie to him.

Maybe I was lucky, thanks to Garbiñe.

When I took off my shirt to put on another one, I was struck by those intense blue eyes running down my torso.

I found it hard to swallow. Not that I felt bad. On the contrary, I was flattered to see admiration flickering in his sea-colored eyes. He was very handsome, with slanted eyes and skin so dark that his teeth sparkled.

"You're not bad," he stated bluntly, smirking.

"How?" I stammered.

The corners of his lips turned up playfully.

"What you heard. You're handsome and hot, although you'll have to put on factor-fifty sunscreen, or they'll end up mistaking you for a boiled crab. Shall we go?"

"Yes."

I wasn't sure what that was about. No guy had ever come on to me, let alone one like that. He *had* come on to me, hadn't he? My friends didn't say things like that, only the girls at the skating club to tease me. Maybe Mr. Surf was messing with me.

I grabbed a towel, hung it around my neck, and we left. Outside, parked with two helmets dangling, was a motorbike.

He grabbed both helmets, handed me the first one, and helped me buckle it on, gently brushing my face with his fingertips.

I was out of breath. That simple gesture, added to the intensity of his eyes, incapacitated me. If I felt this way after an involuntary caress, what would it be like if he kissed me?

He pulled away, and I climbed on the back. He suggested that I grab him by the waist if I didn't want to fall off, and all my ghosts were unleashed in the form of an erection against his ass.

What bad luck! Why was I getting a hard-on now? If he noticed, he could fling me into a ditch. I tried to leave space, but he kept pressing back against me. I didn't know if he was aware, but I was freaking out. I had never felt this way with a guy, not even with Diego. It was impossible for him not to perceive what was going on under my swimsuit. The fabric of his suit was as thin as mine, so there wasn't much left to the imagination.

When we got to the beach, I was sweating. His black hair also stuck to his face. I felt like pushing it back.

"Did you enjoy riding with me?" he asked, biting his lower lip.

"Yes, it was good."

"Great, because I'm going to teach you how to ride any way you let me. On the waves, on the bike, or..."

He waggled his eyebrows, causing a thousand butterflies to flutter in my stomach. I was emboldened since that told me he knew we had chemistry.

"How about anywhere else?" I questioned, all fired up. He laughed softly, tousling his hair.

"We'll see. It depends on how much fun we have together. Right now, I'm too hot to think. Let's see what you can do on the waves."

"If the boards had wheels, I could blow your mind," I boasted.

"You'll have to teach me." He intertwined his fingers with mine to pull me along. "Come on. My friends are waiting for us."

I smiled. It had been months since I had felt so alive. My mother had taken my will to live with her. The world had come to a stop, but only for me. For others, it was still spinning, and that had made me feel very small...until now.

Kyle introduced me to his friends, several guys and girls dressed in wetsuits who looked at him adoringly. For a king of the waves, he was a very down-to-earth guy. I liked that.

He lent me a suit, and while I was putting it on, I asked him to give us a demonstration. He didn't make me beg. He threw himself into the water as if he were part of it, the foam on the waves kissing his body.

It was magical to watch him. I could tell he had the same passion as I did on skates.

I could say that the world disappeared, but it wasn't like that. Rather everything began to spin on a colorful Ferris wheel. I spent the whole day at his side, taking advantage of his patience to teach me how to balance on the water. We celebrated the first time I was able to stand up.

It was easy to talk to him. To unburden myself and let him in on what my life had been like.

I liked that he listened to me. He didn't judge me, just gave his opinion about what had happened so far.

"Your old man can't reproach you for being suspicious of his new situation. You were raised by your mother. It's normal for you to have mixed feelings. I will also say that if they were no longer together, he had the right to rebuild his life. I don't know Garbiñe well, but she seems like a great person, and she's made sure you didn't have a shitty few days. That says a lot."

I didn't contradict him. It's not that I didn't like my father's girlfriend. She was collateral damage. If it hadn't been Garbiñe, it would have been someone else.

Kyle continued, now serious. "It must have been fucked up to see your mother die and almost lose your father twice to terminal cancer. I wouldn't want to be in your shoes. You're a brave person. A lot of guys wouldn't have been able to handle that."

"Thank you for your understanding. It has not been easy. Sometimes I think no one understands me. I thought so until this morning."

His frank smile was dazzling. "Being different is what you make it. I've always been different. As you can see, I'm of mixed race. As a child, I felt different, and since I grew up, I have swum between two waters. How about you?"

"Me?" I asked, not understanding.

It was late. We had eaten some hamburgers that Kyle's friends had brought, and now we were around a campfire, drinking sodas before it was time to drive me home.

"Yes, you. Are you bi or gay?"

Fuck! Did my sexuality show that much?

"Hey, not me." I couldn't be honest. I was afraid of screwing up.

"Don't kid me. At this point, you're going to lie to me or hide from me? If there's one thing I like about you, it's your honesty. Don't fuck it up since I know damn well what I had behind me on the bike, rubbing my ass."

"I didn't rub! You did!" I complained.

"So what? It doesn't matter. I've seen how you look at me. How your eyes dilate when I touch you. You like me, and I like you. I just want to know if we're in sync. At first, I fooled around with the opposite sex, but not anymore. I like boys, and I like you."

My heart rate had skyrocketed. Kyle had just told me that he liked me straight out, looking me in the eye and without a tremor.

"I think I'm gay," I confessed with difficulty. For the first time, I told someone other than my mother.

"You haven't come out of the closet, or do you like girls too?"

"I like girls as friends, but I'm not attracted to them. I say I think since I've never been with a guy. I don't know what I really am. I may be hetero-curious, an amoeba, or just plain gay."

Kyle laughed. "You're a lot of fun, Chris. Your witticisms fascinate me." He took the last sip of his soda and set it down. "I'm going to help you narrow your choices. You don't look like an amoeba, so we're left with hetero-curious or homosexual. What's it going to be?"

He brought his face close to mine, placing his hand on my cheek to grab my chin.

His warm breath mingled with mine. When his tongue invaded my mouth, first cautiously and then brazenly, I could do nothing but tangle my fingers in his hair and let myself be carried away in the most exciting adventure in my existence.

My life had definitely turned around.

Nakama: Aspiring to fly high through thoughts of peace and liberation.

<u>**Áxel**</u>

Days went by, and I barely saw my son. There *were* signs of life in the Batcave. Otherwise, I would have put him on the missing person list.

He got on so well with Kyle that he hardly slept. He came home in the wee hours of the morning and left at dawn. He was gone during the day, and rather than making me angry, that made me very happy.

Forging new friends could help all of us make the transition to our new life more easily.

We had found the ideal home for our growing family, and I was anxious for things to fall into place.

We almost threw in the towel since Guacis had not been able to find what we were looking for, and it was already Sunday. Either the miracle would work, which was unlikely, or I would return to my apartment empty-handed. Tired and defeated, we went for a drink at a beautiful bar with a view where they made fresh fruit smoothies and sweets to die for. The kids were hungry, and I was too.

The waitress approached us kindly. She knew Garbi since this was Ruben's favorite place to have a snack.

"What can I get you, partner and company?" she said, looking at the children, who were glued to the cake counter.

"Four multifruit smoothies, two homemade cheesecakes, a couple of *rosquetes laguneros,* and two strawberry tartlets."

"Nothing else?" she asked with a smile.

"If you have a four-bedroom house with some land and a view of the cliff at a good price, we'll take that, too."

She raised her eyebrows. "Another move?"

"My family is growing," Garbi said, rubbing her belly.

"Congratulations! I didn't know."

"We just wanted to make sure everything was going well," Garbi said.

"It's logical. We all do the same thing. What a surprise! You make a wonderful couple. Let me give it a couple of spins. I can't think of the name right now, but I'm sure Quique remembers it. We have a good client, a stranger, who put his property up for sale a few months ago. I will consult him and tell you. Maybe he can fit you in."

"We won't lose anything by trying." I thanked her and grabbed Garbi's hand across the table.

The waitress smiled and left to prepare our order. When she returned to the table with the loaded tray, she took a slip of paper out of her pocket.

"You are in luck. His name is Johan, and he is here for some days. So I didn't give you false hope, I spoke to him, and he is willing to show you the property today. I figured you would be in a hurry. As soon as you finish your food, he'll be waiting for you. I told him not to go overboard with the price. You are friends, and you are in a hurry. I don't think he's going to give you much trouble. That guy has plenty of money. He is selling the house because he bought another one. They are remodeling it, and they will finish in a couple of months."

"Fantastic! We don't need it until July or early August, so we don't mind waiting."

"I hope I helped you. If you buy the house, you owe me a coffee with a view. They say the property has amazing views."

"That's great," I said, crossing my fingers.

We gobbled down our snack. We were so nervous about the possibility of this being our dream house that we didn't savor the food as it deserved. Even Andrea rushed us with a face full of crumbs.

We left a generous tip for the waitress and headed to the house, which was ten minutes away.

When we arrived, we all held our breath. The location was wonderful, right on the cliff. It also had about nine hundred square meters of land that had endless possibilities.

We rang the doorbell in a state of agitation. This property seemed too expensive for us to afford. The garden was very well kept, with enough space to put in a swimming pool if one wanted to.

The house was almost entirely on one floor, except for a covered part of about forty square meters. The terrace over-looked an immense yard, making it the best place to contemplate the best sunsets in history.

Johan shook our hands and welcomed us. He was a Hungarian widower with no children, a self-made man and a doctor by profession. He was no longer working since Alzheimer's had taken hold of him, and although he had it under control for the time being, he had decided that it was best to retire before the disease took its toll. That was why he had bought another type of property, more practical, closer to the hospital, and without so much land to take care of. The house was too big for him since his wife was no longer with him, and he did not feel like inviting people over as they had when she was alive.

He told me that my face rang a bell, but he wasn't sure why. I told him I had been on some TV show or other explaining my case. He was interested and opened his eyes wide when I told him about my journey with cancer.

"So, that's you! You don't ring a bell from TV but from a meeting I attended this year. I am an oncologist, and though I no longer practice, I like to stay informed. They showed your case and a picture of you to show how well you were doing now. You are a survivor and have given hope to many."

"Thank you. It is an honor."

"The honor is mine to have you in my house, but please come in. I'll be happy to show it to you, and you can see if it suits you. You can let the children continue playing in the garden. Nothing will happen to them here. I like to think this house has a soul. I spent the best moments with my wife here, and I am not willing to sell it to just anyone. But you are not just anyone, are you?"

"We hope we aren't," I admitted without letting go of Garbi's hand. That made her smile.

Given the amount of land outside, it was not a big house. The size was just right. A large living room led to an open kitchen. There were three double bedrooms downstairs plus a full bathroom, and up the stairs was the jewel in the crown, a suite with a dressing room, a private bathroom, and a huge terrace overlooking the ocean. It seemed as if the sea were part of the house.

"This was my wife's favorite place. We used to have a glass of wine every evening to watch the sunset, sitting at this little table we bought in an antique shop on one of our trips."

That was exactly what we wanted to do. This house was made for us.

"It's the perfect place, although I don't know if we can meet the asking price," I told him.

Johan offered us a restrained smile. "Life has taught me that its true value is in moments, experiences, and people who enrich it. Money is a vehicle that is not enough many times. I do not intend to get rich on the sale of this house but to find a family that deserves it. What is your offer?"

"I'm ashamed to even propose it to you. This place is worth three times what we can afford."

"Will you take care of this house, honor the memory of my happiness with your own, and fill it with love and children?"

"That's the idea," I replied, pressing Garbi's fingers.

"Then do not be afraid. Make an offer from the heart."

With a knot in my stomach and hoping Johan really didn't care about the money, I made my proposal.

***

"Can you believe he accepted? That property is a bargain for the amount we offered!"

"It is, but he signed the purchase contract, so we can almost say it's ours." We were home. I held her tight, her heartbeat racing with excitement against mine.

"That means you're clear about the move. There's no going back unless you want to lose the money we gave him."

"What is clear to me is that you are the center of my world, along with our children. I need to be where you are, and that is on this island, so be it."

The happiness in her smile enchanted me. "You don't know how many times I thank the universe that I went to the Taser course that day. Nothing made sense until I met you. I had thrown in the towel. My life was a dark pit I didn't know how to get out of."

"You just needed a shock to turn on the bulb and make you realize that even in the greatest adversity, there is room for hope."

"You gave me that shock."

"I would not have let anyone else electrocute you."

"You are a romantic."

"And you are a beauty who is still my favorite color."

The corners of her lips turned up. "I love you, Áxel."

We were kissing when the roar of a motorcycle and the laughter of two teenagers made us look up.

"It seems that the boys have arrived. Talk to your son and see if Kyle has softened him up." She stroked the back of my neck.

"Do you think this is the best time?"

"No doubt about it."

"Wish me luck, then."

The boys' laughter could no longer be heard. They must have gone into the cellar since the bike had not started up again. Garbi gave me a brief but intense kiss to give me the confidence I needed.

"Go get him. Just talk to him from the heart. He'll surely listen to you this time."

"I hope so. We don't have any more time for him to react." I kissed her again and went to face Christian.

I walked down the three steps to the garage. There was loud music playing in the background. Too loud. I didn't shout his name over the music since he wouldn't hear me. I didn't recognize the band, but I was sure it was one of the alternative groups the kids liked so much. That kind of music gave me a headache.

I turned the corner to the makeshift room to find myself faced with something I was not expecting.

He and his new friend were shirtless, holding each other's faces and kissing. My son's hands were curled in the surfer's long hair. Their bodies were glued together, and their lust was obvious.

That took my breath away. Not because I saw two boys kissing. That was the least of it.

It was because I realized that I didn't know my son.

Chris liked boys! How many unintentional jokes had he put

up with from me? I wasn't homophobic, just an asshole. Sometimes people blurted things out without thinking. We are not aware that we are hurting the person with us, especially if we do not know him or her well enough to know what would affect him or her.

My blindfold had just fallen off.

Christian's eyes opened lazily and met mine. His panicked expression hurt me more than anything else in the world. Fear! My son was afraid because of what I had discovered. Fuck, as if that mattered. All I wanted was for my son to be happy. I didn't care if he was happy with a man or a woman.

I turned my face away, not knowing how to behave, then blurted, "I'm sorry. I didn't mean to interrupt." It tasted like a burned horn as I retraced my steps the way I had come. I had to restore the privacy I had stolen from them. I should have shouted their names and warned them, not burdened the moment.

You could say I ran away. Not because of the kiss but because of my ignorance. Whenever I discovered a new side of my son, I realized what a bad father I had been. I hadn't even realized that he liked boys, and those things showed, didn't they?

I felt like banging my head against the wall after apologizing to him for what I hadn't given him, what I hadn't seen, and what I'd ignored.

Fuck! Fuck! Fuck!

Christian

"Shit!" I howled, jerking away from Kyle.

"What's wrong?" he asked, his eyes still glazed from the intensity of the kiss.

"My father, that's what's going on! I can't believe he spied on us!"

"Spy?" He turned to the door without understanding. "He was there a second ago, watching you and me."

I cut the sentence short and looked for my shirt, which was on the floor. We had been fooling around all day, enjoying ourselves on the beach, holding back the desire to be alone to offer each other more. Or so I hoped until my father stuck his nose where it wasn't wanted.

"Does it bother you that he saw us kissing?"

"Yes! No! I don't know! I didn't think about it. Until I met you, I wasn't sure what I wanted," I admitted angrily. I missed the sleeve when I pulled the shirt on.

Kyle carefully approached and put his hands on my exposed skin.

"And now you do?" he asked patiently.

"Now I know that I like you. When you touch me and when you kiss me, I feel things."

His smile widened. "I like you too, and you make me feel many things." The dark hand was on the spot where my heart was beating. "I want to get to know you, Chris. I want you to teach me how to skate while I keep showing you how to catch waves. I want to show you that to fly, you just feel the peace and release that will lift you to another plane, the plane of acceptance, and you will stop being angry at the world. If my mother was here, I am sure she would offer you one of her favorite proverbs."

"Which one?" I asked, clinging to hope.

Kyle fixed me with his blue eyes. "'If the sea breeze gives you a push, follow it. You will see that there are paths that lead you to the perfect wave.' The proverb, although it seems to speak of surfing, does not."

"Are you my perfect wave?" I asked, more lost than ever.

"Me, your father, and all of us who care about you. Don't shut yourself off, Chris. If he saw us and didn't confront us, it's because he didn't think it was bad. Otherwise, he would have screamed his head off.

"Maybe this is what we all needed—you to realize who you are and what you want, and him to get to know you a little better.

He doesn't seem like a bad guy, so what if you give him a chance instead of barricading yourself behind that anger? You can't spend your life being mad at him for not being in the car with you.

"He might not be perfect. We all make mistakes, but the important thing is that he hasn't stopped trying. He's still here, still by your side, and that says a lot about him. Maybe life didn't want him to be there so you wouldn't become an orphan. Forgive him, and forgive yourself. Only that will set you free."

"Is that also a Hawaiian proverb?"

"In Hawaii, they say, 'Forgive me before the sun goes down.' It hasn't set yet. You have a few minutes left." He clicked his tongue. "I'm leaving. I'll see you tomorrow since I don't want you to spend your last hours on the island without us seeing each other."

Kyle kissed me thoroughly, leaving me in a state that was hard to categorize.

"I don't want to stop seeing you," I confessed, embarrassed.

"I don't either. It's up to you. If you like me as much as you say, do something to remedy this situation. Aloha, skater," he said, stroking my face.

"Aloha, surfer. Thank you for your words."

He waved his hand with his fingers together, little finger and thumb extended. I returned the gesture, watching his body as he left the room.

***

I pulled myself together before I left my cave.

I concluded that Kyle had a point. I was not doing myself any favors with the attitude I had adopted since the accident. My mother's death still hurt, and I doubted it would stop, but I couldn't ignore my new reality. I had to assume that she would never return, and I had only him to fill the void. An absent father I considered a hero, even though he was not *my* hero.

I stepped outside, and the last rays of sunshine and the salt breeze stinging the back of my nose reminded me of Kyle, who always smelled of the sea.

Three steps separated me from what I could become. My father was sitting on the rocker. Alone, squinting, with his eyes on the fingers of his hands, which were intertwined. If I didn't know better, I'd swear he was praying.

I stood in front of him without knowing what to say. I did it the way I had become accustomed to, which seemed to be the only way I could handle things.

"Praying to God to expel the demon from my body?" I interjected derisively.

My father looked sad and dejected. I'm sure he was disappointed that I didn't like boobs.

"You know I'm not much for praying, and if I *was* praying, it wouldn't be for that."

"No? Wouldn't you rather have a normal son than one who likes dicks?" My tone dripped anger.

It wasn't going well, but the need to hurt him was more powerful than the need to forgive him.

"Normality or the lack thereof is not determined by a person's sexuality. I'm sorry if my jokes led you to believe I felt like that. I didn't mean to. If I had known your preference, I would never have joked about it. I'm sorry for so many things that I don't even know where to begin, son." The redness of his eyes, which were about to overflow, shook me.

"I am lost," he confessed. "I don't know how I could have done so badly. Well, I do. I am the worst father in the universe. Even Darth Vader wasn't that bad."

"You don't need to crucify yourself or appeal to the dark side. I have not been easy."

"You are not to blame for anything. I received from you what I gave you. You ignored me as I ignored you. I have felt what it is like to be ignored, even judged. I should never have compared you to your sister or not given enough weight to your skating by extolling her judo. I have been a lousy father, an egotist who was only concerned with navel-gazing until cancer put me in my place. I didn't make my wife happy, and I ignored my children. That was me. I don't know how you can look me in the face."

"Dad."

"No, let me. I need to do this. I need to vomit out the bad to make room for the good, if there is still anything positive you can give me. I understand why you were so sorry to lose your mother. She was all you had. I was just a name with a position in your life that I didn't live up to. A father is not that, Chris. He is so much more, and I have not been one."

"It's not about beating yourself up either."

"I deserve your hatred and contempt since I did nothing to earn anything else, only believed that I had the right to be loved by you for having given you life. Raising a child is much more than that."

My father stood up to look me in the face, then did something I never thought I'd see. He got down on his knees in front of me and grabbed my feet.

"Forgive me, son. Forgive me for not being up to the task, for failing you when you needed me. For not supporting you in the sport you loved, for ignoring who you were and overlooking your needs and feelings. Forgive me for failing you, for robbing you of the trust you should have had in me to tell me what you were worried about.

"I'm sorry I wasn't in that accident. I'm sorry I wasn't the one who died, and I wasn't able to bring back to the person who knew how to be there for you. I'm sorry life has been such a bastard to you, son," he murmured, voice broken by the tears that sparkled on the ground—a drizzle that took on the importance of an epic storm

Seeing him prostrate at my feet, disconsolate, without

strength, broke the walls I had erected around me because even though I felt ignored by him, I still loved him.

"Get off the floor please, Dad." My lower lip trembled. There was nothing left of my reticence toward him, only a need for him to accept me once and for all.

"Not until you forgive me. Not until you understand how bad I feel for everything I've done to you. I didn't want your mother to die. I didn't want you to lose her."

I took a breath. It was hard to do, and I didn't realize why until two thick tears rushed down my cheeks. "I know, and I'm sorry I accused you for no reason. I was very angry. I needed to blame someone, and you were the perfect target. Get up, Dad. Please!" I begged.

I dropped to his level. My father's shoulders shook. He was crying, letting go of the frustration that enveloped us both.

"Please, Dad, get up," I insisted. "I'm sorry too. I'm so sorry. I know it wasn't your fault, and if you had been in the car, it would have made things worse. But it hurt so much. It still hurts."

"I know, son, I know." He hugged me.

I ended up breaking down in his arms, letting go of the pain that gripped me and was not letting me be who I was. There were no longer thick enough walls or barriers to keep me away from him. As Kyle said, he wasn't perfect, just my father, and he too had the right to be wrong and to be forgiven. Just like me.

CHAPTER THIRTY-SEVEN

Sarang: The desire to be with someone until death.

<u>Garbiñe</u>

"Paula, I think my water just broke, or I have the worst urinary incontinence in history."

My friend's eyes almost popped out of their sockets. She looked at the puddle forming on the mall floor and then at me.

"Incontinence! You won't deliver for two weeks. You can't be in labor!"

"Superman doesn't seem to feel the same way."

"Will you stop calling him that? In the end, he'll get that ridiculous nickname instead of his precious name."

"He hasn't got any name yet!" I moaned, holding back the first contraction and feeling another torrent rushing down my legs. Paula grabbed my hands when she saw my grimace of pain.

"What? What is it?"

"A contraction."

"Oh, my God! You can't just go off in the shower curtain

section. Let's at least get to the towel section and see if someone from the kitchen can get us a pot of hot water."

"What are you talking about? You're crazy! You watch too many movies. When a woman's water breaks, she has time to take a shower."

"Okay, but not in the shopping mall. The ones here are glued to the wall! They are not connected to pipes."

"Please stay calm, focus, and call Áxel to bring the bag to the clinic. You're talking nonsense."

"Áxel? You mean an ambulance."

"No, call Áxel and someone from the cleaners. I'm losing everything. Not even in the sinking of the *Titanic* was there so much water." Finally, my friend took her cell phone out of her purse. "Oh, and then buy a couple of towels."

"To help you in childbirth?"

"No! To get me to the clinic without staining your upholstery with amniotic fluid. Do things in that order, please."

"Look at you, thinking about my upholstery at this time. When you're in sergeant mode, no one can contradict you."

"Well, take heed and stop running around like a headless chicken."

"In my case, cock." She giggled and I couldn't answer her because I got another contraction stronger than the previous one.

Dr. Ulloa's clinic

I finally got Paula to come to her senses.

After carrying out my orders, she took me to the place at which I was to be treated.

I was taken care of as soon as I walked through the door. Mino was not there. A midwife did the first examination. She said it was very early, and that I would be in labor for the long haul. She would try to reach the doctor to see what he wanted to do.

Paula was nervous. She told the poor woman, "What do you mean, what does he want to do? Bring her son into the world!" she ordered. The midwife just smiled and told her that she knew the doctor wanted to personally attend my delivery because it was risky.

Paula looked at her blankly. I didn't tell her anything about the delicate circumstances when I gave birth either, which led to a small argument after the midwife walked out the door. Since misfortunes never come by themselves, Áxel walked through the door.

It's not that seeing us argue was strange for him, but when he heard the topic of the discussion, my boy's face changed color like a chameleon's from red to green and from green to white. Paula didn't shut up. An unfiltered person never shuts up when they should. On the contrary, they double down. That was exactly what happened. She brought him fully into the conversation, making him a participant. I had enough to do, dealing with the pain that went through me from my lower back to my belly and was not in the mood for drama. I didn't want to get angry, but since I was swollen, soaked in amniotic fluid, and having labor pains, my inner bitch came out and roared.

I screamed so loudly and so many times that a nurse and an orderly came into the room and asked them to leave.

I stayed there, alone and folded in two. They tried to talk to me again a few minutes later.

"Why didn't you tell us anything? Áxel murmured with restraint, moving to the edge of the bed with a worried look on his face.

"Because I love this child, and if I had told you that my life was in danger, you would have tried to convince me not to have him. Ouch," I complained, putting my hands to my belly again.

"Call the nurse. Tell her it hurts a lot and to give her something!" exclaimed Áxel, looking at Paula.

"They can't give me anything," I mumbled.

"Why not?"

"Because they only do that when you've dilated enough, and I'm very green."

"You look red," he said, peering at my sweaty, flushed face.

"They don't mean that. They mean that she is not ripe to give birth. They say 'green' when dilation has not reached the optimum point," Paula clarified.

"What's that damn point, when the baby's head pops out? Can't you see what she's going through? They'll have to give her something."

"Do you no longer remember the birth of your children? Childbirth is like that. Luckily, one forgets. Otherwise, the human species would become extinct," I pointed out.

The matron reappeared, knocking softly on the door. We ushered her in. "Dr. Ulloa says not to worry. He will take the first flight to the island. In the meantime, Marín and I will help you hold on until he arrives and can take care of the delivery. If that is not possible, we will do it."

"Help her hold on?" Áxel asked. "What do you think, that we're going to push my son's head back in because the damn doctor's flight is delayed?"

"Calm down. That is not the point. We will see how the dilatation is going and monitor it, but in no case will we accelerate it. Those were the doctor's orders, and that's how we are going to act. We will monitor the mother and the baby. Only if there is fetal distress or the mother is at risk will we induce the delivery. Don't worry; you are in the best hands. If you need anything, just press the button."

"What we need is a doctor who wants my child to be born!" growled Áxel, chewing on the words.

If the matron heard him, she gave no sign of it. She disappeared the way she had come in.

"With the money they charge here, they could give better care." Paula snorted.

"Do you think it's not enough for my doctor to take a flight to treat me personally?"

"I don't know, but if you are at risk, they should make you give birth now, shouldn't they?" she complained uneasily.

"They know exactly what they are doing. We should listen to them, which, for your peace of mind, is what I have been doing during the whole pregnancy. It doesn't have to go wrong. Mino told me that we were going to take all the precautions in the world."

"The doctors also told us that we couldn't be parents, and look," Áxel contradicted me. "I'm going to file a complaint against that doctor. I'm the father. He should have told me that I could lose you, not leave me out of it."

"He didn't tell you because I asked him to. Don't blame him. Mino tried to insist several times, and he only respected my will."

"What about mine?"

"Would it have changed anything? Would you have asked me to have an abortion if you had known?" I asked, my brow beading with sweat.

"Maybe. I don't know."

"Well, that's it. What's done is done. We're going to have Superman and everything is going to be fine. And I say this to both of you, so get it into your heads. There's no Murphy's law here. Nothing is going to go wrong. Do you hear me?"

Paula and Áxel looked at each other and nodded, realizing that it was too late for alternatives. They had to stand by my side and support me. Nothing else.

It was Saturday Kyle and Chris were at the movies with their friends. It wasn't just any movie but a marathon of four *Lord of the Rings*, so they both had their cell phones turned off. Ruben was with his father, and Andrea had gone camping with the Girl Scouts. Luckily, we had the kids secured. Having to take care of them at this time would not have been easy.

I didn't want my mother to be called. I could already imagine her bitching at me. When everything was all right and I had my child in my arms, I would let her know. She would pretend to be offended, but at this point, that was the least of my concerns. Just like my sisters, who, for that matter, were just like her.

We alerted Colmenares, who asked if we needed anything. We told him no, that we would let him know when Superman had landed.

Six hours after he set foot in the clinic, Dr. Ulloa delivered the baby. Yeray, which means big in Guanche, was born.

At six pounds eight ounces, with his father's dark hair and my green eyes, he stole our hearts when we saw him for the first time.

"You've done very well. You're a champion." Mino exulted proudly as Áxel ran his hand over my forehead.

"I didn't want to complicate it, and I'm a strong girl. Is the baby okay?"

"Perfect. As soon as he's cleaned up, he'll be taken to your room. I just gave you the last stitch, so you'll be up in no time."

"Is she all right, Doctor?" asked a worried Áxel, who didn't stop caressing me.

"It seems so. The monitors don't indicate otherwise. Anyway, we will monitor Garbiñe for the couple of nights she will spend with us. As I told her, nothing should happen, but with her history, taking precautions is necessary."

Áxel let out the air he was holding in.

"Thank you so much for everything. We couldn't have had a better doctor who would have gone to the trouble of taking a flight just to make sure everything went well."

Mino smiled at him. "The best patients deserve the best doctors, but the credit goes to her. She has done very well. Take care of her. You have a great wife, and I have given her no less than she deserves. I'm just doing my job."

"I will, I promise."

Áxel looked at me tenderly and kissed me softly. "Thank you for giving me a son."

<u>Garbiñe, one week after delivery</u>

I woke up suddenly. Something wasn't right. I was not sure what it was, but I was having a hard time breathing. Oxygen was barely getting into my lungs and I didn't feel strong enough to call Áxel, who was sleeping peacefully next to me.

Andrea was upset that her baby brother had arrived unannounced. Ruben had looked at him in amazement, and Chris was a potential mini-parent as he fearlessly took him in his arms. He was the one who had changed the most since the move.

The island had changed Kyle. He didn't seem like the same person as the one who arrived, angry at the world, on that May long weekend.

Now he was always smiling. He did not stop doing things all day long. The high school teachers were very happy with his performance, even though he had just started the school year.

His relationship with Áxel was stronger, and he made a point of teaching his father how to skate. It wasn't uncommon for them to put on their skates and go out together, me walking Oreo while enjoying watching them glide.

Teresa did not take well to Christian accepting me, although in the end, she had to give in. First, because she did not have custody of her grandson. Second, because it was Chris's will, and third, because her husband put her in her place by telling her that what she should care about as a good practicing Christian was the happiness of her grandchildren.

We moved in July and had Paula and Colmenares give us a hand with the painting and decoration. At the end of August, the property looked very different. We did not hesitate to invite Marta, the waitress who discovered the house for us, and Johan, the former owner, for coffee with a view.

Life smiled at us, not because we had the house of our dreams or an enviable family, but because we had smiles, hugs, arguments, reconciliations, and infinite affection watering our days.

It is true that the one who has the most is not the happiest, but the one who needs the least. We didn't need anything else because we had the most important things: health, love, and family.

I turned my head to look at the crib, where Yeray was sleeping peacefully. It wouldn't be long before he woke up demanding my breast. How could I give it to him if I could barely move?

My eyesight was beginning to blur. The lack of oxygen and the loss of strength and vision were not good signs.

I made an effort to move my arm, without success. The exhaustion was so extreme that I had no strength to do anything but contemplate the love of my life for the last time.

Yes, I said last. I was leaving unannounced, out the back door but with a full soul.

I felt bad for him, for not being able to offer him more time. I would have loved to share more moments with Áxel. I had been given twenty-five years, but death seemed to be in a hurry.

You have to know when to get off the train, and that was my stop. I was sure that Áxel would take perfect care of our family because my love was a great man and a born fighter.

I would have to make do with the "I love you" we had whispered to each other that evening as we watched the sunset. With the reflection of my eyes in his dark eyes. With the warmth of his body next to me. Who could have known it would be the last time?

My eyes were closing. Air no longer reached me. With my last breath, I stretched out my hand leaving it defeated on a chest that rose and fell. His sleeping chest.

There it was—that pure and firm heart on which I would drop my last I love you, the one that had been his alone since the day I first saw him.

"I will wait for you always. Take care of them."

Áxel

"I will wait for you always. Take care of them."

I was dreaming about Garbi. I had wanted to surprise her by asking her to marry me in New York. We were at the top of the Empire State Building. I was on my knees, dressed in a dark suit chosen for the occasion, holding out a little green velvet box containing a ring that was meant to steal the color from her eyes.

She was smiling. Her eyes were shining, and when I popped the question, waiting for the long-awaited "I do," she surprised me with an unusual answer.

"I will wait for you always. Take care of them."

Everything went black. I ran out of air, the building vanished, and Garbiñe disappeared from my side.

I woke up with the uneasy feeling that something was wrong. I turned my face toward the one I considered my wife, even though I didn't have the ring on her finger. Her hand rested on my chest.

I smiled to see that she was sleeping so peacefully that she seemed to be in another world. I did not want to disturb her. She was exhausted, for our son gave her no respite. He seemed to be perpetually hungry and chained to her breasts continuously.

Yeray burst into screams, demanding his ration of food as if he had sensed my thoughts. He was a born gobbler, a worthy son of his father, who also coveted the breasts of the woman lying next to him. As much as I felt sorry for her, I had to wake her up.

"Garbi, honey, wake up. Yeray is hungry," I whispered, watching her. She didn't react. She slept as if she didn't hear the child's thunderous crying. That was logical. These days she was exhausted from breastfeeding on demand. "Garbi, my darling, Yeray is hungry." I moved her and realized that something was wrong.

The moonlight filtered through the window giving a faint glow that let me see that her torso did not rise and fall. It was deathly still.

No! It couldn't be. She couldn't leave me!

Without hesitation, I jumped in to perform CPR. The boy kept crying as if he knew his mother was gone. A few minutes later, Chris appeared in the doorway, drowsy.

"Dad, Garbi, the baby is crying."

I stopped giving her oxygen for a moment to talk to him. "Quickly, Chris! Call an ambulance! Garbi is dying!"

Two things could have happened. Either my son went blank, reliving what happened to his mother, or he reacted as he did. He took to his heels and took care of everything including the child while I tried to get her back.

"I'm sorry. She suffered a pulmonary embolism and deep vein thrombosis."

"She was fine! Dr. Ulloa told me the delivery went well!" I exclaimed, out of my mind.

The emergency department doctor looked at me with regret.

"Your wife was an at-risk patient, so this could happen. A very high percentage of thrombotic episodes occur in the first six weeks after delivery. Venous thromboembolic disease and pulmonary emboli are the main causes of maternal mortality. With a disease like the patient's, it could easily happen."

I processed the data in dribs and drabs. There was one thing I had marveled at since the man uttered it. *Was? Why did he say "was?"* My head was spinning. When I'd started resuscitation, Garbi had no pulse, but several minutes after the cardiac massage, I managed to get her back. The heartbeat was weak, but it was there.

"I'm not going to deceive you. I'm not one of those who gives false hopes. She is very bad. If I were you, I'd say goodbye."

"You don't know her. You have no fucking idea what Garbiñe is like! She's not leaving without me! Do you hear me?" I was shouting at the doctor. Maybe it wasn't the right thing to do, but what he was implying wasn't right either.

Chris had stayed home with the children, all except Yeray, whom I had brought to the hospital. Since Garbi wanted nothing to do with formula, I had implored them to pump some so I could give it to my son. Luckily, they listened to me and the baby was now resting in Paula's arms.

When we arrived at the hospital, she was there. She lived nearby, and my son had let her know so she wouldn't be alone. It was a good decision, even if I didn't to realize it now.

"Calm down, please! This is a hospital, and there are many other patients."

"But none of them is my wife, and you just told me to say goodbye to her!"

"Sir, I understand your pain. In a hospital, we deal with cases like hers on a regular basis. Dealing with the loss of a loved one is one of the hardest things anyone faces, but from experience, I will tell you that you are better off if you can talk, even through glass, to the person you love before they go. If you don't want to do that, I can't force you to say goodbye, although I believe it would relieve you. Good night."

"Wait!" I stopped him before the doctor turned around. "I want to do it," I admitted in defeat, looking at Paula sideways.

She just kept feeding Yeray with tears streaming down her cheeks in silence.

"Go," she muttered. "We will wait for you."

I shook my head, looking at the baby. "I want him to go. Garbi would want us to go together. May I?" I asked the doctor, who nodded with a serious look on his face.

Walking toward death did not frighten me. I had traveled that road many times. What terrified me was living without her. Until now, I had not wanted to live with someone until death, but now I did, and the thought of moving forward without her broke my soul.

I leaned against the glass, placing my forehead on the vitrified coldness, looking at the aseptic room in which she lay connected to countless machines, tubes, and a monitor.

She couldn't hear me unless I screamed like a man possessed, and that wasn't the point. I appealed to our mental connection, the one that had led us to have dream dates when distance was imposed on us.

"Hi, I'm here, waiting for you on our date night. I don't see you've dressed up much unless you intend to go to a Halloween party," I joked. "I know you know I'm kidding, and you've seen my date. Yes, he's younger, better looking, and looks better in pajamas than me, I admit. But he's not that interesting. He lacks experience and wrinkles," I muttered, imagining her smiling at me.

"Today you gave me a big scare. When I told you I liked surprises, I didn't mean these. I meant taking me to a spa. Next time I'll specify. Remember when I told you my favorite color was to see you? I don't know how many times I have to tell you that it still is. Green is just a color, but seeing you floods my life with colors. I need you, Garbi, like I need the air I breathe, and so does he."

I held our son up. Maybe he was a bigger reason for her, and I didn't care if it brought her back.

"Yeray misses you, even if he doesn't know how to say it. I know he will learn soon, and I need you to be here so we can compete for your attention. We all want you to stay, even Chris. You should have seen him run to call the ambulance. You've earned a place in everyone's heart, and that's not easy when it comes to my children."

My eyes were stinging, but I was holding back the tears.

"I want you to come home. I want you to take the trip of my dreams with me. I don't mean to New York. That trip can go to hell. I mean the one of our life together. Waking up because sleep has exhausted us, the one of red sunsets in the green of your eyes. Of the sea foam kissing the tips of your toes as we gaze from the dark sand at Kyle, Chris, and Ruben dominating the waves. The one that will take us to see Andrea win medals throwing judo moves on the tatami or this brunet stealing your attention.

"Don't stop fighting. Don't stop breathing, because if I could become air I would give it to you completely. I love you, Sergeant Tennis Player, and death can't separate us, so give a message from me to the Grim Reaper and tell him to fuck off. Fight! Don't give up, and I promise you that we will live for this family you have wanted to build until we have no life left to live."

Tears no longer welled in my eyes. The monitor that marked her heart rate stopped and a flat line appeared on the screen. The nurses rushed to her.

"We're losing her," I read on the lips of the oldest. My heart exploded.

EPILOGUE

Gigil: The uncontrollable desire to squeeze someone just because you love them.

<u>Yeray, forty years later</u>

Every year, to celebrate my birthday, my siblings and I gather around a bonfire and toast marshmallows in honor of the first night my sister Andrea spent on the island with Ruben.

We always do the same thing. Christian, being the oldest, is in charge of the firewood and lighting the bonfire. Andrea buys the marshmallows and the bottles of limoncello we drink afterward. Ruben is in charge of the hot chocolate, and I arrange the blankets and cushions to be comfortable.

It was our night, the four of us together, on that property that still meant so much to us. We wouldn't even let my brother-in-law Kyle or my wife Belén participate in the sibling evening.

Our wives or husbands were left with the children as we revived the memory of who we were and who we became.

Christian and Kyle were a perfect match. They got married,

adopted Zoe, and founded a surf school. Chris became a skating coach and accumulated many accolades from his students.

Andrea continued with judo. She was selected to participate two consecutive times in the Olympics, achieving an enviable record. In the first one in which she participated, she got the silver medal, and in the next, she won gold.

She now worked training future Olympic judoists. She married her coach, but things did not go well. Fortunately, they had no children to complicate their separation. Years later, at a seminar she attended as a teacher, she fell in love with one of her students, to whom she is still married. With Fran, she had a daughter and a son who followed in her footsteps. All four have made sports their profession.

Ruben works for an association that fights for animal rights. He is a free soul, and we always joke about who he will bring to dinner. My brothers and I think he's into that thing called polyamory, because he says love is universal, and he has a lot to share.

I married Belén and followed in my mother's footsteps. I am a civil guard, and my wife is a police officer. No, don't laugh. Life seems to want to repeat history. We have three children. The middle one is a girl, and we are pregnant with our fourth. Yes, that's how much alike my parents and I are. Three boys and a girl who bears my sister's name. Where do we live? In Barcelona, although we look for any excuse to return to the island.

"Do you think they were happy?" I asked my brothers, staring into the crackling flames.

Andrea moved the stick to bring the candy to her mouth, blowing hard. She scrunched her eyebrows and looked at me with conviction to answer the question I had just posed.

"Of course they were happy! Well, maybe Christian being an asshole made things difficult for them, but when Dad caught him with Kyle's tongue, giving him a tracheotomy, everything fell into place." Christian snorted, rolling his eyes. "What? I'm not lying.

The best part was seeing Chris with his tail between his legs, apologizing to Mom Garbi."

"I've always had my dick between my legs," answered my brother Christian. "I also know when I've screwed up. Garbi was the best thing that could have happened to our father, along with Mom."

"I agree with that," Andrea added. "They did incredible things in their lives! Like having us or, in the case of Mom Garbi, raising Chris and me without making distinctions between Ruben or you. She persevered a lot for us to be the family we are today, and if there are people who can't stand their mother, I couldn't be happier for the two mothers that touched me," she clarified, putting the marshmallow dipped in chocolate to her lips.

"Can you imagine if Dad hadn't woken up in time that night? If Yeray hadn't started crying, or if Christian hadn't entered the room to alert them?" Ruben interceded, hugging his legs.

"He had to wake up. As Mom said, it's not that his destiny was written in the stars, but that we have two guardians who always watch over us. They were watching over us that night, too," I said, raising my eyes to the sky as my brothers did.

My mother always told us all that Claudia and Grandfather were there to protect us when we were sleeping. They had been doing it that night, too. The point is that Dad managed to revive Mom and get her to the hospital in time, and although she suffered a heart attack that almost took her away, the doctors were able to bring her back.

When she woke up, the first thing she said was that Grandfather and Claudia had forced her to return. That she had wanted to be with them resting, but they did not let her because she still had too much to do. That her time had not yet come. In that, they were right.

There were very hard weeks in which everyone feared the worst, and I say that because I didn't know about it. However, my father, my siblings, and Aunt Paula had a terrible time.

However, the result gave rise to an annual celebration: Mom's Unbirthday. We called it that because we didn't celebrate her birthday but the days of her life. When we were little, we had a family party. As soon as we started earning money and stopped living with them, they became family trips to places we all wanted to visit.

At those times the people who had been growing the family would join in. It didn't have to be in the month when everything fell apart. We would choose the destination, and we would schedule vacations so we could all spend four or five days together.

I still remember when we went to Lapland with the kids to meet Santa Claus and my dad forced Mom to sit on the poor man's knee to ask for her present.

They always had this kind of relationship that, when you see it, makes you sigh. No one in this world loves each other as much as my parents, not even me and Belén, and I would give my life for her. Their love is special, one of those that last. My parents' love was a solid feeling that illuminated every sunset they accumulated in their eyes.

We heard their shy footsteps behind us. They never came down before finishing the glass of wine they were drinking on their terrace, watching the view.

The four of us turned to look at them with the same fascination as they looked at each other.

Both with white hair, faces full of wrinkles and happiness, and an intense glow that left no doubt that they were very happy.

"What are you doing, kids?" my father asked, squeezing my mother against his body with that uncontrollable desire that makes you imprison the person you love. I'm forty, and the oldest one is almost sixty, but to him, we'll always be kids.

"Toasting marshmallows. Would you like one?"

There was no better place than our family home on the hillside, which would always be ours.

"You know we prefer to drink a glass of wine at sunset until the stars come out. I stopped eating those things when they started to stick to my teeth."

My mother giggled and kissed him on the cheek.

"My poor toothless. It's true. The last time he ate one, it stuck to one of his molars, forming a paste we couldn't remove. We had no choice but to let the teeth soak for several hours. The damned thing seemed to be made of reinforced concrete."

"Damn my luck!"

The four of us laughed out of pure happiness.

We had a lot to take care of, but they looked like a couple of beautiful roses.

No one remembered the twenty-five years of life they had predicted for my mother. It was forty-something years later, and medicine had advanced quite a bit. The doctors assured us that she would die from anything other than her illness. My parents joked that if they had survived a worldwide pandemic as at-risk patients, they had to come from Krypton and were the improved version of Superman, so we had nothing to worry about. When they left this world, it would be because they had nothing left to do, and they would do it together.

I couldn't imagine how they would survive each other's deaths. They would be one of those couples that, when the first went, the other would go soon after.

The thought of that moment filled me with sadness, but as my father used to say, there was still a long way to go before we would be left with the inheritance and have to scatter his ashes on the cliff at sunset.

My father had made a promise during the days that Mom was so ill in the hospital. He'd said that when she recovered, he would take her to New York to ask her to marry him.

Did he do it? Yes. They had the most romantic proposal ever, but that's better left to them to tell you, don't you think?

"Dad, why don't you tell us about your trip to New York?" I suggested.

"Do you want me to? I've told you a million times."

"We don't get tired of hearing it," Andrea said.

"That's fine, but for that, you'll have to go find us a couple of chairs, kids. These bones are no longer strong enough to sit like Indians on the ground."

"Speak for yourself. With my yoga classes, I can sit anywhere," said my mother, making a space between us. "I told you that you should try it. You can barely reach your shoelaces."

"I wear those canvas ones that you bought me, and the day I can't, I'll wear those wooden clogs from Cantabria. The ones Revilla showed on TV."

"That was in the Pleistocene when you still had teeth and could lose them if you bit yourself," my mother rebuked him. "Now if you fall, they will put in a new hip."

Ruben brought a chair our my father, and he sat down.

<u>Áxel, forty years earlier</u>

"New York!" exclaimed Garbiñe, gazing at a gigantic pink helium balloon with the words "We're going on a trip to New York!" floating in the hospital room to celebrate her discharge.

"Not now, next year, and it will only be for four days," I clarified when I saw her looking at Yeray in horror. My little boy was latched to her breast, suckling like crazy.

"He is very small. Next year, he will still be small."

"We'll go when he starts eating porridge, and we'll milk you until the freezer is full. If there's a pandemic, he'll have milk to drink until he goes to college."

Garbiñe wrinkled her nose. To see her alive, even if she was sulking, when I thought I would lose her, was a wonderful gift. Still, she wasn't about to give up. "Paula has agreed to stay with the children when we have the date. We're not going to make a nuisance of ourselves now. Please, Garbi, it's a promise." I pouted.

"A promise?" she asked without understanding.

"Uh-huh. I promised the Big Boss that if you got out of this, I'd take you to New York."

"You told God that if I made it out alive, you would take me on a trip you've been wanting to take for years?"

"When you put it like that, it sounds bad, but yes. Although I wasn't referring to God, but to your father, who was the one who brought you back from the tunnel. I think he liked the Big Apple, too."

"My father liked the apple in the form of *El Gaitero* cider."

"Well, there you have it. Galicians go everywhere, even to the moon."

"But cider is Asturian!"

"Asturias, Galicia...what difference does it make? They are neighbors."

Garbi snorted. "That thing about passing by the light has made you itchy. I'm sure there was a light bulb out. We can't leave Yeray in Paula's hands so young. I'm sure she'll have pierced his foreskin by the time we get back."

"Or I'll convert him to Judaism and cut it off," she said, coming through the door. "Hello, Mr. Deodorant. I told you it wasn't a good promise since she wouldn't want to part with the baby so soon. And if you thought getting my name out would give you an advantage, you were wrong. Paula and babies is not a good association. Paula and drink it until you can't remember the name of the guy you woke up with is more to the point."

"You're a cracker with the kids! They all love you, and you accepted."

"I was sure that mother lioness would not want to. If I repeat my exact words, they were that I would stay with the baby if Garbi asked me to. You can see she won't." She clicked her tongue.

I rolled my eyes, thinking about the fortune I had spent on the engagement ring. I saw it in a store and knew it was the right one, with a huge emerald in the center. It would not be the same to give it to her on the terrace of the house, no matter how beautiful it was, as on the Empire State Building.

Paula was holding in her laughter. She loved teasing me. I think it had become her favorite pastime since she met me.

"All right, then. We'll all go to New York," I said.

"Have you gone mad?" Garbi shouted, thinking about the fortune that would entail.

"I don't care. I'll throw the house out the window, even if we spend a year sucking on the dumbbells at the gym to get enough iron. I won't break my promise. I'm a man of my word, so if you don't agree to go alone with me, we'll take the whole family."

"We'll fly first class and stay in a five-star hotel," Paula added, giving Garbi two kisses.

"If you want to go on a trip, you pay for it, Lady Carrington. You are not considered part of the family," I provoked her.

She looked at me scornfully. "That's not what you said a week ago. Should I remind you? 'Please, Aunt Paula, please!'"

"Stop it!" Garbi howled, putting her free hand to her temple. "I accept if it will end this argument that is going to make my head explode." I smiled triumphantly, and Paula looked defeated.

"You can't accept!"

"Too late. She's already said yes, and you're in a hurry to organize everything," I interceded, grabbing her by the elbow to pull her out.

As soon as I closed the door behind us, Paula burst out laughing.

"You see how you needed my intervention? I know her!"

"I don't know how you managed."

"Practice. Start organizing the coolest proposal in history because for me to stay alone for four days with your kids, it has to be amazing."

"It will be. Don't doubt it." I hugged her tightly and kissed her cheek.

"To think that I told her to fuck you because you would die soon. The grief you're giving me!"

"You are unique. I owe you one."

"You mean one after the other," she corrected me, pulling away from me with a smile twinkling in her eyes.

Paula was great about taking care of my children while Garbi was in danger. I couldn't ask for more. "I won't have enough life-times to repay you."

"You know I'd do anything for you."

"I know. Go on, go inside. We've finished with the theatrics."

Garbiñe, Central Park, one year later

I have never been in a place as intimidating as the Big Apple.

The skyscrapers engulfed you in a hungry crowd of other people's lives wrapped in exclusive clothes or wearing absolute poverty as a garment. This was the city of inequality, where the big brands fought for a place on Fifth Avenue and the homeless fought to survive in a city full of greed.

We strolled past extravagant shop windows. We visited the Great Lady of Freedom, always ready to welcome us with her eternal torch and the overwhelming Ground Zero, where the stillness of the souls pervaded us in a strange harmony of broken lives.

A day before we left, Áxel insisted on a picnic in the city's great green lung, Central Park.

"Don't you think it's incredible?" he asked, putting grapes in his mouth.

"It is impressive," I acknowledged. "But I wouldn't trade our island life for a month here. I'm not cut out for a day-to-day life full of noise, screams, sirens, and rushing around. I like our warm sunrises, the long walks on the beach, and the laughter of our children in the garden at home when we sit on the terrace in silence because there are no words to define the spectacle of light and color that comes from the sea breaking on the beach and a sky that takes your breath away. There is no painting on display at MoMA that can match the island's changing beauty."

Áxel had stopped eating. The wind was caressing his new haircut. He looked handsome like he always did, but today he had a special gleam in his eyes that I was unable to decipher. I attributed it to the joy he felt at making the trip he had always longed for.

"You know, when you say things like that, I love you even more. I'd lay you down here in the grass to cover you with kisses and make love to you."

"We haven't stopped doing it," I protested, sipping from my wine glass.

"We should never stop doing it."

"Yeah, well, I'd love to live in a hippie commune too. Fill my hair with flowers and dedicate myself to making love and not war, but our reality is different. Sometimes the day-to-day life overcomes us, and we are too exhausted. Work, your courses, the house, and the children make us forget about ourselves on many occasions."

"Well, let's fix it. Let's do something to have more time together."

"Like what?"

"An *au pair*. I've been thinking about it for a while, and I think it's just what we need. The children will improve their English, and she'll give us a hand with the housework and take the kids to school. We can have some evenings to ourselves." He waggled his eyebrows.

"It sounds too good, but we have a problem. We are short of rooms unless the *au pair* is a hippie and sleeps outdoors in the garden."

"You're not wrong. We have a lot of land, and instead of

letting her sleep in a sack, we could put up a small house. A prefabricated wooden house with enough room and furniture for the girl to be comfortable."

"Or boy," I pointed out.

"Is that a yes?"

"That's an 'I'll think about it.' We have to crunch the numbers."

"What if I tell you I already did them, and we can afford it? If you're okay with the idea, I'll show them to you when we get home, and we can talk about it some more."

"That's all right. In the end, you always end up doing what you want."

"Perfect, because right now, I want something else."

He stood up and held out his hand for me to do the same. "Shall we go? There is still food left."

"No. I just want to dance."

"There's no music, and they'll think we're crazy! At the least, you'll be arrested for public scandal."

"I said dance, not fuck. And don't worry about the music. I'll take care of it."

Áxel pressed me against his body, grabbing me by the waist and giving me no choice but to grab him by the back of the neck. He took the opportunity to strategically place his mouth close to my ear. He started humming a Luis Miguel song that we had made our own when we'd lived apart, *Contigo en la Distancia*. My boy's raspy voice made the hairs on my body stand on end.

You have become part of my soul. Nothing comforts me anymore
if you are not there too. Beyond your lips,
of the sun and the stars. With you in the distance, my beloved, I am.

When he stopped singing, he dragged his lips down my cheeks until he reached the final stop, my mouth, gently seizing it until it intoxicated me more than the wine we had drunk.

I could never have imagined a love like the one Áxel offered me. To give without receiving, to be without demanding, to love without waiting. No one completed me more than he did.

We picked up the food since the appetite he had awakened in me was different. We spent part of the afternoon loving each other slowly, going over each other centimeter by centimeter, with lips, skin, and soul.

When it was time for dinner, he surprised me with a beautiful party dress that was delivered to our room.

Áxel had left me in a relaxing bubble bath, rose petals included. When I got out of the tub and wrapped myself in a white terry cloth bathrobe, the room service girl knocked on the door to deliver it to me.

"Mr. Montoya is waiting downstairs to take you to dinner. He told me to tell you to take as much time as you need," she said in perfect Spanish.

"Thank you. I didn't know we were going out to dinner."

She smiled kindly and left the way she had come. I didn't expect anything like that. Áxel had told me that we would get something to eat in the room, and he would keep making love to me until dawn found us, so we would spend the flight home sated and sleeping.

The dress was scandalous, green silk with a strapless neckline and a skirt that fell to the floor.

I did what I could to make an updo that didn't look like a bird's nest. I wished Paula was here. She could have done much better.

I put on mascara, blush, and gloss. Áxel knew I wasn't a makeup person. A little perfume in the right places, and I was ready to go.

When I got to the front desk, I didn't see him, but the bellhop saw me. He asked me to accompany him outside. There, standing beside a white horse-drawn buggy and dressed in a breathtaking black suit, was Áxel, smiling and excited.

"You look beautiful," he greeted me. "The dress suits you very well. I got the size and color right."

I smiled like a fool and nodded. "You look very handsome yourself. Thank you. Shall we go upstairs?"

"What about this?" he asked, pointing at the vehicle he had chosen. "You came to conquer my kingdom, so tonight, I'm going to treat you like the princess you are."

"Please don't let it be Cinderella, who loses a shoe, tears her dress, and ends up with soot up to her eyebrows."

Áxel burst out laughing. "In our case, this princess has a story to write. I asked for it blank so we could write it as we went along."

"What a weight off my shoulders." I sighed, accepting his hand to climb up and take the seat.

The carriage returned to the place where we had picnicked, Central Park. Seeing it at night was very different, almost a trip to the past where I could feel what it would have been like to walk in another time in those places.

We continued our ride, huddled together and lost in the night lights until we stopped at the Empire State Building. Áxel stopped the driver and made us get down.

We rose the elevator to the eighty-sixth floor, the scene of countless movies. It had sweeping views.

It was just us and a small table lit by candles.

"What is this?" I asked, my excitement spilling over. My heart rate accelerated.

"This is the place I chose for dinner."

"But it's not a restaurant!"

"Today, it is. Just for you."

"God bless. It must have cost you a fortune."

"You'll never know. More than money, it's taken a few favors and the invaluable help of the Taser people, who have impressive contacts. And now, Sergeant Princess, would you do me the great honor of dining with me?"

I fluttered my eyelashes. "I'm not sure. I'm a bit dizzy this high in the sky."

"Don't worry. I'll always be here."

"But you can't fly."

Áxel winked at me and undid a couple of buttons on his shirt. "I was hoping to tell you later, but look closely! This time, I bought the original Superman costume!" He buttoned his buttons again. "The guy at the store assured me that I could really fly in this one."

My laughter came on its own. "Just in case, we'll wait until we get to the hotel so you can make me fly another way, okay?"

"That's done, dear Lois."

Smiling, we sat at the table and ate a dinner full of small dishes that filled our mouths with unique flavors.

A violinist livened up the evening, and when dessert arrived, Áxel got up to stand in front of me, then knelt on the floor and opened a little green velvet box containing an impressive ring.

"As soon as I saw you, I knew you were for me, and as soon as I saw this, I knew it was yours. I can't promise you eternity because it would be too ephemeral, but I *can* promise you that I won't stop trying for a second to fill you with smiles."

My lips quirked as he pulled out the ring and took my hand. "Life has taught me that I am nothing, but with you, I am everything. Garbi, will you do me the honor of becoming my wife?"

Tears filled my eyes. My heart was bursting with emotion, and this time, I was short of breath from the love I felt, not because of an illness.

"Yes! Yes! I do!" I forgot the ring and threw my arms around him.

If there was one thing I had learned, it was that there was no greater gem than the Taser instructor I met at my lowest point, and he had been given three months to live. Áxel taught me that life is capable of changing color if you meet the right person, and now he will always be mine.

· · ·

<u>Yeray, present day</u>

No one was able to hold back tears.

It still moved us all as it had the first time we heard it. My mother got up from the ground and walked over to the love of her life to sit on his knees, wrap her arms around his neck, and place on his lips a kiss that contained the truth of the story.

True love needs no tricks because it is pure magic. It doesn't matter if the person you love doesn't know how to dance. The important thing is that they want to dance with you forever, even if things are not easy.

They were my parents, and they would live in each other's smiles until the end of their days.

THAT FLIGHT FROM LONDON TO
MADRID

If you enjoyed this book, you might also enjoy *That Flight From London to Madrid*, from Claudia Velasco.

Grab your copy today!

A chance encounter will change the lives of two strangers forever.

Daniela Mendoza makes a snap decision to get away from it all after a betrayal makes her reevaluate her life.

She meets Edward Dankworth on her flight from London to Madrid. Her unexpected traveling companion offers the comfort she needs, then disappears from her life when their plane lands.

Two years later, coincidence reunites them in Rome. Edward does his best to distance himself from Daniela, but fate has other plans for them...

Their chance encounter unleashes a series of events that immerses Daniela in Edward's world. She finds herself caught in the tangled web of smuggling and spies, secrets and lies that has prevented Edward from letting anyone in.

As their thrilling adventure takes them through Rome, Madrid, and London, Daniela and Edward discover more than the source of the international mystery and espionage that brought them back together.

Can they learn to trust and rely on each other? Or will their pasts get in the way of falling in love?

Grab your copy today!